ROBIN MITCHELL was born in a Fife schoolhouse in 1963 – the same year the Great Train Robbers bagged £2.5 million and cassette recorders were introduced to Scotland. His early claim to fame was curling into the shape of a ball and rolling down the nearest set of stairs.

Robin was always encouraged by his English teacher at school – encouraged to do something else. This positive feedback was just the 'confidence tonic' an aspiring fourteen-year-old scribe required. The football field duly beckoned. In 1977, during Scotland's belated skirmish with Punk Rock, Mitchell's silky poaching skills were noticed by top English soccer legends Aston Villa. Invited to sign for the Midlands side, Mitchell declined the offer and became a rare breed of Scottish schoolboy – uninterested in playing full-time football for a living.

School unsurprisingly led to college – moving to Edinburgh in 1980 to study Hotel Catering and Institutional Management. After successfully gaining his Higher Diploma at Napier University, Robin made a logical step to further his catering career by setting up a walking tour company – The Cadies and Witchery Tours. In 1986, he gained membership of the Scottish Tourist Guide Association after completing a course at the University of Edinburgh. His small ghostly business has gone from strength to strength – still providing light-hearted ghoulish tours around Scotland's capital city. Following the success of the ghastly evening walks, a compilation of stories from the city's dark past – *The Witchery Tales* – was published in 1988 and two more guide-books – *About a Mile* and *The Secret Life of Edinburgh Castle* – were launched in 1994. Dabbling in book publishing led him to produce and release four fifty-minute videos – *Adam Lyal's Royal Mile, Georgian Edinburgh, St. Andrews* and *The Ghosts of Scotland*.

Confirming his fascination with the darker side of Scotland's gory past, Robin purchased at auction a card case made from the skin of infamous bodysnatcher, William Burke. This gruesome relic can be viewed at the Police Information Centre in Edinburgh's Royal Mile.

In 1999, Robin set up his own political party – The Witchery Tour Party – and stood for the Scottish Parliament in the guise of 213 year old highway robber, Adam Lyal (deceased). His policies included a campaign to reduce MSPs salaries from £40,000 a year to £3.60 an hour and a pledge to wear white make up for the full term of the Parliament. He gained 1,184 votes, finishing ninth out of the seventeen parties registered on the Lothians list.

Robin lives in Midlothian with his wife Alison and a huge black and white cat.

Grave Robbers

ROBIN MITCHELL

Luath Press Limited

EDINBURGH

www.luath.co.uk

First Published 1999

The paper used in this book is acid-free, neutral-sized and recyclable.
It is made from low chlorine pulps produced in a low energy,
low emission manner from sustainable forests.

Printed and bound by
Bell & Bain Ltd., Glasgow

Typeset in 10.5 point Sabon by
S. Fairgrieve, Edinburgh 0131 658 1763

This book is dedicated to Alison, Aidan, Brother Brian, Cameron, Elaine, James, Jenny, Jeremy, Judy, Lorna and Pat. I'd also like to thank Rollo and May.

Chapter One

THE AIR WAS TEEMING with the trail of freshly trimmed grass.

The ageing stone outlook tower, watching over the city cemetery for one hundred and fifty years, was falling apart. The turreted watchtower, constructed with the express purpose of denying the enterprising Victorian grave robbers, was now a derelict shadow of its former self. The crumbling steps, clutched together by cement, led to an old decaying wooden door, the rusty handle remaining sealed for over forty years. The black painted iron banister attached to the steps was in a bad state of repair, dangerously loose.

Cameron was on his tea break. Digging graves was bloody hard work, especially on a damp humid day. His place of rest was the top of the tower steps where he could sit in solitude and enjoy his ritual cheese sandwich and flask of milky tea. Ever since his near-death experience at Edinburgh's Commonwealth swimming pool eleven years earlier, he required a special quiet moment in the day to relax and collect his thoughts.

The accident occurred when Cameron, after a momentary lapse of concentration, dived into the shallow end of the swimming pool and cracked open his head. As blood gushed out of him like a cascading fountain, his friend, Andrew, jumped into the water and hauled him to the corner of the baths. He was unconscious for ten minutes and in that time had a near-death experience. When the bleeding wouldn't stop, Cameron thought he was dying and felt totally at peace. He followed a bright golden light to the top of some stairs where he could clearly observe his own body below lying limp and motionless beside a group of anxious spectators. He encountered a strong sensation of peace and painlessness, feeling a reluctance to return from the dead. Then, clear as day, he heard his deceased grandmother's voice echo out with the words. 'It's not your time yet son. Go back and continue your life.' At this point, he felt himself being slammed back into his body and recalls the rapid dart of extreme pain engulfing his head and slicing his whole frame like a knife through butter. After two weeks recuperating in the Royal Infirmary Hospital, he was back home recovering from what was a profoundly life-changing experience.

The view from the Calton graveyard on to the city of Edinburgh was quite magnificent, although Cameron took little notice of Hibernian Football Club's Easter Road Stadium. He instead enthused over Holyrood House and the imposing hill of Arthur's Seat.

'Cammy, are you up there?' A breathy voice emerged from the foot of the tower.

'Yes, up here, Matty, looks like they're late.' This was a regular visit from one of Cameron's best friends.

Ilona was a tall, blond, strong-minded, good looking twenty-nine year old with a tendency to swear a lot. On burial days she kept her choice language to a minimum, a kind of respectful gesture to the dead. Matty was her nickname, derived from two formative hours she spent as a baby on a synthetic doormat only a stone's throw away from the cemetery in Regent Terrace. Today she shared a flat with two work mates, Rebecca and Shona. Her abrupt cynical humour was a symptom of having been abandoned at birth, found on a doorstep, cast away by parents she'd never met. The Smith family adopted her as an eight-month old infant. Her new brother Adam, an only child and five years her senior, wasn't as charitable to the new arrival, temporarily jealous of the attention shown to the new baby.

Cammy, although the same age, had become a sort of father figure to Matty. Perhaps it was because he was reliable, perhaps it was because he was caring, or perhaps it was just because he liked her a lot. Whatever it was, they shared a passion for wake watching.

Matty was a local tourist guide who'd been friends with Cameron since their innocent primary school days. She was Cammy's miniature minder, stepping in to finish any argument he'd started. She was more a rough and tumble tomboy than a petite Barbie doll girl, carrying with her a set of football cards in her jacket pocket. At six years of age her street credentials were secured the day she cleared the pavement by riding her bicycle at full speed through a group of rapidly dispersing teachers. Cammy played the violin; Matty played the drums. Cammy liked nature documentaries; Matty preferred pulling the legs off spiders. While playing Cowboys and Indians, Matty could be excessively vicious, throwing home made spears at passing cars. Cammy meanwhile would observe her antics from afar, preferring to read his crime novel from the safety of a nearby tree house.

These days Matty would visit the churchyard whenever a funeral was booked to watch the burials from the top of the tower. 'Who's it today, Cammy?'

'It's not a who, it's a *they*.'

'Eh?'

'It is a *they*, a double burial, husband and wife, gas explosion.'

'The one in Victoria Street last week?'

'Yeah, that's the one.'

'Should be a few tears today then.' Matty clasped her hands together. 'Any tea left?'

'Yeah, in the flask.'

'Cammy.'

'Yeah?'

'When a couple die, whose buried on top?'

'*What*?'

'Who's buried on top?' repeated Matty.

'Why do you want to know that?'

'I'm just showing a little interest in your job.'

'Well,' responded Cammy. 'The husband's buried on top.'

'That's sexist!'

'Why?'

'The man on top. That's bloody sexist.'

'Yeah, but the woman goes in first and that's not sexist.'

'Yes it is,' said Matty. 'That's like opening doors and getting up in a bus to give us a seat. We don't need that rubbish any more.'

'Some ladies still like that,' replied Cammy in a tone akin to an upper crust viscount. 'So let me get this right. If a woman is buried first it's termed sexist and if a woman is buried second, it's also termed sexist. Why do I feel you're going to win this argument?'

'It's the sexual connotations that worry me.'

'*What*!'

'The man being on top,' continued Matty. 'That is stereotypically a male position.'

'For God's sake, Matty,' uttered Cammy in disbelief. 'They're both on their backs. They're friggin' dead.'

The view of most burials from the top of the tower was superb. 'Here they come. That's a good turnout today. There must be a big will,' conveyed Matty, in her usual cynical way.

The funeral procession of fifty people dressed in black from head to toe proceeded down the steep gravel path to the newly prepared grave. The burial ground on this occasion was located directly below the outlook tower. Cammy and Matty crouched down behind the iron banister and continued to watch through the gaps in the bars. They hoped no one would look up during the service as the sight of two prying faces peering down like lost children, hands tightly clasped to the railings, could cause unnecessary alarm.

'This must go straight to the top of the 'nearest funeral to the watchtower' chart,' declared Matty.

'Quiet! Would you give your active big gob a rest for a minute or try something you have never done before.'

'What's that?'

'Try and whisper for once.'

'*For once*,' whispered Matty.

'Not funny.'

'Fairly funny,' whispered Matty again. 'What the bloody hell is that?'

The ensuing sight was a mix of the surreal, the bizarre, and the plain odd. Digging graves in Edinburgh for over ten years provided Cammy with a variety of astonishing incidents, however none as peculiar as this. Even Matty for once was lost for words, her mouth wide open, teeth and gums in full view, with nothing coming out. They were about to witness an out of the ordinary incident. This was far more than a break with tradition. This was tradition being exiled to the outer solar system, perhaps further. Cammy had never seen anything like this in all of his twenty-nine years residing on this earthly plane.

The long thick oak coffins were being carefully transported to the graveside on the back of two brightly coloured motorised golf buggies, driven by middle aged men in full Highland dress. The coffins were placed side by side on wooden planks above the sodden grave and a full set of golf clubs was perched up against a vandalised tombstone. The minister in his regular church garb, black suit and dog collar, stepped forward, selected a three iron from the Wilson golf bag, teed up a green Slazenger golf ball and hit it with considerable accuracy towards the Stevenson family tomb. Then, as if by magic, a set of bagpipes and an accordion appeared from the centre of the crowded group of mourners and a medley of hits from the Rogers and Hammerstein musical Oklahoma echoed around the Calton Cemetery. This musical tribute struggled to compete with the noise generated by the open-top tourist buses running nearby in the Royal Mile.

The young minister, the Rev. Tommy Weir, stepped forward and started to speak. 'We are gathered here today in the presence of God to celebrate the lives of David and Catherine who, as you all know, were not a conventional couple. As members of the Braid Hills Golf club and co-founders of the Morningside Amateur Dramatic Society, they asked me some time ago to perform an unorthodox service in the event of their death. As there are no children or close relatives, I was happy to agree. Sadly I did not realise I would have to undertake this duty so soon. They signed up to gas only last week.'

Matty was trying to contain her laughter. 'This is brilliant, what a send off. I'd love a funeral like this when I go.'

'I can get you a good price,' retorted Cammy. 'I'd be more than happy to fit you with a wooden overcoat.'

'I am the resurrection and the life, saith the Lord,' continued the minister. 'He that believeth in me, though he were dead, yet he shall live, and whosoever believeth in me shall never die. For as much as it has pleased Almighty God to receive to himself the souls of his servants David and Catherine Duncan, we therefore commit their bodies to the grave.'

At this point of there were two unplanned happenings. Firstly, a line of swallows, quietly perched on a nearby telephone wire, swooped down over the graveside in what appeared to be an orchestrated fly-past in memory of the newly expired. Secondly, when the planks of wood were removed and the bearers slowly released the cords, the coffins wouldn't fit in the grave – the hole wasn't big enough.

'Oh shit, I do not believe this, what a bloody nightmare,' grunted Cammy. He slid back from the banister, clutched his face in his hands, screwed his eyes shut and hoped this was a bad dream. Alas, it was not. 'That shouldn't bloody well happen. The funeral director has given me the wrong sizes.'

Matty chuckled. 'That's right, blame the funeral director. This is absolutely priceless, bloody hilarious. Make sure you add this to my burial arrangements.'

Cameron's moment of complete and utter disaster was saved by the mourners' spontaneous ripple of applause. They thought this was all part of the morbid presentation. Staying hidden until the funeral director, minister and mourners vacated the cemetery, Cameron, seriously annoyed by his mistake, returned to the grave-side. He'd once prepared the wrong plot after a mix-up with a similar surname. He'd never miscalculated the size of a grave before. Matty loved every minute. She was lapping it up. 'Will I get you a bigger spade for Christmas?'

'It's not funny,' mumbled Cammy.

'Oh I think you'll find that this is exceptionally funny,' insisted Matty. 'Very very funny.'

'Piss off.'

'Language, language, language, Cammy.'

'Piss right off.'

'Can I call you cack-handed Cammy from now on,' pursued Matty. 'Or how about cock-up Cammy?'

'*Right*, that's it,' snapped Cammy. 'I've had enough of this.' He stormed off to the far side of the graveyard. Matty thought Cammy might need a few moments to himself, so after more jibes relating to measuring tapes and poor eyesight, she departed the kirkyard and headed off to work. Cammy took twenty thoughtful minutes grumbling out loud before setting about finishing the job he'd started earlier in the day. As the evening sky merged with the onset of night the moon drifted into view from behind the darkening clouds, illuminating the brass nameplates tightly screwed to the coffin lids.

DAVID AND CATHERINE DUNCAN R.I.P

As he started to fill in the grave with the surrounding damp earth, his spade became jammed in the gap under one of the coffin lids. It took his entire six-foot frame to release the spade. In doing so he cracked open the lid.

Chapter Two

NOISY DRILLS, ROAD WORKS and buildings disguised by scaffolding meant only one thing – June. The city seemed to be packed to capacity. Everywhere you looked there were streams of tourists and locals going about their daily chores. There were queues of taxis patiently waiting to enter the over-crowded Waverley railway station and the skirl of several sets of bagpipes fought bravely with the blaring Princes Street traffic. Half a dozen plump pigeons fought over scraps of crusty bread. Rapid digestion led to healthy bird droppings, which in turn covered the statue of Scottish missionary, David Livingstone. The visitors couldn't make out the peculiar pungency in the air. The locals, though, were well aware of this daily aroma – the nearby brewery. The smell was akin to a potent bowl of thick lentil soup.

The day was hot, the sun was not. The open-top bus was full to the brim with a colourful collection of tourists from the four corners of the globe. This was quite simply the United Nations on wheels. The bus, hired the previous day by a provincial charity, was bearing the scars of a teenage outing. The Emergency Door sign had miraculously transformed its name to 'Emergency Loo', while 'Lift to open' was altered to 'Lift to pee'.

Sitting untroubled amongst the variety of international visitors was a certain local by the name of Cammy, who often sneaked on the open-top buses in an attempt to observe Matty at work. He enjoyed chatting to the coach customers, advising them on the finer points of grave digging, not grasping that this specific topic of dialogue was not automatically uppermost on the average tourist's confabulation list. Tact was not a term subscribed to in the Cameron Carter household.

Cammy lived with his parents in a small stone bungalow in the leafy suburbs of Edinburgh. He moved back home eleven years earlier from a rented flat in Easter Road to recuperate from his life-threatening accident at the swimming pool. At about the same time he resigned his position as assistant manager at the five-star

Royal Hotel and to the astonishment of his family and friends took up a full-time grave-digging job with the City Council. Moving from long stressful shifts in a hotel to regular therapeutic hours in a cemetery was the best thing he ever did.

Cammy's narrow upbringing was conservative to say the least. His father left the army to become a local primary school teacher. He was a man of strict routine, keeping an eager eye on Cammy's every move. He never allowed his son out to play, especially if he suspected his lad was mixing with a mischievous crowd. In effect, Cammy was under house arrest for most of his teens, not enjoying a pint of beer and a cigarette until he was eighteen. His worrying mother was a traditional protective mum, doing everything under the sun – working full-time, washing the dishes, shopping, cleaning, sewing clothes and cooking. The trouble with Mrs Carter's cooking was the fact that she couldn't. Neither could anyone else in the house. This lack of culinary expertise was an impetus to Cammy's future catering intentions and meant the Carters were seldom overweight. His mum, after leaving school at fifteen and playing housewife for twenty years, studied at college to become a social worker. Both parents, now retired, still mourned their first son's cot death, who died at three months of age, before Cammy was born.

As Cammy sat quietly beside a group of German tourists he noticed Princes Street Gardens' bustling putting green. The site of golf putters reminded him of his grave error at the previous week's bizarre funeral service. Not wishing to be reminded of this personal disaster, he turned his eyes away from the gardens and focused on a nearby ice cream van. The tune reverberating from the crackling speakers sounded familiar. 'I don't *believe* this,' he mumbled to himself. 'Okla-bloody-homa.'

Everywhere Cammy glanced there seemed to be a reminder of his disastrous day at the cemetery. The white walkway on the first level of a Princes Street store looked like a minister's dog collar. The roof of the headquarters of the Bank of Scotland resembled a coffin lid. The columns of the National Gallery of Scotland were the cords attached to the coffins and however hard he tried they wouldn't fit in the grave. 'Ahh,' blurted Cammy, much to the consternation of his fellow passengers. He took a huge intake of fresh air and tried to settle his over-sensitive mind.

'Ladies and gentlemen, boys and girls, Cameron.'

As Matty uttered Cammy's name, she stared in silence in his direction for fifteen seconds with the intention of embarrassing him. The stony silence seemed like an eternity to him. She succeeded in her quest. Clutching a fluffy yellow microphone under her chin, Matty commenced her City of Edinburgh tour. 'Hit the road, Dave.'

The microphone was connected to both decks so the commentary could be heard in all sections of the bus. With the weather clearly on the humid side, most of the customers were sitting upstairs. 'Hello everyone, my name is Ilona Smith,' announced Matty in a confident manner. 'I'm your guide this afternoon. I suppose you might have guessed that by now.'

Matty was wearing black trousers, moccasins, a white sleeveless shirt and tartan waistcoat. 'We commence our trip today on top of Waverley Bridge, right beside the main railway station, named after Sir Walter Scott's Waverley novels. I suppose there aren't too many railway stations in the world named after books. We can see the Scott Monument from here, built between the years 1840 and 1846. Decorated with the same number of small statues as there are local councillors in the city chambers. Some say the statues are more active. If you look to the right hand side, the four clock-faces of the Balmoral Hotel are perpetually two-and-a-half minutes fast. This location - adjacent to the railway station – is a priceless aid to weary travellers. The idea is to help you catch your train on time. So picture the scene. You think you're late for your connection to London. Having checked the hotel's clock, you go galloping along Princes Street at full speed like a mad woman on heat. Run straight past Jenners department store without shopping – don't you just hate that ladies – and reach the station with two and a half minutes to spare. What a super system. Mind you, the train's then an hour late.' A polite murmur of laughter was lost in the city sky.

Matty was in full descriptive flow. 'Appearing now on your left-hand side from the shadow of the classical National Gallery, is the impregnable site of the capital's imposing fortress, Edinburgh Castle. Built on a volcanic plug, four hundred and forty feet above sea level, the stronghold houses the oldest remaining building in Edinburgh, the eleventh-century Chapel of St Margaret. Remember to go and see the time gun. It's fired every day at one o'clock. They say that we have a one o'clock gun in Scotland as a gun set off at twelve would be too expensive.'

Matty was sitting upstairs at the front of the bus, unsure whether the groans and hissing were emerging from the vehicle's engine or from the expectant group of tourists. She thoroughly enjoyed working as a tour guide on open-top buses. Her old fashioned manager, who everyone called 'mum', had offered her a new contract with extra financial arrangements – a pension plan and a number of additional fully paid holidays. The tour company knew she was a walking, talking, historical asset. Countless complimentary letters arrived at head office acclaiming Matty on her light-hearted yet professional guiding skills. The tour she conducted around the town, derived from a basic script, was a clever mix of history and humour with an adaptable style to suit a variety of groups. There could have been no better job for her. Talking all the time for a living was heaven on earth. How she managed to speak at the same pace out of work after five seventy-five minute trips around the city centre was a mystery to one and all. If the Olympic committee were ever to introduce talking to the international world of sport then Matty could easily represent her country in every speech category with a genuine hope of a medal.

The socialising after work was first-rate. All the guides, mostly women, hit the town two or three times a week for a damn good drinking session. Invariably the girls bitched about the one person at work they hated the most – Jenny. She was a fat cow, according to Matty, a slagheap according to Rebecca and a smelly slut, according to Shona.

The more the alcohol flowed, the more the insults flew. The girls, outrageously boisterous by the end of the night, would drink until they fell over. No one was able to go out for one pint, it was all or nothing. One for all and none for Jenny. The jokes were fly-ing and the gawking men were plentiful. Boys would swan over, chat up the guides, or so they thought, and the girls would twirl them around their little fingers as quickly as you could say boo to a goose. This wasn't a problem as the male species would gladly be the centre of the girls' wicked amusement. Sometimes they were used to satisfy sexual needs, other times played with like little toy action men. When asked by a man what her occupation might be, Matty would have a different answer for each night of the week. Her employment details invariably depended on how much cider she'd consumed. Her jobs seemingly ranged from air traffic controller and part-time bingo caller to trainee redcoat at Butlins, on account of having a green jacket.

'On the left hand side, opposite the Caledonian Hotel where a famous man called Cameron Carter used to work as a porter, is a small stone outlook tower.'

Matty was notorious for including information on friends during her tour of the town. The visitors didn't seem to mind or maybe they didn't notice. 'Families used this watchtower in days gone by, during the time of the grave robbers. This was an absorbing period in the history of Edinburgh, when bodysnatchers, or resurrectionists as they were called, would visit cemeteries late into the night and dig up newly buried bodies. The corpses were then transported to the medical school and peddled at considerable profit to the doctors of anatomy. The small towers were a lookout point where the wealthier families employed men to watch over their loved ones for a few weeks after the funeral. Poor relations would undertake this task themselves. After a period of time, when the body was well past its 'sell-by date', the family could head home in the comforting knowledge that their newly deceased relative was quietly decomposing in peace without interference from disagreeable hands. The tower would then wait patiently for the next funeral. There are of course other towers in this city, principally the one located in the Calton graveyard. This specific watchtower is in need of considerable renovation.'

The last comment was aimed solely at Cammy. He knew exactly what she was talking about even if the rest of the bus looked slightly blank for a second or two. Cammy was listening intently to the tour commentary and even though he'd heard the selfsame stories fifty times before, Matty still possessed a way of making the information sound fresh and spontaneous. She did wonder though, why Cammy attended so many of her trips especially when there was little time to speak to him at the end of a tour.

'Greyfriars Kirkyard and of course Greyfriars Kirk,' persisted Matty. 'They have Gaelic services here on a Sunday. If you wish to go to a sermon where you have no idea what the minister's talking about, then this is the place for you. If you like wandering around graveyards late at night in the pitch dark, then this is definitely the place for you. Watch out for the mortsafes – bars built over graves to stop the dead getting out. I mean, to prevent the bodysnatchers getting in.' Cammy was pleased Matty was including more references to cemeteries on her city tour.

'There are seven hundred and seventeen pubs in Edinburgh and six hundred and thirty-four letter boxes.'

Matty often interjected worthless facts and figures in mid-sentence. This technique was used with the express design of regaining the attention of anyone who was beginning to drift off into another world. The system seemed to work. Her knowledge of irrelevant data and useless narrative was second to none. This was partly due to her effortless retention of historical and anecdotal information. Anything she read about Edinburgh was somehow instantly stored in her brain's huge filing cabinet of facts. The visitors loved her style.

'There are more famous people buried in this cemetery than I've had hot dinners, and let me tell you salads are never served in Ilona Smith's house.' The bus slowed down to a halt exactly on cue. What a difference it made when the driver was fully aware of the tour guide's route and order of stories. This advanced knowledge made the whole journey smooth and professional. On the other side of the coin, when Matty was paired with a new driver, the tour was often less than brilliant. This drove her to despair. Thankfully, Dave, the man behind the wheel on this particular tour, was an old hand at the job. Matty started to list the famous folk who were buried in the Greyfriars Cemetery.

'James Craig – architect of Edinburgh's New Town. Sir Walter

Scott's father, Walter Scott. Allan Ramsay – the Scots poet and writer. William Creech – Robert Burns' Edinburgh publisher, and there's actually an old actor interred in this graveyard who was buried in full theatrical costume, complete with a green flowing gown and gold buckled shoes. And let us not forget the statue and gravestone to our distinguished dog Greyfriars Bobby who was made famous by the popularity of a Walt Disney film of the same name. After the death of its master, old Jock Grey, this dedicated Skye terrier kept vigil at his grave for fourteen years. There's no truth in the rumour that the dog was still attached to the lead.'

Cammy laughed out loud, he'd never heard that line before. 'I must admit that's quite funny.'

'You are visiting Edinburgh?' asked a tourist in a marked Germanic accent.

'No, I live here.'

'You are a *local* on a tour bus?'

'Well, I'm a friend of the tour guide. I come along now and again for the ride.'

The tourist smiled. 'The guide is your girlfriend?'

'No, she's a friend that happens to be a girl.'

'I do not fully understand.'

'She's a friend,' whispered Cammy. 'Although between you and me I wouldn't mind if she became my girlfriend.'

There, he'd finally said it, something he was craving to announce for years. Cammy, secretly in love with Matty for some time, kept his pent up emotions to himself. He was too scared to tell her his true feelings, fearing the loss of what was a fantastic friendship. They'd been close companions for what seemed a lifetime and she'd been so kind to him after his accident. Life wasn't about fortune or wealth but love and trust. If Cammy had Matty's love, food for dinner and a roof over his head, he'd be a millionaire.

What a dilemma to be in. Fearful of spoiling their life-long companionship, he consigned all romantic notions firmly to the back of his mind. Daily deciphering of any potential amorous signal was par for the course. There seemed to be no evidence of this to date, or so he thought. Would he ever build up the courage to ask her out on a date? Cammy certainly didn't envisage that his first public announcement of his true feelings towards Matty would be aimed at a complete stranger from Germany, his devotion unveiled to all and sundry except the person that really mattered.

'Ah *I see*,' The tourist nodded his head. 'I think I know what you mean.'

Cammy smiled. 'Where are you from?'

'Cologne, in Germany.'

'Is that where they make the perfume?'

'I'm sorry?'

'It's okay, just a bad joke.' Then without a thought for tact, he launched into a lengthy speech about his grandfather. 'My grandfather bombed Cologne during the last war. He was a navigator in the RAF. He flew sixty sorties in Lancaster and Wellington bombers, which was a remarkable achievement in the 1940s. He preferred the Lancaster. Oh, and he also bombed Dresden and the Ruhr valley. Do you know the movie The Dambusters? Well, that was grandpops. He wasn't in the film but he was one of the bombers portrayed in the film. Amazing, eh? He said that they bombed the shite out of the Nazis.'

'I think this is our stop. Why are you people still obsessed with the war?' The German couple, suitably offended, stood up and promptly left the bus.

Cammy turned to another unsuspecting tourist. 'Where are you from?'

Luckily the tour was reaching a finale, so Cammy had no time to plant his diplomatic seeds anywhere else. The bus was heading up the Lawnmarket towards Edinburgh Castle where the trip would finish.

'On the right hand side is a pub called Deacon Brodie's named after, believe it or not, a man called Deacon Brodie. You learn something new each day,' remarked Matty sarcastically. 'Brodie by day was a cabinetmaker and member of the town council. By night he was a robber, gambler, crook, cockfighter and womaniser. As I said, a member of the Town Council.' Her drip-dry humour was lost on this raggle taggle band of foreigners. 'He was eventually caught and publicly hanged on a gibbet, which he assisted in introducing to Edinburgh as a Councillor. Robert Louis Stevenson, another native of this fine city, based his book, The Strange case of Dr Jekyll and Mr Hyde on this two-faced character. He sounds a bit like my brother Adam, apart from the cabinet making section that is. Someone once asked me if Deacon Brodie were two people – Deek and Brodie. I've had a few interesting questions in my time.' Cammy knew this throw-away line about Matty's brother, Adam, to be true. He was indeed a petty crook who was always up to no good most days of the year. The bus came to a concluding halt in front of Edinburgh Castle. There was a well received round of applause. Many of the tourists approached Matty personally to thank her for what was in their eyes a first-class tour. As the visitors streamed off the bus onto the bustling castle esplanade, many happily thrust coins into Matty's sweaty palms. Gratuities were commonplace and gratefully accepted.

Cammy pulled on the arm of Matty's jacket. 'I've something to tell you.'

'Not now Cammy, can you not see I'm busy?'

'No, I have to tell you now.'

'*Later*, tell me later, I've got another tour to do. I'll meet you down the pub tonight.'

'The Shovel Inn?'

'Yeah, The Shovel Inn at eight o'clock.'

Chapter Three

MATTY WAS BEHIND SCHEDULE, the time was already twenty past eight. Andrew was otherwise detained. The only person who could be later than Matty was Cammy's friend Andrew. This was unusual, as they'd studied hotel catering and institutional management together and entered the wonderful world of hotels on the same day. Their training taught them the importance of punctuality.

Matty was Matty. She could be late or exceptionally late.

Cammy despised sitting in pubs on his own. In fact he despised sitting anywhere on his own apart from his secluded spot at the top of the watchtower steps. He was already on his second pint of beer. Drinking gave him something to do while waiting.

'The Shovel Inn' was a nickname derived from its location – there was a graveyard on either side of the building. The boozer's real name was The Auld Arms. The gravediggers in days gone by frequented this watering hole after a hard day's slog in the nearby cemeteries. The only establishment near Cammy's place of work was a quaint tearoom some fifteen minutes walk into the heart of the Royal Mile. Standing out like a sore thumb wasn't one of his best-loved pastimes, so he avoided this tourists' tearoom like the plague. The Shovel Inn was more his style. The pub, although recently renovated, remained a working man's bar. The sawdust was long gone from the cracked stone floor, replaced by cheap linoleum tiles. The bygone custom of raising fingers in the air on arrival at the front door prevailed. This was to alert the barman to the number of pints required. By the time you reached the main bar your drinks were sitting on the counter. The retired owner only sold beer, cider and whisky. If anyone asked for another type of drink, they were sent to the lounge bar next door. Unfortunately there wasn't a lounge bar next door and this provided much amusement to the bar staff. One day an unwitting tourist arrived in the pub and requested a steak pie. He was promptly informed, 'I'm not a fuckin' baker.' The till was an accountant's nightmare, consisting of a dusty wooden drawer hidden under the spirit-stained counter.

There was a gruff murmur reverberating around the tavern's smoky atmosphere. The antique clock, precariously attached to the back wall, was slowly shifting towards half-past eight.

'Phone call for a Cameron Carter,' barked the barman at the top of his voice.

Cammy held up his hand. 'Yeah, that's me, guv.' He bypassed the broken jukebox and picked up the receiver. 'Hello?'

'It's Andrew.'

Andrew was Cameron's best male friend. He detested being called Andy, as this sounded uncouth. They'd kept in touch after initially meeting at catering college. The turning point in both their lives occurred after Andrew saved Cammy from drowning at the commonwealth pool. The whole incident seemingly affected Andrew more than his best friend. He resigned his position at the Prince James Hotel and returned to college to study funeral directing, which he was now undertaking with high-minded efficiency. The coffins didn't necessarily arrive at the graveyards on time but when they did, the service was slick and sensitive.

'Hi, where are you?' asked Cammy staring at the pub's clock.

'I'm still at work. Look, I'm sorry, there's no way I can frequent the public house this fine evening. There are three new bodies arriving tonight.'

'People have no consideration.'

'I know. They die willy nilly at all sorts of inconvenient times. It's a disgrace.'

'I think I've one of your lot at the Calton tomorrow, don't I?'

'Yes, you do. Make sure you prepare a large enough grave.' Andrew started laughing down the phone.

'Don't you start. I've had enough for one year.'

'I'm only jesting, try not to take everything to heart. It could have happened to anyone, although it's more likely to happen to you!'

Cammy was fed up with the never-ending jibes. 'Ha fuckin' ha.'

'Look Cameron, you should know I'm only teasing. I'll communicate with you tomorrow.'

'Okay Andy boy.'

'The name is *Andrew*.'

'I'm only joking, try and not take everything to heart, Andy.' Cammy was turning the tables.

'Goodbye Cameron.'

'Yeah, bye.' As Cammy placed the phone receiver back down and returned to his seat, Matty appeared at the front door. 'Sorry I'm late.' She kissed him on the cheek. 'My last tour was held up in traffic at the West End.'

'That's all right, I'm used to you by now. What are you drinking?'

'Pint of cider.'

'Woodpecker?'

'No, Strongbow.'

'Strongbow?'

'Yes Strongbow, are you deaf?'

'A pint of Strongbow coming right up.'

Cammy headed back to the bar to order the drinks. Matty threw her green jacket onto the back of the grubby chair, lit up a cigarette and gazed with pleasure at Cammy standing at the bar. She was more than fond of him. If Cammy wants to be more involved in a romantic way, she thought to herself, then I would jump at the chance. However, it's up to him to make the first move, as I've no intention of spoiling a special relationship. Anyway, there's no sign of him asking me out. Perhaps it's best retaining the status quo. Imagine if we were thrown together and the whole thing fell apart. That would be unbearable. Matty was intrigued to find out what Cammy needed to tell her. He seemed agitated earlier in the day. Was he finally going to ask her out? She certainly hoped so. Cammy returned to the table clutching a pint of cider and a bottle of beer. As he placed the pints down onto the table, a little splashed onto the front of his trousers.

'You're a bloody midden!'

'Bugger it,' snapped Cammy rubbing his cords.

'They'll dry okay.'

'I'm annoyed at that, they're my new trousers.' Cammy was looking fairly smart for a change, kind of handsome in a rugged sort of way. His appearance certainly improved when he made an effort. Matty was now convinced. All the signs were there. Buying drinks, dressing up, not being annoyed with her being late. He was going to ask her out!

'Matty.'

'Cammy.'

'I need to tell you something.'

'Carry on.'

'Something I need to share with you.'

'Go on.'

Cammy paused and looked directly into Matty's hazel eyes. This is it, Matty thought. How would she react, should she play it cool? Maybe she could say how much she was in love with him.

'Matty, something occurred last week, you know when we were both at this odd funeral.'

'How can I forget.'

'Well em.' This was the moment when their love would surely hatch into the public domain.

'Spit it out man, I *feel* the same way if that helps.'

'What do you mean you *feel* the same way?' Cammy was confused. He arrived at the pub with the intention to make known what he'd uncovered in the graveyard on the day of the funeral. They seemed to have their wires crossed. Cammy, true to form, missed his chance while Matty true to form, shut up shop.

'I ... felt the same way ... about the funeral,' stammered Matty, trying to cover her tracks. She was obviously mistaken. He had no intention of asking her out. She was upset but relieved in a funny sort of way.

'Yeah, a mad funeral. Well, what I need to say is this. When I was filling in the graves with earth my spade caught in the rim of one of the coffin lids and jarred the bloody thing open. I unlocked the coffin and couldn't believe what I saw.'

'What did you see?'

'A body.'

'That's not that unusual, a body being in a coffin at a funeral.'

'*No*, the woman's body was covered from head to toe in gold jewellery, necklaces, bracelets, rings and anklets.'

'Well, what's unusual about that?'

'What's *unusual* about that is the fact that the fingers on both hands were covered in gold. You couldn't actually see the skin for jewels. There must have been over fifty rings. Her arms were awash with rattlesnake skin bracelets and there were silver anklets which ran halfway up her leg. She was wearing five or six snake bone necklaces and the biggest silver earrings I've ever seen in my whole life. Then in the guy's coffin...'

'What do you mean the *guy's* coffin?' grilled Matty appalled by his disclosure. 'You're not telling me your spade was caught up in *two* coffins?'

'No, after what I saw in the first one, I had to open the second.'

'Cammy, that's *terrible*.'

'I had to. Inside the bloke's coffin was a carrier bag containing three thousand pounds.'

'How do you know there was three thousand pounds?'

'I counted it.'

'You took the bag *out* the coffin and counted it?'

'Yeah, and I forgot to put it back.' Although intrigued by this disclosure, Matty was dismayed by the news. Any romantic notions for the evening were relegated to the fourth division of love.

'Now, let me get this right.' Matty rubbed her forehead. 'You *stole* money from the coffin of a dead man.'

'And jewellery.'

'You *stole* all the jewellery too?'

'It's not really stealing. I mean, they're dead after all.'

'What the bloody hell did you do that for?' Matty was hoping for a reasonable answer.

'I have no idea why I did this. I can't really dig them back up, so I'm stuck with the stuff. This has been bugging me so much, I had to tell someone.'

This was not what Matty was expecting to hear. 'A bit of a shocker, Cammy. Where's the stuff?'

'It's in behind the small door at the top of the watchtower. I broke in and chained the handle with a new padlock.'

'Did you not think you'd broken into enough things for one day?' Matty was still trying to digest Cammy's crooked confession.

'Look, I'm sorry, what's done is done,' reasoned Cammy. 'Do you think your brother could help me sell the stuff?'

'I don't believe what I am hearing. *Hello*, is this the Cameron Carter that I know? Dr Jekyll and Mr Hyde, or what? Don't you even think about getting Adam involved, he's in enough trouble as it is. It's one thing graverobbing – it's another handling stolen goods. What the bloody hell were you thinking of?'

Cammy shook his head, took a deep purposeful breath and looked sky high to the ceiling. 'Don't think I haven't thought about it a lot since, I have. Maybe it's greed, maybe I wanted to liven up my life, you know, a kind of buzz. Adam says he gets a buzz when he robs a house.'

'Leave my brother out of this. What he does should not be condoned or followed for that matter. Adam is a selfish petty crook absorbed in his own pathetic little world. You don't need to rob a house to get a buzz. Cammy, I can't believe what you've done. Why?'

'I've said I don't know why and that's what I mean, I *do not* know why. It's maybe similar to people buying lottery tickets. That's a kind of greed.'

'It's one thing buying a lottery ticket, it's another digging up a body, stealing cash and jewellery with the hope of selling it. This is not comparable.'

'I thought you would be more understanding.'

'*Understanding*, under bloody standing? You've lost it, Cammy. You're not the sharpest knife in the drawer, are you? I'm away home to have a glass of cider and go to bed. When I wake up in the morning I hope this is all a bad dream.' Matty stood up, grabbed her jacket and stormed out of the pub in full view of the gawking locals. They enjoyed a little bit of domestic toil.

'Don't worry, son, that's women for you. You can't live with them and you can't stab them,' joked the barman. 'Never mind son,' he continued in a menacing manner. 'She might have sliced your head off with an ornate Japanese sword and set you alight with paraffin fuel.' The barman started to laugh moronically.

Cammy turned to face the bar. 'You're new. Is it true you fell out your family tree? What's your name?'

'Jim.'

'Well, Jim,' proclaimed Cammy. 'I hear your wife is in the *Guinness Book of Records.*'

'Why's that, son?'

'I understand she's got two fannies.'

'What do you mean by that, pal?'

'Your wife has two fannies,' repeated Cammy. 'And you're *one* of them.' He stormed out the pub.

Not one the best evenings Cammy had ever enjoyed. The same could be said for Matty.

Chapter Four

ADAM'S FLAT WAS PRESUMABLY by any stretch of the imagination the dirtiest in Edinburgh. Newspapers, food, shoes, empty cans of beer, toilet rolls and clothes were amongst the objects strewn all over the living room floor. He'd lived on his own since his adopted sister Matty expressed a desire to vacate the premises for fear of catching a horrid disease, or so she said. Adam's bathroom entrance resembled a block of Emmenthal cheese thanks to his hobby of repetitively bouncing a ball hard against the toilet door. He spent many a happy hour crouched on the hallway floor, throwing his symmetrically shaped, full-grain leather baseball down the corridor. The neighbours were all elderly and, luckily for Adam, shared the collective low volume impairment of deafness. An active village of Scottish spiders inhabited his frilly peach curtains.

Adam was thirty-four years old and had never in all his limited working life remained in a job long enough to find out his work-mates' surnames. He'd certainly attempted most conceivable occupations available to man yet resisted the temptation to explore any of his jobs past the two-week settling-in period. Although, to be fair, he did on one occasion stay in the same place of employment – a city centre pub – for two months. This was primarily due to the attentions of a female workmate who happened to be a pouting blond bimbo. She took an instant shine to Adam, lured by his devil-may-care attitude. Their brief encounter prolonged his interest in the food and beverage industry for an extended period of time. Their relationship fell apart when she detected the expensive jewellery Adam had given her was stolen from her next door neighbour's house.

Adam was short and slightly overweight with bleached blond hair. His clothes were remarkably clean, tidy and decidedly lavish. His red designer shirt and matching trousers were somewhat ruined by the wearing of white sports' socks and slip-on shoes. Most of his expensive wardrobe arrived from other people's expensive wardrobes, the fruitful labours of many successful break-ins. He had a fetish for footwear; the corridor was awash with shoes of all makes and sizes.

Adam's father was dead. His mother was apparently alive and well and according to Adam an important part of his life. His dad passed on at the age of 39 and this was one of the factors that influenced Adam's personal lifestyle. Most male members of the Smith household died before reaching forty years of age and Adam, now in his mid thirties, was well aware of this unfortunate family trait. The kindred tree quite clearly influenced his daily dose of paranoia. He was truly convinced his life would end at forty and was living accordingly – to the full and in excess. He inherited his parent's flat when his dad died and took on the responsibility of looking after Matty. If truth were told, Matty looked after Adam.

He was a heavy drinker, smoked twenty-five cigarettes a day and had a chocolate, curry and hamburger diet which any kid would die for. His life balanced on a high wire with no safety net below. One fulfilling light shining through Adam's unwholesome lifestyle was his achievement over fifteen years in visiting all of Edinburgh's seven hundred and seventeen pubs, an accomplishment made all the more remarkable by the customary changing of public house names and the habitual opening of new hostelries.

The front door was slightly ajar. Cammy wiped his shoes on the spanking new mat, rattled the letterbox and peeked around the corner. Stepping into a dark hallway, he coughed loudly before moving gingerly into the squalid surrounds of Adam's living room. After viewing the untidy domestic scene, he thought it might be advisable to clean his feet on the way out.

Adam was destroying a plate of greasy food. He stuffed the last five or six thickly cut chips in his mouth and began licking the remaining tomato sauce from the cracked white plate. 'Hi, Cammy, do you want something to eat?'

'No, I'll pass, I've heard about your personal hygiene.'

'Oh, been talking to Matty?' asked Adam poking his finger-nails between his teeth in an attempt to loosen some food.

'Not recently.'

'Why is that then?'

'We've fallen out.'

'Fallen out, what about?'

'That's why I'm here.'

Although Cammy knew Matty's brother reasonably well, he wasn't in a habit of calling at Adam's home. This was only the second time he'd visited the flat in three years. Examining the mouldy baked potato cartons, discarded cigarette ends and the empty Irn Bru bottles he was reminded of why his visits to this address had been few and far between. Adam wiped the dribbling sauce from the side of his mouth with his shirtsleeve. 'That's what God gave you sleeves for.'

'What's the pong, Adam?'

'I managed to spill some yoghurt down the back of the settee last week and the stink won't go away.'

'Did you not give it a good scrub?'

'No way, I didn't go near it! I'm not putting my hand down the back of that settee. Don't know what you might find. I was rummaging once and a mouse ran over my arm. So, never again.'

'Lovely. The girls must adore coming here for a romantic candle-lit dinner.' Cammy's tongue was firmly pushed into the side of his cheek.

'No, I never bring dames back here, it's too personal.'

'Mmm.'

Cammy was hoping that Adam could dispose of the jewellery. He reached deep into his coat pocket, grabbed a handful of rings, bracelets and anklets and placed them down on the stained tablecloth in front of Adam's nose. Picking up every item of jewellery one by one, Adam meticulously examined each piece. A broad smile emerged from his thin lips. The articles were of great value. 'Very nice. Where on earth did you dig this stuff up from?'

'Not so far from the truth. It's a tall tale.'

'I've plenty of time.'

'Well, to cut a long story short, I took the jewellery from a coffin at the kirkyard last week and that's why Matty and I aren't speaking.'

'Why?' Adam paused. 'Did you not give her any of the

jewellery?' He genuinely believed this could be the reason for their fall-out.

'No, she wasn't happy with what I did.'

'Ah, she's an idiot. This stuff is top notch. I suppose you want me to flog it for you?'

'Yeah that was the general idea. Can you?' Cammy observed Adam's piercing eyes.

'No problem at all.'

'Where will you sell it?'

'None of your business. I'll get you a good price. Remember, I'll expect a decent cut.'

'Goes without saying. I just want you to get rid of the stuff.'

'So let me get this clear. You dug someone's corpse up and stole their belongings?'

'*No*. I was about to fill in their grave when my spade jammed in the coffin lid. And by the way, it's *not* stealing. They're dead after all. I opened the other one and . . . '

'You opened a *second* coffin!'

'Yeah, found some money.'

'How much?'

'About three thousand pounds.'

'*Really*.'

'Yeah, three grand, all in crisp twenty pound notes. Apparently the bloke was a bank manager. This was his last request.'

'Dig up graves and steal the valuables buried with the bodies,' affirmed Adam licking his lips. 'That is truly a *brilliant* idea. I suppose most people must be buried with their favourite belongings. You're a genius, Cammy. This could be the scam of the century. The scam to beat all other scams.'

'Now hold on, Adam. All I want you to do is sell this stuff. I'm not planning to do it again. It was a one-off, a moment of madness.'

'A moment of sheer fuckin' brilliance you mean.' Adam was trying desperately to contain his excitement. 'We're onto something here, Cammy. This could be the big time and as you say, it's not stealing because they're dead.' Adam's eyes lit up like sparklers, the lure of money feeding his greed. He grabbed his crotch and let out a wailing sound similar to a lustful pheasant. 'Bingo!'

Cammy looked perplexed. 'Dream on. Get a grip of yourself.'

'Come through here for a second.' Adam pointed to the hall door. 'I've something to show you.'

They left the squalor of the front room and headed a short distance down a dark corridor, past Adam's impressive shoe collection and into his bedroom. The room was amazingly tidy in comparison to the rest of his living quarters. Two cats were fast asleep on the bed. There was a brand new computer and printer beside a bookcase bulging with multicoloured files. A silver whisky flask lay on the bedside table. Four bicycles were leaning against the side of his double bed and the top of the wardrobe was brimming with videotapes and CDs. Everywhere you looked, there was something of value. Adam called his bedroom the 'inner sanctum'. At the back of the room beside the window was a stack of twenty empty ice-cream tubs. Beside the containers, a bundle of adult magazines stood firm and erect in front of a small cupboard.

In a virtuoso attempt to recreate the Union Jack, Adam had painted the wooden door red, white and blue. An old-fashioned sign displaying the words STALAG LUFT III – *PRISONERS WILL BE SHOT BEYOND THIS POINT* was pinned onto the adjoining wall. Captivated by the notice, Cammy moved three garden gnomes to one side and pulled hard on the brass door handle. He was clearly unaware of the large padlock attached to the frame. Adam, proud of his covert collection, threw over the cupboard keys and encouraged Cammy to open the door. The base of the doorway triggered a switch under the carpet, which in turn activated four spotlights. Music bellowed out a rhythmical tune from the 1940s and a voice emanating from a hidden speaker instructed Cammy in a poor German accent to put his hands up. The cubbyhole was full of Second World War memorabilia. Six gas masks, two pairs of field binoculars and an expertly constructed model Spitfire were hanging on hooks from the cupboard ceiling. The shelves were full of maps, ration books, old gun shells and military medals. A grey army kitbag contained further wartime relics including a Luftwaffe pilot's badge and two worse for wear German combat boots. When Adam was asked where he'd purchased the noteworthy artefacts, Cammy was abruptly told in no uncertain terms to mind his own business.

Edinburgh War Museum was temporarily exhibiting two empty glass display-cases.

A dainty leather-covered beanbag lay tattered and neglected in the far corner of the room. Due to age and years of misuse, the patterned cushion was split, revealing soiled foam. 'That's an old pouffe,' claimed Cammy.

'What did you say?' snapped Adam quick as a flash.

'Your pouffe,' replied Cammy, pointing at the beanbag. 'The bottom's fallen out.'

'It's not a poofy, it's a bean bag!' Adam looked annoyed. His tone of voice was bordering on the hateful. 'I'd never have a poof in this house.' What an odd thing to say thought Cammy.

Stealing was a craft which Adam practised with great guile and proficiency. He was proud of his so-called profession. Nothing was too troublesome. He was clever, alert and planned to make a name for himself, already building up a useful network of petty crooks and dodgy dealers around the city. Adam perpetrated many a crime in Edinburgh without being apprehended. Evading the authorities and avoiding convictions was an art in itself. He was indeed a Jekyll and Hyde character, by day a big slob, by night a master criminal of the localised variety. He was desperate to hit the big time and Cammy's unwitting graverobbing concept set his mind loose on a wild criminal goose chase. 'Cammy, your idea is sheer class.'

'Wait a minute,' remarked Cammy bluntly. 'Before you drag me into your sordid little world of crime, I don't want to take this so-called idea any further.' Cammy's protests were falling on deaf ears.

'Nonsense, man, I can see you're tempted. I'll turn this into a big money-making business and we'd never be caught.'

'That's easy for you to say. It so happens that I'm a grave digger and it wouldn't take the local police too long to associate graverobbing with grave digging.'

'I'm not so sure about that,' stated Adam calling his bluff. 'I'd say you'd probably be the last person they'd suspect. You could fill in the grave after we take the stuff.'

'You've *no idea* what's involved in grave digging, have you?'

'No, not really,' He was clueless as to the work involved.

'Well, Adam, in this day and age we use purpose-built excavators which help us dig the exact size of grave.'

'So, how come you managed to underestimate the size of the Calton plot?'

'Who told you that?'

'Who do you think?'

'Matty,' affirmed Cammy, answering his own question. Telling her anything is like advertising in the *Gazette*. 'Anyway, in my own defence, the soil structure at the Calton is so grainy we're not allowed to use a digger. It's all sweat, spit and spade. I miscalculated, *okay?*'

'Okay, Cammy. It doesn't bother me if you a dig a grave too small.' Adam scratched his crotch. 'How long does it take to prepare a burial plot by hand?'

'A long bloody time.'

'You'd have to fill it in again,' persisted Adam, not really listening to what was being said.

'It's bad enough digging a grave, but filling it in too is bloody hard work. Perhaps we should roll up in the middle of the night with a mechanical digger? Anyway, this is all pie in the sky. It will never happen.' Cammy pointed at the bookcase, desperately trying to change the subject. 'What's all the files for?'

'They're *my* salvation,' expounded Adam proudly.

'What do you mean your *salvation?*'

'The folders are the lifeline of my business activities. I keep everything in my files. This one here for example is a complete dossier on regular overseas holidays taken by residents living in various parts of Edinburgh. I can tell you when people are away from home, where they're going to, whom they are with and more importantly, when they're coming back. While they enjoy the delights of Spain or the pleasures of Brighton Beach, I'll do a little housework.'

'How do you get this information?'

'None of your bloody business,' retorted Adam. 'As Matty would say, it's good solid research that counts.'

Adam's contact with a local travel agency provided him with pertinent information on the globetrotting arrangements of various bureau clients. There was even an occasion when a recently married couple left keys to their new premises with the agency and Adam with great delight removed all their wedding presents from the flat. When asked if he had any feelings of guilt, he justified robbing the newlyweds by the remark 'Who needs three toasters anyway?'

'What's this file all about?' inquired Cammy, flicking through a gaudy gold-rimmed folder.

'That's my 'bell-file'. It shows who has a house alarm and who doesn't. I prefer the folk who do, as they've more to hide. This information is all about good reconnaissance.' Lifting down yet another file, Adam continued. 'And this is my press cuttings file.'

Any of his break-ins reported in the local newspaper were cut out and stuck into a clear plastic folder in alphabetical order. 'I'm onto my third press file. I'm really proud of these articles. Gives me a sense of belonging. Have a look at this snippet.' The newspaper heading read: '*Dirty robber has a chocolate chip on his shoulder*'. Cammy read the *Lothian Gazette and Journal* article and started to laugh.

'You are joking, Adam. Tell me you're joking?'

'No,' replied Adam bluntly. 'What a scoop!'

'That was you?'

'Sure was. Let's say it's my calling card.'

Cammy turned up his nose. 'That's disgusting.' Although the article was unpleasant, he still found it funny.

Adam's bedroom was a shrine to petty crime. One of his files listed forthcoming city weddings. He attended evening receptions to enjoy free food and drink, knowing full well that the happy couple would believe he was a friend of the other family. The main purpose of this scam was to give him a quick-fix adrenaline rush. On the one occasion he was rumbled, Adam claimed to be in the wrong hotel.

Even more obscure was the 'take-away, blood and casino' folder – dedicated to the appetising quest for free nosh. For fast food at no expense, Adam phoned a pizza delivery service requesting a tasty carryout. While the motorcyclist delivered to a fictitious top floor neighbour, Adam helped himself to a deep panned crusty pizza from the back of the bike. From time to time, when experiencing midday hunger pangs, he'd sneak into the hospital under the pretence of waiting for a friend. Fresh orange juice, chocolate teacakes and custard creams were then unknowingly donated courtesy of the blood transfusion service. The same could be said for the casino. Free membership meant complimentary snacks and all without placing a single bet. With nothing at stake, he was always evens money favourite to clear the buffet table. Adam was never afraid of adventurous assignments.

'Does breaking into houses really give you a huge buzz?' probed Cammy.

'A bigger buzz than sex.'

'Oh really?' His eyes were wide open. Cammy had never been with a girl in an intimate way. This was highly unusual for a twenty-nine-year-old man who'd worked in the notoriously promiscuous hotel industry. Cammy maintained a pure strongly held belief. He'd only sleep with the woman he married.

'You should come with me house hunting one night,' suggested Adam. 'The invitation's an open one.'

Deep down Cammy found the idea tempting. 'Naw. No way. Definitely no way! Not a snowball in hell's chance.'

Chapter Five

THE STATIONARY WHITE TRANSIT van was merely yards from the wooden gateway leading to an impressively large Georgian house. The summer's night was laden with anticipation. Adam and Cammy were sitting quietly side by side in the front of the hired van. 'I can't *believe* I'm doing this, Adam.'

'You'll love every minute.'

Cammy, nervous yet excited, had given in to temptation and agreed to accompany Adam on one of his break-ins. He was looking forward to the evening's excitement. His sudden change in decision was the result of a niggling teenage demon. At the age of fifteen, accompanied by a volatile gang of troublesome schoolmates, Cammy prepared to break into an old people's home. At the last moment, too nervous for words, he decided to abandon the robbery and was subsequently branded a coward during his final two years at school.

'The van is a bit conspicuous here, isn't it?' suggested Cammy.

'Yes, very conspicuous. I want people to see this van and link the vehicle to the robbery.'

'Why? The van's not stolen, is it?'

'No, not at all. Remember the first rule of dishonesty is honesty. The van is hired. I've changed the front and back number plates and used the registration of a similar vehicle I saw yesterday parked in Heriot Row. You must keep untruths to a minimum or this can ultimately lead to confusion.'

'Thanks for the advice. Ever thought of lecturing at Police College on petty crime? What's that on the windscreen?'

'That's my disabled sticker,' explained Adam. 'Means I can park anywhere in the town.'

'Oh,' muttered Cammy, not impressed with the oldest scam in the book.

Perched in the back of the van were two smart red bicycles and an empty ice cream tub. Earlier in the evening Adam spotted two unlocked bikes beside school railings. Before you could say 'stop, police' the bikes were neatly stacked in the back and Adam proceeded on his merry criminal way.

He had a tendency to relieve owners of their modes of pedal-power, invariably using a large set of wire cutters to clip through the inadequate security chains. He once helped a friend steal motorbikes, lifting them from the street onto the back of a large lorry. The bikes were disassembled and peddled as parts. This mechanism was utilised when Adam, at the merciless age of seventeen, stole his own 50cc moped from the front door of his flat. After reporting his misfortune to the police, he subsequently made a successful insurance claim before selling sections of the stripped machine to a local garage. This was a short-lived job for Adam as he found the whole process boring and lacking any form of excitement. Breaking into houses was a different kettle of fish altogether. The thrill was always there.

'Are you excited?'

'What was that?' Cammy was daydreaming.

'Are you excited?' repeated Adam.

'Suppose I am.'

'Remember, think of your best shag ever and this will come close . . . Come close, get it?' After containing his laughter for a couple of seconds, he started to snigger out loud. Adam possessed a genuine lack of wit. He repeatedly laughed at his own jokes, even if they weren't funny.

'Mmm, okay, Adam, I shall do that.'

'What's that in your hand, Cammy?'

'It's my ketchup top.'

'Your ketchup top?' Adam was surprised by the reply.

'Yeah, my ketchup top, my security ketchup top.'

'A ketchup top,' said Adam. 'I'm a bit worried about you. Are you on some form of medication?'

Cammy carried with him an old lid taken from a bottle of tomato sauce. The top dispensed a feeling of collective calm, similar to a child's security blanket. While recuperating at home from his near-death experience, he knocked over and shattered a bottle of sauce. After extracting the glass from his cut-pile moulded carpet and cleaning up the mess on the floor, he washed the bottle lid and put it in his pocket. 'It's like a lucky charm.'

'You're definitely on medication. If you're not, you should be.'

Cammy ignored the puerile remark. 'Do you always use a van like this?'

'No, that's the last thing you should do. Variation is a man's best friend.' Adam, along with his substandard joke telling, had a nasty habit of either making up proverbs or just getting them badly wrong. 'No, I never use the same vehicle. The reason I've hired this van is because I've a scam on the go tomorrow.'

'You haven't even started tonight's job and you're thinking about tomorrow?'

'Patience is a virtue, my dear Roger.'

'*What?*'

'*The Great Escape*,' yelled Adam punching the air. 'That movie is the tops. There's a line when the SBO – Senior British Officer – says 'patience is a virtue, my dear Roger'. Richard Attenborough played Roger, or Big 'X'. What a cool film.'

'And you were worried about me?'

Adam was obsessed with *The Great Escape*. He had watched the film on countless occasions and knew large sections of the script off by heart. Now and again, for no apparent reason, he would impulsively interject a slice of prisoner-of-war dialogue taken from the feature film into a conversation. This could happen at any time and routinely had the impact of bringing rational chinwags to an abrupt halt. Often when Adam was drunk, his party piece would be the re-enactment of various sections of *The Great Escape*. Even for those who didn't know the film, his entertaining descriptions and long uninterrupted soliloquies couldn't fail to impress.

'Adam, a miracle has fallen to earth and landed on our laps.' Cammy was rolling his eyes up towards the clouds. He fell to his hands and knees and with the glove compartment hard against his face, raised his arms to the heavens 'Hallelujah, praise the Lord. You managed to get a proverb right. What will befall the world next!'

'What do you mean by that?' barked Adam in an aggressive manner, his nicotine stained teeth in full view. He didn't realise that his conglomeration of mottoes and proverbs were constantly erroneous. Sadly, the only reason he'd succeeded this time round in quoting a correct sentence was due to memory proficiency rather than being master of phrase and fable.

'Nothing,' muttered Cammy changing the subject yet again. 'You were talking about a scam you have on tomorrow?'

'Yeah, I've done this a few times before in Fife, Midlothian and down in the Borders and it worked a treat. What I'm going to do tomorrow is head down to the auction rooms in George Street and pretend to be from a small firm that delivers furniture. Here, I've got a few official looking business cards made.' Adam fished into his pocket and handed Cammy one of his cards.

'During the bidding, as the punters buy items from the auction room floor, I'll go up to individuals and pass on my card. For a small charge I'll deliver the goods direct to their home. There's always some rich bastard in need of this service, especially when I tell them no payment is required in advance. So, off I go with some nice pieces of furniture to my associate up in St Andrews who runs an antique shop and he'll be happy to take things on from there. Easy peasy, nice and easy.'

'What's the phone number on the card?'

'The Police Station.'

'You're bloody *unbelievable*. Do you never give that big scamming mind of yours a rest?'

'No rest for the busy. Gloves on and let's get to it.' Adam started up the van, released the handbrake and slowly drove up the gravel drive to the front of the large stone house. 'We'll go through the back.'

The night was bright. Summer was well under way. The residence was conveniently surrounded and adequately protected by a large green hedge on one side and a six-foot brick wall on the other. Prying eyes could not see into the well-kept back garden, ideal for residents and robbers alike. Adam disconnected the alarm system, a quick job for him, and crudely smashed the back door's glass panel. 'These doors are fuckin' hopeless. If I were a crime prevention officer, I would . . .'

'Well you're *not*, so get on with it.'

Adam opened the back door and entered the large kitchen.

The house was dark inside. Most of the curtains were firmly closed. The occupants were away to New York for a long weekend. Cammy, making his way to the main sitting room, noticed a shape moving in the darkness. A skinny black and white cat darted through from one of the bedrooms, brushing Cammy's leg on its way to the kitchen. 'What the hell was that?' shouted Cammy grabbing hold of Adam's arm. 'I nearly shat myself.'

'No *that's* for later. They've gone away for the weekend and left the moggy on its own,' Adam was annoyed by the cat's condition. 'That's a friggin' disgrace, poor wee beast. I've a good mind to phone the RSPCA or the Cats Protection League. It's not even a short weekend they're on; I was told Thursday to Tuesday. I mean, come on, if they went away on Thursday morning and don't come back till Tuesday night, then that's . . .' Adam needed his fingers to work out this perplexing mathematical conundrum. 'That's em . . . that's one, two... em Thursday, Friday, em... six days. Poor bloody cat.'

'Never mind that flea-bitten bag of worms.' Cammy was still in shock. 'Let's get on with it. The little bugger gave me the fright of my life.'

'You've no heart, Cammy. Look, the cat's sitting in the kitchen beside its food bowls. Must have finished all its grub. I'll feed the poor thing. Now where do you think they keep the cat food?' Adam loved animals. Even in the middle of a break-in, he had time to feed the cat. Every time he saw a Rentokil van he let the tyres down.

'Adam, will you hurry up?' Cammy's heart was beating faster, his pores filling with sweat.

'I'll be there in a minute. See if you can find some bags or pillowcases.'

'What for?'

'To put the stuff in, that's what for.'

They seized as many precious objects as possible from each room of the house, turning out drawers and cupboards in the process. There was a fine array of valuables to choose from including jewellery, a couple of expensive watches and some very exotic-looking ornaments. The CD player, TV, video recorder and computer added a traditional look to their haul. Trying to avoid the bulkier items, they snatched as much as the van could take. Cammy was enjoying himself. He was indeed experiencing 'the buzz'. Suddenly, a light appeared from the box-room. They could see a shadow emanating from the base of the door. 'Shit, let's go,' blurted Cammy. 'There's someone in.'

'No there isn't.'

'A light came on,' whispered Cammy 'I'm out of here.'

'Calm down!' Adam confidently stepped forward and opened the box-room door. 'There you go, one light on one timer. Useless bloody things these are anyway. All they do is tell people like me, people like them aren't in. I mean, they come on at the same time each day. All you have to do is watch a house for a couple of days, take some notes and Bob's your Auntie Beanie.'

'Thank goodness for that, I nearly deposited something in my pants.'

'Well, reminded Cammy. Would you go and fetch my ice-cream carton from the van? As the old proverb goes, every tub must stand on its own bottom.'

Juvenile urinary competition led to post-burglary stool deposits. Adam was the unofficial 'school champion of piss', slashing higher than any of his companions, although to be fair Fat Davie after three cans of cheap fizzy cola could blast his pee a respectable distance. His threat to Adam's 'wee' crown was briskly eradicated the day he accidentally urinated onto an electric fence. Fat Dave's shocking aim caused severe jarring to his genitalia and retired him from full competition. At break time and after school, Adam and a group of comparable renegades vanished to a rugged section of isolated wasteland behind the regional library. They would partake in a light-hearted peeing competition, seeing who could discharge their water furthest over a crumbling brick wall. The residents walking on the other side of this wall did not appreciate receiving a free public penny, especially when yellow rain from time to time sprinkled down from above. The boy who sprayed highest won a rock hard toffee stolen from the local newsagent's shop. On one occasion prior to his bout of towering urination, Adam placed a fish supper wrapped in newspaper on top of the wall. Sadly the food fell foul of a gusty blow and tumbled to the ground. Adam, now in full flow, couldn't stop his lofty fire and despondently pished into his haddock and chips. He thought about rinsing his nosh in a nearby puddle but thankfully gave in to common sense. After weighing up his options, he slapped the mushy food on the maths teacher's car windscreen.

Adam was preparing to leave his calling card. Some criminals would try hard to produce a number two and excrete on the living room carpet. Adam was different. After breaking into a house, he evacuated his bowels into an empty chocolate-chip ice-cream tub, placed the lid back on the carton and popped it into the victim's freezer. He pictured the householder some weeks later, looking for a tasty snack in the fridge-freezer and coming across this less than sweet surprise. He hoped one day to gain notoriety as 'the shite robber' or 'the freezer king'.

The notion of defecating in a carton was conceived a decade earlier when Adam and his former partner-in-crime, big Aidan from St. Andrews, broke into a house and prior to leaving invented a game called 'Hunt the shit'. The contest was simple. One of them ran off to have a serious toilet visit somewhere in the house while the other person counted to fifty, ahead of searching for the fresh deposit. Neither was allowed to use the sense of smell to aid their pursuit, so a clothes peg was introduced to the game and hide and seek with a superfluous discharge was born.

They should have sold the rights to a major sports manufacturer.

On the evening in question, Adam produced a runny mess in the householder's walk-in-wardrobe, which Aidan found within five minutes. When Adam's turn emerged to 'hunt the shit', he couldn't locate Aidan's healthy droppings anywhere. For the best part of an hour, he hunted high and low in every room of the house with no success until, looking for a cold drink, opened the fridge and was met with the sight of a thick brown mixture oozing from a white Perspex butter dish. The evening's entertainment was completed when Adam propelled the owner's toothbrush up his bottom and asked Aidan to take a photograph of his backside's brush with hygiene. Two weeks later the photo was sent in the post to the to the householder with a note which said 'brush flush brush'.

Adam dropped his trousers and manoeuvred himself into a position three feet above the carton. Cammy couldn't watch this part of the job. He hoped Adam wouldn't miss. 'I ate several plates of bran, a large tin of sweet corn and a big glass of orange juice yesterday. This could be a good one. You know, I'm a modern day Robin Hood. I steal from the rich to give to the poor, i.e. me.'

'I don't remember Robin Hood shitting in ice-cream tubs.'

Adam marked the base of his carton with a thick red **X**. He'd often judge himself on the accuracy of his aim, awarding points out of ten. As the excrement dropped from his pale spotty bum, Adam shouted, 'Tally Ho chaps, bombs away.'

Cammy vacated the room and remained outside in the corridor until Mr Whippy's ice-cream carton was safely deposited in the freezer. While waiting he realised that an anagram for Adam Smith was 'Ma Mad Shit'. When he returned, Adam was wiping his bottom on the arm of the sofa whilst speaking on the phone. Cammy couldn't believe his eyes. 'I think you're crossing the boundary of decency. Can you not go to the toilet to do this?'

'No way! This is my traditional routine. That was an eight out of ten. I think the cat thought I was using his litter tray.'

'You're disgusting. I hope you washed your hands.' Cammy was appalled by Adam's germ-ridden antics. 'Who were you phoning?'

'My mum. I always phone her at this time of night and to think I'm saving this household money by calling out of peak hours.' After supposedly speaking to his mother for ten minutes, Adam phoned a variety of premium telephone numbers. He would often call special chat lines, which no doubt cost the householders a small fortune. On one occasion he phoned the speaking clock and left the phone off the hook.

'That's it, Cammy, good fun, eh? Bit of a buzz?'

'Not bad,' said Cammy. 'Not bad.'

Chapter Six

MATTY WAS LOOKING FORWARD to seeing Andrew. He had a dreadful habit of keeping people waiting, whether it was clients or friends. 'He's running a few minutes behind schedule today, Miss Smith,' announced the bronzed male receptionist.

The funeral parlour's waiting room was expensively decorated with hand painted wallpaper and matching curtains. A wooden table was positioned in front of four comfy leather seats. Two robust cheese plants flourished in the corner of the room. On top of the counter surrounding the room was a computer screen connected to the Internet. Clients were encouraged to view Fitzpatrick and Sons new web page ahead of linking to other funeral related sites. Andrew's website dispensed helpful information on arranging a funeral, details of cremations and suggestions on caring for the bereaved. His page, although laced with large words and over-elaborate images, contained a useful guide to funeral charges, information for social fund claimants and in effect provided the 'suffering surfer' with a practical A-Z on how to bury a loved one. The ambience was somewhat spoiled by the painful piped organ music originating from the primitive loudspeaker system. Suspended from the low ceiling was a close-circuit security camera.

The thought of a mourning relative running out with a cheese plant seemed most unlikely.

'What have I done with my lottery ticket?' Matty checked the pocket of her favourite green jacket. She religiously invested in the National Lottery each weekend, choosing the same numbers – nine, twelve, fifteen, fourteen, one and nineteen. Her regular formula for choosing lottery numbers related to the initials in her first name and the first of her surname. She then calculated at what place each letter appeared in the alphabet. 'I' for nine, 'L' for twelve and so on. This was not the most original formula available to woman.

Matty glanced up, cast her eyes across the room and gawked in disbelief. The computer screen was displaying a colour photograph of six scantily clad models in see-through yellow bras. Seemingly the last customer to grace the waiting room hooked onto the Internet had bypassed Andrew's funeral pages and viewed a site dedicated to women's underwear. Matty grabbed the mouse, scrolled down the page and clicked onto an order form imparting a sizeable range of lingerie gifts. What a brilliant idea she thought – 'virtual pants'. The company was plugging a colossal catalogue of products by well-known brand names such as Berlei, Sloggi, Gossard, and Playtex. Bras, briefs, corsets and suspender belts were available in all colours, styles, shapes and sizes.

The good-looking male receptionist entered the waiting room. His arrival coincided with a pair of crotchless red panties appearing on the screen. He stared at the monitor, raised an eyebrow and said in an embellished effeminate voice. 'Mr Fitzpatrick will see you now, second door on the left.'

'Yes I *know* where his office is.' Matty was a little embarrassed.

Andrew was of Irish extract, his grandparents originating from Drogheda and his immediate family from further north in Strabane. He was dispatched to an Edinburgh public school at the tender age of eight. Andrew would only see his mother and father during the school holidays and even then they'd often embark on European vacations, leaving him behind with a nanny. His parents appeared to have no interest in him, and to Andrew they might as well have been dead. His schooling suffered; academic results were poor. The only further education course he managed to scrape into was a three-year diploma in hotel management, which he passed with flying colours. Needless to say, none of his family bothered attending the graduation ceremony.

After Cammy's misadventure, Andrew turned his back on the hotel trade and took up the profession, which would irritate his parents the most. He attained a diploma in funeral directing by completing a correspondence course. Then for one evening a week over two years he memorised the theory and practice behind embalming. Membership to the Institute of Embalmers promptly followed.

'Hello, Andrew,' said Matty smiling. 'Your piped music is shite.'

'Charming as usual,' retorted Andrew. 'Matty, How are you?'

'Could be better.' They gave each other a huge hug. 'Nice-looking new receptionist you have. Bit of alright. Shame he's bent as a nine-bob bit. What a waste.'

'Gives an old man like me something to look at.' Andrew, far from old, was thirty-two years of age and noticeably gay. He was wearing a black suit with starched shirt, silk tie and a pocket handkerchief. Apart from employing a full-time embalmer, he only hired part-time men at his funeral parlour, often travellers from around the globe who were searching for short-term work. Andrew, who suffered from delusions of grandeur, had no distinct accent. His superior demeanour, pristine appearance and perfect manners were exaggerated by his habit of turning his nose up at rude remarks. Matty's bad language was always a bone of contention between them but he secretly liked her basic approach.

Keeping people waiting was part of a more multifarious superiority complex.

'You're the sweetest big bugger I know.'

'Matty, please refrain from using such wording in my parlour surrounds.'

Andrew, wise without the wrinkles, had an unusual way of speaking, as if he were back in the days of Queen Victoria. It was a flamboyant vernacular from the 1890s. He normally took twice as long as anyone else to convey a simple statement. Andrew's mind was like a finely tuned instrument, yet his ancient speech pattern was hiding a darker side of his personality. 'Would you care to partake of a glass of something or other?'

'What have you got?'

'I have an array of choice wines and spirits from around the world.' Andrew opened up a small oak cabinet positioned beside two security screens to reveal a concealed fridge. Lying on top of the counter was a pile of colour brochures advertising the benefits of a funeral pre-payment plan. 'My latest little acquisition. You must always be equipped for grieving relatives. It's either a cup of tea or a tumbler of whisky.'

'Do you not have any cider?'

He turned his nose up at the mere thought and gave Matty a condescending glare. 'One does not stock sweet fizzy mush.'

'A tumbler of whisky sounds good then. Should spice up my tours this afternoon.'

'Certainly spices up my day after having a drink with lamenting relatives. By the time I reach my five o'clock appointment, I'm invariably away with the fairies.'

'You're always away with fairies.'

'Very droll my dear Matty. So tell me, what's the problem?'

'What do you mean what's the problem?'

'My dear Matty, your visitations to my fine professional abode are few and far between. Albert Einstein does not have to be in attendance for a chap like me to retain intelligence from preceding visits. They perpetually pertain to a problem on your side of the fence. I have calculated that plausibly on this occasion there may be a wire fence and possibly a problem.'

'You mean, I always come and see you if there is a problem.'

'If you have to relay the meaning of my testimony in that manner, yes.'

'You don't mind me coming here do you?'

'Of course I do not mind you coming here. You should know me better by now. Come on, tell Uncle Andrew today's woes.'

'I've fallen out with Cammy.'

'Again?'

'Yeah, I stormed out the pub the other week. I've not spoken to him since. I thought about calling him. I'll wait until he phones me.' Andrew had heard this scenario so many times before. Although she never told him what her true feelings towards Cammy were, he was aware of the situation. Being best friends to Cammy and Matty had its benefits as well as its drawbacks. He knew exactly what was going on. Matty was in love with Cammy. Cammy was in love with Matty. As a reluctant member of this pretence triangle, he refused to play Cupid, believing they should work out their own problems.

Matty looked troubled. 'I presume he's told you?'

'Told me what?'

'About taking jewellery and money from two coffins. I was pretty shocked at that.'

Andrew wasn't expecting this reply. 'Sorry, say that again?'

'He stole from a couple of coffins.'

'Well, I never. The wretched old rogue. This is more like it, Matty, a juicy slice of parochial gossip.'

'You mean you didn't know?'

'No, this is refreshingly newsworthy.'

'Well what do you make of that?'

He took a few seconds to compose himself. Then in a manner similar to a highly-strung classical actor said, 'I am overwhelmed. I am overwhelmed beyond belief.'

He was far from overwhelmed, having heard of gravediggers plundering graves before. Even Andrew had given into temptation on a few occasions while preparing bodies for burial. Often relatives would ask him to place personal belongings in a coffin with the recently departed. One day, having agreed to position a gold candlestick beside the deceased, he noticed the antique was similar to one displayed in his house. So, to balance up the mantelpiece at his country cottage, he took it home. Other small mementos followed, including a silver pocket watch, a silk tie and a crystal decanter. Andrew thought this was neither the time nor the place to reveal this

'So, I did the right thing by storming out?'

'Oh yes, my poppet, I would have acted in a similar manner. Even splashing a little beer on him would have been permissible in my book. You poor dear.'

'Will you definitely have a word with him? Don't let on I've told you this.'

'Your wish is my command. I'm a double for the fairy godmother in Cinderella. Now changing this sordid subject, how is that coarse, crude, ill-bred, loutish, unrefined, oafish, imbecile brother of yours?' Andrew and Adam had two things in common, a love of animals and a short-lived sexual secret. A broad smile appeared on Matty's pale face. Andrew knew how to cheer her up.

'Oh, same as usual, nothing changes there.'

'And how is your work?'

'Oh fine. Had a weirdo on board the bus the other day though.'

'Tell me the grisly details.' His eyes lit up in the midday sun.

'I was conducting my last tour of the day when I realised there was only one man left on the bus.' Matty was shaking her head. 'All the other tourists left the bus at the East End of Princes Street.'

'Sounds like my kind of bus.'

'The man, only about twenty-five or so, was sitting two seats down. He stared directly at me with a broad smile over his face. He seemed to be moving his arm quite a lot and then started to moan.'

'No, he wasn't was he?' giggled Andrew.

'Yeah, he was!'

Andrew laughed out loud and endeavoured to compose himself. 'That's frightful. What did you do?'

'I ran downstairs and asked the driver to sort it out.'

'Very wise, my dear. So that's the *five* p.m. tour is it?' Andrew suddenly gave out a huge yawn. He stretched his arms high into the air.

'You'll tell me if I'm boring you, won't you?'

'Of course you're not boring me. The dawn chorus woke me up exceptionally early this morning. Plus, one is on call twenty-four hours a day, three hundred and sixty-five days a year. I wish there could be one weekend when someone didn't decide to die.'

Andrew lived twenty miles south of Edinburgh in an old farm labourer's cottage. The house was fairly remote. The only noises heard were the local cacophony of crows and a postal van, arriving each morning at twenty past seven. The whole of the locality was so silent, he found the dawn chorus on certain mornings too noisy for words. Considering he once lived in the clangorous city centre, this was kind of odd. The forty-mile round trip also contributed to his tiredness, not to mention his vibrant sex life. 'You really do seem to be down,' suggested Andrew. 'Have you been 'stepping' again?'

'Yeah, last Tuesday. What a difference it makes.' When Matty required peace to regain her weary thoughts, she went 'stepping'. This was her own term given to the custom of sitting on a doorstep in the street where she was found as a baby. The residents of Regent Terrace didn't mind. She'd become a frequent visitor to the stylish street. This was her place of solitude, similar to Cammy's watchtower retreat. Andrew's place of privacy was his bathroom. This was an actuality only known to himself. 'My dear Matty, I have another appointment looming. Would you mind being a dear and running along?'

'No problem, thanks for the chat. You'll speak to Cammy for me won't you?'

'I shall make this my foremost quest of the week.' Do not despair, I shall be there. Do embrace one of my business cards.' Andrew passed Matty one of his new cards. It read, Andrew Fitzpatrick DIP FD, HDHCIM – Higher Diploma in Hotel Catering and Institutional Management.

'I always laugh at the initials after your name,' said Matty. 'Has anyone asked you what they mean?'

'No, not as yet. Clients prefer dealing with directors who have initials after their names. They're not too troubled with what they mean. I will ascertain the availability of my new funeral operative and request the boy to fetch you a complimentary taxi courtesy of Fitzpatrick and Sons.'

Matty grinned. 'Where are the sons going to come from?'

'Wouldn't you like to know?' responded Andrew, rolling his eyes. He pressed a large yellow button on his desk and spoke into a plastic microphone sticking up from the table. 'Attention all staff. Would Eric please call a taxi for Miss Smith.' His voice blared out all over the building. The elaborate loudspeaker system was an earlier link between Andrew and Matty's brother. He'd acquired the old device from Adam who'd purloined it from, oddly enough, the taxi firm they were about to call. Andrew loved the power of switching on his loudspeaker system and controlling the whole office at the touch of a button. Matty hurriedly left the funeral parlour feeling a little happier inside and headed off to work. Andrew picked up the phone and dialled Cammy's telephone number.

Chapter Seven

ADAM WAS RADIANTLY ATTIRED in a superior blue linen suit, immaculately pressed trousers, white socks and grey slip-on shoes. For a man who possessed an uncontrollable fetish for shoes, he still had the ability to choose footwear which was inferior, inexpensive and falling apart. 'I have called you here on this nineteenth day of July for the first meeting of our company, whose name is yet to be defined, to officially launch our credentials to the world of commerce. As company chairman . . .'

'Wait a minute, who voted *you* in as company chairman?' quizzed Cammy.

'I had a secret ballot yesterday which was orchestrated by my good self in the presence of my good self and witnessed by a certain Mr Adam Smith, who seconded my motion.'

Adam made a big effort to look smart looking for their inaugural engagement. He relished the notion of faking company chairmanship. Graverobbing was top of the agenda. He was temporarily living in a swindle-tinged fantasyland. Cammy was less enthusiastic, tired and late for work. He just wanted to get on with their discussion and was not overly impressed with Adam's play-acting.

'Adam, would you like some tea?' Cammy was unable to focus properly without his daily dose of milky tea. A large silver stainless-steel flask accompanied him on his travels to work and beyond.

'No, you're okay.'

Adam was standing tall and proud with a large black folder under one arm and a bundle of business-like papers in the other. He was frantically pointing to an array of spoof charts, prepared earlier in the day by photocopying an old school accounts book and highlighting the least pertinent sections with a bright orange pen. 'We must with a majority of two choose our trading name today, among other applicable negotiations. I shall endeavour to take notes of this meeting. As you can see from the charts, we must always reach a sixty-two percent gross profit of base national product and net profit can never be thirty-four percent of the distribution supplies. There will be three tunnels, Tom, Dick and Harry. Tom goes out directly east from one hundred and four, Dick goes north from the kitchen and Harry goes parallel to Tom from one hundred and five. If the Goons find one we'll move into the other. How many men do you plan to take out, Roger? Two hundred and fifty.'

None of this grand statement made any sense whatsoever apart from the lines taken from *The Great Escape*. Adam was enjoying the silly moment. He hoped one day to be a famous company director with international recognition. Without rationality Adam wanted to be famous, or perhaps he just wanted to be noticed.

'What a *fantastic* meeting room,' proclaimed Adam. 'I'm sure you agree with the choice. Excellent facilities, adequate space, air conditioning, lovely views, relaxing surrounds, ice-cream van and hotdog stand.'

'Adam, cut the bullshit,' growled Cammy. 'We're in the fuckin' gardens!' They were sitting on a new park bench under the dramatic fortress of Edinburgh Castle in the majestic surrounds of Princes Street Gardens. They elected this leafy location ahead of any other as they didn't want to be overheard while conferring on important corporation matters. Adam never discussed business in restaurants or bars, fearing the presence of unwelcome nosy ears. They intended meeting at Adam's flat. However his sacred bedroom was temporarily full of small brown microwave ovens and the space available in his room was unsuitable for a small child, never mind two grown men. Adam placed his bag on the end of the bench to prevent strangers from sitting down.

'What's in the bag?'

'Papers, pens and pencils. I borrowed them from a shop in Princes Street.'

'Borrowed?' Cammy pulled out a leather-bound full-sized desk-diary. 'And what's this?'

'That's a diary'.

'I can see it's a diary, I'm not *completely* thick you know.'

'That's open to debate,' mumbled Adam. 'It's a diary for our new business.'

'Oh, you're planning on taking bookings?' remarked Cammy sarcastically. 'Are you hopeful some dead geezer is going to phone up from his coffin mobile and tell us that his beautiful nineteenth century Georgian chest of drawers is buried with him in plot sixty-eight of Candlewick Cemetery?'

'Don't be silly.'

'*Me*, silly. I'm not the one with the hocus-pocus bogus flow-charts or the daft bastard who shits in chocolate-chip ice-cream cartons. That's like the pot calling the kettle black.'

'Come on, let's get on,' proposed Adam.

'*Get on, Get on.* I've been sitting here for twenty minutes listening to your made-up rubbish, which frankly is only funny to you and a deranged squirrel. So don't tell me to come along.' Cammy wasn't angry. He was gifted with a social technique giving him the power to sound exasperated when he wasn't necessarily upset. The resulting climb-down by the other party involved in the discussion was the inescapable conclusion. This was his control button over Adam, who himself felt very much in control of Cammy.

'The diary is so we can be organised,' claimed Adam.

'I know, I'm not bothered by the diary.'

'Well then, can we get on? I mean can we commence our meeting?'

'I suppose so.'

'The way I see it, after much thought, the plan of action should be thus:' Adam paused, rubbed his sweaty hands together and looked Cammy straight in the eye. 'We *steal* the goods.'

'It's not stealing,' interrupted Cammy.

'We appropriate the goods, sell them to my antiques contact in St Andrews and collect the profits.'

'You must have taken *days*, even *weeks* working out this comprehensive master plan,' voiced Cammy derisively. 'I suppose you want me to have a look in every coffin I bury?'

'No, that's overly obvious, too much of a limited market. There's nothing to say there will be anything of value in these coffins. We somehow need to know in advance what is in each and every coffin before we decide to act. Firstly, I would recommend we dig in cemeteries that have no connection with your work whatsoever.' Adam, contrary to his earlier statement, was now showing his true criminal colours. He was leaving no stone unturned. 'Then you can dig six feet under to your heart's content.'

'Six feet, six inches under.' Cammy corrected his partner in crime.

'*What?*'

'The hole should be six feet, six inches deep and twenty-six inches wide to accommodate the standard coffin. The 'six feet under' line bandied about is complete myth. In fact it's sometimes seven feet under if it's a family plot.'

'Okay, save us the lecture.'

'A standard coffin,' continued Cammy. 'Is six feet three inches long and twenty-two inches wide.' Cammy was nit-picking.

'So it wouldn't be possible to dig a grave too small?' Adam was commenting on Cammy's funereal blunder.

'We should apply for a government grant,' recommended Cammy, ignoring Adam's comment.

'What?'

'We should apply for a business start-up scheme and we'd receive funding to print up leaflets and things.'

'You're *not* serious are you?'

Cammy laughed. 'Of course not.'

'Can we get on then?'

'Carry on, mein Führer.'

'Now, the main thing to remember is that unlike the graverobbers of old, we're not looking for bodies, so there is no hurry to plunder a grave directly after the funeral. In fact, I recommend we do a little historical research on inhabitants buried a hundred years ago, as I would imagine their belongings will be more valuable in today's world.'

'Can we trust your antique shop friend?'

'No troubles there.'

'We could use the bodies for another purpose,' suggested Cammy, trying to derail Adam's good ideas.

'How's that, then?'

'I've heard that a few car companies are using dead bodies as test dummies to ascertain the impact motor accidents have on human heads. We could dig up a few corpses, take them along to our local car dealer and sell them for mechanical research.' Cammy was winding him up. He knew Adam had worked out a competent plan of action but nevertheless savoured throwing small human spanners in the works. The only distressing thing about alluding to test dummies was the thoughtful look which materialised on Adam's face, as if weighing up this absurd proposition. 'Interesting idea, I'll have a think about that later. Meantime we need to do some research. I'm sure Matty could help us out.' As soon as her name was uttered, she appeared in the busy Princes Street traffic on a sluggish open-top bus. The bright yellow microphone and pale green jacket were the distant clues.

'That's spooky,' claimed Cammy. 'You mentioned Matty and she appeared.'

'I could also mention pigeons and bingo; we suddenly have hundreds.'

'Not the same; there's more pigeons than Mattys. In fact a friend of a friend's brother was watching TV one morning and the boy's dad asked him what he wanted for breakfast. He replied 'eighty sausage rolls', which was an odd thing to say at the best of times. Then the doorbell rang and lo and behold there was the neighbour with two packs of forty sausage rolls. Spooky, eh?'

'Not really. It's known as coincidence.'

'I think there must be more to it.'

Cammy was more open minded to the unknown since his misadventure at the swimming pool. He'd been attending a regular therapy group with people who'd undergone similar ordeals. Many within the circle believed in some form of life after death. Adam was only interested in himself in the here and in the now. His main aim on earth was to look after number one.

'Do you think Matty will help us with our research?'

'No.'

'Are you speaking to her yet, Cammy?'

'No.'

'So I'll take that as a *no*.'

'*Yes*, take that as a *no*. To be fair, she does tell the tourists about citizens who were buried with an assortment of treasures. That would be worth checking out. Apparently there was a man consigned to the grave in 1865 with six bottles of red Burgundy and a small case of vintage port. Another fellow was buried with a golden goblet. There must be more folk like that. I also remember Matty mentioning an iron coffin which has never gone underground. This was a final protection from the bodysnatchers. Following death, the corpse was padlocked in this iron coffin. After a period of time, when the body was of no use to the doctors of anatomy, the remains were buried properly in the cemetery.'

The whole plan was fermenting in Adam's over-active brain. 'Great stuff, Cammy, whoopee fuckin' do.' Excitement was overtaking his sense of reality. 'Let's forget the present-day dead for now and concentrate on the long since deceased. No real need to tell Matty about our master plan. We should involve Andrew at some point. Of course you'd have to deal with him, as we don't see eye to eye. Imagine if he knew where the precious objects were going to be buried. In fact he could seize the valuables out the coffin in advance and we could brush aside the digging bit.'

'Very good, Adam.'

'What?'

'Brush aside the digging bit. Not a bad pun.'

Adam was pleased with his subconscious humour. 'Yes I'm a real wag.'

'More like a real wank,' mumbled Cammy.

'What was that?'

'Nothing Adam, nothing. What were you saying about Andrew?'

'He's owing me a favour. I equipped his funeral parlour with a proficient loudspeaker system.'

'And where did you pinch that from?'

'I wouldn't say pinched, I would say purloined.'

'Same difference, Adam.'

'That loudspeaker system is *cherished* by Andrew.'

'Yeah, but robbing a coffin in exchange for installing a loudspeaker system is not the best of deals and a proposition Andrew wouldn't be party to.'

'You should speak to the bummer boy. Could save us a bit of time.'

'You're disgusting. Anyway, I wasn't going to tell him about this.'

'Okay, fair enough, first things first. We need to undertake . . . undertake . . . get it!'

Adam stopped in mid-sentence and elbowed Cammy in the ribs, alerting him to another comic moment. His stand-up comedy career was a prime candidate for de-selection. Adam saw himself as the prince of puns. In reality he was a joke that fell out the Christmas cracker. 'We need to tackle some research and since Matty spends half her life studying in the Central Library, that *must* be the place to start.'

'Yeah, there's a whole floor dedicated to Edinburgh. So anything we need to know should be found there.' They both sat back, stretched their arms in the air and placed their hands behind their heads. The boys were growing to like this idea more and more. Adam opened the bulky diary and started to scribble additional notes and suggestions. 'Cammy.'

'Yeah.'

'If we get this scheme together, you should move into my flat.'

'Thanks but *no* bloody thanks.' Cammy gazed into the summer sky, took a deep breath and sighed in a contented fashion. He observed with great interest the men cutting the expansive Princes Street Garden lawns. This was pure therapy next to cutting the grass himself. Then it happened, yet again. For the second time this week he was experiencing *déjà vu*. Cammy sat bolt upright. A shiver ran down his spine. 'Adam, I've just had *déjà vu*. I've definitely been here before.'

'It's Princes Street Gardens; we've *all* been here before.'

'No, I've *done* this before.'

'Oh, you mean sitting on a bench. Yes, I would imagine you've sat on a bench before.' Adam was providing Cammy with a little of his own obstinate medicine.

'Never mind.' Cammy grappled with the sensation of *déjà vu* on a regular basis. He also experienced lucid dreams and was convinced he'd observed his deceased grandmother on half a dozen different occasions. Before his near-death experience, he'd never encountered *déjà vu* before. A large bang suspended Cammy's day dreaming and echoed around the castle ramparts. 'One o'clock.'

'One o'clock,' acknowledged Adam.

The time gun served the citizens of Edinburgh, providing the local populace with an audible lunchtime signal. 'Adam, you know why it's a one o'clock gun? Well a twelve o'clock gun . . . no never mind, it's a shite joke.'

'Too expensive, I know. Look, remember Matty's my sister. We might not see too much of each other but nevertheless I've heard her tour spiel enough times to know a shit joke when I hear one.'

'That's rich coming from you.'

'What do you mean by that?'

'Nothing Adam, nothing, merely messing.'

Adam was making illegible notes. 'I think we need to decide on a business name. Any ideas?'

'How about something similar to Burke and Hare? How does Burt and Player sound? Kurt and Dare? Or, em . . . Lurk and Bare?'

'Mmm. What about Snatchers and Co or Graves and Sons?'

'Snatch U Like, Bodies R Us?'

'No, I've got it.' Adam leant over, grabbed Cammy on the shoulder and announced with great gusto. 'We should be called . . . The Body Shop.' They both started to laugh out loud. For Adam, that was funny.

'Tell you what. We should use our own names. How about Carter and Smith?'

Adam was born with the ill-fated surname of Smith. Not that the name Smith on its own was ill-fated, but when attached to a first name of Adam, it furnished him with many hours of grief. Having the same name as the famous Scots economist and author of *The Wealth of Nations* equipped many probing parties with ammunition over the years. Firstly in the school playground, secondly in the mathematics classroom, especially as he was poor at arithmetic, and thirdly to everyone he met who'd heard of the original Adam Smith. '*Is that like the economist Adam Smith*' would ring in his ears day in and day out. He'd thought about changing his name yet resisted the temptation, knowing full well that he enjoyed the notoriety. The modern day Adam Smith supplied televisions, video games, CD players, dishwashers and tin openers, among other stolen goods. He'd cornered the electrical market where supply quite clearly outweighed demand. 'Smith and Carter sounds better.'

'No, it doesn't.'

'Yes, it does.'

'No, it doesn't.'

'Yes, it friggin' well does.'

'All right then, how about our first names, Cameron and Adam? Em no, forget that one, it sounds pants.'

'I've got it,' bellowed Adam smirking. 'How about the Adams family . . . get it. Adam's family!' He started to laugh. The crooked jester was on his own this time. His funny quip career had only lasted fifteen seconds. The number of good gags told by Adam remained at the grand total of one.

'How about Dig it and Co, em . . . The Shovel Society,' Adam was beginning to rant. 'Robber Hood, The Gravy Train, Spade and Whistle, no that sounds like a pub. What about the Borrowers?'

'No that's a book, film and TV series.'

The deliberation over a popular company title proceeded for fifty minutes. It seemed peculiar spending such a long time finding a fitting name, considering they couldn't wholly advertise their future business plans and were unlikely to register the new speculative venture at Companies House. The dialogue was important none the less, as a title provided Adam with a sense of worth and Cammy with a mistaken sense of legitimacy. They suddenly realised how long they'd been talking when a lady in an open top bus wearing a green jacket and holding a large yellow microphone appeared on the horizon.

'Bloody hell, that's Matty going round again,' spurted Cammy. 'Look, I better shoot the crow.'

'Okay pal, I'll check out the library. Thanks for coming. Speak to you later.'

Cammy speedily headed off to work. Adam remained seated on the park bench.

To commemorate what was an historic affair in Adam's blue eyes, he took out a small Swiss army knife and carved his initials into the back of the wooden bench. The letters 'AS' were now visible beside the official bench plaque, which read 'DEDICATED TO THE MEMORY OF DAVID AND CATHERINE DUNCAN'.

Chapter Eight

THE CENTRAL LIBRARY ON George IV Bridge was a novel building. You entered the block on the third floor and descended to the section dedicated to the City of Edinburgh. Adam hadn't entered a library during daylight hours since his primary school days, when such excursions were mandatory. He'd visited a couple of local libraries after midnight before with intentions less than educational. He went out with a librarian once who always wanted to have sex on a pile of dusty science-fiction books. Adam didn't find this a lot of fun, so he made his excuses and left her matchless in a forsaken world of words.

The Edinburgh Room was packed. Adam waited patiently for someone to help him with his weighty request. He flicked through a few pamphlets scattered on shelves at the rear of the room and picked up a local Edinburgh property paper. He believed this would be of use to him in the days to come. You could clearly observe from a small decorated balcony the main Scottish library below.

This would make a dazzling nightclub, thought Adam. Mirrors, dry ice, sticky carpets and neon lights flashed through his skull. He opened the local newspaper – available in the library for public consumption – and flicked to the page dedicated to regional crime. Huh, five people have been arrested after cannabis resin worth more than one million pounds was found in a joint police operation. Very funny that, in a joint . . .police operation. He laughed out loud and made a mental note of the story. Then in the corner of the page he noticed a tiny mention of his previous week's break-in at the big Georgian house. Not all of Adam's crimes were reported. On this occasion the newspaper evidently created an angle to the story. The heading read, 'House victim reprimanded by the RSPCA – Andy Macmillan reports.' 'That's fabbie! One for the press file.' The noise generated by the column being ripped from the newspaper was disguised by a sharp outburst of coughing.

Adam was wearing an expensive pair of fine leather shoes.

Sadly, the rest of his garments were nothing to write home about. He never managed to wear his best clothes and footwear at the same time. Maybe tomorrow, then again maybe not. Like a conscientious boy scout, Adam was suitably equipped for his long wait. He was working on a petty project. The scam involved his former pen pal from school. Alexis from Switzerland had been a charming little boy, a prodigious writer with an excellent grasp of the English language. In effect a model child. On numerous occasions as a young lad Alexis visited Scotland and stayed with the Smiths. Adam's mother would regularly say, 'what a lovely child, if only you could turn out like him'. He did turn out like this lovely Swiss boy – Alexis was as much a charlatan as Adam.

Adam was posting spurious invoices to businesses all over the United Kingdom. The bogus statement was a well-designed and neatly printed document requesting payment for the company's inclusion within a fictitious European e-mail directory. Adam's correspondence address was a PO Box number in Zurich. The letter-headed paper was copied from a legitimate Swiss directory. Many establishments didn't pay. Other firms happily settled their invoices without the requisite validation and this furnished Adam and Alexis with additional pocket money.

Imagine if I was to invite Alexis into the graverobbing scam, thought Adam. We could have a European branch and open antique shops all over the world. I would become like Richard Branson. Adam's merry-go mind was working on an extra dose of overtime. We could get big Aidan from St Andrews to advise us on the shop front. He was pleased with the furniture from the George Street auction. And if we . . .

The bulky librarian interrupted Adam's cortege of crooked deliberations. His head, saturated to the brim with villainy, was liable to explode and this sort of mess wouldn't be applauded in the library.

'Can I help you sir?'

'Yeah, I'm interested in Edinburgh graveyards. Do you have any books?'

'Yes, indeed. If you check through the small wooden trays, fill in the code and category numbers on one of the sheets I'll fetch the books for you.' This sounded a trifle convoluted for Adam. The Edinburgh room retained many valuable books under lock and key. The library staff collected them from the back room.

'I'm . . . em . . . not too sure what I should do?'

'Never mind,' said the librarian. 'I'll bring you a selection of books. Will that be okay?'

'Will I need to fill in one of the forms?'

'No, you'll be fine, no time for that.'

'You're the boss,' wisecracked Adam wiping his nose.

Kevin the librarian, attired with a shiny pair of brown brogues, was run off his feet. He mumbled under his breath 'I've only one pair of fuckin' hands. It's testicles I have madam, not tentacles.' With the queue extending by the minute, the photocopier and phones buzzing, buzzing and buzzing, bending the rules to save time was firmly on the staff's agenda. Kevin was a helpful slim bearded man with an undesirable body odour. He was a self-confessed environmentalist, not using any form of deodorant. Kevin planned on saving the world by killing the rest of us on the way. As he marched through the building a number of people screwed up their faces.

'He's *truly* stinking,' stated Adam to an elderly lady examining an old newspaper on microfilm.

'Yes, it is quite awful,' agreed the lady. 'Each time he walks past he trails his underarm odours through the whole block. Mind you, none of us has mustered up the courage to tell him. It's not something you tend to say.'

'If my friend Cameron was here, he'd tell him straight away about his dodgy armpits and then call him a smelly bastard. Sorry, excuse my Spanish.'

'That's all right son, I've heard it all before. Young people forget that we've experienced all sorts in life. It's nice and sweet that kids try now and again not to swear in front of their Granny. Fuck, isn't a new word you know.'

'Hey language, there's a naive youngster present,' quipped Adam. He was enjoying this brief conversation. They smiled at each other. Adam sat down at a desk and waited for the books to arrive. What a cool granny he thought. She's right, you forget that grannies were once young and shagged around like the rest of us. Mind you, why do old women always smell of ginger nuts? The stale smell of BO heralded the arrival of eight large volumes on the City Cemeteries of Edinburgh. Bad body odour in a confined space within a busy warm library wasn't the best of working conditions. Funnily enough, Adam's mouldy settee imparted a similar sort of whiff.

'There you are, all you need to know about graveyards. Return them to the front table when you've finished.'

'Thanks.'

The seconds, minutes and hours ticked away in a predictable daily routine. Adam hadn't concentrated this hard since stealing a full-sized arcade quiz game from a bar in Leith. From the safety of his flat he attempted to memorise the answers appearing on the screen in the hope of winning the jackpot. Each time he played the quiz, fifty pence was lost in the slot. This was a deliberate ploy to win all the money resting in the machine. As Adam grew nearer the jackpot, his grey matter created a hair-brained idea of visiting pubs that housed this particular quiz machine to win top prize. He didn't, however, plan for such a diverse range of questions; there seemed to be several thousand. So he gave in to academic temptation and hacked the machine open with an axe.

Adam was making copious notes. He'd located the graves where wine, gold goblets and buckled shoes were buried. Details of two Highland swords, a silver walking stick and a man who'd been buried in a full set of armour followed. Many of the books imparted flowing descriptions of the citizens occupying the graves rather than details of the objects they were entombed with. None the less, he jotted down particulars of the more salubrious characters as he thought there could be circumstances when they might have to take a chance. He even recorded information on the city's pet cemetery.

If we dig up a famous individual or perhaps a rich person, we'll discover more valuable stuff, thought Adam. Certainly I'd be famous if I robbed from Sir Walter Scott, Robert Burns or Robert Louis Stevenson. No, I'll forget Stevenson; it says in this book he's buried in Western Samoa. Then again, I could go on a business trip to the South Seas. His thoughts were once again sprinting into the distance.

His research persisted over the lunchtime period and well into the afternoon. There were two fifteen-minute intervals when the fetid smell of BO instantly disappeared from the room, courtesy of the bearded man's tea breaks. Adam became engrossed in a book dealing with grave robbing. Reading the publication with zest, he discovered that in the early 1800s the study of anatomy in Edinburgh surged forward thanks to surgeons like Dr Robert Knox who attracted up to five hundred people to his class. There was a time when each medical school in Scotland was only allowed the body of one executed criminal per year. This did not meet the demands of the scholars; thus the sinister trade of body-snatching was born. Suspicious characters, sometimes the medical students themselves, became well known at the time, masquerading under the title of 'The Resurrectionists'. In city graveyards on dark moonless nights, shadowy figures were seen flitting amongst the gravestones, going about their gory pursuit.

Burke and Hare were different, missing out the middleman (death by natural causes) and instead murdering their victims in a premeditated effort to provide the doctors with the freshest bodies in town. Nobody to this day knows exactly how many people disappeared; estimates at the time were running somewhere between thirteen and thirty. Only three murders were discussed at the trial, the case beginning on a cold December's day in 1828. Large crowds gathered outside the High Courts waiting for any pertinent news. The report of William Hare's turning King's evidence and walking free from sentence outraged the fiery Edinburgh mob. His dubious partner in crime, William Burke, carried the can and was hanged for his crimes on the 28th January 1829 in front of twenty-five thousand people. Afterwards, his body was cut down, whisked away and used to further medical science.

Adam was altogether self-satisfied with his library achievements to date. He became somewhat anxious when life was proceeding to plan, fearing a calamity around the next corner. As a friend once said, 'There's always some bastard lurking about to spoil your day'.

Emerging at the main door of the Edinburgh Room and heading in Adam's direction was Matty clad in her always worn, lucky green jacket. She didn't initially notice her brother. When she did her face turned scarlet like a beetroot at a red paint convention. Adam tried in vain to hide his array of books. It was too late, Matty was already at his table planning a war. 'What are you up to?'

'Hello, Adam, how are you? might be better.'

'Hello, Adam. What the hell are you doing here?'

'Watch your language, there's a granny present.' Adam glanced over to the corner of the room. 'No, you're okay, she's gone.'

'You're a *disgrace*.'

There was a gentle collective 'Shh' which echoed round the room.

'Shh, yourselves. You dirty sods,' roared Matty. She was blowing a human gasket.

'Quiet, please,' screeched the librarian, running towards Adam's table.

'I'm sorry, but you *really* need to do something about your boggin' armpits,' snapped Matty. 'You smell like rancid butter.' The staff looked on in stunned silence as Adam grabbed hold of Matty's arm, dragged her up the stairs and out onto the street. The librarian ran into the back room to have a quick sniff of his shirt.

'What are you playing at Matty?' She stormed over the busy George IV Bridge. Adam tried desperately to keep up. 'What's up?'

'You know friggin' well what's up!'

'No, I've no idea.' Adam shrugged his shoulders in an innocent manner. 'Slow down would you?'

Matty grabbed hold of the lapels on Adam's cheap white shirt and stared straight into his piercing blue eyes. 'It's Cammy. I hear you're leading him astray. Leave him alone. I don't want him getting mixed up with a twat like you.'

'I'm not leading anyone astray. It's up to Cammy what he does, he's a big boy now.' He'd always secretly liked his adopted sister but encountered difficulty in showing his love, their relationship rarely travelling beyond a bitter argument. Adam was a self-centred scoundrel through circumstances rather than choice. Matty was instantly crippled by Adam's persona, never able to pass her brother's barricaded door.

Matty and Andrew had tried without success on a number of occasions to phone the Carter household. When they eventually managed to speak to Cammy's parents, they were both informed of his change of residence: he had moved into a flat with Adam. This set alarm bells ringing and meant only one thing in their eyes – disaster. Matty knew only too well the traits of her deceitful brother. She was convinced his conniving expertise would lead Cammy a merry criminal dance.

'Look, let's go for a beer and chat about this,' proposed Adam.

'I don't want a beer.'

'What about a coffee, then?'

'I prefer tea.'

'Whatever. Shall we go in here?' Adam grasped Matty by the hand and led her into a small coffee shop. They sat down by the window and he spent the next twenty minutes trying to calm her down. Two cups of tea and a sticky jam bun later the conversation became less heated. 'What are you up to?' asked Matty.

'Something is coming, I can feel it, and it's coming right around the corner at me, Squadron Leader,' replied Adam in a poor American accent.

'Fuck Steve McQueen and fuck *The Great Escape*!'

'Steady on, that's a bit harsh.'

'I've never seen you in the library before, what are you up to?'

'Give me credit for some recreational activities.'

'Look, I didn't sail up the Firth of Forth on a banana boat. You're definitely up to something.'

'Might be.'

'Is Cammy involved?'

'Might be.'

'Has it anything to do with the stuff he found in the grave-yard?'

'What *stuff* found in the graveyard?' Adam was pretending not to know.

'Oh, nothing important. Don't tell him I said anything.'

'What *stuff* did he find?' Adam took this opportunity to turn the conversation on its head and slice the ball firmly back into Matty's court.

'Nothing, Adam, forget I said anything.'

'Go on, tell me. What's Cammy's wee secret?'

'Don't you *dare* say anything to him!'

'Okay,' sighed Adam knowing the worst of the storm was over for the time being. 'Why were you up in the library?'

She paused for a few seconds. 'I'm . . . em . . . wanting to find out who my real parents are or at least I think I want to find out. I'm not sure. Thought I might make a start, though. I'll probably have to go down to the Records Office at the East End but I wanted to check the library first.'

'Oh, right,' acknowledged Adam trying to appear interested. 'That's very good.'

'Can't be arsed looking today now. That's *your* fault. You've upset me.'

'Sorry, Matty.'

'So Cammy has really moved in with you?'

'Yeah, of his own free will.'

'Where does he sleep?'

'He's avoided the settee for some reason and sleeps on a camp bed on the floor. It's up to him, I didn't force him to move in.'

'Well, watch it, cause I'll be watching you.'

'So you haven't phoned him yet?'

'No.'

'Phone him, he'll tell you he's fine.'

'No, it's up to him to phone me.'

Adam was yet another person who knew Matty's true feelings towards Cammy. Although he wasn't bothered whether they went out with each other or not, he was pissed off listening to her continually moaning on about him all the time. Was Cammy the only person left in Edinburgh who didn't know Matty's true feelings towards him? 'Look, phone him, ask him out, shag him and get this whole bloody nonsense sorted out once and for all.'

'Say that again?'

'Shag him. Shag him!'

'He doesn't even fancy me.' She was blushing brighter than a crystal coloured marble.

'Oh, I see, yeah, right.' Adam was disguising the truth.

The thought of making love with Cammy entered Matty's mind. This was handy for Adam, as he didn't have to answer any more demanding questions.

'Look, I've got to go back and get my stuff from the library, are you coming?' Adam hoped the answer would be no. He checked his pockets and delivered his standard leaving line. 'Wallet, keys, fags, cock.' This was an adapted expression taken from his dad who used to say, 'spectacles, testicles, wallet and watch.'

'No, I'm fine here for the moment.' A glazed look appeared over Matty's face. She was enjoying her sexual fantasy.

'Bye then, Matty.'

'Em, yes, bye.'

Adam returned to the library via a chemist's shop, purchasing roll-on deodorant and a bar of soap. He collected his scribbled notes and placed the books on the front desk. He took the paper bag out of his jacket pocket and handed it to the librarian. 'Kevin, something for you. Don't open it till later. A small thank you for all the help you've given me today. Sorry about the hullabaloo earlier, I think my sister has the painters in this week, you know, surfing the crimson wave. She's like a dragon at the moment, you'd need dynamite to move her.'

'I don't mean to be rude,' divulged the librarian, 'Your fly is open.'

'Oh thanks. But remember, dead men don't fall out of windows.' Kevin looked somewhat baffled. Adam headed out of the building and home for his dinner.

Chapter Nine

THE DARING DUO RETURNED to Adam's flat with the intent to plan the next stage of 'operation gravedigger'. The classical sound of Elgar's Cello Concerto gently filled the four corners of the dirty living room. Sadly, the hideous racket of Adam trying to eat his dinner in double quick time wrecked the harmony. What a talented man! He could effortlessly make innumerable noises from several orifices, all at the same time.

'Adam, why have you bought a beef curry and a pizza?'

'I'm normally still hungry after my curry,' spluttered Adam trying desperately to keep the food in his mouth. He then broke wind with such ferocity the cutlery on the table was in fear of rattling. 'Have that on me duchess.' He aimed his backside towards the corridor door. This was another of Adam's quaint old irreverent customs.

'You know, you must be the filthiest, most disgusting person I've ever met in my whole life.'

'Flattery will get you nowhere, but flatulence will. Huh . . . flatulence will, get it . . . funny eh? Adam stood up, bent over and pointed his backside in Cammy's direction. 'Through the lips, round the gums, look out stomach, here she comes.'

Cammy was trying to decipher Adam's speech through the array of curry, poppadoms and nan bread, being stuffed with aggressive haste into his mouth. The sights and smells did not merge comfortably with the music. 'Is this Edward Elgar's Cello Concerto, which includes the fine Adagio – Moderato?' challenged Cammy reading from the back of the CD cover.

'You like football, don't you? Edward Elgar supported Wolverhampton Wanderers. At the stadium there's a plaque commemorating him. I love symphonies. That's the trouble with present-day society. People like me are pigeonholed. Everyone is so judgmental. I love all sorts of classical music. What's wrong with that?'

'Nothing whatsoever.' Cammy was momentarily impressed.

'This is a surprise. Do you really love classical music?'

'No, It's shite! I hate the pishy stuff. Long drawn-out snobby crap. No, I'm making sure this batch of CDs are okay before I flog them.'

'Thought as much. Where are you going to sell classical CDs?'

'I have my contacts. It's Bach to basics.'

'Mmm,' retorted Cammy, unimpressed with his attempt at a pun.

Adam would ferry his choice collection of classical records and CDs up to the High Court buildings in the Royal Mile. This was the only time he visited the courts. Lawyers and advocates made up the flawless market for this type of melodious merchandise. He even accepted orders from certain court officials. Whether it is Holst or Chopin, Beethoven or Monteverdi, Adam was your man. It was funny to think that he may have stolen CDs from one lawyer to sell to another. This was the securest scam around, as the advocates were unlikely to announce their illegitimate insider emporium sprees. The court security guard preferred Johnny Cash. The phone rang. Cammy answered.

'This is your finest friend on earth,' announced Andrew in his usual way. 'Are you living well?'

'Yes, I'm fine, Andrew,' conceded Cammy holding the phone under his chin.

'Are you sure?'

'Yes I'm sure, *quite* sure.' Cammy was pushing two fingers into his mouth pretending to be sick. 'Adam's flat is beautiful.'

'Matty requested me to bestow you with a call. She's eminently anxious about your predicament.'

'Did she tell you about the library?'

'Oh yes, the little library incident.'

'Yes, the little library incident. Adam thinks she's off her fuckin' rocker.'

'Please, patrol your language, Cameron.' A pregnant pause followed.

'Is there something wrong?' inquired Cammy.

'I heard today my father is unwell.' Andrew was happy to get this news off his chest. 'My father is indisposed.'

'What's wrong with him?'

'He's had a stroke.'

'I'm sorry.'

'I'm not,' admitted Andrew. 'I hardly know the man.' There was another short pause.

'Still,' imparted Cammy. 'He's *your* father.'

Andrew ignored Cammy's comment. 'Cameron, one must proceed with the day ahead.'

'Yeah, I must go too, I've a lot on.'

'Yes, go and wash your mouth out with Simple soap and a bottle of chilled mineral water. Oh and send my love to Adam.'

'I'll see you soon, Andy.'

'I'll disregard that last comment. There is no one with that name residing here. We should partake in further dialogue in the near future. Goodbye, Cameron.'

'Goodbye Andrew.' Cammy was mimicking his friend.

'Why are you pals with that big poofter?' asked Adam.

'We get on really well, I've known him since college. He also happened to save my life.'

'But he's a nancy boy shirt lifter. Backs to the wall and all that. Here, listen to this joke. Why do gays like American football?' Cammy didn't want to know the punch line. 'Because they can play wide receiver. That's funny, eh?' Adam's limited repartee fell on deaf ears.

'You are *so* homophobic, it's unreal.'

'Come on, Cammy, It's not natural waking up to a couple of hairy legs. Mind you, a couple of girls together is okay. Don't mind a little toupee licking.'

'You're filthy and *such* a bigot Adam. You should listen to yourself sometime. It's *unbelievable*. You're a primitive version of neanderthal man's ancestors and that's an insult to Stone Age man. If you were stupider I'd have to water you twice a day.'

Adam's anti-gay rhetoric was repressing a closely guarded secret of five years – sexual relations with another man. Admittedly he was out of his head on drink and drugs at the time but this couldn't disguise the fact that a tiny part of him enjoyed the homosexual experience, and this he hated.

'Andrew is the same as you and me,' affirmed Cammy. 'A *real* person, there's no difference.'

'There's a huge difference,' contested Adam. 'It's not right.'

'And being like *you* is right?' voiced Cammy in disbelief.

'Yeah.'

'Adam, your narrow-mindedness is *unbelievable*. If I stood any closer to you, I'd hear the ocean. Surely you don't genuinely believe what you're saying?'

'Yeah.'

'How can you have so much prejudice in your body? I thought narrow attitudes like yours went out with the dinosaurs.'

'No, not at all, I know a lot of people like me.'

'I believe you and *that's* worrying. I think you're quietly gay,' imparted Cammy unaware of Adam's secret. He was hoping to wind him up.

'Like bollocks!' blurted Adam quick as a flash.

'So you are gay.' Cammy was tormenting his prey. 'You've admitted liking bollocks.'

'Piss off! You know what I mean,' rumbled Adam, flying off the handle. 'I'd never be seen dead with a poof.'

'They say denial can hide the truth,' maintained Cammy, enjoying his line of attack. 'Perhaps you're homosexual. It's a great life.'

'Bugger off!'

'You seem to know the right words. With your wide vocabulary,' Cammy was happily turning the screw, 'you should apply for a job with the Oxford English Dictionary. You'd be such a *gay* editor. You could change your name to Mr Adam Camp.'

'Fuck right off!' yelped Adam. There was genuine hate in his eyes. Cammy noticed this and decided to back off. An imaginary white flag heralded another cooling off period. Their simmering relationship returned to a dormant state. For Adam, there was no surrender. After ten minutes, a bulky belch was followed by a babble that sounded like a beached whale with a ticky tummy. Adam lifted his shirt, rubbed his stomach and picked the head off a large spot. 'Milk, milk, lemonade, round the corner chocolate's made.'

'Delightful, Adam. The girls must flock to experience your marvellous array of social skills.'

'I don't fart in front of girls, apart from Matty, but then she's not a girl, she's my sister. Grubs gone, time for our big meeting.'

'Hope you'll miss out the flow chart rubbish?'

'I shall.'

'And no references to *The Great Escape*, okay?'

'Wait a minute, you aren't seriously suggesting that if I get through the wire and case everything out there and don't get picked up. I turn myself in and get thrown back into the cooler for a couple of months, so you can get the information you need.'

Cammy shook his head. That's what happens when you show a red rag to a bull.

'No, Cammy. I'll be serious for this meeting. No mention of flowcharts, corporation names or any references to prison-of-war camps. Business is business. Too many crooks spoil the brothel. So the time has come to commence our new partnership and tomorrow night is the big one. You know, choosing people who died a long time ago is a sensitive thing to do.'

'*Sensitive*, how do you work that one out?'

'Well, people who are long gone won't have any relatives.'

'Of course they'll have relatives.'

'You know what I mean, they won't have any living relatives.'

'Of course they'll have living relatives. Everyone will always have some sort of distant living relative.'

'No, but people buried ages ago are more likely not . . .'

'I know what you mean,' interrupted Cammy. His pedantic constitution gave way to the call for progress. 'I was wondering what we should wear?'

Normally that would be like asking a twenty stone rugby player to become a ballet dancer yet when it came to bent business, Adam was well prepared. His life fell off the back of a lorry.

'Here's how I see it. We both wear a set of clothes which we don't normally wear and after the robbery we burn them, boots and all. In fact I've a couple of pairs of dual density boots with non-metallic toe caps,' Adam was attempting to sound vaguely intelligent. 'We'll only select disused graveyards on the outskirts of town to avoid unnecessary attention. I propose we dig up the geezer in the suit of armour to start. Any objections to that?'

'No, but what does dual density mean?'

'Never mind.' Adam didn't know either. 'Big Aidan in St Andrews said he'd get a good price for a suit of armour. We need to single out the most lucrative plots first.

'Have you considered the mess we'll make,' warned Cammy. 'Even if I neatly cut the turf, put it to one side and place it back on top of the grave once we're finished, it'll still be noticeable. Remember, people still walk through disused graveyards during the day.'

'I've thought about this problem and this is what I think we should do. We take an array of cut flowers to the cemetery and place them on top of the turf to disguise our little activity. We then leave a small sign beside the flowers; here, I've made one.' Adam handed him a small printed and laminated sign which read 'The American Society of Scholars remembers a fine family'. Cammy looked confused. 'What's that meant to mean?'

'Nothing much. Sounds plausible, though. Why would this bother anyone walking through the churchyard? And no one's going to move the flowers. It's not the done thing.'

'What if a council official sees them?'

'Well, again, why would a council official be bothered about an odd society leaving flowers at a grave?'

'I suppose so. We can probably visit the city centre graveyards, then?'

'I don't think that's a good idea. Lots of the churchyards have superintendents and of course regular visitors, too. A little risky!'

Cammy was firing an abundance of queries in Adam's general direction. 'How will we see in the dark?'

'I've bought two lightweight cap-lamps.'

'You've done what? Did you say *bought*?'

'Yeah, hard to believe. You know what they say, a money less man goes fast through the market.'

'Oh I see.' He was fairly sure Adam had quoted a correct proverb. 'Did you *buy* any spades?'

'Come on! I can't buy everything!' They both smiled.

'How will we get the spades up to the cemetery? Isn't it a bit obvious if someone walks into a graveyard complete with shovel in the middle of the night?'

'We're hardly going to be taking the bus. I'm going to hire a van.'

'Number plate job,' proclaimed Cammy.

'Bingo! That's the one. You're getting good at this.' For a man who originally refused to be part of such a scam, Cammy was beginning to enjoy the unlawful lingo, savouring every minute.

'Cammy, once we finish in the graveyard tomorrow you should hide the spade for the next time we're there. We could dig people up all over the town.'

'Did you say spade?'

'Yeah.'

'Meaning *one* spade?'

'Yeah, you're the grave digger, I'm the look out. You know, like a sentry.'

'You're the look out? The churchyard's deserted; what are you planning to look out at?'

'You never know who might come wandering into the cemetery. And if I see someone, I'll give a signal to alert you. I'll make the sound of an owl. No, I'm no good at owls. I'll make the noise of a sheep and when you hear a baa you can shut up shop.'

'A sheep, a shagging sheep! What good is that? If I'm four-feet down with a mound of earth beside me, there's not much I can do.'

'You can clamp your tongue for starters.'

'Anyway, we'll need both of us digging.'

'All right, we'll alternate between digging and watching.'

'You will my arse! We need *both* of us digging! That means two spades, for two people, *right*? By the way, I prefer a flat shovel with a long handle.'

'Right,' acknowledged Adam reluctantly. He enjoyed the notion of accumulating vast profits without breaking into a sweat. Then again, he thought, this would be like starting his own escape tunnel. Imagine being remembered in the same breath as Steve McQueen, Charles Bronson and Richard Attenborough. Fan-bloodytastic. 'You're right Cammy, we should both dig.' Adam began whistling the tune to *The Great Escape*.

'I hope you aren't going to bring a chocolate chip ice-cream carton with you?'

'No, I have my standards to keep, although . . .' A thoughtful look emerged on Adam's scamming face.

'Don't even *think* about it.'

The following evening's escapades would activate a catalogue of events they had no way of stopping, circumstances overtaking them like a snowball rolling down a steep icy hill.

Chapter Ten

THE DISMAL NIGHT WAS DARK, cold and windy. Distant orange streetlights flickered on the foggy horizon. The rain was streaming down in a torrid fashion like a gushing waterfall. Deep puddles and sludge were the order of the night. The short summer months could sometimes bring the fine citizens of Edinburgh all four seasons in one day and this blustery July evening was indubitably bordering on winter. Two shimmering lights suddenly appeared and then disappeared from the middle of the muddy graveyard. The contemporary Resurrectionists, wearing dark overalls, black ski masks and cap-lamps, were a couple of shadowy figures hard at work.

Well, *Cammy* was hard at work as his partner's initial effort was described as 'a dog's dinner'. He took over the spadework and implied that the best contribution Adam could make was to stay out the way. Whether Adam meant to make a complete hash of the digging to lessen his workload or if this was a natural self-inflicted shambles was open to debate. Cammy was deeply submerged in water, five-feet down in the sodden grave with a mound of earth and clay neatly piled beside him. The green turf, adeptly cut into sections, was arranged in a way to ensure the exact pieces of grass were returned to their original place. The next grave along was protected by a mortsafe. 'Good job that's not our man under those bars, you'd need a welder to get in. Could be a good omen.'

'What was that, Adam?' cried Cammy from the watery grave.

'The mortsafe, it's a sort of good omen.'

'If you say so.' He wasn't entirely sure what Adam was chattering about. Cammy's mind at times meandered while in other people's company. He knew exactly what was happening yet couldn't help himself. He would be gazing at the other person, nodding his head from time to time with no idea what was being said. This caused embarrassment when the other person paused, until Cammy invented a way of side-stepping this predicament by asking the date and saying, 'My goodness, doesn't time fly?'

'Adam.'

'Yes.'

'What was that you were saying?'

'Nothing much, doesn't matter.'

'Adam.'

'Yes.'

'Hope you don't mind me saying this. Your driving tonight was a heap of shite. In fact it was a complete shambles the other night too.' Cammy was being his usual tactful self. 'I'd swear you didn't have a licence.'

'I bloody do have a licence!'

'Oh, just wondering.'

'I've got a bloody licence all right; I'll show you if you want.'

'No, it's okay, I'm a bit busy at the moment.'

Adam obtained his driver's licence without sitting his driving test. No one ever asked him for a photograph, so he sent somebody else in his place to sit the test for him. This somebody else was big Aidan, an advanced driver as well as crooked antiques dealer. In return, Adam furnished Aidan with a stolen mahogany piano.

'Adam.'

'What *now*?'

'Do you think this person minds if we dig him up?'

'No, I think you'll find he's dead.' Adam wasn't sure where the conversation was heading. 'Died in 1846, it says so on the grave-stone. This seems to suggest he's pretty much deceased.'

Cammy bent over and adopted a creepy voice. 'He might be watching us at this very moment.'

'You're *not* listening, Cammy. The guy is dead." A conde-scending tone reverberated through his cheeky grin. 'We're in a graveyard, which is where they bury dead people. You should *know* that by now.'

Cammy stopped digging, lifted himself out of the grave and grabbed hold of his flask of tea. The friendly banter didn't hide the evening's tension. The boys were unsettled, yet at the same time excited.

'Want some tea?'

'No, you're okay.'

'Right enough, being look out to nothing doesn't make you thirsty.'

'Bugger off!'

'Adam, don't you believe in life after death?'

'Cammy, what's all this Adam, Adam, Adam stuff tonight? I don't go Cammy, Cammy, Cammy all the time.' He was clearly irritated.

'Ah, just the mood I'm in. Well, do you believe in life after death?'

'Cammy, as far as I am concerned, when you're dead you're dead. Gone, gone, gone. You're here and then you're not. You come from nothing and you go back to nothing. Quite simple really. You're born, you live, you die.'

'No, there must be more to it than that.'

'Why must there be more to it than that? Who says so? People waste so much time wondering about what might happen next and miss out on the here and now. You should be out shagging when you can. Dead means dead, so you best get on with your life.'

'I can't believe what you're saying is true,' said Cammy. 'It makes perfect sense to me that there's something to follow on from this life.'

'It's makes no sense at all.' Adam was laying down the law. His tough talking tonsils were holding court. 'All this mumbo-jumbo has caused more harm than good. It's given people false hope, leading them astray and what about these new so-called religious groups, they're all fuckin' woo woo.'

'That's a bit narrow minded.'

'No more narrow minded than the brainwashing ministers, priests and high altar idiots or whatever they are called. You see, all these bloody dogmatic witch doctors attract the weak and vulnerable in our society and proceed to blow their brains out with absolute shite. They're all a disgrace, should be shot.' Adam was fully seated in the saddle of his high horse. His strong views were galloping out of control in a Ramboesque direction. He was forever at odds with his world of demons. 'I'd fuckin' shoot them all in public or even burn them like the witches of old. I'd take them to Murrayfield stadium, sell tickets, shoot the idiots and blow them up with friggin' land mines. Yah bastards!'

What had Cammy started? He only wanted to ascertain Adam's opinion on death.

'All these wars and deaths through the years, courtesy of religion.' Adam clenched his fists tightly. 'It was shite then and it's still shite now. When you're dead, you're dead. Ashes to ashes, dust to dust, earth to earth.'

'It's earth to earth first. You said ashes to ashes.'

'That's what I said.'

'No, the phrase starts with earth to earth.'

'So what!' Adam stormed off in the direction of the old cemetery gates.

'Fairly strong views,' thought Cammy, 'maybe I touched on a sensitive nerve? I didn't expect him to go ballistic'. He started to laugh inwardly, picturing in his mind sixty-five thousand blood-thirsty people gathering at the home of the Scottish Rugby Union for a public shooting. What could you charge? Would it catch on? Who would print the programmes? Would they sell steak pies? Cammy's flask reflected in the darkly luminous half-light. He took another sip of milky tea out of his metallic cup, jumped back down into the grave and continued to dig. There couldn't be far to go. Another couple of feet and I'll be there. The rain was teeming down like sheets of jagged ice, creating a mud bath reminiscent of an outdoor rock concert. The sweat was gushing out of Cammy's mucky pores. His nose was full of earth and his less than weather-resistant boots were full of water. His hands, although clad in heavy industrial gloves, were feeling the bitter chill of the night. He pushed a hand firmly against one of his nostrils and cleaned out the other with a loud snort.

Having recovered from his recent ranting session, Adam returned to the scene of the crime. 'What the fuck was that noise?'

Cammy was annoyed by the interruption. 'I was clearing my nose out.'

'Oh, was that all? Are we near the coffin yet?'

'*We?*'

'I mean, are *you* near the coffin yet?'

'Not far off.'

Another loud snort heralded the departure of further grime from Cammy's mucky nose. 'Is there a lot of snot?' queried Adam.

'*What?*'

'Wondering how much stuff came out your nose?'

Cammy stuck the top of his head out of the grave. 'Why the *hell* would you want to know that?'

'Just interested.'

'You're a weird bastard, Adam.'

'Piss off.'

Cammy jumped back down into the grave.

Believe it or not, Adam as a boy was a lavish devotee of snot. He gratefully received rich pickings from his nose and placed them in a jam jar beside his bed, hoping one day to sell his phlegm as glue. When everything in the jar dried up, Adam realised the scheme should be abandoned, so posted a batch of mucus to his grumpy maths teacher. Although a ridiculous idea, this was one of the many early pranks that helped shape the present-day Adam Smith. A loud breaking of wind broke the silence.

'Was that you Adam?'

'I'm the only one here, have a guess? Have that one on me, Duchess.'

'You've no manners. You'll wake the dead.'

'Don't start me on that topic again.'

'Right Adam, I'm going to stop for another break, finish off my tea and then I'll dig through to the coffin. I think I've got pins and needles.' Cammy sat down, rested his weary back against the barely legible gravestone and rubbed the rain off his brow. He unscrewed the top from his flask. 'Want some tea?'

'No. I'm not that hot on tea. I'll get a beer later.' Adam pushed both his hands onto the handle of the spade and tried in vain to light up a soggy cigarette. Sadly his matches were damp and his lighter wasn't working. He sat down facing Cammy on the edge of the plot, dangled both his legs in the grave and wiped the moisture off the end of his nose. 'This must be like a trench from the first war.'

'More like the second war,' corrected Cammy. 'My grandad said they were called foxholes.'

'Was your grandad *really* shot down during the war?'

'Yes.'

'*Really*?'

'Yes, *really*.'

'What happened?'

Cammy took another sip of his milky tea. 'Another Lancaster dropping a bomb from above clobbered him. Imagine being hit by your own side. The device went straight through their plane, knocking out one of the engines. They were over Germany at the time, so they had to turn round and fly back to England.'

'That's amazing!' Adam was obsessed with any stories relating to the Second World War.

'So my grandad, who was the navigator . . .'

'How many on board the Lancaster?'

'Seven. My grandad had to guide them safely back to the English coast on two engines. They lost another engine on route.'

'How many engines did the Lancaster have?'

'Four.'

'That's *amazing*! You might have never been born if he'd crashed.'

'Suppose not. The thing was, though, his best memory of this whole event wasn't being shot down but meeting Rex Harrison at the airfield.'

'Who's Rex Harrison?'

'*My Fair Lady*?'

'Oh, it was a girl?'

'No, Rex Harrison the actor. He was in the film *My Fair Lady* and happened to be stationed at West Malling airfield where my grandad's crew landed.'

'He wasn't in *The Great Escape*, I'll tell you that for nothing.'

'Here, Adam.'

'What?'

'Tell me, what's your favourite scam been?'

'Difficult one that, there've been so many.'

'There must be a couple that stick out in your mind or have a special place in your heart?'

'One of my early scams was pretty good. I used to have a paper round when I was a kid. The newsagent's shop was full of chocolates, books, magazines and annuals; you know, like the *Beano*, *Dandy* or the *Victor*. Do you remember the *Victor Annual*?'

'The one with all the army commando stories?'

'That's the one. When I packed my newspapers into my bag each morning I used to help myself to magazines and chocolates. When some of my mates found out what I was doing, they started to place orders, and when Christmas arrived I was doing a roaring trade.'

'Did the newsagent ever find out?'

'No, it was a big city centre shop. The manager changed every few weeks and nobody had a scooby. Piss-easy scam. Anyway, they paid us peanuts. We got up at six in the morning to deliver their shagging papers. I also used to steal flowers from our local cemetery and sell them outside the hospital gates to people visiting relatives. I always felt flowers were more useful to the living. One of the funniest scams, though, was up by the castle. A tourist came up and asked me to take a photograph of himself and his wife.'

'What happened?'

'I ran off with his camera. *Classic*, eh? In fact on the same day I saw a coach in Johnston Terrace reversing into a parking space. I waved him in and as soon as he hit the bus behind, I ran off.'

'Not bad, Adam. Your never cease to amaze me. Oh shit!'

'What's up, Cammy?'

'I've dropped my ketchup top . . . oh it's okay, I see it.' He picked up the lid and placed it back into his trouser pocket.

'That story,' said Adam, 'reminds me of my free runs home from school. Do you remember the biscuit factory beside the games hall?'

'Yeah, used to steal the rejects from their industrial bins.' Cammy was licking his lips.

'There was a one-way street where all the workers parked. I used to help them reverse onto the main road by waving them out. As soon as the back tyre passed my feet, I fell to the ground clutching my ankle, pretending to have been run over. The driver would always get out his car, check if I was okay and give me a run home. Saved on the bus fare.'

Cammy sniggered. 'How many times did you do that?'

'Five or six. The workers eventually got wise to my ruse.'

'Has anything ever gone wrong with one of your schemes?'

'Oh,' sighed Adam, insulted by the question. 'Never in a month of Tuesdays.' Adam didn't want to tell *anyone* about his most disastrous scam to date, as the plan ended in farce. He arranged to test drive a 125cc motorcycle, producing false documents to secure his ride. He planned to pick up big Aidan and travel through to Glasgow to knock off a chemist's shop. He'd then return the bike at the end of the day and the police would be none the wiser. Unfortunately Adam crashed the bike on the way to Aidan's flat, broke both his legs and spent three weeks in hospital.

Cammy and Adam were disparate people with contrasting views, yet seemed to be getting on exceptionally well. They somehow managed to find a side of each other's character to home in on. Their relationship was fairly odd, bordering on the offensive at times. Mixed in with this aggression was a peculiar affection, which couldn't be explained by either party.

Cammy jumped back into the sodden grave to complete the task in hand – the first great grave robbery. 'Shit, coffin, I've reached the wood,' shouted Cammy, brushing away the damp soil. Adam peered over the side of the grave, his cap-lamp reflecting on the rusty nameplate. With little effort, Cammy managed to open the decaying coffin and as he did, a mouse scurried up the side of the grave and shot into the distant night.

'This is something else,' crowed Adam. They stared in wonderment. The shiny armour seemed to be in exemplary condition for its age.

Cammy lifted the visor of the helmet to reveal the stagnant skull of the deceased. We need to remove the armour.'

'Looks pretty well attached if you ask me.'

'Why don't we try to remove his boots first?'

'I'm not sure about that.'

Adam leapt down into the burial plot, grabbed hold of both feet and started to tug at the boots with all his might. 'Oh tits, a slight mishap, I've taken his fuckin' feet off!'

'Yaw eejit. Look, let's get him in the van, I'll fill in the grave and then we can have a better look.' The van was parked at the cemetery gate. They lifted the armour-clad skeleton down the gravel path and positioned him to the rear of the vehicle.

They returned for the feet.

Both the boys filled in the flooded hole with earth and placed the turf neatly on top of the grave. They positioned the array of cut flowers complete with home-made sign on top of the grass. Cammy looked closely at the laminated sign. 'What does that say?'

'I told you before, 'The American Society of Scholars remembers a fine family', that's what it says!'

'No, underneath that.'

'Oh yeah, I've signed it Danny. I've decided this is our grave-yard calling card. Better than an ice-cream carton job, I think.'

'Why Danny?'

'Danny! Tunnel King! *The Great Escape*!'

'Oh, of course,' Cammy nodded his head, not sure what Adam was talking about. 'Oh yeah Danny, tunnel thing.'

'Tunnel King!' snapped Adam.

'Oh yeah, Burger King.'

'Piss off, Cammy.'

'Piss off yourself.'

They hastily returned to the van, viewed their prize lying still and dead in the back of the vehicle and released the breastplate. In doing so they uncovered a mouldy diary. The age-old book had been placed inside the armour plating.

'Oh shit,' screeched Adam.

'What now!'

'You won't believe this.'

'Try me.'

'My flat keys are on top of the coffin. We've fuckin' buried them!'

'You *stupid* arse. Well that's where they're staying. I'm not doing any more digging tonight!'

Thankfully the neighbours didn't notice the boys carrying their newly found friend into the block at three o'clock in the morning. The main entrance to the building was open, although Adam's flat door required a little intricate picking. They eventually stripped the skeleton free from his armour, spliced off a couple of gold rings from the bony fingers and placed the dead soldier in a soapy bath. 'I think I'll scrub him up, glue the feet back on and hang him up in my room.'

'Very nice, Adam.'

'You know what they say.'

'No, what do they say?'

'Death is a great healer.'

Cammy was too tired to correct him. 'I'm going to turn in for the night.'

'We should celebrate tomorrow, fancy going to a restaurant?'

'Yeah, could do.'

'Now, I've a list somewhere of places which have toilets near the entrance.' Adam's purple file listed the restaurants in Edinburgh where the gents' toilets were situated near the front door. Towards the end of a meal he would visit the relevant facilities and then leave the building through the main entrance or a toilet window. He tended only to use this scam when he was dining alone.

'No you don't, Adam. If I go out for a meal with you, I plan on paying the bill.'

'Thanks very much, Cammy, very good of you to offer.'

'You know what I mean.'

'Here Cammy, we could invite a couple of birds. I could phone an old girlfriend and you could phone Matty.'

'I've not spoken to her for a month.'

'I wish you two would get it together.'

'What do you mean?' questioned Cammy, a quizzical look appearing on his face. 'We're only pals. Former pals at this rate.'

'Get real, are you completely friggin' dense?' Adam tapped two fingers on Cammy's forehead. 'Are you sorely lacking in any sort of brains? She fancies the pants off you. I can't believe you don't know that?'

Cammy looked stunned as a startled rabbit in the headlights of a car. 'You're winding me up.'

'Why would I wind you up? I don't give a toss whether you get together with my sister or not. You should at least know she fancies you. I mean the rest of Central Scotland does.'

'What, fancy me?'

'*No*,' retorted Adam. 'The rest of Central Scotland knows that she fancies you.'

'You *genuine*, Adam?'

'Cross my hat and hope to die.'

'Heart.'

'Yeah, whatever.'

'That is the *best* news I've ever heard,' proclaimed Cammy smiling. 'Matty fancies me!'

Adam was pleased he'd told him. 'She sure does.' He reached for his cigarettes. 'So do something about it as I'm fed up listening to her prattling on about you. It's getting beyond a joke. No disrespect.' Cammy was ecstatic with this sudden news. Although mentally and physically shattered from the evening's endeavours, he was too delirious to sleep. He climbed into his camp bed, placed his arms behind his head and stared into space.

'I'll phone my mum,' stated Adam.

'You can't phone your mum, it's three o'clock in the morning!'

Adam hesitated for a few seconds. 'Oh, she doesn't sleep well, she'll be awake. I'll nip through to my bedroom and give her a quick call on the mobile.'

'What's wrong with the phone in here?'

'I'll let you get to sleep.'

Chapter Eleven

THE DAY WAS COLD AND damp and the bracing wind dispatched an icy shiver down Matty's back. She spent the morning 'stepping' in Regent Terrace, crouched alone, hands tightly clasped between her legs, attempting to keep the chills at bay. This was the last point of contact with her real parents and the nearest she'd ever be to her own family. There was a struggle in Matty's head, a war of attrition, a family tree dilemma. Her unusual place of solitude provided her with a sense of security.

Cammy, after purchasing an expensive multipurpose vacuum cleaner and a set of thick yellow dusters, was busy cleaning Adam's flat from head to toe and back again. This was a significant undertaking, as most of the dirt-ridden surfaces had not seen the light of day for a number of years. Even the smelly settee was dismantled. An extra-large scrubbing brush was employed to tackle this less than hygienic chair.

Cammy washed the oily kitchen walls and stepped back to admire his handiwork. To his horror, several black streaks appeared on the red paint. He was probably making matters worse. Ten black bin-bags were filled with an assortment of rubbish including a potential three-course meal. This concealed culinary feast was discovered in a gap behind the cooker. No wonder the mice flocked to Adam's flat, they must have thought their entire rodent Christmases had come at once. Never mind Edam or Gorgonzola, we're off to Adam's pad. Retiring from oven duties was imperative as the dirt, grease and grime were thickly set and the powerful industrial spray only dislodged the top layer. As there was so much work to do, Cammy started cleaning the flat at eight in the morning. The worst part of this job was finding chunks of Adam's toe nails scattered around the house. The bog-standard bathroom proved to be a challenge. The basin and rim of the toilet was a pale colour of yellow, the wooden seat cracking at the edges. The bowl was fractured, seeping water onto the fluffy green carpet. Due to a broken handle, a bucket of water had to be carried from the kitchen to flush the toilet. A small plastic bag full of ten-pound notes lived in the cistern.

Adam stepped into the living room without Cammy noticing. He'd just returned from St Andrews where big Aidan from the antique shop was very impressed with the suit of armour. He was certain to find a buyer within the week. 'Switch the vacuum cleaner off, would you.'

Cammy couldn't hear him, he was too engrossed in his labours, trying hopelessly to clean up every conceivable piece of fluff. Adam tapped Cammy gently on the shoulder.

'Bloody hell, I nearly jumped out my skin.' He switched off the hoover and sat down on a chair beside the television. 'Happy birthday to you, squashed tomatoes and stew, bread and butter in the gutter, happy 'birds day' for you.' Cammy was deliberately singing out of tune.

'Thanks mate, touching tribute.'

'Thirty-five?'

'Yeah, thirty friggin' five. Middle bloody age. I'm no spring duck anymore. Here, have a look at the card I received from my mum.' The large brown birthday card had a picture of a fuzzy bear on the front with some fitting words written on the inside, '*I love you more than choc-chip ice-cream*'.

'She surely doesn't know about your shitting activities?'

'No, not at all, just coincidence or as you would call it, spooky. Funny though, eh?'

'Funny all right. How did you get on?'

'Guess.'

'One thousand pounds?'

'More.'

'Two thousand pounds?'

'More.'

'Twenty-five million pounds?'

'Don't be stupid, three thousand quid, not bad for a night's work.'

'Three thousand pounds! Bloody brilliant for a night's work. What about the diary,' quizzed Cammy. 'Did he take that too?'

'No, he said the diary wouldn't be of much interest to anyone except a few Edinburgh historians. So I packed the damn thing in an envelope and popped it through the door of the library. Remember the guy with the doggy armpits? I put it for his attention.'

'What? You wrote on the envelope – for the attention of the man with the smelly armpits?'

'No, I wrote – please pass this on to the big hairy bastard that stinks to high heaven and who needs to wash before the world dies from asphyxiation.'

'Will they know who to give the diary to?'

'I reckon they'll know. It's hard not to know.'

'That was really good of you to do that.'

'What, call him a big hairy bastard?'

'No, hand in the diary to the library. You're showing a side I've not readily seen before.'

'Goes to show,' claimed Adam. 'I'm absolutely perfect after all and not the rotten apple in the barrel people think I am.'

'Yeah,' responded Cammy. 'But you know what they say about scraping the bottom of the barrel.'

Ignoring this comment, Adam stood up on the coffee table, puffed out his chest and saluted Cammy in a style not dissimilar to a British Colonel. The recently glued front leg buckled under Adam's sizeable frame and sent him tumbling to the floor. No worse for wear, he dusted himself down and doubled over in a fit of laughter. Then bizarrely, lifting an imaginary pint of ale to his lips gulped down a mouthful of illusory liquor and commenced crooning in the style of a demented pub singer. 'Cammy, Cammy, Cammy boy, I have done the dirty deed.'

'What dirty deed?'

'The dirty deed. You know the *big* one.'

'You've been to the toilet?'

'No, thick head,' roared Adam. 'I've done the dirty deed!'

'I don't follow.'

'Well, what do you think I've done?'

'You haven't, have you?' Cammy exuded oodles of excitement. 'You've done it, have you?'

'I've done it, all right. I've asked Matty round.'

'You've asked Matty round?' repeated Cammy.

'I sure have. It's funny how it only takes a simple invitation to get people together.' Adam was feeling pleased. 'You make things so difficult for yourself. I think I'll open a dating agency.'

Adam had removed his scamming hat for one day to replace it with Cupid's bow and arrow. He'd summoned his sister round for a birthday celebration and although she was slightly suspicious of this unlikely invitation, Matty agreed to attend. The birthday party was of course phoney, as the intention was to bring Cammy and Matty together once and for all. Adam would withdraw to the pub and leave the dubious duo in the company of Mr and Mrs Romance. How they'd never managed to get together before now was one of those little human mysteries.

'Where's all my shoes gone?'

'I've stacked them neatly inside the microwave ovens in your bedroom. Space is at a premium, you know?'

'And what have you done with Virgil?'

'Oh, he's in your bed, I couldn't have him dangling in the front room during dinner.'

Steve McQueen's character, Virgil, taken from *The Great Escape* was the name given to Adam's new friendly skeleton. 'I must say Cammy, you've done a reasonable job on the flat, not how I like it, but nevertheless it's still fairly good.'

'Here, birthday boy, I found a dead mouse under the fridge.'

'Really, where is it?'

'I threw it out.'

'Oh that's a shame, I could have sent it to my old maths teacher.'

Adam walked into the small kitchen and for the first time in years was amazed to see – a small kitchen. Cammy followed him through. 'My God you've been busy in here too. What are you making for dinner?'

'Melon balls in avocado to start, followed by home-made parsley and almond soup.' Cammy was playing chef. 'For main course we have chicken in a white cider sauce with all the trimmings and then for pudding, orange sorbet.'

'Your hotel training comes in handy, doesn't it?'

'I suppose it does.'

'One thing though, Cammy.'

'What?'

'Matty's vegetarian.'

'*Is she*?' A shocked look appeared on Cammy's face.

'No.'

'Shit, you nearly gave me a heart attack.'

'Look, you should know she's not vegetarian. God, you're slow at times.'

'Oh right enough, I wasn't thinking.' Cammy resumed his cooking and cleaning chores while Adam changed for his visit to the pub. The main dining room table, highly polished and covered with a linen tablecloth was the focus of the room. Two place settings were arranged with stainless steel cutlery, the napkins were expertly folded into the shape of fans and the central yellow candle was already burning bright. Cammy positioned beer glasses on the table, as Matty loathed all types of wines. One taste invariably made her stomach churn. The thought of her violently throwing up in the toilet basin was not part of the evening's romantic plan.

'Cammy, remember to feed the cats,' barked Adam from his bedroom. 'There's food in the fridge. I've got some prawns for Cavendish and salmon for Ives.' The diets of Adam's cats were considerably superior to their owner's. His affection for animals far outweighed his feelings for anything else. In effect, Adam was a devious, conniving, unscrupulous, scamming, big animal lover.

'No problem, Adam, I'll feed them.'

'And remember the goldfish has been fed.'

'When did you feed Roger?'

'Earlier today.'

'Okay.'

The time eventually arrived. The purple Mickey Mouse clock was showing eight-thirty. As Matty promised to appear at eight o'clock, the doorbell would presumably ring at any moment. Adam had left the flat at seven. Everything was in place. The food would be perfect and the flat was cleaner than new, apart from the oven. Cammy was looking smart yet casual. He was wearing black trousers, a crisp white shirt and his hair was slicked back with gel. The sound of *The Great Escape* theme tune echoed around the flat courtesy of Adam's home made doorbell. This is it, thought Cammy to himself. He opened the door and was somewhat disappointed to see a dotty grey-haired lady with a clipboard. 'I'm doing a survey for the local council, can I have five minutes of your time?'

'No you can't. Go away,' snapped Cammy slamming the door shut.

He'd been a tense child, spending many hours of his younger years watching television on his own. On blazing summer days you'd more than likely find him in the living room, curtains closed, stretched out on the settee watching sport. The only interruption to his daily dose of viewing was his mother opening the drapes to vacuum the carpet. Through hard work and an inner struggle against the dreaded disease of shyness, Cammy succeeded in confronting his nerves and became a disciplined young man. At the start of catering college he couldn't give a presentation to the class without feeling violently sick. By the time he graduated from his management course, though, Cammy confidently delivered a two-hour lecture, only blushing twice. Although still a nervous man, the worst symptoms were left back in the distant days of his childhood. His sporadic outbursts of abruptness were part of the on-going fight against his reserved persona.

The bell rang again. He quickly opened the door and shouted, 'Go away. Are you deaf as well as . . .'

Matty was standing on the doorstep. 'Charming.'

'Sorry, thought it was someone else.'

'Nice door mat,' Matty raised her left eyebrow. The woven mat read, 'I can see your pubic hair'.

'Yes, your brother's latest acquisition.'

'Is Adam in?'

'No, he's not.'

'Oh, he invited me round for his birthday.'

'He's gone out.'

'When will he be back?'

'I think he said about midnight.'

'Should have bloody well known. I knew something was up when he cajoled me here tonight. I mean, Adam doesn't normally ask me round on his birthday. Bugger it, I'll go back home.'

'No no . . . no, don't,' stammered. 'Come in anyway.'

Without a second invitation, Matty marched into the front room. 'Are you expecting someone?'

'Yes, I am.'

'I won't stay long then.'

'Please stay as long as you like.'

'No, I wouldn't want to be a gooseberry, three's a crowd and all that.'

'No, I want you to stay.' Cammy prepared for his important announcement by standing up straight and clasping his hands together. 'This is all set up for you. A kind of apology.' His voice quivered with nervous anticipation. 'I want us to make up. You're too good a friend to lose.'

Matty appeared genuinely gobsmacked. Twice in one year, this was verging on a world record.

Cammy was glowing inside. 'Would you like a drink?' The excitement was building up in his body

'Em . . . Any cider?'

'I sure do. Big one, wee one?'

'Pint, please.'

Cammy was preparing Matty's favourite food while two bottles of cider, her favourite tipple, were chilling in the fridge. He pulled a chair out from under the table. The legs were in full working order. 'Have a seat at the table, are you hungry?'

'Starving, I've just finished my work.'

She took off her jacket, stuffed her yellow microphone into the pocket, unclipped her name badge and placed it on the dining room table. Her shabby old green jacket, tattered and torn, was Matty's lucky garb; she'd lost her virginity while wearing it. She was fifteen at the time and the boy in question was a man twenty-two years her senior. Mr Paul Gordon was his name. He taught technical drawing at school – in between dating third-year girls. Matty had sex with him on a Saturday evening, completed her homework on a Sunday night and sat in his class as a pupil on the Monday morning. To add spice to this human jigsaw, Mr Gordon was happily married with three children. The eldest, Sandra, sat beside her in Mr Houston's maths class. This brief affair lasted three months, the teacher calling a halt to their secret meetings, fearing serious repercussions at the high school. Although upset, Matty had found this attention from an older man both assuring and exhilarating. For a quarter of one teenage year, she saw Mr Gordon as a replacement father. Cammy knew about this liaison, discovering the truth by complete chance. A steamed up, bouncing Volvo Estate in the local woods, with Matty's smiling face squashed hard against the front windscreen was the conclusive evidence. Heartbroken by his find, Cammy ran all the way home crying his eyes out.

He never told her he knew and Matty never knew he knew.

The relationship with Mr Gordon gave Matty the biggest scare of her adolescent life – she was three weeks late for her period. This daily distress led her to visit the local chemist's shop with a urine sample, seeking a pregnancy test. She couldn't find a small receptacle in the house, so handed over her sample in a sauce bottle. One wonders what Cammy would have thought of a ketchup container being used in such a fashion. If that wasn't bad enough, the pharmacist shouting out at the top of her voice in a packed shop extended her agony. 'We've lost the label off the tomato sauce bottle, is this urine for a pregnancy test?' Returning home after this humiliating ordeal, her period started. She ran into the public toilets, which happened to be 'men only' and locked herself in the nearest cubicle. For several minutes all you could hear was cheering, laughing and crying. This was one of the few occasions when Matty was actually glad to have her period. After this stressful turn of events she went on the pill and wore her lucky green jacket whenever she could. 'Cammy, this is very good of you.'

'No problem, I'm sorry about what happened in the Shovel Inn.'

'Yes and I'm sorry I stormed out the pub. I'm sure you understand why I was upset.'

'Yeah, I *do* understand. I don't know what I was thinking about.'

Cammy stepped into the kitchen. Matty followed him. 'What did you do with the jewellery and money?'

'You'll be glad to hear I sold the jewellery and donated all the proceeds to charity.' He was uncomfortable with lying. She was impressed with his honesty. 'Oh, I'm glad you did that.'

'I've put some chicken in the oven,' said Cammy. 'It's better than a bun in the oven, eh?'

'Yum, yum... Pigs bum.'

'*No*, chicken.'

Cammy paused and gazed into Matty's hazel eyes. My goodness, she thought. Is he going to say something romantic?

'I had a bad dose of diarrhoea yesterday, a real feud with the back door trots.' A strained look crossed his face. 'On the pan all day. I didn't eat much so I'm looking forward to dinner.'

Matty returned to the main room, once again mistaking eye contact for flirtation.

'So, Adam *hasn't* got a birthday party on?' shouted Matty.

'No, not here,' retorted Cammy, sticking his head round the kitchen door, a tea towel draped over his shoulder. 'He's meeting a few mates down the pub. It was his idea to set this up.'

'I still find that suspicious. He must be up to something.'

'No, he's not. I promise you this was a genuine act. Maybe he's changing?'

'I find that hard to believe.' Matty lit up a cigarette, put her name badge into her jacket pocket and gazed in astonishment at the spick-and-span flat. Cammy appeared from the kitchen carrying two plates of food.

'Do you know what someone asked me on the bus today?'

'What?'

'They asked if Edinburgh Castle goes up every year for the Festival.'

'Oh really,' he muttered, concentrating on placing the starters on the table. 'Now, put your ciggy out and prepare yourself for a culinary feast. It's your favourite, avocado with melon. The meal took longer than I thought to prepare. I'm sorry.'

'You don't need to apologise.'

'I'm sorry.'

'Cammy, stop apologising.'

'I'm really sorry.' They both laughed.

'I presume this is your doing?' asked Matty, pointing at the tidy room.

'Would hardly be Adam,' scoffed Cammy. 'He's not changed *that* much.'

Matty took one more drag from her cigarette, stubbed it out in the elephant shaped ashtray, picked up her spoon and started to eat. Cammy, although exceedingly tense, felt in a confident mood. Knowing she fancied him was pure ecstasy in motion and gave him a level of control he'd never experienced before. In past relationships, he would wait until the girl made the move, fearing rejection. This was the same for Matty; she also waited to be asked out, dating around twenty men in her time, sleeping with nine. Cammy stepped out with four girls and slept with none, determined to save himself for the one he'd marry. He was shy with women, never sure what to say. The topics of Hibernian Football Club and the finer points of grave digging rarely excited the other sex. His habit of not listening to people at times didn't help either.

One day, while walking down George Street, Cammy noticed an attractive girl staring at him from a bookshop window. He instantly fell in love and commenced his three-month 'Mills and Boon' quest to woo a new girlfriend. Two weeks were lost in deciding to go into the shop, another passed without him buying a book. He only found out her name, Nicola, by complete chance, overhearing her colleagues chatting. Then in a sudden act of bravery, Cammy purchased a crime novel and she asked him if he would like the receipt in his bag. This was it, she'd spoken to him. Cammy thought it would be only a matter of time before love blossomed.

To justify seeing Nicola, he attended readings, book signings and joined the shop's literary club. This was an expensive romance, as he didn't read much! When queuing at the till, he made sure Nicola served him. Words uttered like, 'There's your change' and 'Have you anything smaller?' convinced Cammy that a liaison was imminent. When another assistant was working with Nicola at the desk and the line was moving out of sequence, Cammy moved back a place or temporarily paused at the section dedicated to science fiction. He'd do anything to see Nicola, her face occupying his thought for months. This fixation ended in tragedy. On the day he finally plucked up the courage to ask her out, she was nowhere to be seen, having moved to another job in Aberdeen – with her husband. Cammy was devastated. He'd built up an imaginary romance in which was so real that the news of Nicola's departure affected him in the same way a real parting of the ways would.

Whenever Matty stepped out with a boyfriend, Cammy kept a low profile, more out of jealousy than anything else. Little did Cammy know that whenever he dated a girl she was dead jealous too.

'How's work been?' asked Cammy.

'Hectic, I'll be glad when the Festival's over. I'm looking forward to having a break. I've booked a holiday with Andrew.'

'*What?*'

'Andrew and I are going to Sicily at the end of the month for two weeks. Should be fab.' This announcement somewhat deflated Cammy's amorous intentions. The thought of getting together with Matty and then for her to be whisked away abroad was unbearable. Then again, they weren't an item and hadn't spoken for weeks. He could hardly complain.

'Terrific.' Cammy attempted to sound enthusiastic.

'Yes, We're going to shack up with a friend of Andrew's in Sicily,' added Matty. 'In fact you'll know him. Graham used to be at college with you both.'

'Oh yeah, 'Camp' Graham, really nice guy.'

'He's working at a hotel in a place called Taormina and has offered us free food and lodgings. All we have to do is book our flights to Catania and the rest of the holiday's virtually paid for.'

'Pretty good deal. How's your Italian?'

'Portacenere,' pronounced Matty in a poor Italian accent.

'What?' replied Cammy in a down-to-earth Scottish dialect.

'Portacenere.'

'What does that mean?'

'Ash tray.'

'That's a start.'

'Just need to learn the word for cider and I'll be happy as Larry. Anyway, Andrew is better at Italian. We'll get by. At school,

I was shit-hot at French, so I took Spanish in the third year. No good at Italian, though.'

'Sidro.'

'What?'

'Sidro is cider.'

'Oh right, excellent, sidro, fab.' She sipped from her chilled glass of cider. 'Fantastic history over there.'

Cammy was exceptionally jealous of Matty's future trip to the sunny Mediterranean. Maybe he could go too. Then again, work was busy and Adam was organising another cemetery excursion. Anyway, one thing at a time, he thought to himself. When will be the best time to ask Matty out? Should I wait until she comes back from Sicily?

With great gusto, they tucked into their main course of chicken in a cider and mushroom sauce, roast potatoes, broccoli and peas. Matty thought the dinner was fantastic, although in her opinion the whole evening was a bit over the top for a simple apology. Why was Cammy pressing all the right buttons? Was he going to ask her out? She immediately dismissed this from her thoughts, having been wrong so many times before.

'Hello, Cavendish, you daft duck of a cat, where's Ives?' whimpered Matty, in a baby voice. 'You realise, these cats are better fed than Adam.'

'That's not hard.'

'You know, Cammy, if I'm ever reincarnated I'd like to come back as a big ginger cat.'

'Why is that?'

'I just do,' whined Matty. 'I love cats.'

'So you believe in reincarnation?'

'Sort of.'

'Did you know, I was once regressed?'

'No, you never told me that before.' Matty was interested to find out more.

'I was taken back to previous lives.'

'*Lives?*'

'Yeah, apparently I was a musician, writer, calligrapher and reader of poetry in France during the Crusades and died without having any family. Then in Elizabethan times, I was a female dancer entertaining the court of the king, leading a frivolous lifestyle.'

'A *woman*!' Matty was exceptionally surprised by the idea. 'Do you *believe* that?'

'Parts of it. Have you ever had the feeling you've known someone for years when in actual fact you've only been acquainted for a few days? It's possible we've all met each other before. I think you, Adam, Andrew and me could have crossed paths in previous lives. Imagine if you were a man, Adam was your wife and I happened to be your mother.'

'What a horrible thought, Adam being my wife and I'm not too sure about you being my mother.'

'I'd make a good mother,' screeched Cammy in a high-pitched voice. 'I'd cook your dinner and do your washing.' She laughed.

'Where did you go to be regressed?' asked Matty, in a deep booming voice. 'Is the place in town?'

'No,' answered Cammy. 'I signed up on a correspondence course.'

'What do you mean by that?'

'By post,' responded Cammy. 'I was regressed on a postal self-development course. I saw an advert in the *Gazette*, sent away for details and after filling in an application form, received a tape through the mail.'

'A video tape?'

'No, an audio tape with details of my past lives recorded by a clairvoyant.'

'Surely you can't do this sort of thing by post?' questioned Matty in a cynical way. 'That all sounds a little bogus.'

'Not at all,' declared Cammy. 'A clairvoyant works with several guides.'

'I also work with several guides,' interrupted Matty. 'And they couldn't tell you about past lives. They have trouble with their present day ones!'

'You're just being awkward, aren't you?'

'Well, come on,' claimed Matty. 'By letter? An audio tape? Did you ever speak to the clairvoyant?'

'No, you don't have to speak to her.'

'Well there you go, then. What if you lose a life in the post? Is a well-to-do life sent recorded delivery?'

'Don't be *silly*.'

'*Me* silly. You're the woman dancer.'

'Was,' corrected Cammy. '*Was* a woman dancer.'

'Yeah, and I'm Florence Nightingale.'

'You might have been,' informed Cammy. 'Anything's possible. Anyway, draw your own conclusions. My Elizabethan days are on tape if you want to listen.'

'Maybe another time,' suggested Matty preferring to eat. The conversation persisted on this subject for a few more minutes. She wondered if Cammy would ever pluck up the courage to ask her out.

'My mate Rebecca is forever checking packets and tins to see how much sugar they contain,' declared Matty changing the subject. 'It takes from here to eternity to walk around the supermarket together and that really irritates me.' Matty could eat as much as she wanted but never gained any weight.

'Pudding, Matty?'

'How dare you call me a pudding.' She was enjoying the food. 'Yes, please.'

'Sorbet and strawberries.' He placed the sweet bowl in front of her and poured double cream on top of the freshly prepared fruit. 'Say when.'

'When.'

'What else have you been up to apart from work?'

Matty paused for a few seconds. 'Em... I've been trying to find out who my real parents are. Well, to be honest, I've been thinking about it; not done much yet. All I know is my real surname is Duncan. I discovered this a couple of weeks ago. Didn't take the search any further.' She was flushed and confused. 'I'm not sure whether I want to find out who they are and even if I do, I'm not convinced I want to see them. They might not want to see me. Why did they abandon me at birth?'

'Only your parents can answer that question.' This offspring dilemma had been on Matty's mind for years. She'd recently written to the adoption section at New Registrar House. She didn't post the letter.

'Take your time, for goodness sake,' advised Cammy. 'Don't rush into anything you might regret.'

'I *am* taking my time, that's the problem.'

'What about Adam's mum, do you get on with her?'

'What do you *mean*?' Matty was confused by the question.

'I know Adam's close to her. Are you close to her, too? If you are, then is she not your real mum? Well, not real in the *real* sense, nevertheless she's been your mother from day one, hasn't she?' Cammy was getting a little mixed up.

'She was a great mum when she was alive.'

'What do you mean *alive*?'

'Mrs Smith's dead, she died when I was five.'

'*What*!'

'Did you not know that?'

'Admittedly I've never heard you talking about her. I presumed this was because she was your adopted mother rather than your real mum.' Cammy was shocked. He couldn't understand why Adam was pretending to phone his dead mother. Did this mean he was sending birthday cards to himself?

'Cammy, I can't believe, considering how long we've known each other, that you didn't realise Adam's mother was dead. She passed away before I started at primary school, Adam was eleven at the time. He took it very badly, crying himself to sleep at night. I don't remember much myself. Then of course when Adam's dad died, we were both devastated.'

'You were about fourteen, weren't you?'

'I'd be fifteen, Adam was twenty-one. It happened on his twenty-first birthday. His father, standing on the bar counter making a small speech, clutched at his chest, keeled over and died. No warning, no nothing. A bloody heart attack. The man was fit as a fiddle, jogged through the town every other day. Since then on his birthday Adam has drunk himself senseless until he falls over. That's why I was surprised he asked me over here tonight. I'm sure you're aware that all male members of the Smith family have died before reaching the age of forty?'

'Yeah, I knew that.'

Adam's annual booze induced pilgrimage was a tribute to his late lamented dad who, prior to his death, ran a small hearty bar in Leith. The pub locals held the late Mr Smith in high esteem due to his legendary lock-ins. Thick dark blinds were drawn at closing time, keeping the night out and the locals in. On the stroke of midnight, free liquor was lavishly dispensed among his patrons for thirty minutes. Adam's dad believed the day should always start with a nip of whisky. He'd often cite the incorrect proverb, 'You can take a horse to whisky but you can't make him drink'. Like father, like son.

Each year Adam literally stepped into the old boy's shoes and returned to his father's last port of call to resurrect his dearly held image. Drinking his old man's favourite pint, playing Elvis on the jukebox and chatting to old beer swigging buddies was all part and parcel of the evening's batch of nostalgia. The regulars accepted Adam's annual alcoholic antics, turning a blind eye to him falling off the counter and spewing on the linoleum.

'Although you can't condone Adam's behaviour,' said Matty. 'You can perhaps understand where he's coming from. His Mum dies when he's eleven, his father dies at the age of thirty-eight and to add insult to injury, his cat Scrounger died two weeks later. With Adam now in his mid-thirties, maybe pretending his mother's alive is a way of coping.'

Norman Bates from Hitchcock's chiller *Psycho* entered Cammy's head. 'Tea, mother...em...I mean Matty?' To ease the tension, unsure how to express a heartfelt response, Cammy picked up a butter knife, placed a napkin on his head and uttered in a squeaky voice, 'Mother...Norman...mother...Norman...tea Matty?

'That's not terribly funny.' She was barely able to keep a straight face.

'So you do want coffee?' inquired Cammy, dropping his puerile mask.

'Yeah, and have you any more cider?'

'Coming right up.'

'I'm out of fags. Has Adam got any?'

'There's some in his bedroom. I'll get them for you.' Cammy

had no intention of letting Matty anywhere near Adam's bedroom, especially as Virgil was tucked up in bed and the pack of cigarettes would come from a stolen Cash and Carry carton of five thousand. While rummaging in the bedroom, he unearthed four old photograph albums. A fleeting flick through the collection revealed the same faces, snapshot after snapshot. None of the pictures seemed to show anybody else apart from Adam's mum and dad, their photographs emerging again and again. My God, thought Cammy. Adam must really miss his parents.

Returning to the main room, he placed a pack of twenty on the dining room table. 'There you are, Matty.'

'Thanks. See, when I'm away . . .'

'Yeah.'

'Would you do the lottery for me?'

'No problem, what's your numbers?'

'You know my numbers.'

'Oh yes... em... One, nine, twelve, fourteen, fifteen and nineteen.'

'That's the ones. I'll leave you money.' Matty lifted her hands to rub her face. 'I've a bit of a sore head.'

'Must be the cider,' suggested Cammy. 'Too much cider.'

'No, the head aches have been hitting me more and more, even in the middle of the night.'

'I'm sure they'll pass.'

The kettle was boiling. 'It's true what they say about a watched kettle,' affirmed Matty. 'Oh, I feel cold.'

'Try some yoga breathing.'

'Why?'

'It regulates your temperature.'

'Is that true?'

'Yeah, my cousin told me.'

They walked through to the kitchen. Cammy pulled down two large cups from the hooks hanging on the oily wall and Matty opened the cutlery drawer looking for teaspoons. They reached for the sugar at the same time and as they did their hands touched. The feeling was joyous for both of them, releasing their sensual emotions. They turned, gazed knowingly into each other's eyes and as the electricity grid prepared to rush out of control, the doorbell rang. *The Great Escape* theme tune was beginning to sound bearable. Although this was an unwanted interruption, the romantic contact had been made and that was all that mattered. They rushed to open the front door and in doing so, Adam fell across the natural tan doormat on to the corridor floor. 'Hello love birds. I'm pished out my fuckin' tree. Pished out my tree, big time. Someone on the bus said I was an imbecile. I don't know what that means.'

This was a less than coherent end to a splendidly amorous evening.

Chapter Twelve

SOAKING PEACEFULLY IN A spacious old tin bath was Andrew, savouring the solitude of his special place – the bathroom. It was hardly surprising the man was always tired, considering he spent two hours each morning preening himself for the day ahead. The whole process was like an ancient ritual. The first task of the day was to bathe his feet in a small foot spa for twenty minutes while sitting on the toilet seat. He would then shave twice, clip his nasal hair and clean his teeth with an electric toothbrush. After completing these bodily tasks, a short shower paved the way for a hot soothing bath. A strong coffee was then followed by a quick look at the *Times* crossword. Behind closed doors Andrew could drop all guards, place his mask to one side and be himself.

His morning timetable was without a doubt a reaction to a stern public school routine where only twenty minutes were allocated to shower, dress and be ready for class. As this was never enough time, the boys arrived late, often in a less than presentable manner. Unfortunately, a sloppy appearance was frowned upon and led many students to be punished. On a number of occasions Andrew's rump was a reluctant guest to a severe caning. No wonder this had a lasting effect on him. He was making up for lost time. Each second of the ticking clock spent in his tastefully designed cottage bathroom was two fingers up to his old school.

While steeped in the warm soapy water he often pondered life's rich tapestry and contemplated what might be in store after death. The subject was like a second skin, due to the nature of his occupation. Day in and day out, death was very much part of his life. Perhaps working in the funeral industry made dying more acceptable; he certainly wasn't afraid of mortality.

Death was odd, thought Andrew. For all one knows, the only way of achieving life after death was by fathering children in the hope that part of your soul lived on. Andrew considered it a great shame for people who desperately wanted a family but couldn't. It was unlikely he would be a father, so this avenue was closed off in his complex mind.

He once entertained a theory. He thought when someone died in the world, at the same time someone else was being born. It was a possibility that other souls remained in limbo until a suitable body was found. God or a peerless being operated an intricate swap programme for human and animal spirits to enter new bodies after a period of time, ranging from one second to a thousand years. So he picked up a bible and started to hunt for religious clues. Andrew's research to give life a meaning was sadly interrupted by the premature death of his grandfather. Believing he was treading along a secret path, investigating matters that were best left alone, he didn't read the bible for a further four years. He returned to biblical texts when desperately unhappy, working at a large hotel in the English countryside. The mind-numbing daily routine, unsociable hours and ill-mannered staff fuelled his desire to return home. Then all of a sudden, like a bolt out of the blue, his cousin died and this put him off the bible once and for all. Talk about lightening striking in the same place twice. This was too close for Andrew's comfort.

From that day on, he was convinced relatives might sometimes die to help their family and perhaps guiding spirits would provide added strength. He believed his young cousin was watching over him, an unseen helping hand in times of trouble.

There was a large bang on Andrew's front door. 'Surely they're not here already.' Andrew had reluctantly agreed with Matty to be driven to the airport in Adam's hired transit van. 'Rather low class,' he thought 'but at least I won't have to leave my Mercedes at the airport for a week.' Cammy said he would come along for the ride, having spent the last two weeks in Matty's arms. Mind you, he probably had to come along, as they were practically attached at the hips and only the precision of a skilled surgeon's scalpel would uncouple them. 'Come, my liege,' bellowed Andrew from the bathroom. 'The door is unattached from the lock.'

Adam pushed the front door so hard, it bounced off the corridor wall. 'Oops a fuckin' daisy.'

'I will not be any spacious length of time. Please make your-selves at home.'

The trio marched into the front room of the cottage. Cammy and Matty sat hand in hand on the black leather sofa. Adam, with an eye for the main chance, set about scrutinising the fine collection of antiques. He stood in front of Andrew's freestanding stove. 'There's some pretty impressive stuff here, especially these candle-sticks. Matty, how long are you away on holiday?'

'Don't even joke about it.'

Matty stepped into the hallway, walked down the corridor and tapped lightly with her fingernails on the bathroom door. 'Andrew...'

'Yes, my poppet?'

'Remember the plane is at eleven.'

'One comprehends this pertinent fact,' he conveyed in a wry tone. 'Do not seek consternation and alarm your winsome features. I shall powder my nose and be in your fine company shortly.'

Adam overheard Andrew's flowery language. 'He really does speak weird, doesn't he?'

'So what if he does.' Matty returned to the main room. 'He's our best friend. End of story.'

Adam was busy examining Andrew's expensive Asian rug. Like a human gaming machine eagerly awaiting the next jackpot, gleaming gold bars lit up his eyes. 'Big Aidan would shift this quite easily... if he had to, that is,' remarked Adam coughing, an innocent look appearing on his face. Matty glowered at him.

Andrew appeared at the living room door like a camp knight in shining armour

'What happened to you?' asked Matty. He was sporting a rather noticeable black eye.

'I was set upon up by one of my less salubrious clients. A ven-erable lady, around eighty years of age, smacked me rather hard on the face. She was overly distressed about her recently departed husband. People reciprocate in disparate ways, you know. Yesterday was a complete and utter nightmare. One of the small rubber wheels uncoupled itself from the funeral trolley, causing our newly expired to take a tumble and enjoy a fleeting seat with the grieving congregation. A *disastrous* day.' Adam started to laugh. 'The day was no laughing matter, my dear commoner.'

'You've got to laugh though, haven't you?' quipped Adam.

'As I said, the day was no laughing matter. There is a time and place for laughter and yesterday at work was neither the time nor the place. So Adam, please refrain from mocking the afflicted.'

'Lighten up Andy, eh?'

Andrew turned his back. 'Matty, let us call a taxi cab, as I do not wish to voyage with this rather vulgar, disrespectful brother of yours. His buffoonery is pathetic. What a second class nincompoop.'

'I didn't have to volunteer to take you to the airport, you big bender,' muttered Adam. 'You can walk for all I fuckin' care.' Adam shook his head, picked up a magazine and headed out the front door to the van. Matty stood up and tried to retrieve the situation. 'Andrew, we're running out of time. Look, I know you don't see eye to eye with Adam. However, would you just grin and bear a journey to the airport? Before you know it, we'll be in Sicily. You sit in the back with Cammy and I'll sit in the front with Adam. You don't even have to speak to him.'

'I find Adam somewhat tiresome and crude. Why I agreed to this, I do not know. He makes one's blood boil.'

'So is that a yes?'

Andrew replied in a sulky tone. 'Under severe protest.'

'Get your skates on or we'll miss the plane.' Andrew headed off to the bedroom to check off his holiday list. He had three suitcases full to the brim with an outfit for every conceivable occasion. Adam ran back into the cottage. 'Can I use your bog, missus?' Andrew ignored his question. 'Can I use your bog?' repeated Adam. 'I need to feed the fishes.'

Andrew rolled his eyes in despair. 'If you must.'

Allowing any visitor into his peaceful place of solitude was unsettling. Permitting Adam to use his toilet sanctuary was intolerable. Before Adam had time to zip up his trousers and flush the toilet, Andrew burst into the bathroom and pinned him up against the wall. 'If you ever talk about gays in a defamatory manner ever again, I'll maim you for life,' said Andrew in a broad Irish accent.

'I'll break your legs and kick the shit out of you before telling everyone our special secret. You're an ignorant little fucker.' Talk about being at a loss for words. Adam was dumbfounded. The darker side of Andrew had raised its ugly head. His cultivated voice concealed an Irish brogue.

The journey to the airport was made in unabridged silence. Adam, still in a state of shock, didn't attempt go inside the main terminal, preferring instead to sit outside in the van. Andrew had problems wrenching Matty away from Cammy's firm grip. Thankfully he managed this in time to board the plane. Cammy watched the jet take off from the viewing gallery. He was missing her already.

Back in the van, Adam was more relaxed. 'Isn't life good?'

'You seem to be in a better mood.' Cammy jumped into the passenger seat.

'Yeah, just been talking to someone.'

'Who?'

'Believe it or not, Kevin from the library.'

'Mr Smelly?'

'Not Mr Smelly anymore, more like Mr Fragrance. He thanked me for the diary and was glad I'd pointed out his bad body odour, although he didn't like being called a hairy bastard. He's shaved his beard off and looks fifty times smarter. He's even joined a health club.'

'There you go, you've done some good for a change. Honesty is the best policy.'

'No, *not* convinced by that one.' Adam started up the van, departed the airport and drove back into town.

'Well, Adam, if you ever wanted Andrew to join our scam, you haven't a hope in hell now.'

'I've gone off the idea of including Andrew in our business plans.' Adam didn't wish to disclose Andrew's alter ego. 'He rubs me up the wrong way.'

'Oh, something to tell me? Coming out the closet?'

'Piss off, you know what I mean. He talks like an over-edu-cated Victorian butler. I was in a pub with him one night and he couldn't even order a drink and a pack of cigarettes properly. He goes up to the barman and says 'My dear innkeeper, what ales do you stock within this fine establishment? Can you also present me with a choice array of smoking materials?' I mean he's a weird up-hill gardener. An Oscar Wilde-reading pillow-biter.'

'Andrew is weird? What about mister shit in cartons? That's not a normal practice, is it? Have a look in your own backyard before you throw stones in glass houses.'

Adam's mind had already moved on a couple of paces. His bent brain was beginning to scheme. 'New scam, Cammy.'

'Go on.'

'Visit a row of houses with a fist full of dodgy leaflets. Put them halfway through the letterbox, so some of the paper can still be seen. Return a couple of days later and the homes which still have the leaflets hanging from the letterboxes are probably empty.'

'Not bad. What about the folks who haven't noticed the leaflet? Or houses that are unoccupied, waiting to be sold or people who are returning home the day you plan to break in?' Cammy was trying to make Adam work for his money.

'All right, Cammy, how about this one? I fake my own death. I take out a load of insurance policies in, say, my mother's name.'

'Mmm.'

'Find a friendly doctor who signs my death certificate, slip the funeral director a few quid and he then pretends to bury me.'

'Probably not Andrew, though.'

'No, probably not,' agreed Adam. 'So I return in another part of the country under a new name taken from the Records Office. Conceivably a kid that died at birth. Then I live the life of Riley, happy as Larry.'

'Yes, Adam, I suspect it's not as easy as it sounds. You're involving too many people for a start.'

Adam mirthfully rattled on with scamming hypothesis after scamming hypothesis, while Cammy simultaneously threw large logical obstacles in his way. 'So Adam, tonight is grave two.'

'Grave two and hopefully two antique pistols.'

'What time is kick-off?'

'I think we should start a bit earlier this evening. How about midnight?'

'Sounds good to me.'

Adam and Cammy spent the rest of the day sitting at the Mound soaking up the special atmosphere of the Edinburgh International Festival. The annual event attracted artists from all over the world and provided an assortment of street theatre for thousands of spectators. 'Is this the last day of the festival, Adam?'

'I don't know. I hope so. Might get rid of these pansy bastards.'

'Have you ever thought about joining the Scottish Tourist Board? I'm sure you would provide them with an alternative marketing strategy.'

'Piss off!'

They were sitting under the awe-inspiring Georgian pillars of the National Gallery of Scotland on the last day of August. Fire-eaters, comedians, men on stilts and a couple of over-elaborate acrobats were plying their artistic trade. 'You've got to say this is impressive, haven't you Adam?'

'No, this event attracts crooks from all over the country onto our patch. That's not impressive. It's a pain in the arse, dull as dishwater. And another thing, I can't get my van parked. The whole thing's a nuisance.'

Cammy lay down on the gallery steps, positioned his hands over his face and fell fast asleep in the shadow of Edinburgh Castle. Adam scowled at a few tourists sitting beside him until they took to their feet and sauntered off. As far as Adam was concerned, this was a complete waste of time. To relieve the boredom, he tied Cammy's shoelaces together, covered him in an old newspaper and placed an empty bottle of sherry beside his head. Rescuing a soggy cardboard box from a wire bin, Adam hastily scrawled the words, 'Hungry and Homeless – please help'. He then balanced a polystyrene cup between Cammy's feet and left him unattended for an hour. On his return, Adam found £3.28 and an old Italian coin in the cup. With Cammy wheezing his face off, Adam bought two tubs of choc-chip ice cream, threw the bottle onto the gallery roof and thumped Cammy hard in the ribs. Waving the ice cream under his nose, Adam shouted, 'Surprise, surprise. I brought you a present.' Shielding the sun from his eyes,

Cammy retorted, 'You haven't a hope in hell's chance of me taking a tub of ice-cream from you.' As the he stood up to walk away, he fell over.

Later the same night the daring lads were once again hard at work excavating grave number two. The freshly cut flowers and American society sign were close at hand. Adam thought, everything is going to plan. Aidan is pleased with the merchandise and if we can get a couple of thousand quid for the pistols – presuming they're buried where they're supposed to be buried – then we'll be more than happy. This feeling of wellbeing was a sensation Adam didn't like. Often in the past, his positive thoughts were cut short by something going wrong. He hoped this was coincidence or perhaps he possessed a foreboding sixth sense. True to form, the dark night was unexpectedly lit up by a display of glowing lanterns and the derelict cemetery gradually filled up with people. 'Quick Cammy, have a look at this.' He poked his head out of the grave. 'What's all this about?'

A gathering of about forty-five people were walking, lanterns in hand, in the direction of Adam and Cammy. Little did the boys know this group was part of a Fringe Festival show – a poet hiring the cemetery from the local council. As the party advanced like ghouls in the night, Cammy began to panic. 'What do we do?'

'Em.'

'Come on, you're the look out.'

'Em... baa'

'Come on, quick!'

'Em...*hide*!' stuttered Adam.

They leapt down into the three-foot grave and tried to cover themselves in loose earth. Cammy grabbed his flask. 'They're going to see us.'

'Switch your lamp off.'

'They're still going to see us.'

'Not necessarily, now shut up!'

'Who the hell are they?'

'How the hell should I know. Bite your lip!'

Each member of the group paid £10 to attend this 2 a.m. poetry recital. They'd been encouraged to wear fancy dress to this 'evening of modern poetic horror' and were handed a candle-lit lantern on arrival at the cemetery. Lucky it wasn't daylight, as the site of a grim reaper, Dracula and a headless drummer would cause alarm to many a local citizen. Unfortunately the gathering stopped next to the newly exhumed grave. All the boys could do was keep quiet, keep still and listen to the show.

'Thank you for attending Dave's wonderful world of horror. My name is Dave Wokowlski, I'm from Texas, and this is my first time at the Edinburgh Fringe. I've been writing poetry since I was eleven and I've recently published my first book, entitled 'Bury My Laundry – A Study of Dead Clothes'. I thought it would be a fun idea to recite my work, which I call 'new millennium poetry', in a cemetery. So take in the night and let the show begin.' A flash of light lit up the dark sky. The forty-five paying customers seemed to be enjoying the evening, although the fits of giggles could be attributed more to alcohol than to the poet's wit.

'My horse is a clothes line,
My shirt is a panel of butter,
My death is for the living,
My powder is for the breeding.'
'This is absolute shite,' whispered Adam.
'Shh.'
'Oh will my shoes ever return to this mortal shop
And will the seeds of my shorts grow into long pants?
Devastation, outrages and fear.
Don't worry about the orange head-dress
As he is here.'
A gentle ripple of applause could be heard courtesy of the forty-five brave souls. Whether they understood anything that was being said didn't seem to matter. This was all part and parcel of the Festival. Then, quick as a flash, another cheap pyrotechnic shot off in the wrong direction and landed, still lit, in the half-dug grave.

'Shit, what do we do now?' challenged Cammy.
'Only one thing to do.'
'What?'
'*Run!*' They jumped out the grave and ran at full speed

towards the cemetery gates. Luckily the paying audience thought the boys' hasty exit was all part of the show and the poet, doing his best to light the firecrackers, didn't notice.

'My flask, I've left my flask,' cried Cammy trying to keep up with Adam. He stopped, turned round and attempted to return for his prized possession. Adam grabbed hold of his arm.

'Never mind the friggin' flask, let's get the hell out of here.' They reached the rusty graveyard gateway completely out of breath and were alarmed to see two young girls with pale faces and scarlet lips standing in front of the van.

'Are you the poet?' asked one of the girls. 'We're late for the show.'

'No, he's in the graveyard, follow the path.' Cammy tried to hide his exhaustion. 'Adam do you have your keys this time?'

'Piss off!' They jumped in the van and took off as quickly as they could. Adam rolled down the window and shouted in a weak American drawl.

'Hey, girls.'

'What?'

'Some advice.'

'What?'

'The poet's a crock of shit.'

Chapter Thirteen

MR CAMERON CARTER RETURNED to his daily spadework. Andrew Fitzpatrick and Ilona 'Matty' Duncan were happily lying in the hot Mediterranean sun. Adam Smith, Cavendish and Ives were fast asleep in his double bed – they didn't do mornings. Virgil Hiltz was hanging quietly from the living room ceiling. Andy Macmillan was twirling a red pen around his fat fingers. Lorna Nicol was waving the smoke away from her attractive face.

The non-smoking policy implemented by the local newspaper's innovative new owner, Sir Richard Normans, was a complete sham. The main newsroom resembled a cinema from the 1970s, one side of the room smoking and the other side non-smoking. The smoking section was so full of smoke it was impossible for the non-smoking section to remain in a smoke-free zone. Of the sixteen people who were employed with the *Lothian Gazette*, fifteen smoked and Lorna didn't. Although with the present inadequate set-up, maybe Lorna inhaled more than the rest. Andy and Lorna were temporary trainee journalists with Edinburgh's premier evening rag, *The Lothian Gazette and Journal*. Their daily duties included twiddling their thumbs, seeing if they could stick chewed paper onto the ceiling and reporting on stories none of the other journalists would touch with a barge pole. During their first two and a half weeks in the job they covered nail-biting and knicker-gripping incidents of the highest magnitude. The heady heights of page thirty-six was now their home with stunning headlines like 'Fence broken in Morningside', 'Festival brings more traffic to the city centre' and 'Cow escapes from field'. Both Andy and Lorna longed to find the 'scoop of the year' or the 'scoop of the month' or the 'scoop of the week'. The 'scoop of the afternoon' would be fine for now.

Andy sat back in his swivel chair. 'Lorna, If you had a choice, what would your big story be?'

'I'd like to report on a serious road accident, some sort of huge big disaster or perhaps a massive fire. It would have to be a catastrophe, like.' Lorna was twenty-two, used the word 'like' too often and collected books and magazines covering detailed articles on any form of horrific accident. Her passion for calamity was born out of a childhood love of rubber monsters and scary movies, when she was unable to differentiate between fact and fiction. 'What about you, like?'

'I think I'd like to uncover the man or woman who's invented a cure for the common cold and then have my story published over the Internet and in every newspaper world wide.' Andy was twenty-three, originated from Devon, always had a blocked-up nose and hated being called Andrew. This was too formal for his working class ears.

'Not asking for too much then, like,' acknowledged Lorna.

'No, not too much. By the way, Lorna.'

'Aye.'

'An old lady phoned me up yesterday, wanting to put an obituary notice in the paper for her recently deceased spouse. She lived in a small village outside Edinburgh. Everyone in the parish had known her husband for many years, so all she wanted to say in the ad was 'Frank dead, funeral Friday'. I mentioned that she'd chosen the least expensive line advert and suggested she could use a further four words if need be and do you know what she put in?'

'No, What?'

'She added 'Citroën Saxo for sale'. What do you make of that?

'My goodness, that's not very sensitive.'

'No Lorna, that was a *joke.*'

'But it's not very funny, like, if she's trying to sell a car, like, in the same advert as a death notice. She should be ashamed of herself.'

'No, the whole thing was a *joke.*'

'She shouldn't make jokes about her dead husband like that. You should never tempt fate.'

'No, *I* was telling the joke.'

'Oh, so there wasn't an old lady, like?'

'No.'

'No Frank?'

'No Frank.'

'Oh.'

Telling Lorna jokes was like talking to a crispy ham and peach pizza or a medium sized loaf of wholemeal bread – futile. Every gag would soar miles over her head and the witticisms were in danger of knocking Russian astronauts off their motorised moon buggies. The humorous lines would go whoosh, whoosh, whoosh as far away from Lorna's head as was physically possible. Her lights were on low-power, dimmer than most, running on a permanent back-up battery. Some drank from the fountain of satire, Lorna only gargled, preferring instead to laugh at natural disasters. 'I don't find that joke very funny,' blurted Lorna 'Not in the slightest bit funny.'

'Come on, Lorna,' said Andy. 'It's not a *bad* joke.'

'It is a *bad* joke, a *bad taste* joke, especially as my auntie has recently died.'

'Oh, I'm sorry,' conceded Andy. 'I didn't realise your auntie was dead. You didn't say anything.'

'I was too upset, I didn't feel like saying anything.' Lorna began rubbing her eyes. 'It was a tragic death that happened last week. She was still a young woman.'

'What happened?' asked Andy in a sympathetic way.

'An extremely nasty accident. Her new tractor and trailer toppled over and she was crushed by ten tons of cabbages.' Lorna was covering her face with her hands.

'How old was she?'

'She was 170 years old and a black belt at folding clothes.' Lorna appeared to snigger out loud. 'Then aliens came down from the sky and redecorated her house with yellow paint.' She was clutching her side, trying not to cackle any louder.

'Okay,' mumbled Andy. 'Very funny.'

'And giant pigeons,' added Lorna in stitches, 'flew down and sang Michael Jackson songs out of tune.' She was out of control, bent double over her desk.

'Okay, Lorna, point taken,' confessed Andy, 'I was reeled in hook, line and sinker.'

'That'll teach you,' warned Lorna containing her laughter. 'Okay, sometimes it takes me an hour and a half to experience sixty minutes. Nevertheless, don't think I'm not a match, like, for your jokes. I'm not just tits and a bum.'

You're not even tits and a bum, thought Andy already formulating a retaliatory joke. 'I'll bear that in mind.'

Big blustering footsteps could be heard parading through the journalistic corridors of local media power. The editor was on the move. This meant only one thing, a new assignment for Lorna and Andy. Would they be asked to interview a huge Hollywood star visiting a new city centre restaurant? Would Lorna be sent to a four hundred and sixty-eight car pile up on the M90? Would Andy be asked to interview an old Norwegian professor working on a cold cure remedy, ending all colds forever?

'Andrew, Lorna,' announced Mr Editor. 'I would like you both to go up to the Caledonian Cemetery near Lyal Street to have a look at a vandalised grave. I've had a call from a Mrs Diamond who walks her dog through the derelict kirkyard every day and she says vandals have been digging up a grave at the back of the cemetery.' The editor's name was actually Mr Brian Editor. After taking up his new Edinburgh media post, he changed his real name from Brian Healy to Brian Editor, with the express intention of generating much needed publicity for the local newspaper. Sales were down.

'Right you are, sir,' voiced Andy.

'Aye, like, okay,' added Lorna. They both picked up a pad of paper and a couple of pens from the empty desk, looked at each other knowingly as if to say, not another dead-end job.

The graveyard was deserted. Lorna opened the cemetery gates. 'Andy, should we, like, speak to the old dear first or have a look round the cemetery, like?'

'Let's have a look at the vandalised grave.'

'Aye, okay.'

Andy was fairly good at piecing news stories together. Lorna was fairly poor at writing. Her spelling was atrocious. Andy was keen to leave journalism and join the fire brigade. Lorna hoped for a career in television.

'Lorna, what do you observe from this act of vandalism? Where are the clues?'

Andy had watched too many Sherlock Holmes movies as a

child. At the age of twelve he played Dr Watson in a church play. Seven people attended. As Andy sauntered home from the show, a Plymouth police car picked him up from the side of the road and drove him home. He knew something was wrong as soon as he walked into the silent house. After a lengthy composed speech by his father, he was informed of his older brother's death – murdered in the local woods, literally kicked to death. A boulder had been dropped on his head. Clues were few. Even an appeal on BBC's *Crimewatch* produced no significant leads and fifteen years on the guilty party remained unknown. For Andy as a child, numerous nightmares preceded a perpetual flow of panic attacks and for two years he was terrified of being buried alive. Andy's brother Simon always wanted to be a reporter so Andy, after completing his schooling and in memory of his older brother, reluctantly joined the journalistic profession. This present-day graveyard investigation would *not* spark a flow of bad memories, as Andy for many years had learned to live with his past.

'Em, Andy, vandals are vandals, like. Let's speak to Mrs Diamond and get back to the warmth of the office. I don't think we even have to look here, like.'

'Elementary, my dear Lorna. The clues are here in abundance. Actually, joking aside, do you not notice anything out of place?'

'No,' answered Lorna, wiping dog dirt off her shoes.

'The grave is neatly dug.'

'So, like, tidy vandals or the council have been at work?'

'Look at the turf, immaculately cut. And what about this flower arrangement?'

Andy and Lorna noticed the sign attached to the cut flowers. 'The American Society of Scholars remembers a fine family'. 'Lorna, this seems to be signed. Does that say Dandy?'

'Aye, like, I think it does.' Lorna was scraping her shoes on the edge of the kerb.

'Here, Andy, look what I've found.'

'*Like*,' added Andy.

'What?'

'*Like*. You never said the word 'like' in the last sentence.'

'Sorry.'

'No don't worry, I'd prefer if you decided to drop the word 'like' from your vocabulary. You're a walking simile.'

'You know, Andy, I don't notice I'm saying it, I'll try and make a mental note.'

'Great.'

'I'll drop 'like', if you drop 'great',' suggested Lorna. 'That's the one word you say all the time.'

'No I don't,' argued Andy, disputing the point.

'Like, I think you'll find that you do.'

'Oh, that's a surprise to me. I say 'great' all the time, *great*? Okay, I can't say I'm conscious of saying 'great'. Okay we have a deal. Is there a forfeit?'

'What do you mean by a forfeit?' Lorna wasn't sure of the meaning.

'Well, if you say 'like' and I say 'great', we have to pay the other person money or give up something for a month.'

'Every time 'like' and 'great' are said, I think we should give £1 to charity,' proposed Lorna.

'Steady on, twenty-five pence might be better.'

'Seventy-five pence.'

'Fifty-pence.'

'Fifty-pence it is then.'

'Shake on it.' They shook hands.

'Like, great,' spouted Andy in a jocular manner.

'You said 'great', you said 'great',' bellowed Lorna. 'That's £1, no... em... I mean fifty-pence for charity.' If you'd given Lorna a penny for her thoughts, you'd probably get change. She'd be out of her depth in a car park puddle.

'No, Lorna that was a *joke*, an amusing aside. Look never mind. What have you found?'

'This looks like the remains of fireworks and down here is a stainless-steel flask.' Ding! Fifty pence was deposited in Andy's brain. Lorna opened the lid of the flask and sniffed. 'Tea.'

'Lorna. This is all very suspicious, don't you think?'

'No, not really.'

'There's more to it. Neatly dug grave, freshly cut flowers, fireworks, flasks.'

'*A* flask.'

'A flask, and who's Dandy? Maybe we've discovered some sort of witches coven and Dandy is the leader. Now that would be a big story. Let's go and speak to Mrs Diamond.' Andy was beginning to experience genuine excitement.

'You mean, that would be a good *fairy* story.'

Mrs Diamond was walking briskly out her front gate as Lorna and Andy approached her house.

'Mrs Diamond?' asked Lorna.

'It's Mrs Dimond, without the 'a'.'

'Mrs Dimond?' remarked Andy in a professional way.

'Yes, dear.'

'Can we speak to you?'

'Depends on who you are. If you're a double-glazing salesman, then my name is not Mrs Dimond, it's Mrs Smith and I live next door. However if you are an agent from the football pools with a large cheque, then I could probably locate Mrs Dimond for you.'

'We're from the *Gazette*,' announced Andy. 'You phoned Mr Editor.'

'Oh yes, indeed I did. Is that his real name?'

'Yes, I'm afraid it is,' added Lorna.

'He's sounds like a charming man, I'd love to cook some cheese scones for him sometime. In fact anytime.'

'We'll pass on the message,' affirmed Andy nodding his head.

Mrs Dimond was a sprightly eighty-three year old with a mind sharper than a razor. She pointed down to her Skye terrier dog. 'This is Hector.'

'Hello Hector,' blubbered Lorna in a baby-like voice.

'Hello Hector,' repeated Andy reluctantly. He was allergic to dogs, cats, lentil soup, penicillin, wool and synthetic fibres.

'He won't bite you son,' reassured Mrs Dimond in a high pitched tone.

'We were wondering about last night?' questioned Andy. 'When you were walking your dog.'

'Oh yes, son, would you both walk with me? I'm away to take Hector for a stroll. You don't mind, do you? Hector's very frisky and a bit of a show-off. I used to have two dogs but Max my retriever didn't get on with Hector, so I gave wee Max away to my cousin Keith. Max was getting too strong for me. The cost of dog food didn't help either. Don't get me wrong, that wasn't why I gave him away. I was going to give him to my sisters Katie and Elaine but they live with three cats.'

'Oh, I see.' Lorna was lost. She tried to hide her blank look.

'Cousin Keith is a two-faced so and so.'

'Mrs Dimond,' interrupted Andy. 'About last night?'

'Oh yes. Poor wee Hector was very upset with the fireworks and started barking. I got out of bed. You know it was in the middle of the night. I looked out my back window and saw people in cloaks and masks, funny looking bunch.'

'What did I say about witchcraft?' declared Andy confidently to Lorna.

'No, it wasn't witches,' divulged Mrs Dimond. 'It was some sort of Festival show. Four Saturdays in a row and every week Hector has been woken up from his beauty sleep.'

'*Not* witches, a Festival show?' queried Lorna, looking directly into Andy's eyes. Her empty look became less vacant.

'Yes, thankfully last night was the last night. I couldn't believe it when I took Hector out for his stroll first thing this morning. Imagine someone digging up a grave.'

Lorna temporarily took control. 'So you think the Festival group dug up the grave?'

'Well they all looked strange and Hector didn't like them much, I mean he was barking and Hector doesn't bark at anyone.' She continued to ramble in a dithering tone. 'That counts for a lot. I called the police last night but they said they couldn't do anything as the council had given the Festival people a licence. So I called the council this morning and all I got was one of those awful answering machines with a message saying they're closed till Tuesday, so I called you.'

This was a long answer for Lorna. Andy took over. 'Did you call the police this morning after you found the vandalised grave?'

'No, I only allow myself three calls a day on my phone. Remember I'm a pensioner. You see, I've made all my calls today already. Mrs Thompson wasn't in, so I phoned Jessie at the baker's instead. I suppose I could phone the police tomorrow.'

'Don't worry, Mrs Dimond,' assured Lorna, trying to put the old lady's mind at ease. 'We shall inform the police, like.' Ding! Another fifty-pence clicked up in Andy's eyes.

'You've been great, Mrs Dimond.' Andy was forgetting his side of the bet. He touched the back of her hand in mock affection. 'Thank you very much indeed, you've been more than helpful. If you don't mind I'll send a photographer down for a shot of you and the grave. Not together though!' An image of the havering pensioner lying in a sodden plot with lively Hector still attached to the lead entered his thoughts.

'Aye, son, I'm not ready to drop off yet. I'm determined to out-live that old bugger Keith if it is the last thing I ever do. Remember to ask Mr Editor out for me.'

'We'll tell him,' promised Andy. 'But he's a terribly busy man.'

'He wouldn't be busy if he tasted my home-made shortbread.' You'd swear a twinkle appeared in her eye. 'Do you think Hector looks like Greyfriars Bobby?'

'Bye Mrs Dimond,' yelled Andy and Lorna as they briskly walked off in the opposite direction.

'It's not her dog that's barking,' declared Andy. 'There's plenty of bats in her belfry.'

Back in the small smoke-filled office, Andy and Lorna pursued their preliminary investigations. Andy thought they might be onto a good story while Lorna wasn't initially persuaded. The only human being who literally mattered in the selection of an article was Mr Editor. He was the man you had to convince.

'Lorna, if we try to contact the Festival people, have a word with the Council and check the Web for an American society, that would be a start?'

'I actually saw that graveyard show advertised in the Fringe programme.'

'Why didn't you say anything?' Andy was flabbergasted by her latest confession. 'You should have mentioned this earlier.'

'Only came back to my mind this very minute. I saw the programme lying on my desk.' 'Dizzy dame dreaming' was another active pastime.

'Lorna, have you ever considered another type of career?'

'No.'

'Did you speak to Mr Editor earlier?'

'He said at worst he'd print a photograph of the grave in the paper and we could compile a little article on vandalism. That's not too bad, Andy.'

'The trouble is, I think there's more to it than meets the eye.'

Chapter Fourteen

JITTERY CAMMY WAS FLUSTERED.

After retreating from the castle, Adam bought a smart pair of brown brogues. Earlier in the week he'd arranged for a small official guide badge to be forged which allowed him free admission into historic buildings around the city centre. More importantly this entitled him to a free mug of freshly ground coffee and a tasty deep-filled sandwich in the castle's cafe. After his morning bout of scamming sustenance he dropped in on the law courts to sell a CD collection of Wagner's orchestral favourites to a young defence lawyer. It would take more than a tiny mishap with a North American bard to unsettle Mr Adam Smith.

A dog seemed to be carrying half a tree in its mouth over the railway bridge near the foot of Edinburgh Castle. A can of Virgin Cola was spiked on a black railing. A ragged Union Jack, clearly visible above a Princes Street store, was flapping in the gusty breeze. A stack of rubbish was blown onto the garden's luscious green lawns. A park attendant now had the thankless task of retrieving the flying paper and juice cans. The swirling wind added extra work to the attendant's already fruitless duties and each time he missed a fluttering piece of paper a group of Italian school children bellowed out an almighty cheer. Mother Nature was cruelly teasing and tormenting its prey like a drawn-out game of cat and mouse.

Their beloved Princes Street Gardens' bench was the setting for Adam and Cammy's 'Festival fiasco post mortem'. For a man so well established in all matters perfidious, the graveyard botch-up was of huge embarrassment to Adam. For a man normally overwrought at the best of times the cemetery shambles and midnight dash was causing great movement of Cammy's ketchup top. Adam's earlier carving of 'AS' on their adopted wooden park bench had been amusingly converted to 'smelly ArSe'. Maybe the delinquents were aware of Adam's shitting capabilities, maybe not. To add insult to injury, a flock of seagulls had left bird droppings on the back of the bench. Cammy's grubby hanky saved the day.

'The wheels have come off, haven't they? We're out on a limb.' Cammy was like a cat on hot bricks. 'We've reached rock bottom and we're still digging.'

'No wheels have come off our business trolley,' claimed Adam, furious with any such suggestion. 'All tyres are still intact. We've even got a spare in the company boot. Might have to lie low for a couple of weeks though, but that's not a problem.'

The meeting was turning into a 'tales of woe around the camp fire' type of event. Cammy's eyes were rapidly closing in on each other and were in danger of colliding if his scowling persisted a minute longer. He'd surely soon, any minute now, have a longer face than a horse. 'Stop fidgeting with that stupid bottle-top,' snapped Adam, his voice converting to a growl.

'I can't help it, we're in serious trouble. The shit has hit the fan. What if the police find our fingerprints on the spades?'

'We were wearing gloves.'

'They might trace us from the flowers. Possibly by your address taken from a visa slip?'

'I always pay by cash.'

'What about our footprints?'

'Remember, I always throw the boots out.'

'What about your handwriting on the note you left with the flowers?'

'What about my handwriting?' countered Adam, screwing up his face.

'They might take that to a person who reads handwriting and she...'

'*She?*' interrupted Adam. '*She?*'

'She or he would discover your characteristics as a person and have you arrested.'

'Get bloody real, Cammy. You're not being serious, are you?'

'What about the silver flask I left behind?'

'Would you ever calm down for a second or two? I'm not your fuckin' nursemaid,' thundered Adam. 'The police will not be interested in a tea flask and remember, in their eyes, they've found an insignificant vandalised grave. They've better things to do, like shopping at twenty-four hour petrol stations and sitting in police cars eating fish and chips. Cammy, forget it. They'll *not* find us. Are you listening to me? I said, they *will not* find us.'

Cammy, preoccupied with his own nervous tension, was staring into empty space. He was passing his white ketchup top from one hand to the other and back again similar to the final stages of the 'hot potato Olympics'. He was not a happy man, convinced the police would establish a detailed crime scene at the cemetery, find traces of his snot and compose a DNA sample. He'd probably watched too many low budget crime flicks in his day. Cammy was more nervous than a freshly opened tin of tuna in tomcat alley. If nerves were sold in theatre bars, he'd order a juice-less cocktail of first night fright.

'My flask was a limited edition, you know,' mumbled Cammy grinding his teeth.

'Cammy, forget your flask, forget all your nonsense and calm down. We have no problems with the police. Have you got that?'

Cammy was taking deep breaths trying desperately to regain his aplomb.

'Are you calming down?'

'Slowly.'

'Your bottle-top is moving slower.'

'That's a good sign, a good, good, good sign. My bottle top retreating from stress is a good sign,' muttered Cammy between long laborious breaths.

Adam gave him a reassuring slap on the back 'Well done, Cammy, you're getting there.'

'So no police.'

'No police Cammy, definitely no police for now.'

'For now, what do you mean for now?' blurted Cammy as if he'd taken a bath with an electric toaster. 'You mean, the police might eventually catch up with us?'

'No, not at all. Definitely no police Cammy,' assured Adam. 'You were doing so well a minute or two ago. Deep breathes now. Ketchup top into your pocket. Well done. Calm, calm, calm Cammy.'

Adam was intentionally cooling him down and playing with his over-emotional human strings. He was about to set Cammy's high pressure steam train loose on the rickety tracks of anxiety only seconds after bringing his apprehensive rolling locomotive to a near halt. 'Cammy, we don't have to worry about the police... but we might have to worry about the newspaper.' Adam produced a copy of the *Lothian Gazette and Journal* from the inside pocket of his black and white jacket and turned to page thirty-six.

'Here, have a look at this.' He placed the newspaper on Cammy's lap and waited for the eruption. The article, written by Andy Macmillan and Lorna Nicol, was at least half a page in size and consisted of two large colour photographs and one small black and white print. This was great media exposure in Adam's enterprising blue eyes.

'That's my friggin' flask they've printed in the paper,' spluttered Cammy. He placed his elbows on his knees, cupped both hands around his face and let out a weary sigh. 'I miss my silver flask and I'm missing Matty too.' He stood up and marched passed the Council's unattractive wire bins, kicking an aluminium-recycling container on the way. Adam followed his every move.

'Oh shit, we are in the shit, shit, shit, shit,' bemoaned Cammy.

Adam laughed. 'Want an ice-cream carton?'

Cammy was attempting to read the paper on the hoof. Between each couple of sentences he curled the newspaper up into a makeshift baton and violently whacked the side of his right leg, hoping to make the article disappear. Adam followed Cammy up and down the length of Princes Street Gardens, interjecting soothing words of calm followed briskly by harrowing words of doom. 'They've printed photographs of an old woman with a dog, the hand-cut flowers and a copy of your hand written note,' declared Cammy. 'I told you the handwriting was a shitting problem.'

'Okay, you're right,' agreed Adam, sticking his tongue out and making a mocking face behind Cammy's back.

The newspaper headline read, 'Mystery American Society – Who is Dandy?' The local rag, trying to make a story out of nothing, unwittingly stumbled onto the boys' chary trail. Adam wasn't overly worried. He was more concerned with adding this fine piece of parochial journalism to his expanding villainous press file. Cammy had little interest in plastic sleeves, scissors and sticky tape at this exact moment in time.

'Adam, this is nightmare stuff. We're now in the thick curry soup big time, are we not?'

'Not at all Cammy, look, sit down and read the article. There is nothing of any significance in this piece. No real story whatsoever, except for that reference to vandals slap-bang in the middle of the page. They've even spelt Danny wrong, ignorant fuckers!'

After playing with the emotional side of Cammy's brain for a few more minutes, Adam started the calming process all over again and soon had deep breathing back on the agenda. Without needlessly burning up shoe leather or continually clobbering his leg with a folded newspaper, Cammy sat down on the adopted company bench and attempted to read the article. Adam was right, there were no admissible details to link the boys to the scene of the crime. In fact, there were no particulars of any relevance in the story. In short there was no story. How do newspapers manage to do that?

'Imagine spelling Danny wrong,' snarled Adam. 'Bunch of fuckin' morons.'

'It's your handwriting.' Cammy pointed to the picture in the paper.

'What do you mean?'

'It's shit,' added Cammy. 'Like your driving.'

'What is?'

'Your handwriting. Your 'N' looks like a 'D'. In fact your Danny looks more like Daddy not Dandy.'

'Bollocks! My Danny looks like Danny.'

'Look at the picture Adam. That looks like Daddy.'

'It's a shite picture,' retorted Adam 'And it looks like Danny.'

'Daddy.'

'Danny.'

'Daddy.'

'Danny.'

'Daddy, daddy, daddy,' shouted Cammy. 'In fact the 'A' looks a bit like a 'U'. So your name looks like Duddy.'

'No way, you tossing piss pot.'

Cammy was consciously turning the affliction tables around. It was his turn to badger and bait. They both sat silently for about ten minutes.

Adam's handwriting was noticeably poor. He'd been expelled from all educational establishments by the age of fifteen. Oddly, his English at school had been more than satisfactory. Maths was the problem – not the subject but the teacher. Mr Houston had taken an instant dislike to Adam as soon as his feet stepped into the stern tutor's strict classroom. Adam experienced a severe baptism of mathematics and embarked upon his short time at the high school with the wrong teacher, in the wrong place at the wrong time. Adam was far from a perfect pupil, yet this was no reason for a senior schoolmaster to single out and pick on one specific struggling child. Sometimes the chemistry is wrong. Sometimes people cannot get along. Sometimes gut feeling takes over from logical sensations.

Extra homework, weekly detention coupled with regular beatings by the intimidating Mr Houston were the impetus to Adam's expulsion from school. He more than likely deserved some of the administered punishments - but no more than any of the other kids in his class. Mr Houston should have never started his nasty tricks' campaign against Adam, as retaliation was high on the Smith hit list and much merry devilment would precede his academic exile. After pushing Adam over the browbeating edge with one detention too many, Mr Houston received his comeuppance. Adam thought, what goes around comes around or was it what comes around goes around? For Mr Houston, he was about to experience a nasty little merry-go-round.

Adam launched his harassment by sending a local builder around to demolish the front garden wall of the maths teacher's semi-detached bungalow while the teacher was at school. He then arranged for a funeral director to arrive at the tutor's house at three in the morning to collect the recently deceased occupant. Mr Houston was alarmed to be notified of his death, especially in the middle of the night. An ambulance and four fire engines later, Adam was enjoying his revenge and his mind was beginning to cultivate additional inventive thoughts. Date-line registration forms and a bumper set of pornographic magazines were sent to the teacher care of the school. Admittedly the ideas were not overly positive, nevertheless for once in his life he was learning to think for himself.

Adam then moved on to catering, arranging for various types of carryout food to be delivered to Mr Houston's house. Pizza, chow mein, tandoori bread and baked potatoes weaned their nutritious way to the arithmetic-minded bully. The joiners, plumbers and double-glazing salesmen arrived at the teacher's house at regular intervals. Adam couldn't believe the number of people who agreed to go direct to Mr Houston's address without asking any pertinent questions or even requesting a telephone number. Book offers, videos and clothes were sent through the post and on one occasion Adam managed to arrange for a prostitute to visit the teacher's house in the middle of the family's traditional Sunday lunch. She was instructed to give him a forty-five minute audiocassette containing a rich variety of Adam's burps and farts, including an original rendition of Elton John's 'Rocket Man'. It was so easy to make someone's life a misery when you put your mind to it.

Adam wasn't expelled from school because of the torturous activities administered towards Mr Houston, as nothing was ever proved. Instead, he was ejected for swearing in the classroom and gluing the teacher's new hat to the blackboard. Mr Houston served not only as a catalyst to Adam's expulsion but proved also to be an impetus to Adam's favourite pastime...scamming.

'This note, without doubt, is clearly *Danny*, not Daddy or Dandy. I should know, I wrote the fuckin' thing.'

'Whatever, Adam, two wrongs doesn't help you write,' quipped Cammy.

'Oh yeah, that's a proverb.'

'Yes Adam, that is nearly a proverb. Now, spelling aside, what went wrong the other night? Why didn't you know the graveyard was going to be used by a Festival group? You of all people should have been organised. The whole thing was plain amateurish.'

'I put my hands in the air and bow to my mistake,' declared

Adam. 'I'm annoyed about this, but apart from a pishy newspaper article no harm has been done. Believe me, I'm really pissed off I messed up. I'm not sure you could have planned for that shitty poet's piss-awful show.'

'Mind you, you're the one that keeps going on about being prepared,' replied Cammy reminding Adam of his earlier lecture. 'You were far from prepared. You were as set as a watery jelly.'

'Leave it out, Cammy, I'm not going to know about crappy Festival shite am I?'

'Having the privilege of eavesdropping on your eloquent artistic reply to my question, you probably have a point.'

'The bugger is,' said Adam. 'Aidan was on the phone today asking about the pistols.'

'How much would he have bought them for?'

'That's between me and the gate post.'

'I must have a word with this gate post one day.' Cammy was fed up with Adam's secrecy.

'Here Cammy.'

'What?'

'Have a look at this funny article in the paper.'

Cammy picked up the newspaper and started to read. 'A jar of artist's excrement has been sold at auction in Paris for twenty-eight thousand pounds. 'Le Artistes Merd' was one of twenty-three works by Dutch artist Jacob Van Brockelle.'

'Look at the headline.'

'Oh yeah, mildly amusing, 'Artist's excrement goes under the hammer – Auctioneer lacks moral fibre'. Here, I hope this doesn't give you any funny ideas. 'Le carton de schect' or 'whippy le tubby shit'.'

'If I'm ever famous, I'll give you some of my shit with compliments, in a lovely glass case,' scoffed Adam. 'I'll even sign my name in it.'

'You'll need to print your name or it might look like Alan Smitt.'

'Fuck off, I'm trying to give you a valuable piece of shite free of charge.'

'You can keep your shite to yourself, thank you very much.'

Chapter Fifteen

A FULL-PAGE ADVERTISEMENT was being drafted for the *Lothian Gazette and Journal*. The Edinburgh evening newspaper was normally printed by eleven-thirty in the morning, which meant that any breaking news during the day would break first in all the other newsrooms around the world. The *Gazette* would pick up the pieces and publish an updated version of the story in the following day's edition. Most people bought the paper for the lonely hearts column and the football. Mr Editor had carried out some primitive market research. From the one thousand forms sent out, only twenty-two were returned. Still, this did not deter Mr Brian Editor, as the twenty-two responses were eminently positive and according to the figures published from this limited data on the front page of the tabloid, ninety-five percent of *Gazette* readers bought no other newspaper.

A full-page advertisement was still being drafted for the *Lothian Gazette and Journal*. Lorna relocated her tawdry plastic desk into the grubby external corridor outside the main newsroom, stretching her telephone and computer wires under the door and in behind the carpet. She was hopefully saying goodbye to cigarette smoke once and for all. No one seemed to mind.

A full-page advertisement was nearing completion in the less than pressing surrounds of the *Lothian Gazette and Journal*. Mr Andrew Fitzpatrick arranged the advert prior to his sun holiday in Sicily. He decided to market his funeral and burial services in the newspaper, on the Internet and at the cinema, taking an advert on the big screen. He loved the idea of his thirty seconds of fame ahead of an Oscar-winning Hollywood blockbuster. The advertising campaign was more to do with personal acclaim than boosting business revenue. Whether anyone understood his weighty wordstock was another matter.

FITZPATRICK AND SONS - SOLACE WITH A SIMPER

Avail yourself of our superior and empathetic embedding and entombing service.

Have you suffered a sorrowful bereavement, a misfortune or an affliction?

Though shalt not be melancholy as we consign your associates to the grave with prudence.

I intimately attest to a steadfast, proficient and sympathetic service of the highest magnitude. We provide a top quality after-death service.

LAY TO REST WITH THE BEST

Andrew personally signed the advert. This marketing technique was more commonly employed when selling used cars. He was trying hard to be stylish, although his way of promoting funerals was simply tacky.

'Lorna.'

'Yes.'

'Did you hear I had a phone call from the hospital?' Andy was embarking on another one of his jokes.

'No, what was it about?'

'There's a chap in ward seven who has part of a vacuum cleaner stuck up his bottom.'

'No way, that's beastly.'

'Yeah, it's true. It's okay, though, the doctor said he was picking up.'

'That's a terrible thing to happen to you.' Lorna was sounding concerned. 'Imagine getting stuck to a vacuum cleaner.'

'Joke, Lorna, joke.' Whoosh, whoosh and whoosh. Conceivably one day, Lorna would understand the meaning of the word joke.

'That's not funny,' claimed Lorna. 'My uncle is recovering in hospital at the moment.'

'Stop right there, Lorna,' replied Andy. 'I'm not going to fall for another one of your made-up stories.'

'This is not a made-up story,' insisted Lorna. 'This is God's honest truth, like. My uncle is genuinely in hospital and his condition isn't good.'

'You're not having me on, are you?' Andy wasn't sure what to believe.

'No, I'm being serious this time.'

'What's wrong with him?'

'Sadly, he fell off a large mountain in Peru.' Lorna was unable to keep a straight face. 'Luckily a polar bear broke his fall.'

'Okay,' retorted Andy. 'Ha ha ha. Looks like I've met my match.'

Lorna didn't always comprehend the daily dialogue unfolding in the news office. Nevertheless, when the conversation clicked she invariably came out fighting with all guns blazing.

'What's the update on the vandalised grave story?'

'The American Society does exist after all. I e-mailed them and they've no knowledge of any flowers being distributed in Edinburgh. In fact, the society is a literary organisation, collecting books from around the USA. To treble check, I also e-mailed the Society of Rogerian Scholars, the Renaissance Society of Scholars and the Society of Women Scholars. They all gave me the same answer. Meanwhile, the Council say they've not worked in that particular graveyard for months, so that rules them out. I also managed to speak to a couple of the people who attended the poet's Festival show. Unfortunately they arrived late for the performance and were too drunk to remember anything.'

'How did you find them?' asked Lorna.

'The Festival Office keep a list of names and addresses of all the people who book a show with them.'

'That's like good detective work.'

'Not too bad eh? Would you believe I've also had a phone call from a florist who recognised her flower arrangement in the paper. That's great news. I've arranged to see her later today.'

'That's excellent Andy. Do you think she'll like remember the person who bought the flowers?'

'You mean Dandy.'

'I don't know if it says Dandy. Have a look at the note again. Lorna passed the card to Andy. 'I think this might say Daddy. Maybe the flowers were from the person's father?'

'The grave was Victorian,' imparted Andy. 'I hardly think that the person's daddy would still be alive!'

'I bet the flowers have, like, nothing to do with the open grave?' volunteered Lorna.

'Perhaps not, but I think they do.' Adam tucked a red pen behind his ear. 'What have you found out?'

'Well, em,' Lorna paused for a second. 'I've been too busy... moving my desk and throwing out old magazines... to do very much on this story.'

'I see.' Andy nodded his head. 'Have you ever thought of taking up recycling as a career?'

'No, why?' Even sarcasm flew over Lorna's hairdo. Mr Editor appeared from his smoke-filled room and launched into a roar before reaching the other side of the office. 'I keep being phoned by a Mrs Diamond, do you know anything about this?'

'It's Mrs Dimond,' declared Lorna.

'Without the 'a',' added Andy.

'Whatever her name is, did you say something to make her call me seven times today?'

'No, we didn't say anything,' replied Lorna, flatly denying any responsibility. 'I even told her you were a very busy man. Apparently she liked your voice on the phone. She makes nice cheese scones.'

'And lovely shortbread,' maintained Andy. They both started to giggle. Mr Editor was not amused, clearly reaching the end of his tether. 'If that old bag Mrs Diamond phones again today, I'm not in! Do you hear me I am *not* in and that goes for everyone else in this blessed newsroom.' His blood pressure was reaching boiling point. 'Why do I have to have an 80-year-old-stalker? Oh and by the way, Lorna, the word 'stalker' has an 'l' in it, *okay.*'

Mr Editor wasn't impressed with Lorna's limited vocabulary, bad grammar and poor spelling. Luckily she was only a temporary member of staff, a trainee journalist, employed for six months. The article she wrote bemoaning a local high school's decision to replace the blackboard with more up-to-date methods of teaching proved the ludicrous point. The story, which never passed the editor's keen eye, had a substandard headline of '*School swaps chak for computer*'. Lorna had difficulty with the letter 'l', which seemed peculiar considering how many times she used the word 'like' in a day. With faulty articles aplenty, there was no chance of the newspaper retaining her services after the training period was fulfilled.

Until then, Mr Editor was content for Lorna to hold on to Andy's more literate coat tail.

The Editor stomped back to the secure four walls of his office. Lorna returned to the unusual working surrounds of the draughty corridor and Andy sauntered off to the florist's.

The florist's shop was, not unusually, full of blooms. The old style emporium overflowed with a balmy bouquet of freshly cut flowers. The floral displays discharged an aromatic scent, blending the rich with the rough. Abundant sprigs of greenery enhanced this wild urban garden, exuding a pleasant spray of bright colours. The effervescent florist, Mrs Baxter, was without a shadow of doubt the consummate professional. 'Do you remember what the man looked like who bought the flowers?' questioned Andy.

'Oh yes,' answered Mrs Baxter. 'I remember the man's blue eyes and nice shoes.'

'Did he give you a name?'

'Yes, he said his name was Mr Burke.'

'Any first name?'

'Yes, I think he said Virgil.'

'Mr Virgil Burke.' Andy was quickly scribbling down every little detail. 'How did he pay for his flowers?'

'Cash.'

'Did he say who the flowers were for?'

'Yes, they were for his mother,' remarked the florist with slushy sentiment. 'In fact he was in not so long ago buying assorted lilies for his mum. What a nice chap, thinking of his mother like that. Has he done anything wrong?'

'He may have. I'm trying to find out if he has or hasn't.'

'So I might be helping in a police enquiry. Gosh, that's something to tell my neighbours!'

'I'm not sure what we are dealing with at this moment in time. Nevertheless, your help is much appreciated. Do you remember anything else, Mrs Baxter?'

'He was driving a white transit van.'

'No, I mean about his description?'

'I'll show you the close-circuit footage if you want?'

'You've a security camera in here?' inquired Andy looking round the shop.

'Yes we do. You can never be too careful.'

'I don't see a security camera,' remarked Andy, scrutinising the top shelves. 'Where's it hidden?'

The florist pointed above Andy's head. 'Do you see that wicker basket?'

'Yes.'

'The camera is concealed behind the chrysanthemums and in front of the roses. My brother Johnny rigged the system up. Some of my roses are imported from Africa, you know. Due to their climate, roses can flower seven times in a year in Uganda. Isn't that interesting?'

'Riveting.' Adam was trying not to appear bored. The strange picture of a bustling Garden Centre, car park full to the brim, in the middle of a dry dusty desert seemed hard to believe. Andy, trying hard to hurry things along, was more excited about seeing the footage of Mr Virgil Burke. Maybe the Editor would print the picture in the paper? The florist retreated to the small back room and reappeared with two videotapes.

'You can borrow these cassettes if you want? The first time he was in the shop is on this tape.' Mrs Baxter passed over the cassettes. 'The tapes are ready to play. You'll see him happily chatting to me and choosing flowers. The shot of him on the first tape is the best.'

'Is the footage in colour or black and white?'

'It's in black and white, actually more greyish to be honest. You can tell it's a man.'

'Mrs Baxter, you have been more than helpful. I shall return the tapes a.s.a.p. Would you mind if the newspaper printed a still from one of the cassettes?'

'Not at all. It would be my pleasure. Would my florist's shop get a wee credit?'

'Not a problem, Mrs Baxter.'

Back in the bustling city centre newsroom, Andy had a look at the images from the security tapes. Admittedly they weren't the clearest he'd ever seen, yet distinct enough to reproduce.

Chapter Sixteen

ROGER COULD SCARCELY SEE the front door from his murky goldfish bowl. A newspaper crashing through the letterbox and tumbling onto the hall floor abruptly suspended his limited swimming endeavours. The paperboy was trying to see how far he could launch the *Gazette* into Adam's hallway and, on this showing, not much further if he tried.

The time was twenty to three in the afternoon. Cammy was wearing his favourite Hibernian football top while languishing in the land of nod. Four days off awaited his awakening. His first day of leisure, without his knowledge, was already well under way. He enjoyed sleeping on his days off.

Adam was also fast asleep. As soon as his head hit the pillow, he was out like a light. He simply savoured slumbering. He could easily on this showing be selected to hibernate for Scotland and win the coveted 'forty winks' trophy. Cavendish was catnapping on top of Adam's right shoulder while his other mog, Ives, was dozing at the foot of Cammy's camp bed. Dangling gracefully from the living room ceiling was Virgil, neither asleep nor awake.

Stationed, pride of place, on the wooden table in the middle of the living room was Cammy's new green and white flask. He'd spent an abundance of time selecting this rather fetching model, which cost eight pounds more than his previous purchase. Perhaps one day he would invest in a new ketchup top?

As Cammy twisted his body to reposition himself in the lumpy camp bed, he noticed a pair of feet at the base of his berth. He looked up in a trance-like state to observe his grandmother gazing down at him. Ives the cat snarled, leapt down onto the floor and shot like a mad hairy projectile into the hall. Although Cammy's granny was dead, he was not frightened to see her standing there, as she'd materialised numerous times before. Mrs Carter commonly emerged to dispense advice and offer guidance. When Cammy awoke from one of his 'sightings', he was never sure whether she'd really surfaced or whether he'd been dreaming. She started to speak. 'Cameron, you need to think about what you are doing, son. If you do decide to go on holiday then for goodness sake be careful, be very careful.' Before the word careful was fully pronounced, Mrs Carter faded slowly into thin air.

'Holiday? Holiday? What holiday,' whispered Cammy. Then quick as a flash fell fast asleep before answering his own question.

Cammy wondered whether his grandmother was a guardian angel and if insects such as flies and daddy long legs were distant ancestors. He'd never kill a bee or a wasp, being opposed to potentially murdering a former relative with a copy of the *Radio Times*. Cammy and Andrew both agreed that some form of reincarnation was conceivable, not through the emergence of any hard driven facts but through gut feeling and a sensitive sense of solidarity.

Cammy had a tendency to sleepwalk. Routinely through his childhood days, he'd go walkabouts in the dark, strolling through the hall to the kitchen, turning round and walking straight back to his bedroom. When Cammy's mum heard him roaming around the house in the middle of the night, she'd arise and coax him back to bed. The most embarrassing moment to befall Cammy during his shut-eye escapades materialised when he walked into his parents' bedroom, opened up their fine antique wardrobe and unconsciously peed with prolonged accuracy into his mum's underwear drawer. What a surprise awaited Mrs Carter when she awoke from her deep slumber and turned on the bedside lamp. In the days that followed, countless scrubbings couldn't displace the rancid smell of urine. The pungent odour wore everyone's senses down to the bone, so the cabinet was hastily dismantled and thrown out with the rubbish.

Adam was exhibiting a talent beyond his station. He was snoring, dribbling and breaking wind – all at the same time. This was a considerable accomplishment. He could presumably apply for a job inflating balloons at children's parties. Then again some of the mothers might be upset with this less than congenial sight.

Joining the circus would be a better bet.

Socialising late into the night at Bankhead's Casino, Adam enjoyed a complimentary glass of wine and salmon sandwich before once again retiring without wagering a penny. On the way home he collected two pints of milk and half-a-dozen rolls for breakfast, courtesy of a couple of city-centre doorsteps.

Adam never had any dreams; if he did, he didn't remember them.

Cavendish jumped down from Adam's bed to check his litter tray. The plastic container – two ice cream tubs glued together – was full to the brim so the cat proceeded directly to the toilet to have a healthy poo in the bath. Both Adam's cats had the habit of visiting the lavatory if all other options were closed off. Adam didn't mind. At least this was better than dumping on the carpet, on his bed or anywhere else for that matter. Taking after their owner wasn't a bad thing. A couple of rules of the house were:

1) Never have a bath when half asleep.
2) Never presume the water is naturally brown.

Adam once had a cat that deposited its watery excrement on the cables and wires behind the television set. Not a pretty sight, nor a pretty smell. He had one hell of a job cleaning the mess up. If truth were told, *Matty* had one hell of a job cleaning the mess up!

Adam awoke from a deep snooze, stretched his arms in the air and farted loudly with immense venom. Forcing the duvet cover over his head to enjoy a good long smell, he screamed 'Have that one on me, duchess. That was a *beauty*.'

Adam took a swig of whisky from his silver flask and placed the family heirloom back on the bedside table. He stumbled out of bed, picked up the newspaper from the hall floor and staggered off to the bathroom. He sat down on the toilet seat, opened the *Gazette* and flicked through its lightweight content. Then before you could say 'ah, that's better', Adam was astonished to see his own features staring back at him from page fourteen. Mr Brian Editor had decided to print a sizeable photograph of Adam with the caption 'Do you know the mysterious Mr Burke?' 'Oh shit,' cursed Adam under his breath. 'Oh shit,' cursed Adam again, this time out loud.

The first thing that crossed his mind was to make sure Cammy didn't see this edition of the newspaper. A story like this would have the capability of blowing Cammy's sensitive gaskets out of the water once and for all and Adam didn't want to be responsible for a worn-out ketchup top. He'd have to prevent Cammy going out during the day in case he stumbled across this press article. The print of Adam's face in the newspaper was distinct enough to be recognised. He thought it might be wise to lie low for a few days or even leave Edinburgh. His scamming ideas were set at full throttle in a defensive mode. All avenues were being investigated in what was, in a strange way, a very logical mind. How can I lure Cammy away with me for a few days? I know, thought Adam. Use Matty as the carrot and suggest we go to Sicily. Now this is Thursday, Cammy is off tomorrow and the weekend. I wonder if he can arrange to have Monday and Tuesday off and we could go for... He paused to count. Em, five days. That should be okay.

Adam briskly washed, shaved, hid the newspaper under his bed and phoned a friend at the travel agency. Luckily, places were available to book at short notice. Unbeknown to Adam, the Italian Tourist Board was currently attracting new customers to their country with the advertising slogan, 'Italy – *The Great Escape*'. Flights and a hotel were reserved for the following day, flying out on Friday morning, returning Tuesday evening. Adam would go down to the travel office later in the day and pay for the holiday by cash. He needed to ask Cammy if he wanted to go on holiday, or perhaps he would just *tell* Cammy he was going?

The unconscious tourist was now awake from his deep slumber, not knowing whether his grandmother's phantom form was for real or simply another translucent dream. Adam sauntered into the living room in an unaccustomed bright and breezy manner as if he'd stepped out of a sickly television commercial advertising a new brand of shampoo. Cammy knew something was up. 'Rise and shine, Cammy boy, it's nearly teatime.'

'What's up with you?'

'I'm nice and cheery today.'

'What's happened?' grumbled Cammy. 'What are you after? What's *wrong*?'

'What do you mean what's wrong?' announced Adam in a bout of denial. 'Am I not allowed to be a smiling happy person?'

'You're never a smiling happy person. That's why there must be something wrong.'

Adam had planned to defer his holiday chat until Cammy was dressed and savouring his morning mug of milky tea. However, due to Mr Carter's suspicious mind and perceptive line of fire the sun-drenched chinwag was brought forward. This was the appropriate time to lay his tanned cards on the table. 'Well if you have to know, I've had a good idea. I've been thinking.'

'God help us.'

I've been thinking you merit a short break. You've been working tirelessly day and night, you deserve a weekend away – a small holiday in the sun. I've arranged for both of us to go to Sicily tomorrow for a few days and you'll be able to meet up with Matty. How does that sound?'

'That's really weird!'

'Why?'

'Well my grandmother, em . . . she . . .em . . .never mind. It's a long story, you wouldn't understand.'

'Try me?'

'No, it's okay, Adam. Call it coincidence.' Cammy was doing his best to move the conversation on. '*Sicily*, that sounds amazing. When will we be back?'

'When do you need to be back?'

'Hopefully Monday, for my therapy class. Definitely Tuesday morning as I've an important burial.'

'No problem.' Adam knew full well that they wouldn't arrive back in Edinburgh until Tuesday night. He'd worry about this little difficulty at a later date. 'Monday evening it is then.' He was delighted Cammy was going along with his holiday scheme.

'Have you got a passport?' quizzed Adam.

'I do.'

'Thank goodness for that. Mind you, I could have probably sorted one out for you.'

'Why the sudden rush for a short break?'

'You deserve it and I know how much you're missing Matty.' Cammy was seeing a nicer side of his flatmate. This was bordering on disbelief. 'I'm off to see Mrs Waddel and ask her if she'll feed the cats when we're away.' Adam stepped out of the front door, drew in a lung full of air and knocked on Mrs Waddel's front door. 'Hello, Mrs Waddel.'

'Hello.'

'We're going on a wee break this weekend.'

'Would you speak up, my hearing aid's on the blink,' answered Mrs Waddel, stepping onto the stair landing. 'Now, what were you saying?'

'We're going on a wee break this weekend,' rumbled Adam. 'I wonder if you could feed Roger and the cats?'

'Oh yes, Adam, no bother. My hearing's getting worse.'

'Oh really,' mouthed Adam silently, unable to resist the temptation.

'Speak up, Adam. I can't hear what you're saying.'

'Here's the new front door key,' added Adam in a louder voice. 'The cat food is in the cupboard above the sink and the goldfish flakes are beside the bowl. I'll also buy extra milk.'

'Don't worry about that. I've plenty of milk. My brother always brings me milk on a Saturday with the fish.'

'The fish?'

'Yes, haddock on a Saturday and cod on a Wednesday.'

'Of course,' acknowledged Adam nodding his head.

'Where are you off too?' asked Mrs Waddel.

'Sunny Sicily.'

'For the weekend? That's not very long, is it?'

'Yeah, it's all the time Cammy can take off.'

'He works too hard. Should be hot in Sicily, much better weather than here. Mind you most places would be hotter than here. Is Sicily in Spain?'

'No, Italy.'

'It's near Brussels isn't it?'

'No, it's an island off Italy.'

'Oh yes, Italy. It's an island isn't it?'

'Yes,' agreed Adam. 'It's an island.'

'Here, Adam.'

'Yeah.'

'There was a picture of a boy in the paper today that looked a wee bit like you.'

'Surely not,' replied Adam trying to feign innocence. 'I've never been in the newspaper. Wouldn't be me.'

'Yes, I'll get the paper and show you.' Mrs Waddel turned her back. 'It's beside the television.'

'No, don't worry Mrs Waddel, I've a lot to do.' Adam was clearly agitated. 'We'll see you when we get back. I really must go.'

'Oh, all right, Adam, have a nice time and tell Cameron to have a lovely time too. He's a charming boy, that Cameron.'

'We'll try our best and I'll send you a postcard.' Adam returned to the relative security of his front door. 'Mind you, we'll probably be home before the postcard arrives.'

'Don't worry, it's the thought that counts.' At least her sentiment was sound.

'Bye, Mrs Waddel.'

'Bye.' Adam swiftly retreated to the semi-safety of his flat. Next on the agenda was the task of keeping Cammy busy, keeping Cammy inside and keeping Cammy away from any newspaper stands.

'What are you up to today, Cammy?'

'Well if we're going away, I'll need to buy some shorts, shirts and toothpaste. Stuff like that.'

'Why don't you get the stuff tomorrow morning before we go?' suggested Adam. 'That's what I'm going to do.'

'That'll be a bit of a rush for me. I'd like to be sorted out tonight. You know, pack my bags this evening. When I'm out, I'll buy some food for tonight's dinner and since the *Gazette* hasn't arrived, I'll also buy a newspaper. You should have words with that paperboy, it's happened before.'

'Why don't I prepare dinner tonight and do your shopping for you?'

'Are you feeling all right?' bawled Cammy. 'Have you had a charm transplant in the night? Has a helpful fairy cast a spell to bypass the lazy side of your personality?'

'Hey, steady on,' retorted Adam, his temper fraying at the edges. 'I never get any credit for my good turns. I'm only trying to be helpful. If that's your attitude, I'll cancel the tickets right now and we can roam around grey Edinburgh all weekend.'

'No, I didn't mean that,' uttered Cammy attempting to retrieve the situation. 'I just meant that you aren't always like this... I mean you're never like this... Oh look, forget it. If you want to do some shopping, then *do* some shopping. Have you any idea where the shops are?'

'Ha bloody ha.'

'Okay, I'll give you a list of things I need. However, under no circumstances will I let you prepare dinner tonight. I've seen your cooking before and it isn't a pretty sight.'

'Fair enough.' Adam was more than happy to soak up the latest insult. He was keeping the bigger picture in perspective. ' I take your point.'

'Glad we sorted that out. Can you buy Matty's lottery ticket when you're out? I said I'd do it when she was away.'

'What's her numbers again?'

'You should know.'

'No, remind me.'

'Come on Adam, how many times have you bought tickets for her?'

'Okay, I know them. One nine twelve fourteen fifteen and nineteen. How can I *forget*?'

'So why did you ask?'

'Just being lazy.'

'There's a first,' muttered Cammy under his breath.

'I don't know why Matty plays the lottery. It's a bloody rip-off. Robbing the poor to fund the rich.'

'How do you work that one out?'

'The punters buy the tickets and the toffs spend the money. What do we get? I'll tell you what we get, Opera houses and shitty theatres. Daylight fuckin' fraud if you ask me. The biggest legitimate scam of all time!'

'Oh I see.' To avoid Adam's head exploding, Cammy shifted the topic of conversation. 'Why are you wearing dark glasses and a baseball cap?'

'Style, Cammy, style.'

'Mmm,' ruminated Cammy. 'You've as much style as a badly dressed scarecrow.'

Adam for the time being was managing to keep his flatmate under lock and key. He hoped Cammy would stay indoors while he was out at the shops. This he did, and Adam returned from the supermarket having purchased every item on the list. 'There's a good film on TV tonight. I've bought a few beers. We can stay in and conserve our energy for tomorrow if you want?'

'Sounds good to me.' Adam was feeling rather pleased with himself. So far, so good.

'Did you get a copy of the *Gazette*?' asked Cammy.

'Em, no . . . em, they were sold out.'

'Sold out? *The Gazette* is never sold out.'

'It was today. I tried four shops and they were all gone.'

Cammy sighed. 'That's unusual.'

'Yes, most unusual.'

'That's a real pity,' grumbled Cammy. 'Andrew has an advert in today's edition. Oh well, I'm sure he'll keep a copy.'

Adam safely detained his graverobbing partner indoors for the entire evening. The next morning, Cammy dragged a large brown suitcase into the hallway. 'Where's your luggage, Adam?'

'I never travel with luggage.'

'How come?'

'I'll show you later.'

Adam, when travelling, would only carry a small bag onto the plane as hand luggage. After arriving at his destination, Adam would poach the first two suitcases he saw appearing from the reclaim section, lift them onto a trolley and promptly leave the airport terminal. This was easy, as security for personal baggage was non-existent. When he reached his final destination, he invariably found a few pieces of clothing to wear. He'd nurtured an eye for 'male looking' luggage rather than 'female looking' luggage, although he once arrived on holiday with two purloined bags revealing only woman's underwear. A shoplifting spree soon cleared up this modest inconvenience. If any of the real owners ever tried to stop him, Adam planned to apologise gracefully and explain that he owned a similar bag. This wasn't an unreasonable excuse. He hadn't been caught to date.

Adam wondered why there were always unclaimed suitcases

rolling around in circles on airport conveyor belts. One of these unknown mysteries, he thought, like odd socks.

'Echo Beach' by Martha and the Muffins was blasting out from Adam's rather impressive state of the art compact disc player.

'Do you know something, Cammy? My mum used to think Martha and the Muffins were singing 'Methil beach', rather than 'Echo beach'. That's funny, isn't it?'

'No, not excessively.'

'Why?'

'Because I don't know the song.'

'Suit yourself.'

'Talking of your mum, Adam.'

'Yes.'

'Have you told her you'll be away?'

Adam paused for a few seconds. 'I have.'

'*Really.*'

'What is that tone of voice meant to mean?' Adam wondered what Cammy was up to.

'Nothing, Adam, nothing whatsoever. Time to go.'

'Oh yeah,' Adam glanced down at his recently stolen watch. 'So it is. One thing, though.'

'What?'

'Final check. Wallet, keys, fags, cock.'

Chapter Seventeen

A LARGE PILE OF UNSOLD Lothian *Gazettes* lay at the side door of the airport shop ready to be returned to the Journal's office.

The daring duo's journey to Sicily, via a long delay in London was fairly uneventful. The only incident of any note was a fine display of Cammy's tactless skills demonstrated on board the plane to the appreciation of a captivated group of fellow passengers. A party of boisterous juveniles, making an abundance of noise behind Cammy's seat, was unsettling. Nobody sitting near the raucous teenagers volunteered to complain. The verbal blasts were accompanied by a loud radio and the six youths were happily snapping their fingers in time with the music. Cammy, no slouch at telling people what he thought, turned round and suggested if the radio wasn't turned off, none of the party would have any fingers left to click and if the commotion continued at any point during the trip, he would break their legs one by one. From then on, the journey was joyously peaceful and the passengers opposite Cammy exchanged polite nods of approval.

Adam was inordinately quiet throughout the journey. He only made one attempt at a joke. This was while awaiting take-off at Heathrow airport. Spotting an Air China jet on the forecourt, he asked if the pilot would need cushions and if Chinese whispers in China were called something else. Cammy was fast asleep.

Meanwhile back in cloudy Edinburgh, Andy and Lorna were listening intently to Mr Brian Editor. 'So you're telling me we haven't had any calls about our Virgil Burke photograph?'

'We've received one call. The bloke hung up,' answered Andy. 'He was from St Andrews and wanted to know if there was a reward. When I explained there wasn't, he slammed the phone down. I tried to trace the call. His number wasn't available.'

'That's *very* pleasing,' replied the editor.

'What?' Andy was confused.

'I'm pleased someone in St Andrews is reading our paper.'

'Oh I see,' acknowledged Lorna blankly. A redundant look

spread across her face. She decided to retire from the conversation in the warm-up lap.

'Now,' continued Mr Editor, 'what's this about another bouquet?'

'Yes,' responded Andy. 'Another batch of cut flowers have been found. They were discovered in a cemetery on the outskirts of town. I've spoken to the florist and she has confirmed the latest display is without doubt her handiwork. It was a similar flower arrangement, with the same American Society notice signed by Dandy.'

'Dandy! Looks more like Diddy to me,' insisted Mr Editor.

'I think it says Daddy,' chimed Lorna, throwing her tuppence worth into the ring.

'Well, whatever it says, are the police involved yet?' countered Mr Editor, trying to establish the heart of the matter

'Indeed they are,' voiced Andy. 'They're finally taking an interest. The turf on this latest tomb was expertly cut and neatly placed back on the grave - similar to the previous plot.'

'What are you saying here, Andy?' asked the Editor. The scent of a good story filled his nostrils with anticipation.

'It seems we're dealing with more than vandals. Someone has clearly broken into both graves.'

'I thought bodysnatching went out of fashion many years ago. Any announcements from the police?'

'Yes, the police have gained permission to exhume the grave to see if anything has been tampered with.'

'By Jove, this is becoming a serious story! Keep your ears to the ground and make sure you pester the local constabulary every hour.'

'No problem, Brian.' Andy was overstepping the mark.

'*Mr Editor* will do. Just because you have a story moving rapidly towards the front page, It doesn't mean you can get friendly with me!'

'Sorry, Mr Editor.' Andy was exceptionally excited. He'd mentioned the 'f' word. That's great! The front page. My God, the friggin' front page! A telling off by the boss was diffused by his own elation.

Mr Editor turned to Lorna and, with the stale air of limited expectancy, asked what she'd found out. 'Well like, I've discovered details relating to the silver flask. Apparently it's a limited edition.' She was proud as punch, surely a pay rise would ensue. The newsroom fell silent with a prolonged pregnant pause. Brian was expecting more to follow. 'And?'

'And that's it so far...'

'Lorna, I have reason to believe that this is the finest piece of journalistic investigation I have ever come across in my twenty-two years working in the media industry.'

'Thank you, sir, you're too kind.' Once again without fail, whoosh, whoosh, whoosh. Lorna's comic shield successfully defended a sarcasm attack. She planted her white flag in the fluffy clouds while the hack to hack combat and journalistic sharp shooting persisted in the media trenches below.

Lorna was a woman in no man's land.

'What next, Andy?'

'I think we should print a grave-robbing type of story, continue the search for Mr Burke and see what the police come up with.'

In a vain attempt to keep her involved, the sympathetic editor encountered 'Operation Deserted Storm'. Any bullets fired from his gun were destined to draw a blank. 'What do you think, Lorna?'

'Yes, I agree with Andy.'

'I thought you might. However, I would say that neither of you are aware of local history, are you?'

'Well I'm from Devon.'

'And I'm from Dundee,' boasted Lorna.

'Mr William Burke happens to be an infamous bodysnatcher from the 1820s. Along with his accomplice, Mr William Hare, they murdered people and sold the corpses to the doctors of anatomy at Edinburgh Medical School. I think our Dandy fellow is taking the piss. Not to worry, this only adds to our story.'

'Was William Burke's first name Virgil?' asked Lorna. Another remarkable question from the poker-faced queen of wooden clubs. The editor couldn't believe his ears. This was a priceless comment for his scrapbook. 'No, funnily enough his first name was

William,' affirmed the editor. 'I have no idea where the name Virgil comes from. Sounds American to me.'

'So do you think we merit a front page spot?' said Andy expectantly.

'We'll see, Andy, we'll see.'

'Mr Editor, sorry to interrupt.' A voice hollered from the newsroom. 'There's a Mrs Diamond on the phone. She says if you don't speak to her she'll bring someone called Hector in to bite you.'

'Thanks,' yelled Mr Editor. 'I'll take the call and sort this woman out once and for all. By the time I'm finished with this old dear, she'll wish she never started pestering me. Put her through, I'll take the call in here. Please excuse me for a few minutes.'

Andy and Lorna left the boss's office and returned to the chaos of the newsroom. The dense smoke lingered with malignant intent. The room's extractor fan was temporarily out of order due to a colossal build-up of soot, dust and grime. Owing to Brian Editor's budgetary restraints, the ageing mechanism was unlikely to be repaired in the foreseeable future, if at all. Adding scorn to detriment, an overzealous painter had recently administered a liberal quota of gloss directly onto the mouldy window frames, sealing the structural cases firmly shut. The venetian blinds overhanging the smeared glass were a deep discoloration of yellow, badly stained by several layers of nicotine and although the *Gazette's* office enjoyed a dazzling view over the city centre skyline, the drapes invariably remained half closed. The part-time janitor, secreting wisdom ahead of his station, refused to venture near the contaminated blinds and with few disputing his resolve, the mire continued to accumulate on a daily basis.

The bins were worse than the windows. Newspapers, polystyrene coffee cups and chewing gum merged with festering tea bags, half-sucked sweets and snotty handkerchiefs. One of the reporters occasionally brought her six-month-old daughter to work and cheerfully deposited full nappies in the nearest bin, adding her litter's litter to the litter. All the staff refused to place their hands anywhere near the buckets for fear of catching a wasting disease. If the cleaning arrangements remained static, the bins might effortlessly gain a substantial grant from the Scottish Arts

Council and be displayed as 'modern trash art' at the Edinburgh International Festival.

On a more mechanical note, the newsroom through the debris contained a wide range of hi-tech state of the art computers, scanners and colour copiers. Technology wouldn't change the day to day life of the city and to prove the point, e-mails endlessly streamed into the office with absorbing details on future car boot sales, women's guild dinners and missing pets.

'Lorna.'

'Yes.'

'Do you think we might get a front page?'

'No, I don't think so.'

'Thanks for the encouragement.' The air had been let out of Andy's tyres.

'I don't think we will. I was only answering your question. Do you want me to, like, lie and say we'll get a front page?'

'No, fair enough.'

'Anyway, it would be more *your* front page than mine,' objected Lorna. 'You've done most of the work.'

'No Lorna, that's not fair,' responded Andy. 'Without you, this story would never have happened.'

'*Really*?' Lorna turned a bright shade of red. She was blushing like a sun baked plum.

'Yes really.' Once again a severe bout of irony missed Lorna by several light years. Her ice-cream sundae was clearly lost in Thursday afternoon. Whoosh, whoosh and whoosh. A lifetime membership to cloud cuckoo land was in the post. Feeling warm and cosy inside, pleased with her seemingly effective journalistic contribution, Lorna turned to matters more charitable.

'Andy.'

'Yes.'

'Have you got your cheque book here?'

'Why?'

'I've detected at least eighty-two 'greats' and that's only when I've been in your company.'

'Lorna, I've lost count of how many 'likes' you've said.'

'How about we both write a cheque for twenty-five pounds,' proposed Lorna.

'Which charity do you want to choose?'

'I don't know. What do you think?'

'I think we should send the money to the American Society of Scholars.'

'I thought you said they weren't a charity?' Whoosh, whoosh and whoosh.

'We'll choose later. On the money front, ten pounds might be more reasonable?'

'How about seven pounds, then?' Andy had no notion of where Lorna had plucked seven-pounds from. Still this was better than paying twenty-five pounds.

'Em..........seven it is then, as long as our forfeit has now expired.' They both shook hands.

'I'll go along with that, like.'

'Great.'

Chapter Eighteen

THE ATMOSPHERE WAS ALIVE with the tangible fragrance of orange, lemon and mandarin trees.

Taormina was awash with seasoned German tourists. The spellbinding little Sicilian town, overlooking the clear blue waters of the Ionian sea, uniquely set in the Province of Messina, was one of the many jewels in Italy's crown.

The swarming town centre, surrounded by steep slopes full of olive trees, was a mere servant to the still active Mount Etna. The towering inferno rumbled its tummy like the roll of distant thunder, emitting sporadic glowing sprays of fire. Taormina was in all respects one of the most celebrated resorts in the Mediterranean.

Cammy and Adam flew from London and landed at Catania on the east coast of Sicily. The primitive airport resembled something from a late 1950s cine film. There was so much clutter at the baggage reclaim section that Adam effortlessly selected his two holiday suitcases. He dragged them clear of the conveyor belt past a jumble of fighting tourists. Staring in from outside the main terminal through large Perspex windows were umpteen Sicilian families awaiting the arrival of their loved ones. You'd swear that half of Italy was standing in the car park. Anxious citizens, faces pressed hard against the window jostled for position by waving small signs above their heads. It all resembled a bizarre scene from the movie *Zombie Flesh Eaters*.

The journey into Taormina from the airport, complete with Scottish tour rep Jeremy, took less than an hour. However, with all the delays they did not arrive at their hotel, the Villa Caterina, until a quarter to midnight. The twin room was barely adequate. An unpleasant sterile smell dogged the air as if they'd booked into a three-star sewerage plant. There was a saving grace: the room opened onto a small sun-trapped balcony looking down to a swimming pool encircled by lush subtropical palm trees. What a majestic sight.

Adam unlocked the two naturally grained calfskin suitcases

with a wire coat hanger and rummaged through the real owner's personal items of clothing. 'Shorts, T-shirts, swimming gear, toothpaste, it's all here. By the looks of the clothes, they'll be a bit big for me. Good, there's a belt to hold everything up. Huh, look at this Cammy – a kilt. I've nicked a Scotsman's bag. Cool bananas.'

'Cool bananas' was Adam's new phrase of the week.

'He's from Glasgow,' mentioned Cammy.

'Who is?'

'The guy who owns this bag.'

'How do you know that?'

'I'm psychic,' divulged Cammy in a spooky voice. 'Gifted with a mind that can predict the future.'

'No you're not.'

'Of course I'm *not*.' Cammy pointed down to the suitcase. 'Check the label, idiot brain.'

'Mr Glenn Spence from Glasgow,' read Adam. 'Glasgow boy, that's fab. Nothing like stealing from a Glaswegian.'

'That looks like a Macduff tartan.' Cammy was familiar with Scottish family plaids, thanks to Matty's sharing of tourist guide knowledge. 'I'm 99% sure it's a Macduff.'

'I wouldn't know.' Adam didn't like Glasgow because he never went. Then again, Adam didn't like lots of places. Come to think about it, he didn't like Edinburgh either. The rumble of Adam's tummy meant only one thing – food. 'I'm starving, I've real bellyache. Shall we try and find somewhere to eat?'

'Should we not find Matty first?' Cammy was desperate to see her as soon as he could.

'It's nearly midnight, she'll be in her scratcher, you know what she's like. You'll see her tomorrow morning. Come on, food and a couple of beers.' Cammy reluctantly agreed.

They were out eating, drinking and being very merry (in between Cammy ranting on about Matty) until 6.30 am. As the boys were going to bed, Matty and Andrew – sharing a twin room in a far superior hotel on the other side of town, were slowly surfacing. All with the compliments of Andrew's college friend, Graham McCrea.

The golden sun climbed majestically above the sublime bay.

The Ionian Sea constantly splashed the land of myth, mystery and legend. The tranquillising drift of cooling water complemented the blissfully warm day. September was pleasant rather than blistering. The view of Mount Etna was breathtaking.

Andrew and Matty were lying stretched out like cats in front of an open fire. Matty was wearing khaki shorts, no socks and sandals, a yellow vest-top and a baseball cap. The warm stone steps within the marvellous ruins of the superbly restored Greco-Roman theatre would be their place of relaxation for the rest of the day. The historic structure carved out of limestone over two thousand years before was an evocative testament to the builders of old and an exalted reminder of Sicily's over-indulgent past. On a less highbrow note, the amphitheatre was also a great place to boost your suntan.

'Matty.'

'Yeah.'

'Have you corresponded with the adoption agency yet?'

'Yeah, I've written a letter. I haven't posted it yet. I found out at the Records Office that my real name is Duncan. My parents are called David and Catherine. Didn't really want to know more, so I aborted the search.'

'Duncan, an exceptionally elevated name. Still pondering the positives and negatives are you?'

'Yeah, they'll send me a birth certificate if I want one with details of my parents' occupations. The thing I don't understand is, if my birth was registered why didn't the authorities find the documents and contact my real parents?'

'God only knows.'

'Part of me wants to find out more. Another part wants me to forget the search.'

'I sincerely understand, Matty. You take as much time as you need.'

'Don't worry, Andrew, I shall, I shall.'

'I'm glad.'

'Andrew, isn't this the business?' Matty shaded the sun from her eyes. 'I've a bit of a sore head, though.'

'My dear girl, this is nirvana on planet earth. I'm sure it's the sun.'

'I suppose you're right. Here Andrew, look at my legs.'

'Your legs?'

'Yeah, I cut them to buggery this morning trying to shave in the bath.'

Andrew peered over the top of his sunglasses and voiced in a nonplussed fashion. 'Oh how awful.'

'Before I left Edinburgh I arranged a bikini wax,' added Matty. 'When I got there, they were closed.'

'What time did you book your appointment?'

'Five o'clock.'

'What time did you arrive?'

'Six o'clock.'

'I rest my case.'

'I wonder how Cammy's getting on in Edinburgh?' Matty rubbed sun lotion onto her scarred legs.

'Matty dear child, if Cameron's name is articulated once more this week, I shall not be answerable for my gesticulations. For goodness sake refrain from persecuting yourself and desist from irritating me any further. Please start to appreciate this holiday.'

'I *am* enjoying the holiday. It's . . .'

'Before you once again bore me to the core, brake, button your lips and savour this exquisite climate.'

'Talking of lips,' uttered Matty in a less than polite manner. 'I need the toilet.'

'You flabbergast me at times with your vulgarity. You can be so common. If I didn't know you better, I'd swear you were endeavouring to rile me.'

'Not at all Andrew, would you hand me my bag. On second thoughts, could you dig your hand in and pass me out a tampon.'

'I despair at times, you are such a trollop,' whined Andrew through a poorly disguised grin. He dipped his left hand into Matty's handbag. 'There's a petit tampon here, is that what you're after?'

'No, that's like throwing a sanitary towel up Princes Street. Here, let me have a look.' Matty grabbed hold of her satchel, rummaged around for a few seconds, found what she was looking for and darted off to the toilet.

Andrew lay motionless, enjoying the mid-day sun. His black eye was gradually fading, his face was turning a deep colour of brown. Some people burned in the sun and become bright red, Andrew instantly bronzed. Squinting through his expensive pair of designer sunglasses he spotted a group of young men entering the amphitheatre with a German-speaking guide.

Spying a choice gaggle of honest looking young specimens, Andrew commenced his private little competition. He scanned every man in the tour party individually and fantasised whether he would have sexual intercourse with them or not. Marks were given out of ten for tanned muscular frames and tidy buttocks. Andrew didn't have a name for his provocative hobby. If a caption were required, the term 'shagging game' would rarely be in contention. Thanks to his impressive grasp of the English language, Andrew's pastime would probably enjoy a courteous title not dissimilar to the 'carnal coupling contest'. Willie Wagner from Stolberg near Aachen was today's unwitting 'champion of copulation'.

There was a man in the group of German sightseers who reminded Andrew of someone he knew. It was frustrating when he recognised a person yet couldn't quite place where he'd met them. This was an annoying feature of Andrew's multiple mind. Then he remembered. 'Wasteland Woods,' he whispered to himself. Stale breath caught in the back of his throat. Perspiration oozed from his brow. 'He looks like the guy I killed in the Wasteland Woods.'

Vicious thoughts flashed through his brain. Fifteen years earlier while on holiday in Devon, he took a stroll through the Wasteland Woods, where he bumped into a group of teenagers hanging a grey cat from a tree. He went ballistic. The site of a poor defenceless animal being strung up and nailed to a branch by some heartless youths was too much to bear. When the gang saw him running towards them, they took to their heels and disappeared from the woods. Andrew managed to catch one of the boys and, like a man possessed, relentlessly kicked the lad until blood seeped out of the youngster's head. He persisted in kicking the boy until he was almost dead. Then, in a fresh bout of rage, he picked up a large muddy boulder and smashed the final semblance of life out of the teenager.

The next morning, after a disturbing night's sleep, Andrew consciously commenced the process of blocking the previous day's Jekyll and Hyde actions from his mind and to protect his sobriety, the refined version of Andrew was assembled. Fifteen years on, bringing with him the burden of a young lad's death, Andrew was uncertain whether the incident had actually taken place or not. Blotting out this gloomy chapter from his life virtually worked. From time to time, though, as in the present case, his virulent actions reappeared to bedevil his convoluted brain. With sustained will power and an organised intellect, Andrew was able to plead his innocence. The crime remained unsolved and Andrew, with courteous caution, kept his shocking secret tucked up in the back of his classified mind.

This brutal murder was in part the consequence of a childhood trauma. He was confronting his demons by slaying the dragon. Andrew's grey cat, Quentin, suffering from a throat tumour, was taken to the local veterinary surgery to be put to sleep. The vet asked if the family wished to be present when the lethal injection was administered. Andrew's father agreed and the poor defence-less animal, crouching in distress, was put down in front of their very eyes. Andrew wrapped Quentin in a tartan rug and held him tight in his arms during the short car journey back to the family home. Although Quentin was dead and motionless, his eyes were wide open to the world and each time the car passed under a street lamp, the yellow light reflected in the deceased cat's eyes. This haunting image had remained with Andrew since the tender age of eight.

Returning from the basic bathroom, Matty noticed an agitated look on Andrew's face and inquired if anything was wrong. The sound of her dulcet tones registered in Andrew's head, jolting him back to the here and now. 'Oh nothing much.' He shifted ner-vously and wiped beads of sweat from his bronzed brow in a determined effort to regain his composure. 'Merely relishing the wonderful views. This locality has an abundance of ambience. I'm dumbfounded by the architecture. You know, I swear I've been here before.'

'Yes, we were here yesterday.'

'No Matty, don't endeavour to be whimsical. The entire vicinity has a magical aura. You can visualise the thrilling days of the gladiators. Giant muscular fighting men parading in front of a packed theatre.'

'Yes, I bet you would queue overnight, just like Wimbledon.'

'I shall disregard your discourteous observations for the ensuing minutes.'

Andrew lay down on the stone steps. Matty headed off to listen to a British tour guide regaling the history of the Greco-Roman theatre. She worshipped history. This was her favoured subject at school, thanks to the passionate teaching techniques employed by the flamboyant Mrs Beath. Her inspirational classes and spellbinding diction brought history alive, nurturing Matty's mind in the ways of the past. The intention to record Mrs Beath's wise words on tape was always top of Matty's list until she heard of her old teacher's death and realised the chance to preserve a piece of local history was lost forever. Since that day, Matty never did tomorrow the things she could do today.

Andrew, wearing a purple T-shirt with matching shorts, was showing no signs of grief. His father had died in the middle of the night, the startling message passed on to him by a hotel porter at three in the morning. Matty was unaware of this shocking news.

Andrew was unlikely to shed many tears. He had nothing in common with either of his parents. For many years he had only visited them on Christmas Day. A polite exchanging of gifts was followed by a mannerly dinner, which was hastily followed by a less than fond farewell. One day a year in the company of his folks was a struggle. He couldn't understand why he was upset, considering how much he detested his father. Even the thought 'well he's still my dad' didn't occupy much space in Andrew's heart. He certainly wouldn't attend his father's funeral. He believed death settled all human failings; death resolved our problems and death conquered all. Even if Andrew was upset for now, he was determined that his deceased dad wouldn't ruin this holiday.

'She's a fuckin' good guide that one,' yelled Matty as she returned to where Andrew was relaxing.

'Matty, your profanity at times is beyond belief,' expressed

Andrew arrogantly, a faint Irish brogue beginning to show. 'You squander far too much time in the company of that unrefined brother of yours. Before any respectable quota of time has elapsed you'll be revving your car engine, playing uncouth ear-splitting music with the windows down and purchasing cheap furry dice. Degenerate human beings like Adam should not be allowed to corrupt fine citizens like you. Inhabitants like Adam should not be permitted to procreate and this would avert moronic dimwits being born into this world. It's the uneducated riffraff that breed like rabbits. Some of them should be put down at birth.' A bee was buzzing in Andrew's right-wing bonnet. This was his way of grieving. 'Don't hold back, Andrew, or can I call you Benito?

As the hours ticked by, Andrew became a richer colour of brown, Matty became a brighter colour of red and Adam and Cammy became aware half the day was over. Cammy looked whiter than a newly washed sheet, his hair tousled like a bird's nest. The previous night's high jinks had taken their toll. To cure his morning hangover, he opened a small bottle of sparkling mineral water and emptied the fizzy contents over his head. 'I'll need to get my act together before I see Matty. I can't believe I've been in the same town as her for so many hours without making contact.'

'You best not see Matty, looking like that. You look like death warmed down.'

'*Up.*'

'Up?'

'Death warmed up, not down.'

'Whatever. You look like shite on a hot tin roof.'

Cammy thought Adam had as much style as a tramp's assistant.

Adam wondered why most of the shops were closed. Cammy happily explained it was siesta time. 'When we were sleeping, they were working and now that we're up, they're off for their afternoon snooze. The shops will be open later.'

They were sitting outside the Café Umberto in Piazza IX Aprile, Taormina's main square. The boys were nursing severe hangovers. The quantity of potent Sicilian wines proving an intoxicating indulgence. 'What were we drinking last night?' croaked Adam, holding his head in his hands. 'I think it was mostly white wine - seemed to disappear like water. I think we tried a bottle of red at about five this morning and then Jeremy bought us a cherry liqueur. Don't remember much after that.' Cammy picked up a copy of the café's menu and ran his finger down the drinks list. 'Yeah, I remember some of these names. We had a glass of Corvo, a half bottle of Donnafugata, a carafe of Solunto and I'm not sure if we had a Regealia or not. What a fantastic selection. You know what they say, choice is the enemy of time.'

Adam wasn't really listening. 'It's all double Dutch to me.'

Cammy looked down and noticed a dark patch on Adam's instep. 'What the hell is that?'

'A tattoo,' answered Adam. 'Fifteen pounds at Bob's tattoo studio, not bad eh?'

'What does it say?' Adam slipped his training shoe off. The tattoo read 'What the fuck are you looking at'.

'Charming, Adam. You know how to win friends. Why did you get that done?'

'To hide my gunshot wound.'

'*What*!'

'I was shot in the foot a few years back,' boasted Adam brushing his left thumb over the instep of his foot. 'I was walking down a country lane and saw a group of twats shooting pheasants. This really pissed me off, so I jumped the stone wall and ran at full speed towards them, screaming my head off.'

A comical image appeared in Cammy's mind, a smirk surfacing on his face. The thought of Adam sprinting towards twenty men holding loaded shotguns was farcical. 'What happened?'

'One of the posh toffs shot me.'

Cammy burst out laughing. He thought Adam must have been out of his skull. At least that would be an excuse for him behaving like a complete idiot.

'It's not funny, you know. The tit nearly blew my foot off. If the bullet had been a few inches the other way, I'd be hopping today.'

'Good job the bullets didn't lodge in your arse.' Cammy chuckled. 'Might have blown your brains out.'

'Piss off.' Yet another well-developed witty reply from Adam.

Cammy couldn't suppress his glee. Adam's love for animals clearly outweighed his lack of common sense. For the rest of the day Cammy retained the image of Adam storming over a muddy field waving his arms frantically in the air.

'At least I got the wax-coated bastards to stop shooting,' said Adam. 'An ambulance was called to take me to the hospital.'

'Should have kept you in,' mumbled Cammy.

The main square was bustling with all nationalities including endless groups of Italian school children. Many people arrived at Piazza IX Aprile to view Mount Etna from the iron balustrade surrounding the square. A French couple approached Adam, handed him a camera and asked if he could take their photograph with Mount Etna in the background.

'Don't you dare run off with the camera!' warned Cammy.

'Been there, done that, bought the teapot.'

'T-shirt!'

'Yeah, that too.'

Adam snapped a couple of photographs of the tourists, handed their camera back and returned to the table giggling.

'What are you laughing at Adam?'

'When they get their photos developed, they'll be really pissed off.'

'Why's that?'

'I cut their heads off!'

'You're such a bastard at times.'

'Yeah, but a funny bastard,' crooned Adam staring at the street sign. 'That's a strange name, isn't it?'

'What is?'

'April the ninth Square. Does that mean you only get served here on April the ninth?'

'At this rate, you could be right.'

The café was packed to the gunnels. Adam tried to attract the attention of the lone waiter who was charging around like a madman looking for the keys to his padded cell. His attempts were fruitless. This was a job for Tactless Man. Cammy stood up, approached the waiter, grabbed hold of his arm and dragged him over to their table.

'Bon giorno.'

'English will do,' said Cammy.

'Ah, you are English?'

'No, Scottish,' proclaimed both boys at the same time, swapping from British to Scottish at the drop of a hat. Unionist one minute, nationalist the next. They were blindfolded civic animals stranded in the middle of the road. From the baffling bag of pick and mix politics, the soft centred romantic notion of freedom was chosen as frequently as the traditional toffee wrapped in the Union Jack.

'Can I have a big mug of coffee?' rasped Adam. 'None of your wee expresso crap.'

'And bring me a pot of tea and a couple of toasted cheese sandwiches,' added Cammy. 'You do want a sandwich, don't you?'

'Yes, and before next April.' Adam looked directly at the waiter, his steely glance resembling that of a medieval witch hunter conveyed a clear message - hurry up. The cowering waiter translated Adam's stare into Italian and scuttled back to the kitchen. Cammy stretched his arms, yawned out loud and mused on the previous night's sleep. 'I slept well last night. There was one point I woke up and was convinced someone was in the room, so I didn't open my eyes. Have you ever had that feeling before?'

'Can't say I have. The only feeling I ever get is wondering where the hell I am. At least I had an excuse this morning.'

The day was warm and breezy. A number of plastic chairs raised by a sharp gust of wind slid into the middle of the square. The distraught Italian waiter rushed after them, tripping over a table in the process. A large bee descended from the café roof and landed on the back of Cammy's chair. He looked round in admiration, smiling at the colourful creature. Adam picked up the laminated menu, folded the 'Carte du jour' in two and prepared to extinguish the bee's hive of activity. Realising the insect's plight, Cammy grabbed hold of Adam's wrist with one hand and ushered the bee away with the other. When Adam less than politely asked 'what the fuck he was doing', Cammy explained that the bee might be his Uncle Jim. Even Adam for once looked concerned. He thought Cammy should be measured for a straightjacket, bundled into a yellow van and driven to the nearest laughing academy.

'I thought you liked animals?'

'I do, but I hate bees.' With a comment like this, Adam would soon to be fitted with wrist restraints and join his business partner in the funny farm's nutcracker suite. 'This town is like Edinburgh,' reflected Cammy. 'There are so many similarities.'

'How do you work that one out?'

'A windy city, Italian school children, full of tourists, lots of alleyways, history, architecture, restaurants, em . . .and . . .'

'Lovely weather, hot sunshine and relaxing,' spouted Adam. 'It's nothing like Edinburgh.'

'Suit yourself.'

'I will.'

Cammy left his seat to avail himself of the toilet facilities located on the other side of the square. A large Hungarian man followed him in. Inside the lavatory, a small chubby Italian sat in the tiniest room you could ever imagine. A grubby sign posted on the wall beside him suggested all visitors should tip the attendant. Peering eyes blocked the will to urinate. Cammy couldn't relieve his bladder when someone was watching, so he found some loose change in the pockets of his shorts, paid the man and hurriedly returned to the café. 'They charge you to have a piss. In fact they charge you *not* to have a piss!'

'Never mind that.' Adam waved the bill above his head. 'Look how much the bandits have charged us for a couple of drinks and a sandwich. No wonder they don't show the prices on the menu. Bunch of thieving bastards.'

'That's rich coming from you, Adam.'

'At least my thieving is legitimate.' Cammy looked somewhat perplexed by this reply. Before leaving the café, Adam spied a video camera sitting unattended on a bench beside the balustrade. He made a hasty procurement and in a moment of plundering madness took up filmmaking.

Back in the Greco-Roman Theatre, Andrew was fashioning notes in regard to a forthcoming funeral, the service of a young teenage boy who died in a car crash. Although on holiday, he didn't mind sorting out some of his business matters. The four-teen-year-old was a keen movie watcher who received a compact video camera for Christmas. He jokingly made a short film about his loves and hates in life, giving detailed funeral arrangements in the unlikely event of his premature death. Never tempt fate, thought Andrew. The film was to be shown to the congregation during the church service prior to the burial. Andrew would have to arrange for a large screen and video recorder to be set up in the kirk. The youngster also wished to be buried with a Christmas stocking full of oranges, apples and five pence coins. The young boy's mother, who survived the car crash, always bought her Christmas presents for the following year in the January sales. By relaying instructions back to Edinburgh, Andrew could make sure all the mother's gifts were placed in the coffin. Fitzpatrick and Sons would surely oblige.

A shrill blast from a whistle echoed around the theatre complex. A security guard removed several children who were climbing over the ancient columns.

'Matty?'

'Yes?'

'You are now permitted to mention Cameron's name.'

'Why the change?'

'Because he's standing behind you.'

'Aye, right. That's not funny.'

'Reasonably funny,' quipped Cammy leaning over her shoulder. Matty, in total shock and bewilderment, turned, threw her arms around Cammy's neck and gave him the biggest kiss she'd ever given anyone in her whole life. They were swapping saliva in the first set of tonsil tennis. Adam and Andrew reluctantly stood side-by-side observing the romantic twosome slobbering all over each other.

'Remind you of anything?' whispered Andrew into Adam's ear.

'Fuck you!' hissed Adam.

'You certainly did,' whispered Andrew. 'And boy didn't you enjoy the night.'

'Fuck right off.' Adam's eyes returned a volley of hate.

'I don't believe this,' screamed Matty. ' I do not believe this! I cannot believe you're here.' She was genuinely experiencing severe shock. 'Why are you here? What are you doing here? It is so good to see you!' Cammy smiled and cheerfully passed on the credit. 'This was Adam's idea. He wanted to surprise you. We're only here for the weekend. I hope you're pleased to see us? Your brother shows a caring side at times. A caring sharing side.'

'I'm ecstatic. Over the moon!'

Adam gave his sister a hug and nodded his head in Andrew's general direction. This was as far as their communication would go. Matty would normally accuse Adam of being up to no good. Today she was too agog to throw incriminations into her brother's path.

'We saw Graham at the hotel and he sent us up here,' said Cammy. 'It is so good to see you. I've missed you so much.' They started to kiss once more. Adam stuffed two fingers down his throat. 'I think I'll need a giant-sized bucket.' Andrew ignored his comment.

The long day merged into evening and the evening merged into night. Graham was on a day off, so he joined Andrew for dinner at the finest restaurant in town. Matty and Cammy, locked hand in hand, enjoyed a lengthy walk around Taormina, stopping briefly for pasta and a glass of cider. Adam, not wishing to play a Sicilian gooseberry, retired to the local pub, ordered vast quantities of alcohol and amid the frivolity regaled the locals with descriptive passages from *The Great Escape*.

Chapter Nineteen

BREAKFAST AT THE HOTEL CATRINA consisted of a spoilt for choice
self-service buffet, full of crisp baguettes, cheese, thinly sliced ham,
fresh melon, cereals, fruit-juice and locally produced yoghurt. The
package deal allowed the hotel residents to eat as much food as
they wanted and Adam followed this ruling to the letter, asking on
four occasions for additional slices of Parma ham. In fact, this was
the only reason Adam agreed to get out of his bed. He was making up for the previous day's extravagant café excursion.

The top floor dining room, filled full of noisy German tourists,
looked out over the sun-drenched bay. Adam, resplendent in his
new extra large kilt, and Cammy, not so resplendent in his pale
green cycling shorts, were the only British let alone Scottish people
to be found in this below average three-star hotel. Cammy hoped
Adam wouldn't break wind in the dining room as his back-end
odours could seriously damage everyone's health.

'Sunday,' announced Cammy, anticipating the days ahead.
'Start of another week.'

'No, the week doesn't start till Monday,' retorted Adam, cor-
recting his holiday companion.

'No, you're wrong, Sunday is officially the start of the new
week, not Monday.'

'Monday, officially, is the start of *my* week and that's all that
matters.'

'You're wrong.'

'No, you're bloody wrong.' Adam was laying down the law.
'I'm right.' They continued their short aggressive argument, agreeing
to disagree and disagreeing to agree. Their relationship bordered
on the absurd.

'Did you see the brochure in the rooms?' inquired Adam.

'What brochure?'

'The Italian Tourist Board brochure. Brilliant! They're advertising Italy as The Great Escape.'

'That's fascinating.'

'It most certainly is.'

Cammy stared ruefully at his teaspoon hoping Adam would be quiet long enough for him to enjoy his breakfast. Realistically this was a futile long shot, especially as Adam's idle banter remained top of the menu.

'Here Cammy. Have you ever seen *The Great Escape 2 – the Untold Story?*'

'No.'

'That's good, 'cause it's a pile of fictional shite.'

'Oh, right.' Cammy scratched his head. Adam's comment was far from noteworthy.

'Yeah, shite! How dare Hollywood tarnish the memory of those brave men who laid down their lives for Great Britain by making a shite sequel. I mean, the acting was more wooden than Long John Silver's leg.' He then proceeded to mutter aggressively under his breath for a few more minutes. Cammy couldn't make head nor tail of Adam's moaning so took this opportunity to finish his breakfast in double quick time. He was glad to finally talk with his mouth free of food. 'What time did you get back last night?'

'I can't really remember, I was rat-arsed, out my friggin' head. Probably about five or so. What about you, I thought you were going to stay the night with Matty?'

'Not at all. She's sharing with Andrew.'

'Right enough, two's company, three's a group.' Cammy overlooked this observation, too bleary-eyed to remedy any sort of inadequate proverb.

'Plus,' added Adam, 'you wouldn't want to be around if big sausage jockey Andy was in the same room. You'd have to lock yourself in the toilet with a cork, in case he jumped you.'

'I hardly think he is going to jump me,' remarked Cammy in disbelief. He'd shaken his head so often at Adam's derisory opinions it was amazing his neck hadn't unravelled.

Matty asked Cammy to stay over at her hotel when Andrew disappeared to Graham's apartment. He gallantly declined the offer and returned to spend the night opposite a snoring, farting, grunting, gurgling Adam. He was sticking to his guns, only wanting to sleep with the woman he married. His dilemma was clear. If he believed wedding bells were on the cards, would he sleep with Matty out of wedlock or would he wait until they were married? Watching Adam's gaping mouth dribbling saliva onto the pillow in the early hours of the morning could well influence his sleeping arrangements for Sunday night. 'Did you notice the film of dust on everything yesterday?' stated Cammy. 'That's Mount Etna leaving grime everywhere.'

'Yeah, I also noticed there wasn't a shower curtain around the bath. Why is that?'

'I don't know. I'm not a fuckin' chambermaid. Ask the waiter.' Cammy was glancing at his new Italian phrase book and dictionary.

'What's that?' asked Adam.

'A phrase book. I'm trying to learn a few words of Italian.'

'Why do you want to do that? They all speak English.'

'That's a bit narrow-minded, isn't it?' whispered Cammy.

'Not at all. Why learn a phrase in Italian if you're not going to understand the answer?' Cammy hated to admit it Adam had a point.

'Cammy.'

'What?'

'Why are you whispering?'

'I always tend to speak quietly in restaurants. I don't want anyone listening in to my conversation.'

'What does it matter here. The room's full of Germans.' Adam loudly hammered home his point.

'Yes and most of them can speak English.'

'So what. See if I care. Don't get me wrong, I've nothing against the fat Nazi bastards.'

Some of the tourists in the dining room gazed towards Adam. To avoid multiple contact, Cammy fleetingly looked away and focused on the swimming pool below. His initial aversion to joining in such a discussion was abruptly altered by the sight of towels covering all the chairs beside the swimming pool. This fuelled his antagonism towards the Germans. 'Look at that, Adam.'

'What?'

'The superior residents of this hotel have claimed all the seats and sun loungers beside the pool. Now that's worse than invading France.' Cammy, unduly irritated by this selfish action, was now ready to join the 'Jerry bashing'. 'My grandad tells me the Lancaster bombers were far superior to the German planes. Old pops said he couldn't get enough of bombing the Hun.'

'Remind me again,' asked Adam. 'Who won the war?'

'We did.'

'Who are we?'

'Britain.'

'I'm sorry, I'm going a wee bit deaf. Could you repeat who won the last war?'

'*Britain*,' thundered Cammy, standing up thumping his fist on the table. The boys fleetingly returned to being British. Staring at the couple opposite, Adam quoted Steve McQueen. 'Are all American officers so ill-mannered? Yeah about ninety-nine percent.'

Who lost the war?' Cammy picked up a fork and thrust it forward like a microphone under Adam's chin.

'Did you say who *lost* the war?'

'Yeah, my question was, who *lost* the war?'

'Oh that's easy,' pronounced Cammy. 'The Germans lost the war.'

'Who?'

'*Germany* lost the war. We whipped their arses.'

'Who whipped whose arses?'

'Britain, Great Britain. The Hun were humped.'

Adam and Cammy were having a whale of a time, loving every minute of their anti-German rhetoric. Some of the residents left the dining room, others ignored them and the few who didn't speak English were none the wiser. 'My grandad,' continued Cammy, 'also bombed Germany in a Wellington bomber.'

'Did you say Wellington?'

'Yes, Wellington, as in the Duke of Wellington. No relation as far as I know.'

'Do you realise twenty-seven million people died during the Second World War and that was Hitler's fault.' History and mathematics had been Adam's poorer subjects at school.

'Twenty-seven million souls. That is unbelievable. Wait a minute, wasn't it fifty million souls?'

'Twenty-seven million, fifty million, one hundred and fifty million. Whatever the figure, it's too many. There is only one good German.'

'Who's that?'

'Beethoven'.

'Why Beethoven?'

'Because he's dead.' They both laughed.

'Quite funny for you, Adam,' remarked Cammy. 'Is that line from *The Great Escape*?'

'No, another war film. Can't remember the title but we won the war in that movie too. We seem to win the war in most Second World War movies.'

'Really, we beat the Germans in every film?'

'Every Second World War film.'

'Or First World War film.'

'Clobbered them in the First World War as well!'

The waiter, who spoke numerous languages including English, understood every word of the boys' conversation and approached their table in a vain attempt to ask them to be quieter. Before the waiter had a chance to open his Mediterranean mouth, Adam pointed to his empty cup of coffee. 'In the three years, seven months and approximately two weeks I've been in the bag, that's the most extraordinary stuff I've ever tasted. It's shattering.' Even Cammy recognised this line from *The Great Escape* and for once in his life, didn't mind Adam rattling on. 'Pass down thirty feet of rope. How many are you taking out? Two hundred and fifty. You're crazy, you ought to be locked up. Two hundred and fifty guys just walking down the road just like that. Why, they're going to swoop down and scoop you up so fast it would make your head swim.' The waiter fathomed he was no match for Adam's wartime patter. He was in danger of making matters worse, so withdrew to the sanctuary of the kitchen.

'That's right, you run backwards like the Italians during the war,' shouted Adam at the waiter. 'I suppose you keep changing hotels. Crazy mixed up kid that Vernor, but I like him.'

'Adam?'

'Cammy.'

'Want to see something drastically funny?'

'Drastically?'

'Yes, drastically.'

'Go on.'

'Go back to your room and watch from the balcony.'

'Cool bananas.' Adam stood up, saluted the catering staff and with outstretched arms ran through the dining room humming the tune to *The Dambusters*. He swooped down with a lunchtime mission in mind, raided ample rations from the buffet table and returned to his bedroom barracks. Cammy took the lift down to the poolside, gathered all the tourist's towels and threw them with boyish delight into the deep end of the swimming pool. Looking up to Adam's balcony, he yelled at the top of his voice, 'Now *that's* funny. I've fucked their towels in the water!'

'Yah beauty!' howled Adam laughing. He clenched his fists and ran around the room as if he'd scored the winning goal during a European Football final. Cammy briskly departed the hotel via the back garden wall, while Adam locked his bedroom door in case the hotel manager wanted to shout stern words in his ear.

Knowing the German tourists from the adjoining room were still at breakfast, Adam jumped over the side of the exterior balcony and entered their apartment through the double doors. They were wide open to the fine weather. This was simple to do, as the rooms were close together, the outside balconies practically touching each other. When inside the suite he stole a watch and some loose change, stuffing the coins into his sporran. He then used the telephone to call Mrs Waddel in Edinburgh to check if Roger and the cats were all right. His pets were indeed relishing the large helpings of food dished out by his neighbour and Adam himself was pleased that his telephone call would be paid for by a couple of German tourists. Feeling like a dusty devil on speed, he plundered the room's mini-bar, consumed three miniature bottles of whisky and replenished the empties with cold tea. From inside the adjacent suite he could hear a knocking at his own apartment door and a key slowly turning in the lock. He thought this might be the seething manager on the warpath. Deciding not to take any chances, he quickly left his neighbours' room and made a hasty exit down the service elevator.

At the less than salubrious tradesman's entrance to the hotel, a green lizard scurried passed Adam's feet. You'd swear the reptile briefly paused to look up his kilt. Adam also noticed two scrawny black and white cats eating from a bowl of pasta kindly left out for them by one of the kitchen staff.

Vespas were whizzing around the scenic Sicilian town, oblivious to the visitors walking on the narrow roads. The smart young Italians seemingly enjoyed playing 'scatter the tourist'. Adam was once again isolated in a strange town. He was wearing, much to the amusement of the locals, an oversized kilt and was fearful of returning to the hotel.

Cammy was with Matty. Andrew was with Graham. Adam was all alone.

Monday morning heralded the onset of Adam's week. His customary hangover welcomed his head into a brand new day with a tapping sound similar to a Morse code convention. His Sunday turned out agreeable, considering the ominous start to the day. The afternoon and most of the night was spent in his new adopted bar where drinks freely flowed as if they were going out of fashion.

Thanks to the novelty of the kilt, others paid for many of the refreshments. This was just as well, as the only cash Adam had in his sporran were a few coins stolen out of the Germans' hotel room. The locals and other visitors were fascinated by the 'tartan skirt', many taking photographs before buying him a couple of double brandies, and Adam for one evening, became the 'toast of Taormina'. His Sean Connery impressions were universally accepted as complete and utter rubbish, although the sentence, 'I was born in the shitty of Edinburgh' raised a couple of wry smiles. He befriended two German girls, having sex with one of them in the ladies' toilet. Leaving the pub last, he staggered back to the hotel at six in the morning, entered by the back stairs to avoid the night porter and crashed out cold, fatigued and intoxicated. A mid-morning telephone call awakened Adam from his alcoholic slumber.

'Hello.'

'Hello.'

'It's you Cammy?'

'Well it's not Rudolph Hess, is it?'

'Honestly, it could be anyone on the phone. You wouldn't believe the noise clattering through my head this morning.'

'Let me have a wild guess, you have a hangover?'

'Just a big, huge, massive one. Hold on, Cammy.' Adam picked up his silver flask and poured a nip of whisky into a tumbler lying on his bedside table. This was a daily ritual passed down from father to son. 'I'm back.'

'I'll take it you were out last night?' queried Cammy.

'Another good guess. I was in at the death. I must have smoked sixty fags.'

'Was it a good night?'

'Brilliant crack. I won the 'dropping your sunglasses from the top of your head on to the end of your nose competition' and at the end of the night I remember banging a German bird.'

'How romantic. What was your chat up line?'

'I think I said, 'Nice ass can I use it as a hat?' Remember, if you don't shag a bird on the first date you're gay.'

'You passionate fiend,' replied Cammy sarcastically.

'What a great ride,' urged Adam. 'She was a pretty young thing with big teeth, although that doesn't normally bother me. Let's face it, you don't look at the mantelpiece when you're poking the fire.'

'Okay, Adam, spare me the details. Do you always have to think with your cock?'

'I haven't got a cock. I've two cats.'

'You know what I mean.'

'Well, it's good to know that both me and my grandad have now officially fucked Germans.'

'*Charming*, Adam, just *charming*.'

'Cammy, what happened to you? Wah hey hey, did you give Matty one?'

'Adam, *please*. I stayed with her and nothing happened.'

'Why was that?' Adam found it hard to believe that couples didn't have sex every night of the week. 'Are you a willie woofer or is it her bad week?' Another subtle question from Mr Adam Smith.

'Neither of them. She wasn't very well. We had a plate of pasta in a restaurant last night and no one told us the dish contained white wine. You know what happens to Matty when she has wine?'

'Throwing up, was she?'

'Like there was no tomorrow. She was green around the gills.'

'Right enough, Cammy, nothing worse than snogging someone who has just puked. I was kissing a girl once, completely plastered and was half-sick in her mouth.'

'That's disgusting! Andrew's right, you are without doubt the most repellent person we know.'

'She wouldn't sleep with me after that. What a prude.'

'I'm not surprised, who in their right mind would?'

'Was Andrew there last night?' questioned Adam.

'No, he's staying at Graham's apartment.'

'Is Graham one of them too?'

'One of what?' asked Cammy.

'You know, a chutney warrior.'

'A *what*?'

'You know,' stated Adam. 'A light-on-his-loafers backend warmer, a bottom basher, a bum chum, a chocolate box poker.'

'You're bloody unreal! What a *sick* mind you have. I thought you knew Graham fancied Andrew at college. He always thought that Andrew and I were an item as we were together most of the time, so he never made a move.'

'You never went fudge packing with Andy at college, did you?'

'No way. I'm not gay. We were just good friends.'

'Just as well or I'd throw you out the flat. In fact if I was about to become a dad and I knew the baby was going to be a dome rider, I'd have it terminated.'

Cammy, dismayed by Adam's never-ending anti-gay stance didn't even attempt to tell him the absurd nature of his comments. If brains were taxed, he'd receive a full rebate. It was hard to believe he'd been faster than a million other sperm, winning the fertilised eggcup in a foetal front crawl.

'Did you phone me through the reception desk?' asked Adam.

'Yeah, why?'

'I think the manager might be after us and they'll know I'm in the room now.'

'Tell them to piss off,' advised Cammy cheekily.

'That's easy for you to say from a hotel on the other side of town!'

'Tell them it was all my fault and you don't know where I've gone.'

'I might do that.' Adam was unaware that the manager wasn't pursuing either of them. Surprisingly, no one had reported the 'towel throwing incident' at the swimming pool and the breakfast waiter was now on his two days off. The person knocking on the apartment door on Sunday was the chambermaid looking for access to clean the room.

'Adam, what time is our flight today?'

'Well.... em . . .flight time.....' This was not a moment Adam had been looking forward to. He knew Cammy was expecting to go home today, not Tuesday. What could he say?

'It's just,' added Cammy. 'I wish I could stay a little longer. Another day would do, until Matty's feeling better.'

'Another day did you say, Cammy?'

"I know that's probably out of the question. However can you speak to the airline and see if this is possible?' Adam couldn't believe his luck and was determined to take advantage of this fortuitous situation.

'Cammy, there's not much hope of changing scheduled flights. I'll see what I can do. In fact, I'll go one better and *guarantee* to organise this especially for you.'

'You would do this for me?'

'With my scamming skills, consider it done. I'll arrange for us to go home on Tuesday.'

'What if this isn't possible? What time are we due away today?'

'Calm down, I'll sort it out. No problems.'

'Are you sure about this, Adam. I'll understand if we have to go home today.'

'Cammy, If you don't shut your face, we will go home today.'

'So you're pretty sure? I'll check with the hotel at lunch time if you want?'

'No, don't do that. Everything will be arranged for Tuesday.

Spend the time with Matty. Can I see you later?'

'Yeah, maybe meet up for dinner?'

'Sounds fine. Speak to you later.'

Adam placed the phone down, flopped onto the bed and dropped off to sleep. Within minutes, there was a tapping on his bedroom door. He jumped up and without thinking locked himself in the bathroom, pushing his ear hard against the hollow wall. The chambermaid unlocked the apartment door and stepped into the stale-smelling room, announcing herself in pidgin English, 'Me here to clean room.' Adam opened the bathroom door. 'Can you come back later? In fact, why don't you leave the room today? I don't mind. You can clean it tomorrow, when I'm gone.'

'Non capisco.'

'Oh shit, you don't speak English.'

'I speak a little.'

Adam held up the five fingers on his right hand. 'Can you give me five minutes?' The chambermaid nodded her head and held up her right hand. 'Cinque.'

'Yeah, whatever.' He ushered the maid out of the room. Adam was about to spend another day on his own relaxing in the hazy sunshine. He picked up a pen and paper from his bedside table and sat outside on the hotel's main balcony. He'd decided not to travel into the town centre as the excesses of the previous night's debauched drunken soiree were beginning to catch up. It would be a day contriving new schemes. 'What if the bedrooms where people had sex were linked up to the national grid,' thought Adam. 'The world could create an amazing amount of electricity. Good idea, but not beneficial to me.'

Adam had a pathological need to deceive himself in order to achieve a desired result.

The ideas continued to flow. 'I place a bet on a golfer bagging a hole-in-one at the Open Championship. I go to the tournament and when the player hits his first shot at a par three I'll run on the green, pick up the ball and place it in the hole.' I wonder if there are any rules forbidding a member of the public doing this.' Adam liked this simple sporting scam. I'll find out which bookmakers take bets on a hole-in-one and try to discover if there are any laws prohibiting spectators touching golf balls during play. This idea truly whetted his appetite and figures were scribbled down on the pad of paper as he worked out potential winnings from a fifty-to-one bet.

The concepts became less plausible as the day advanced. I think I'll produce and market bloodstained hankies and call my new product, 'the get out of awkward situations snot rag'. If you ever happen to be bored in someone's company, take the blood stained hanky out of your pocket and leave the tedious scene under the illusion of a bleeding nose. That's brilliant! By mid-afternoon he was deliberating on the possibility of producing post-cards from dreadful photographs with the front picture complete-ly out of focus. Then as his derangement reached an all time high, the pondering transferred to devising an intricate scheme to steal the Scottish Crown Jewels from Edinburgh Castle. For a man liv-ing for the day, he was always planning ahead. The graverobbing business had great potential and Adam was of the opinion the boys could get straight back to work when they returned home from Sicily. He was unaware the gravedigging episode had a deeper meaning. The whole psychology of digging in a cemetery and his obsession with the tunnelling was a metaphor for trying to resurrect his mother and father. He was trying to break free from the per-sonal distress of their deaths. The actuality was all a rotten night-mare; the more he would delve the further there was to go. The feeling was comparable to attempting a fast run in a dream yet managing only to move a few yards. Living the life Adam did was a buffer from his own reality. Then again, perhaps his reality needed a veil.

Adam's life was complicated enough. A gypsy fortune teller did not aid his existence. Feeling low after his mother's death, he had attended a country fair and invested the grand sum of fifty pence to have his palm read by Madame Izzy. He was only eleven at the time, a vulnerable young boy in a world already turned upside down by the loss of his mum. Adam was at an age and in the appropriate state of mind to grasp hold of every word uttered by the gypsy. Most of the other kids were going to see the eccentric Bohemian for a laugh after capering on the dodgems – not young Adam Smith.

Startling revelations touched his visit. Whether the crystal ball gazer was authentic or not, she certainly was disturbed by Adam's palm. The cranky clairvoyant asked if someone had recently died and predicted another death in the family within a decade. Looking as if she was about to lose her soul to a demon, the travelling seer refused to say any more, knowing she'd already overstepped the mark. Adam was refunded his fifty pence and asked to run along. The New Age mystic boarded up her Romany caravan for a week, claiming to be emotionally drained. Never mind mad Madame Izzy, just imagine how an encounter like this affected a sensitive boy of eleven.

Dinner was taken at Matty's hotel. Andrew was nowhere to be seen. It looked like Graham had swept him off his feet and there was talk of Andrew staying in Taormina for an extra week. Cammy was enjoying the holiday, the ketchup top staying safely locked away in his suitcase. Matty, recuperating after her bout of sickness, was happily tucking into a large plate of spaghetti. 'Are you feeling better?' inquired Adam.

'Much better,' mumbled Matty through a mouth of bolognaise sauce.

'What time's our flight tomorrow?' asked Cammy.

'Four o'clock,' assured Adam.

'It was good of you to change the flight time.'

'Fantastic.' Matty kissed her brother on the cheek. 'You've really come up trumps and it's good to hear from Cammy that you've been undertaking voluntary work in the city cemeteries. By the way, thanks for doing my lottery.' Adam almost choked on his steak and chips. He put his fork and knife down on the plate, looked up at Cammy and grinned like a man possessed by humour. 'Yes, I'm a reformed man. I knew it was the last chance saloon for me. If I didn't change my ways, I'd end up in hot water. Cammy has been an immense help in my rehabilitation.' Adam loved telling lots of lies. What a joy making your life story up as you went along.

Eagle eyed Matty spotted Adam's video camera. 'That's nice, where did you get that?'

'I thought Cammy would have told you. Em . . . this was a gift for my birthday from Aidan. Brilliant present, eh?'

'Without a doubt, brother.'

Adam switched on his new filmmaking toy. 'Here Matty, I'll shoot you and Cammy on video. Pretend you're enjoying yourself. Say 'Scottish cheddar' or 'cool bananas.'

'We *are* enjoying ourselves.' The devoted duo looked like the Catherine and Heathcliffe of East Edinburgh.

The evening passed off without any arguments. Surely Matty would find out about the boys' graveyard venture sooner rather than later? Was it wise of Cammy to avoid telling Matty the truth? Everything seemed perfect for now and no one wanted to alter that. Adam's last significant holiday act was to leave his dirty trademark in the swimming pool, a messy calling card for the beloved nation of Germany. I wonder who'll jump in the pool first tomorrow?

The hotel guests would wake up to a brown swimming pool. The chambermaid would later discover gifts left for her in Adam's room, half a bottle of Martini and two suitcases full of clothes.

Boarding the plane and waving goodbye to Matty was heart-breaking for Cammy. 'She'll be home soon,' reflected Adam, sitting down.

'Hey, *I've* got the window seat ticket,' protested Cammy.

'Doesn't matter.' Adam shrugged his shoulders and looked in the opposite direction.

'Oh, yes it does.'

'No it doesn't. I'm sitting here, okay.'

'No, *not* okay, I want to wave to Matty from the window seat.'

'You can't because I'm sitting here, so piss off.'

'Move, bog face.'

'You can say whatever you want. I'm not moving. Remember you would have gone home yesterday if it hadn't been for me.'

'So what? I need to wave to Matty.' Cammy grabbed hold of Adam's arm and pulled him out of the seat. A few fellow passengers watched on with interest. Adam slapped Cammy on the face and pushed him back into the aisle seat. Adam returned to the window seat and watched sunny Catania fade into the hazy distance. After all this fuss, Matty couldn't see anyone in the plane from her distant position on the airport viewing balcony. Nothing was ever simple.

'What a grand view of Sicily from the air,' gloated Adam.

'I wouldn't know,' replied Cammy. 'That hurt, you know.'

'What did?'

'The slap on the face.'

'I just stroked you, yah big nancy boy.'

'More like a punch than a stroke.'

'Bollocks!'

'It was more like a punch,' scowled Cammy, rubbing the side of his face. 'Definitely more like a punch.'

'Bollocks. I'll show you what a punch is like.' Adam lifted his right clenched fist and aimed a punch in the direction of Cammy's face, missing his forehead by inches. 'Now, if that hit your face, that would be a punch. This is a stroke.' Adam once again slapped Cammy.

'I'll fuckin' have you,' shouted Cammy. His frowning face turned a harrowing shade of purple.

'Yeah right. You and whose battalion?'

'Army. It should be you and whose army.' What a time for Cammy to correct one of Adam's erroneous proverbs – in the middle of an argument! Adam smiled. He knew fine well that this adage was off target. He fired this faulty saying into the combat zone just to provoke a reaction. 'Relax, don't get your Y-fronts in a twist.'

'You're the one throwing punches.'

'Strokes, not punches.'

'*You* started it.'

'I didn't.'

'You did, by stealing my seat.'

'It's my seat. No, it's the airline's seat.' The boys sat in stubborn silence for the best part of an hour. Food and drinks came and went without any words being uttered. Of course time is a great healer. Both of them seemed to mellow at the same moment and a new conversation was soon under way. Cammy was first to break the ice by attempting idle banter. 'Did you notice at the airport when the flight was called everyone rushed forward to the desk and we waited ten minutes before the door opened? I bet there's an air attendant up in the tower watching on closed circuit television who announces the flight ahead of schedule. He probably has a good laugh at the tourists standing by the gate.'

'Could well be.' Adam's bad mood hadn't fully defrosted.

Cammy picked up the in-flight magazine and turned to the back page. 'Do you want to know your horoscope?'

'If you must,' sighed Adam slowly mellowing.

'Adam, what sign are you? No wait, let me guess, em...Virgo.'

'How did you know that?'

'I know your birthday, thicko. Remember my dinner with Matty? It was on your birthday.'

'Oh yeah, so it was.'

'It says here,' read Cammy. 'You're ruled by the planet Mercury, reflecting the qualities of a virgin, shy, nervous, neat, well organised and good in business.' Adam nodded his head in agreement. 'You're modest,' continued Cammy, 'industrious, logical and skilled at seeing all sides of a situation. In love relationships you're devoted and rarely flirtatious.'

'Sounds like me.' Adam rubbed his crotch. 'I'm as pure as the driven snow.'

'Oh and look at this,' remarked Cammy excitedly. 'It says that Virgos are prone to problems with their bowels.'

'No, it doesn't.' Adam grabbed hold of the magazine, ripping the page in the process.

'It does,' assured Cammy pointing at the page.

'Bloody hell, so it does.' Adam let off a fart in agreement. 'Have that one on me, duchess.'

One of the cabin crew was walking briskly up the aisle. 'Is there an Adam Smith here?'

'Yes, I'm Adam Smith.'

'Is that the same as the economist Adam Smith?' commented one of the other passengers sitting nearby.

'Never heard that one before,' stated Adam. 'That's extremely funny. I'll add that to my joke book when I get home. I'm sure you'll receive royalties for an amazingly witty remark like that. Do you by any chance write for children's television?' The young passenger looked away.

The airhostess handed Adam a small white envelope. 'There's a message for you.'

'I wonder what this is?' Adam ripped open the envelope and read the short note. 'It's from Mrs Waddel. It says to give her a call. Oh shit, I hope there isn't anything wrong with Roger and the cats.' Adam was extremely worried. Last night he'd been feeling content with the world. In his book this was always an ominous sign. 'I'll phone when we land in London.'

'Why don't you phone now?'

'I haven't got a mobile.'

Cammy looked slightly exasperated. 'I realise you don't have a mobile. You're not allowed to use a mobile on the plane in case your conversation gets mixed up with the airline's communication system.'

'So why suggest I phone her from here?'

'Because there is a main phone at the front of the cabin.'

'Oh, I didn't realise that. Okay, have you got twenty pence?'

'No, I think you need to use your credit card.'

'You know as well as I do, I don't use credit cards.'

'You can borrow mine.' Cammy handed over his Visa card.

'Oh, I see. I tell you what, I'll go and use the phone once the queue for the toilet has died down.'

'Fair enough.'

Cammy was reading a magazine article entitled 'Forecourt Fear'. 'Do you know you're not allowed to use mobile phones at petrol stations because there is a minuscule chance of blowing the whole place up.'

'I can't believe that. They probably don't want people clogging up the forecourt with mobile phone conversations. This delays potential sales. In all likelihood they want customers to use their payphone?'

'You might have a point there.' Cammy was reluctant to agree. Adam walked slowly down the centre of the aisle to the front of the cabin. He was unsure why Mrs Waddel would want to talk to him. He picked up the receiver and dialled his neighbour's number.

'Hello.'

'Hello, Mrs Waddel?'

'Yes, who's that?'

'It's Adam.'

'Adam who?'

'Adam Smith, your neighbour.'

'Oh hello Adam. I thought you would be flying home today.'

'I am.'

'What time's your flight?'

'I'm on the flight.'

'You're phoning from a plane?'

'Yes.'

'My goodness, whatever will they think of next? I've heard of telephones at airports but never on planes.'

'Why did you phone me, Mrs Waddel?'

'You phoned me.'

'No, you left me a message at the airport. I'm returning your call. Is there anything wrong? Are Roger and the cats okay?'

'Yes they're fine. Ives prefers the chicken in gravy cat food. Cavendish turned his nose up at the tinned stuff so I opened a can of tuna chunks. Roger is fighting fit too.'

'So why were you phoning me?'

'You've had a break-in.'

'*What!*'

'Your flat has been broken into. Don't worry, there's not a lot of damage. The police don't think much has been stolen.'

'*The police!*'

'Yes, I called the police in. I thought you'd be pleased with me calling the police. They've been in the flat, had a good look round and seem very keen to speak to you.' Adam was shocked into silence. His jaw dropped to the floor. The calm was deafening.

'What was that, Adam?'

'Em, nothing. I didn't say anything . . .What else did the police say?'

'Can you speak up, it's a bad line?'

'What else did the police say?' shouted Adam. The first four rows of the plane turned to listen.

'They took a lot of files out the house for some reason. Maybe the robbers left their fingerprints on them. I informed the police when you'd be back.'

'*What*!' This was a bolt from the blue.

'Remember, you gave me all the flight details, so I gave them to a helpful young detective. It's good to see the boys in blue taking so much time over a robbery. A joiner was in to fix your front door. Don't worry, I'll keep an eye on the goldfish and the cats. Sorry about the break-in. That's modern-day society for you. I blame the government. Did you have a nice holiday?'

He ignored Mrs Waddel's question. His hands were shaking. He replaced the receiver without saying goodbye. Adam – weak at the knees – couldn't feel his feet. He staggered into the toilet, sat down and stared at his reflection in the mirror. 'Oh shit, shit, shit, shit, shit. This is a fuckin' disaster! What the hell am I going to do? Think, think, think, think, come on think.' Adam couldn't possibly tell Cammy this news, or could he? If the police had been anywhere near his files, then he was surely in for the chop. Adam's flat was full of evidence relating to the graveyard escapades and what would the authorities make of Virgil? This was an almighty cock-up. All of Adam's thieving life was about to be wiped out by the actions of another thieving bastard. Then again, perhaps he could abscond to London? Adam returned to his seat, his face pale as a sheet.

Cammy smirked. 'You look like you've seen a ghost. Has something happened?'

'Now, if I tell you what Mrs Waddel said, will you promise not to panic?'

Cammy began to fidget, his left eye twitched. 'What's happened?' The smile disappeared from his face.

'The flat has been broken into and it looks like the police have found my files. Now *listen*, if the police arrive at the airport, you have nothing to do with anything. There is zilch in the flat to incriminate you. So, say nought. Keep your lips sealed, I'll sort everything out.' Cammy couldn't believe what he was hearing and started to wriggle uncomfortably in his seat. 'Remember, leave the talking to me.'

'Oh shit,' spluttered Cammy. 'We'll get the jail. I'll be locked up for life and will never see Matty ever again. This is a major nightmare. This is the final nail in my coffin.' A personal explosion was imminent. Adam leant over, clenched his fist and whacked Cammy on the side of the chin. Luckily no one saw him doing this. 'Now, *that's* a punch.'

Cammy was out cold. He slept all the way to Heathrow airport. The Edinburgh constabulary, desperate to solve a catalogue of crimes, travelled from Edinburgh to London. The Scottish detectives were waiting in Terminal One to arrest Adam as soon as he left the plane. Cammy continued on to Edinburgh with a sore jaw. The police weren't interested in him.

Chapter Twenty

CAMMY ENTERED A GIANT whitewashed cavern full of the nosiest and worst behaved children in the world. This was no innocent nursery school, this was Her Majesty's prison, Edinburgh, in the arms of a typical boisterous visiting session. The vast rectangular room seemed to go on forever. As all the prisoners were men, the majority of family callers were women, apart from Cammy. A designated playing area full of building bricks, toys, books and crayons was set aside at the back of the hall for the numerous excitable children who thoroughly enjoyed bouncing on the mini-trampolines oblivious to their parents' plight.

As a fresh inmate, Adam was slowly learning the rules of the house, aware of being a little chip within the global fat fryer. He was making a firm mental note of his table position within the hall, wishing to avoid the possibility of rubbing someone up the wrong way. Each prisoner had his own seat during public visits. Woe betide anyone who sat in the wrong place. While awaiting his court case, Adam was keeping his head firmly down and out of trouble. Avoiding disorder didn't mean abandoning his half-baked ideas to escape. Daily scheming sustained his sanity. He made copious notes on the movements of prisoners and prison guards, timing meals and public visits. Detailed plans were sketched of the kitchen, the prison block and exercise yard. He even managed to calculate the exact distance from the main building to the wire fence. His thoughts on tunnelling were ruined by the position of his cell – unsuitably located on the third floor.

Captured at Heathrow airport, Adam was charged and then questioned in Edinburgh for the best part of seven days. The evidence against him was clear and concise, thanks to the detailed notes found in his bedroom. The police asked several times about Cammy's possible involvement in the grave-digging scam. Adam protected his partner and carried the criminal can. This was his selective amnesia working to its full potential. Adam's collection of punk records was confiscated from his flat. No Sham 69, the Sex Pistols or the Buzzcocks for the time being.

The detectives didn't bother inviting Cammy in for questioning, happy enough with their prize trophy. In the eyes of the law they'd caught a big fish in a sizeable city pond. Their arms at full length wouldn't exaggerate the size of the catch in terms of crimes solved. The long arm of the law after one arrest managed to knock off, for want of a better expression, one hundred and seventeen unsolved crimes. Someone was due for a promotion.

'Hello.' Cammy was clutching a bottle of Irn Bru full of cider. 'This is from Matty, she sends her love.' He sat down opposite Adam. The room was crammed full to the brim.

'I don't think we're allowed booze in here. I'm surprised they didn't confiscate that on the way in. You're allowed as many drugs as you want but no booze.' Adam wasn't wide of the mark. During visiting sessions, in an assortment of ingenious ways, drugs were passed from visitor to prisoner with relative ease. Cammy shoved the bottle of cider back into his plastic bag. 'Here's some cigarettes, Adam.'

'Thanks mate, they're like gold in here.'

Cammy handed over three packs of Benson and Hedges king size cigarettes. Adam nodded his head in appreciation. 'How's your jaw?'

'Oh, fine. The bruise has almost gone. At least I know what your punch is like now.'

'Yeah, sorry about that. It was for your own good.'

'My jaw was pretty sore for a couple of days. I understand why you hit me.'

'I didn't enjoy hitting you. Then again I didn't mind... no only joking. Have the coppers been in touch?'

'No.'

'Good.' Adam was happy to play the villainous martyr to gain more recognition. Cammy noticed Adam fidgeting with his hands. 'What's that?'

'You won't believe this. It's a plastic salad cream top, which I borrowed from the prison kitchens. Not exactly a ketchup top. Seems to do the business. It's extremely therapeutic. Thanks for the idea. We should market this as an aid to stress. How are Roger and the cats?'

'Roger and the cats are fine. Mrs Waddel was telling me a horror story, though.'

'What's wrong? What's happened now?' Adam looked as pale as prison porridge. He tossed the salad cream lid in the air and caught it in his other hand.

'Calm down, Adam, there's nothing wrong. Have a fiddle with your bottle top. What I was trying to tell you was this. Mrs Waddel's friend's son had a nasty accident. He was sitting in his dressing gown on the front of his settee. His bollocks happened to be dangling over the edge of the sofa and his cat....'

'No way,' interrupted Adam. 'You're not going to say what I think you are going to say?'

'I am . . .'

'Oh lord.' Adam clenched his teeth together. A pained expression appeared on his face. 'Your bags caught by a cat. It's *bloody sore* even hearing that story. Talking of bags, does Mrs Waddel know what's happened?'

'I think most people know what's happened. Look at the *Gazette*.' Cammy opened the newspaper and folded page three in half. He passed the paper to Adam who started to read the article. 'Grave robber charged with a myriad of crimes. Adam Ferguson Smith aged 35 of 16 Caddick Square, Edinburgh, was charged today with 117 individual crimes stretching over a fifteen-year period, including an involvement in the recent spate of graverobbing. Smith pleaded not guilty but was refused bail and has been remanded in custody. *The Gazette* was of course first to bring you this story and was first to publish a picture of the accused. We have conducted an opinion poll, asking our readers. 'Does someone desecrating a grave appal you?' Ninety-five percent said yes and five percent said no.'

'Is that it?' Adam was bristling. 'Talk about a loaded opinion poll. Is that all I get? A tiny column, a piss poll and an old picture they've printed before? That's a shite article. I've a good mind to write in and complain.'

The opinion poll was another example of Mr Brian Editor's shambolic attempt to gauge public sentiment. A print deadline was imminent, so rather than speaking to the fine citizens of

Edinburgh he took a show of hands in the office. As Lorna was busy in the toilet, she lost her vote and without realising represented the five percent opposing the question.

'I don't believe they're allowed to print many details before a trial in case they influence the jury,' advised Cammy. 'At least you've made page three. Not many men make page three.'

'Still, I'd expect better coverage than that. Surely I deserve the front page of this shitty rag.' Adam banged his fist on the table.

'Don't worry, I have a funny feeling every newspaper and magazine in the land might cover the trial when they get wind of what's happened, especially the graverobbing bit. By the way, I've not had the chance to say this to you before...' Cammy looked thoughtful, unsure what to say next.

'What? Spit it out.'

'Adam, thanks for taking the blame for me.'

'Shout it from the rooftops, why don't you! For fuck's sake, keep your voice down,' hissed Adam. 'No bother, Cammy, no bother. The way I see it is like this. I'm going down for my other crimes. There is no point in dragging you down with me.'

There was a tear in Cammy's eye. He was genuinely touched. 'I'm really amazed with what you've done. I still have a job, I still have Matty and I still have my freedom. Thanks, mate.' He leant over the table and touched Adam on the back of his right hand.

'Get your sweaty paws off me.' Adam quickly pulled his hand away and looked round to see if anyone else in the room had noticed. All the inmates seemed too engrossed in their own personal traumas. 'Don't start bubbling. It's bad enough being one of the few prisoners in this dump with a male visitor without you starting to cry. If any of the guys in here think I'm a tin roof, then boy, I'm in big trouble. So wipe your eyes, sit up straight and for God's sake look as if you're the world's hardest heterosexual.'

Cammy wiped the tears away from his eyes and took a deep breath. His voice suddenly developed a deeper tone. 'I got pished last night.'

Adam laughed. 'That's more like it. Tell me, have you spoken to the lawyer? I've not seen him for a couple of days. How many years do you think I'll get?'

'Yeah, I've spoken to Mr Kirke. I kind of sensed he didn't really know. He said the court case would happen sooner rather than later because of the number of unsolved crimes and especially because of the grave-digging escapade. The courts have to react to public opinion. He'll be in to see you later. There's no real bench-mark for what you've done. You're one in a million.'

Adam was beaming. The court case was unmatched. His noto-riety dispensed a warm feeling inside. This cosy sensation was tempered by an acute bout of worry.

Neil Kirke, recommended by Andrew, was Adam's lawyer. Neil was gay. Most people would be delighted to have a friend in a position to recommend a successful solicitor - not Adam. 'I can't believe I'm going to be defended by a poof.'

Cammy was exhibiting dismay. 'Don't start this argument again. Neil is a proficient lawyer, the best you'll ever get. He can't perform miracles; nevertheless he'll do the best he can.'

'He's a cocoa shunter.'

'That's plain *disgusting*. You're more than homophobic, you're sick.'

'It's the truth.'

'It's the furthest you can get from the truth. You should be thankful Andrew was kind enough to recommend Neil, consider-ing you aren't exactly best of pals.'

'He probably did it to please Matty.'

'You ungrateful shit.' Cammy was frustrated with Adam's atti-tude. 'So let me get this right. You'd prefer an incompetent lawyer to a gay one?'

'No, I didn't say that. I'd prefer a good lawyer that isn't gay.' Black was black and white was grey with Adam. You'd never win an argument like this. His trench was far too deep to infiltrate. Cammy sat back in his chair, folded his arms and shook his head from side to side. 'Of course, there's worse news about your lawyer.'

'What's that?'

'His mum's German.'

'You're joking!'

'And his dad's Japanese.'

'You're bloody joking!'

'Yes, I'm joking,' retorted Cammy, regaining a little argumentative ground. His counter-attack temporarily diffused Adam's bigotry and a change of subject entered centre stage 'These are for you.' Cammy passed over two letters. 'There's one from the R & A.'

'The who?'

'The Royal and Ancient Golf Club of St Andrews.'

Adam ripped the envelopes open and scanned the basics of the correspondence. In the fleeting time spent in jail, he'd written various letters trying to uncover more about his 'hole-in-one' scam. The note from the R&A highlighted a ruling against someone deliberately interfering with a ball in play. The correspondence from various bookmakers indicated they wouldn't entertain a bet on a golfer achieving a hole-in-one. Perhaps his chance to make a million had gone for now. Leaning over the table, Cammy tried to read the letter upside down.

'Anything interesting?'

'No, not really. Just something I'm working on at the moment.'

'In *here*?'

'No better place. I've so many hours on my hands. I try to make good use of time.'

'Good use?'

'Yeah, good use.'

'An idle brain is in the devil's workshop,' conveyed Cammy, 'and Neil is the devil's advocate.'

'*What*?'

'Better the devil you know. The wages of sin are death. The devil finds work for idle hands.'

'What do you mean, Cammy?' Adam was firmly on the back foot, defending a barrage of proverbs.

'Home is home, as the devil said when he found himself in the Court of Session.'

'Cammy, fuck the devil stuff. What are you on about?'

'Lots of kids in here. The devil's children have the devil's work.' Cammy concluded his devilish rush of proverbial blood to the head. This was a way of getting his own back on Adam, after listening to seven months of his distorted phrases.

'Surely gays are the devil's work,' implied Adam. A retaliatory move was underway.

'How do you work that out?'

'It says in the bible.'

'You're not religious.'

'That's not the point.'

'I don't think it says that in the bible.' Cammy wasn't sure if it did or it didn't. 'You know something Adam?'

'What?'

'You're depriving a village somewhere of an idiot.'

'Piss off!'

'You're so dense, light bends around you.'

'A poof is the devil in disguise,' retorted Adam adding even less to the ridiculous discussion. The boys were throwing imaginary spears at each other. The insults were sharper than razors.

'By the way where is Andy?'

'You mean Andrew.'

'I mean *Andy*.'

'He's gone to Devon for a few days' holiday.'

After Andrew's lucid encounter with his horrific past he decided, fifteen years on, to return to the scene of his crime. Andrew couldn't explain why. Sentiment taking over from sense. He boarded a train bound for Plymouth, strolling the next morning into the Wasteland Woods. Andrew knew precisely where the murder had taken place and stood motionless on the site for over an hour. Bitter emotions seeped out from the veiled assassin. The whole experience was a personal exorcism, providing him with a peculiar feeling of contentment. A visit to the main library revealed his victim's burial site. Simon Macmillan was entombed with his grandparents in a churchyard near the town centre. He visited the graveside to lay a wreath, kneeling down to ask for absolution.

Then the surreal took over from the bizarre. As Andrew stood up, a lady clutching a large bunch of roses bumped into him. This was no meaningless lady. This was Simon Macmillan's mother. She'd visited the graveside every week for the past fifteen years.

Mrs Macmillan introduced herself and thanked Andrew for the lovely flowers. With no time to think, he explained that Simon was one of his old school friends. She had no reason to disbelieve him. With regret written all over his face, Andrew politely said farewell and made a hasty exit from the graveyard.

Mrs Macmillan would never discover that she actually exchanged pleasantries with her son's murderer.

The boys' bittersweet relationship was in full flow. Insults flew around the table like Robin Hood's arrows in gale force conditions. After ten minutes Adam, for no apparent reason, interjected factual details to the discussion. This was his way of calling a truce. 'I heard through the grapevine big Aidan from St Andrews was arrested for possession of stolen goods.'

'Really?'

'No, I made it up, of course *really*. I don't know if he was arrested because of my filing system or if he was nicked independent of this.'

'That's bad.' Cammy tried to appear concerned. It was difficult to be worried about someone you hardly knew. 'I heard your mother was dead.' Ouch. That was below the belt, well out of order. A sinking feeling told Cammy straight away that he'd uttered something best left alone. He'd breached their personal Geneva Convention. This was comparable to waving a white flag ahead of shooting your enemy. 'Adam, I'm sorry. I didn't mean to say that.'

'Cammy, don't worry, my mother is dead. She died when I was young.'

'I know, I'm sorry.'

'I can't get her out of my head.'

'I'm sorry, Adam. I didn't mean to say that.' His remorse was bona fide. No more was said about Adam's mother. Silence prevailed for a further ten minutes. 'Adam,' uttered Cammy, moving the conversation onto the next stage, 'something has been troubling me.'

'Go on.'

'You know how the police picked you up on a Tuesday.'

'Yeah.'

'Why weren't they there on the Monday?'

'Sorry, I don't grasp what you are trying to say.' Adam was following every word.

'Well, if our tickets showed we were arriving in London on Monday, then why were the police not there on Monday instead of Tuesday?'

'Maybe they *were* at Heathrow on Monday and when we didn't arrive at the airport, decided to come back on Tuesday. Or, more than likely they checked with the airline to see when we were actually returning from Sicily.' Adam had long forgotten about his time in Taormina. The supposed changes in flight times were small beer. Sitting in prison awaiting a court case put minor matters into perspective. Adam continued to avoid the truth.

Cammy was content with this explanation. 'I didn't think of that.'

'Cammy.'

'Yeah.'

'Have you told Matty the truth yet?'

'No, not the whole truth.'

'Just as well, I think.'

'She's not daft. She must know I'm involved.'

'Keep your bloody voice down, fuckwit.'

Cammy lowered his voice. 'I was going to tell her everything yesterday but something happened.'

'What?'

Cammy adjusted his shirt collar and leant over the table. A smile appeared on his face. The boys' animosity now seemed a thousand miles away. 'I was on the tour bus yesterday. Halfway through the trip, Matty knelt down in front of all the tourists and proposed marriage to me. The whole of the top-deck applauded and the driver cracked open a bottle of fizzy wine.'

'*What!*' cried Adam. 'Why didn't you tell me when you first came in. That's brilliant news. Fuckin' brilliant. You'll need to wait until I'm out before you get married.' Adam stood up, punched the air and in his excitement grabbed hold of Cammy and gave him a huge hug. 'That has made my day. You're a bloody rascal. Just think, we'll soon be related.'

'There's always drawbacks.' There was a serious tone to his joke. There were other prisoners watching so Adam pushed Cammy away and slapped him on the shoulder in a macho fashion. 'Well done. I can't get over this news. I presume you said yes?'

'Of course I did.'

'Shame I'm in here, I could have organised a few cheap kilts for you and....'

'Leave it Adam... leave it.'

Chapter Twenty-One

WINTER WAS LOOMING. Jock McIvor, one of the regulars who frequented The Shovel Inn every night of the week was a grouchy antiquated man. He tended to arrive later on Sunday as all the family – children, grandchildren and great grandchildren – visited his house for dinner. At the end of this dreary family feast, a pint and a smoke were compulsory. The stench of his piped tobacco was as much a part of 'Shovels bar' as the old football pictures hanging on the wall. Cammy recognised Jock from his earlier visits to the bar yet had never spoken to him. Matty was late, the time was already quarter to nine. Some things were destined never to change.

Cammy and Matty arranged to meet at The Shovel Inn to discuss their wedding plans, even though the big day was months away. The service would take place in the St Nicholas Church, Dalry, as Cammy knew the minister from the many funerals he'd undertaken at the Calton Cemetery. The Reverend Tommy Weir, a trendy young man of the cloth, was the only minister Cammy knew with three rings through his ear. The reception was due to take place at the Royal Hotel where Cammy had worked as an Assistant Manager many moons ago. He eternally vowed to return to his old haunt on the other side of the fence, playing guest instead of servant.

Andrew agreed to give Matty away. This was presumably the only time Andrew would walk down the aisle linking arms with a woman draped in a wedding dress. Cammy wanted Adam to be his best man. For this wish to come true, Adam would have to be released from jail for the day. This looked increasingly unlikely as the court case hadn't yet taken place and public opinion could easily sway this type of request.

Matty appeared at the main door. She was wearing a tight knee-length skirt, stretch silk shirt and black T-bar shoes. 'Sorry I'm late. The clock in the house is fast... I mean slow, and that's thrown me way out. Otherwise I would have been here by now. Have you been here long?'

'Only since eight o'clock, when we arranged to meet.' He was used to Matty being late. She regularly had an excuse formulated. It was never her fault, always someone else's. He was familiar with her customary apologetic performances and this was just as well, since marriage would follow. 'You should know me by now,' said Matty. 'Maybe, you should arrive later to coincide with me being behind time.' Cammy was astonished to find that his punctuality was beginning to sound like the cause of Matty's erratic time-keeping. How was she able to blame him for her lateness? On one occasion he appeared twenty minutes late, hoping to coincide with her appearance. However, this happened to be the day Matty decided to be early and she subsequently gave him a mouthful of abuse. Cammy could never win. This wasn't a problem as he loved her dearly and that was all that mattered. 'Cider?'

'Nice one, Cammy.'

'Which cider are you on these days?' Cammy fumbled in his pockets for change.

'Strongbow.'

'Pint?'

'Do crows shit on your car?'

'I don't know, do they?'

'Of course I want a pint,' asserted Matty. 'It's only girls that drink half-pints.'

Cammy visited the bar via the toilets. He'd recently read in the paper about various germs carried on human fingers by people who didn't wash their hands after using the lavatory. A bowl of appetising peanuts removed by a scientist from a busy bar had been analysed for germs. The scientist detected a high level of bacteria on the snacks, caused by folk sharing the same bowl of peanuts. This article stuck in Cammy's mind. From now on he pledged to regularly wash his hands after visiting the bathroom and to never eat any type of savoury snack offered to him in a pub.

However, the gents' toilet in The Shovel Inn had the smallest wash hand basin in the city, conceivably the country. The hot and cold taps were the size of miniature walnuts and the only person with any chance of feeling a drip of water would have been the local midget, presuming he had the smallest hands in the world.

Obviously it wasn't deemed manly in this part of Edinburgh to wash your hands after availing yourself of the toilet facilities. Cammy manoeuvred round this enormous hygiene problem by taking the tiny cake of soap from the wash hand basin, pushing his hands down the toilet bowl and flushing twice. Not the cleanest practice known to man, woman or child and how Cammy managed to think this was more hygienic than not washing your hands remained a mystery. What would Matty think if she knew? Especially later in the evening when his hands were rummaging around her fair body in a spate of heated passion. 'Cider, Matty.' He placed the drinks on the table. 'And a pint of lager for me.'

'What's wrong with real beer?'

'I wanted a change.'

'Oh, I see. So, what's new?'

'How do you mean?'

'Did you see the guy about the menu?'

'Yes, all sorted. Why are we planning our wedding so far ahead? It's not till next August!'

'Ten months isn't long in wedding terms.'

'Oh really,' expressed Cammy. 'Ten months is a lifetime to me!'

The rather ordinary dinner menu selected for the reception was largely influenced by Matty. In fact, she chose her favourite meal. When asked his opinion on the range of edibles, Cammy repeatedly nodded his head in agreement. He was simply happy to tie the knot. All the finer points of the wedding day were of less importance to him. The startlingly unoriginal menu read:

AVOCADO AND MELON
HOMEMADE PARSLEY SOUP
ORANGE SORBET
ROAST CHICKEN IN A CIDER SAUCE with ROAST
  POTATOES, BROCCOLI, PEAS and CARROTS
STRAWBERRIES AND CREAM
TEA AND MINTS

The guests would be greeted at the hotel reception with a glass of cider and the wedding cake, made by Cammy's mother, would be cut prior to dinner. The happy couple would need a sharp knife to penetrate Mrs Carter's rock-hard icing. Still, it's the thought that counts. Matty contemplated providing the guests with twiglets, cheese puffs and peanuts. Cammy put an abrupt stop to this unsavoury idea. This caused her much puzzlement, considering his concordance to all other wedding decisions. 'Let's go through the check list,' declared Matty in a soon to be wife like manner. 'Kilts?'

'Done.'

'Cars?'

'Done.'

'Bus?'

'Done.'

'Did you see the mistake the printer made with our invitations?' quizzed Matty.

'Yeah.'

'What an idiot, eh?'

'No, it was deliberate.'

'What do you mean?' Matty was confused by the suggestion. 'Why would someone deliberately make a spelling mistake on an invitation?'

'I was speaking to the printer and he said the firm make a couple of errors in their initial work so customers take more care reading the proof. He's convinced this technique works a treat.'

'Really?'

'Yes, really,' added Cammy. 'I seem to remember you double-checked every word after you found the mistake?'

'I suppose I did.'

'There you are, the system works.'

'Here Cammy, what about the disco man?

'He doesn't take distant bookings. I've to phone him in a couple of months.'

'Okay.' Matty was obsessed with the wedding plans. 'Minister, church, hotel.'

'Done, done, done.'

'Did you pick up the paperwork from the Registrar's Office?'

'I thought *you* were going to pick up the stuff from the Registrar's Office.'

'No, I told you to go.'

'No, you didn't.' Cammy was toying with Matty in his usual infuriating way. Of course he'd been to the Registrar's Office, arriving early and waiting twenty minutes before the agency officially opened. No wedding could go ahead without the appropriate documentation. He was well aware of this simple fact.

'I *did* tell you to go,' claimed Matty.

'I don't remember you saying this to me. In fact, I'm sure you told me you were going to go to the office yourself.'

'Bollocks, Cammy. You need your bloody ears examined.'

'What was that?' asked Cammy leaning over the table, pretending to be deaf. 'Can you speak up.'

'*Predictable*, Cammy.'

'Maybe that's why we're getting married?'

'We're not getting married if you don't pick up the forms. Can you go tomorrow?'

'You don't have to fill in the forms and pay the fees until nearer the time!'

'Make sure you go tomorrow,' repeated Matty.

'There's no point going tomorrow.'

'Why?'

'Because I went today.'

'Yah bastard, come here and give me a snog.' Matty grabbed Cammy by the shirt-collar, hauled him round to her side of the table and started to lick his face off. Jock McIvor casually looked round and without uttering a single word, turned back to face the bar. He'd seen a lot in his time and simple snogging was not something to waste his breath over. 'I love you so much, Cammy. Do you know that? You are the only boyfriend I've ever had who has said he loves me when he's sober.'

'I'm not sure if that's a compliment. It doesn't say much for your old boyfriends does it? I've never been happier in my whole life.'

'Same here. We're the symbol of happiness and light. This is as good as it gets.' The conversation was verging on the sickly. Plastic buckets would be provided for the regulars in the event of a full love sharing red-alert. 'Why do you love me?' asked Matty.

'Because I do,' Cammy was feeling ill at ease.

'But why?' quizzed Matty again, this time in a louder voice.

'Well, em...' Cammy realised he should reply to her question before Matty reached full volume. 'I love you because... you're shite at cooking, crap with money, smoke too much – although I like the smoke rings you blow, you lose your keys all the time and you're always late.'

'Yeah, but I'm always late in style,' said Matty. 'What about my bad points?' She began to laugh.

Cammy sat back in his seat slightly embarrassed at her public show of affection. He steered the conversation back onto the wedding plans. 'Have a look at the leaflet I received from the Registrar's Office.' Cammy pulled a green pamphlet from his top pocket. 'It says here that a man cannot marry his great-grandmother.'

'Stranger things have happened.'

'Matty, that's my wedding list checked, what about yours?'

'I think I've done everything.' Matty ran her fingers down the scribbled list. 'Wedding dress, yes. Underwear, yes. Shoes, yes. Going away outfit. Presents for the bridesmaids, yes. Everything is virtually organised. I'll do the rest nearer the time.'

Matty's bridesmaids, Rebecca and Shona, were friends from work, both tall, both good looking and both tourist guides. Cammy's ushers were colleagues from his therapy class, both short, both plain looking and both searching for their own identity. Maybe the bridesmaids and ushers would hit it off?

Cammy's parents were the only relations to receive invitations. As Matty had no close family they opted to ask good friends to the wedding rather than distant relatives. Cammy thought this was better than inviting his numerous uncles, aunts and cousins whom he hadn't seen for years. Admittedly some of Cammy's relatives would be annoyed. Mind you, they were all fairly miserable people anyway.

'The wedding list in Argos has now been amended,' divulged Matty. 'I removed the table football game and fishing rod from the list.'

'I was only joking in the shop when the guy was writing down the presents.'

'He didn't know you were joking. If I can't tell when you're joking, how will a young boy in Argos know?'

'Come on, Matty. Table football and a fishing rod on a wedding present list? Get real!'

'Oh shit,' blurted Matty.

'What?'

'I've forgotten to organise the favours.'

'What the fuck are favours? You've bloody ages to organise favours, whatever favours are.'

'Watch your fuckin' language. Away and wash your mouth out with soap and water.'

'I would but the sink isn't big enough.'

'What?'

'Male joke. Toilet humour.'

'Favours,' apprised Matty. 'Are little sugar almonds which you give out to all the female guests.'

'What about the men? What do they get?'

'They get pished. That's what they get.'

'Talking about getting pished,' voiced Cammy, 'do you know anyone who can operate a video camera?'

'What's that got to do with getting pished?'

'It reminded me of Adam. Pished and Adam go hand in hand.'

'I told you we can't afford a wedding video.'

'I know that, you've told me about twelve times. We could use Adam's video camera if you knew someone who could operate the damn thing.'

'Let me think about that one,' said Matty. Cammy noticed a cream coloured piece of silk sticking out the top of Matty's carrier bag. 'What's that?'

'Keep your eyes off, it's my wedding dress. I've had the seam adjusted today.'

'Can I have a look?'

'No you *cannot* have a look. That would be bad luck. You're not allowed to see the bride's wedding dress until the big day.'

'The bloody wedding's ten months away! Go on, let me have a look,' said Cammy.

'No, it's bad luck. Something will go badly wrong if I show you my dress.'

'You don't believe that, do you?'

'No, not really.'

'Well what's the harm, the wedding's miles away?' In most circumstances, Matty would stick to her guns and tell Cammy to piss off. However, on this occasion, she ignored her better judgement, opened the large bag and without taking the dress out of the satchel, asked Cammy to have a quick look. 'Well, what do you think?'

'Oh doom and gloom and gloom and doom will befall us since I've now seen a tiny section of your dress.' crowed Cammy in a chilling voice directly out of a low-budget horror film. 'Tragedy will strike us both and our children will turn out like monkeys.' He was trying to contain his laughter.

'Don't be an idiot.' Matty objected to his ape-like antics. The choice of a honeymoon destination was made easy by the options available – Blackpool or Sicily. Blackpool finished a credible second, a worthy runner up. Sicily was chosen, thanks once again to the generosity of Graham who'd be travelling to attend their wedding as Andrew's partner. With the preparations in order, Matty finally plucked up the courage to tell Cammy something he wasn't expecting to hear. Matty grabbed hold of his hand. 'Cammy.'

'Yes, dear,' croaked Cammy in the style similar to a henpecked husband.

'I've something to tell you, something important, something which I hope will make you very happy. ...I'm late.'

'Matty, I know you're late. You're always late.'

'No, I'm late. You know, late. I've missed my period. I'm pretty sure I'm pregnant. You're going to be a dad.' Matty was beaming. She hoped he'd be delighted. Cammy opened his mouth as if to reply, then changed his mind. He stared at her in silence. 'How did that happen?'

'I think you know how it happened,' beamed Matty. 'Are you pleased?'

Cammy had decided to sleep with Matty before marriage. It wasn't exactly sleeping. They took advantage of an empty open-top bus and more or less raped each other on the top deck. They were aware of the possible outcome, as Matty after fifteen years on the pill had stopped taking the tablets. They didn't however expect this type of joyous news so quickly. 'My God, that is *brilliant*. I'm over the moon,' proclaimed Cammy. 'I am so happy, so bloody well happy. My God what a *shocker*. Are you sure?'

'It's ninety-nine percent confirmed.' She was grinning like a Cheshire cat who'd had the cream. Their eyes were full of tears. They grabbed each other and fiercely hugged like two grizzly bears playing in the forest. Everything was complete.

Chapter Twenty-Two

THE COLD JANUARY SKY threatened a flurry of snow. There were close to five hundred people gathered outside the high courts in Edinburgh's Parliament Square. The press hounds were setting up their mini media centre within the building at the back of the picturesque Parliament Hall. The whole country seemed to be outraged and yet fascinated by the trial of a modern-day graverobber. On the other hand, the whole country seemed unconcerned and not in the least captivated by the Adam's one hundred and seventeen other charges. Assuming the jail sentence was imposed, someone else would have to cut out the various tabloid articles for his scrapbook. Mr Adam Smith was finally going to be well-known.

The courtroom was bursting to capacity. The court officials turned a queue of curious gossipmongers away from the public gallery, as standing during a court case was not permitted. Adam and his lawyer, Neil Kirke, were sitting side by side at the front of the courtroom awaiting the judge's arrival. The members of the public appearing for jury service were requested to fill in expenses forms and then sent home.

Adam, dressed in a stolen brown suit and dark green suede shoes, was in deep shit - deeper than the world's largest ice-cream tub. His bleached blond hair was rapidly growing out, the former spiky roots becoming full-blown hair. His bowels were playing up, thanks to a burrowing blend of nervous energy and stodgy prison catering. Even Neil Kirke was looking decidedly nervous. Adam recognised the prosecuting advocate from an earlier CD-selling visit to the courts. She'd bought Mahler's Symphony No. 5 and Verdi's *Requiem*, paying over the odds. The prosecuting lawyer did not seem to remember Adam's face. If she did, she wasn't letting on. Adam also recognised the clerk of the court who had purchased Sergei Prokofiev's Cinderella.

Sitting quietly amongst the packed public gallery were Mrs Waddel, Cammy and a three-month pregnant Matty. They didn't attempt to predict the length of jail sentence awaiting Adam.

Having spoken to Mr Kirke earlier in the morning, they were at least aware of Adam changing his plea from not guilty to guilty. His lawyer suggested the police, the court and the judge would look favourably on this decision. Sitting two rows behind Adam was his friend from Switzerland, Alexis. He'd been called in as a character witness – unfortunately a fruitless journey.

Such was the media interest that the press hounds were allocated two rows of seats at the rear of the public benches. Most of the national newspapers were in attendance alongside the local television station. Representing the *Lothian Gazette and Journal* were the infamous journalistic duo of Andy Macmillan and Lorna Nicol. They were now local celebrities in their own right, having initially uncovered the graverobbing story and Lorna, whose help was less than worthless, was relishing the star status. Determined to look her finest for the court, she'd been to the hairdressers in advance of the trial. Her hair was stunningly arranged on the top of her head in a bun, clasped together by a gold coloured bow. This would surely give her a sporting chance of catching some of the judge's summing up speech. *Whoosh. Whoosh. Whoosh.*

Andrew was sitting in front of Andy. Neither realised the connection. Imagine sitting in a courtroom breathing down the neck of the nameless man who'd met your mother and killed your brother. Remaining unknown to each other was the truth of the matter.

In the eyes of the *Gazette* the significance of the event was underlined by the presence of the newspaper's owner, Sir Richard Normans and chief, Mr Brian Editor. Brian's beaming face was shattered by the appearance of Mrs Dimond and her two sisters who waved at him across the crowded courtroom. Mr Editor – attempting to crack a simper over his irritated countenance – reluctantly waved back, avoiding any eye contact. Perhaps the judge would slap a restraining order on old Mrs Dimond for stalking? Or more likely, Brian would have to make a run for it at lunchtime. Luckily the public gallery was congested. Mrs Dimond, Katie and Elaine were unable to sit any closer than three rows away from their darling editor. Cousin Keith was looking after Hector the dog.

The trial exhibits, sealed in clear plastic bags and labelled in numerical order were displayed on a cumbersome table situated at the side of the judge's bench. From where he was seated, Cammy could see his silver flask, Virgil the skeleton, a white spade, an ice-cream carton and a set of Adam's keys, which the police discovered in one of the graves. The exhibits would now be surplus to requirements due to Adam's belated plea of guilt. 'All rise for the judge,' pronounced the clerk of the court. The judge, Lord Gorseman, ambled unhurried into the courtroom from his chambers, which were situated behind the main bench. He was promptly followed into the room by a fussy yet attractive typist who sat down beside him.

As soon as the judge was seated in his heavy oak chair, Adam looked over to the ice-cream carton, unleashed a silent fart and uttered under his breath, 'Have this one on me, duchess.' There were too many people in the courtroom to blame Adam for this stinking act, one charge he'd avoid today. The fart was so putrid, Lord Gorseman cleared the courtroom for ten minutes and asked for air fresheners to be sent up from the cleaners' cupboard.

Adam used to play smelly tricks at school on unsuspecting tutors. If he ever saw two teachers talking to each other, especially if they taught maths, he'd saunter slowly past them, break wind, walk on and then observe their reaction from afar. He loved the idea of two teachers each thinking the other had broken wind. Adam's lawyer, familiar with his client's weak bowel condition, blamed the smell on the local drains and suggested the judge should call in the plumbers.

Having swiftly reconvened, the clerk of the court asked Mr Smith to stand in front of Lord Gorseman. He then commenced reading out the main charges brought against him. Adam blocked out most of the clerk's words and let his grey matter aimlessly meander. This was his own defence against reality.

What would the typist look like stark naked? What would rampant sex be like with her? Does the judge masturbate secretly in his little room while reading dirty magazines? Does Lord Gorseman have illegal drugs hidden under his wig? Wouldn't I just love to ram a rusty sword through the judge's fat stomach. A selection of ludicrous thoughts swept through Adam's disturbed mind.

I'd wager half the guys in this courtroom want to bang the typist, although I suspect Neil and the women won't fancy her. Mind you, simple mathematics would suggest there's probably a lesbian in the courtroom somewhere and she's bound to fancy the pants off the typist. His thoughts then journeyed into a fantasyland of lesbian lovemaking. Adam was beginning to feel an erection. Protruding genitalia were imminent. My god, I can't have a big stiffy pointing at the judge. To counteract his ever-expanding trousers, he scoured his brain and focused on a picture of Queen Victoria's horse. Ever since school, every time he experienced a growing feeling in his pants, he would concentrate on the image of Queen Victoria's horse. This had the desired effect of reducing juvenile swelling and ever since then Adam found this technique to be one hundred percent successful. Why Queen Victoria's horse? He didn't know why. Thankfully the rush of blood in his trousers was beginning to fade.

As the clerk of the court continued reading the collection of charges, Adam's mind strayed in the direction of his late mother. Ever since she died, Adam observed a minute's silence in her memory to coincide with the anniversary of her death. This respectful gesture corresponded to the exact moment of Mrs Smith's demise – recorded on her death certificate as 3.45 a.m. The time was beneficial to Adam as he could normally honour his habitual ritual while immersed in the land of nod.

The judge was famished. He'd never listened to so many allegations in his whole life. As lunchtime approached Lord Gorseman pronounced that a sentence would not be administered until after the break. Adam pictured a stark naked judge following a scantily clad typist out of the courtroom before being escorted himself by two bulky policemen down a neverending set of stairs into one of the small basement cells. Cammy, Matty and Andrew headed off for a seat in the Parliament Hall. Mrs Dimond searched high and low for Mr Editor.

The press charged around like ravenous piranha fish in a vain attempt to relay the latest news to their main offices. This seemed peculiar, considering there wasn't any fresh information to divulge apart from the announcement of lunch. The seventeenth- century

Parliament Hall was full of advocates and lawyers walking up the length of the lobby before turning and walking back down again. Cammy observed this with interest. 'Why do they do that?'

'This is an old custom,' explained Matty. 'The solicitors and lawyers walk up and down the hall chatting to each other to avoid people eavesdropping on their conversations. Other advocates believe it's easier to think on the move.'

'Let's have a shot,' suggested Cammy.

Matty, Andrew and Cammy marched up to the top of the hall and to avoid bumping into the media centre's temporary partition turned and paraded back down. 'No,' complained Matty to Cammy, 'you've to try and turn at the same time, you know, in unison. Watch these two guys.' She pointed over to a couple of advocates spinning in a superb symmetrical style as if part of a synchronised solicitor's team. 'Now it's our turn.' For a fleeting moment they'd placed Adam's dire predicament to the back of their minds and enjoyed several attempts at parallel rotation. Matty and Andrew fine-tuned their turning technique while Cammy languished in the layman's land of mediocrity. As they walked, they talked. 'How many years will he get?' asked Matty.

'My dear pet,' confessed Andrew. 'We have ventured down this topic of discussion on too many occasions. I would counsel you to linger until the judge has concluded his luncheon.'

'I can't help myself,' conceded Matty. 'I wish I could. I am what I am. No, Cammy, try and turn round on your right foot, not your left.'

'Sorry Matty, I was daydreaming.'

'My dearest Matty,' added Andrew. 'You should take your mind off this perilous matter and endeavour to populate your brain with less portentous details. Perhaps you can tell us a short history of this exquisite Parliament Hall?' She reluctantly agreed and an impromptu tour followed. 'The hall has a hammer-beam roof. This was where the Scottish Parliament met for many years up until the Union of the Parliaments in 1707 when Scotland joined England for the first time.'

'You mean, England joined Scotland,' retorted Cammy in a non-British way.

'Whatever. The large window was made in Germany. What a pain that must have been.'

'Nice pun, dear, is it the left foot first?' asked Cammy.

'In the 1840s,' continued Matty. 'Your right foot, Cammy, for goodness sake, try the right foot, not the left. You're friggin' hopeless at turning in time. This is no good.' She stopped in her tracks and stared at the main door. 'The history of the hall is a nice idea, Andrew, however I think I need some fresh air. My head is thumping.' Matty walked out the main entrance of the High Courts into Parliament Square, followed immediately by Andrew and Cammy. They couldn't believe the size of the crowd standing outside, so they turned in perfect unison and returned into the main building. There hadn't been so many people in Parliament Square since Burke and Hare's trial in 1828.

The judge thoroughly enjoyed his roast beef, carrots, peas and boiled potatoes, although the gravy could have been warmer. He turned down the chance to have bread and butter pudding for dessert as a dinner invitation lay in wait and tummy space was at a premium. The court reconvened for the sentencing. The public gallery was hushed. You could hear a silent fart drop. The press hawks were perched like vultures, menacingly nesting with their poisoned pens. 'Adam Ferguson Smith, I have come to my decision.' Lord Gorseman was looking forward to an afternoon snooze. His summing up would be concise. 'You are a nuisance to society and should be locked up for a long time.'

'Oh shit,' thought Adam.

'Your dishonest schemes over a period of fifteen years have been contemptible to the extreme and the attempt to desecrate graves is a disgusting, indefensible act of violation. I have deliberated long and hard on this case and I have no alternative but to send you to prison for six years. After a period of time I shall insist you are involved in a voluntary scheme to tidy up the city's graveyards. Take him down.'

Adam looked pleased, he'd been expecting worse. He turned to his lawyer and was close to hugging him until his bigoted brain decided that a handshake would be more suitable. There was a bemused silence in the courtroom. No one was sure whether this was a strict or lenient sentence as there were no cases to compare this trial with. Matty was in tears. Cammy took hold of her hand and tried valiantly to comfort her.

'Can I say something?' bellowed Adam with daggers in his eyes.

'What is it?' The red-robed judge wanted to retire to his quarters. He had a dinner jacket to brush.

'I just wanted to say, the best thing about winter is the fact that there are no wasps.' He bet twenty pounds with Cammy he'd say this to the judge.

'Take him away!'

As Adam was led from the court he shouted over to Cammy. 'Hey mate, would you tape the news tonight and buy the papers tomorrow?'

'No problem, Danny.'

Adam was led away by two policemen into the heated atmosphere of Parliament Square. Several vegetables were thrown in his direction. The police managed to bundle him into a white prison van before any harm was done. Adam turned to one of the prison guards. 'We should have caught the carrots, then we could have made some soup.' He was whisked away to Edinburgh's Saltown jail and coincidentally placed into a cell looking over the local cemetery.

Mrs Dimond couldn't find Mr Editor anywhere. Andy and Lorna had their front-page story. Adam was now famous or more accurately *infamous*.

Chapter Twenty-Three

SEVEN MONTHS LATER, the August sun was shining down from a clear blue sky. Matty's gorgeous wedding dress was neatly spread on her lumpy bed.

From his cot in the corner of the bedroom, young Cameron junior was crying his eyes out. Admittedly, Cammy senior wasn't adverse to tasty nipple. He'd have to wait his turn. Named after his dad, three-week-old Cameron junior was the spitting image of his mother – hazel eyes and a cheeky grin. Most mornings the wee man was up with the lark.

Graham was fussing. Andrew was fussing more than Graham. Shona and Rebecca the bridesmaids were fussing more than Andrew was. Graham travelled all the way from Sicily to be Andrew's partner at the wedding. His wild nervous energy and blissful enthusiasm were extremely tiring attributes for everyone else to contend with. The calmest of them all was Matty. She was sitting peacefully in front of her bedroom mirror attempting to apply make-up, while the rest of the bridal party fiddled with her hair.

'I'd tie it back in a bow,' advised Shona. 'What do you think, Graham?'

'Oh yes, I'd *definitely* tie it back,' agreed Graham. 'Matty's hair is crying out to be tied back. Then we can fasten a silver bow to the tip of the curls, or perhaps it should be blue. You know how the saying goes, something old, something new, something borrowed, and something blue.'

'No,' objected Rebecca. 'I think Matty should let her hair naturally flop and wave itself into shape. The hairdresser has done such a marvellous job. We shouldn't obliterate his work by tying it back into a bow.'

'One agrees with Rebecca,' conceded Andrew. 'The earthy look is fabulous.'

'You don't destroy the hair if you tie it back into a bow,' growled Shona. 'You just enhance the cut.'

'That's so true, Shona pet,' expressed Graham in a camp tone. 'Shite,' complained Rebecca.

'One embraces Rebecca's argument,' remarked Andrew. 'But not her inauspicious language.'

'I'll shite you,' screeched Shona. The bridesmaids were close to blows. 'Girls, girls, girls,' interrupted Matty. 'Please friggin' well behave yourselves for once. Remember this is *my* wedding day. You may find this an outrageous thing to accept but my intention is to decide how I wear my hair without anyone's advice. If my hair stays as it is or if I put it up in a bow is my decision and my decision alone. Have you got that?' They all sheepishly nodded their heads out of sequence. 'Now let me get on with my make-up. In fact, girls – you don't mind being called a girl, do you Graham?'

'Not in the slightest,' rumbled Graham in deep frisky voice. 'I'm honoured.'

'Well, girls,' ordered Matty. 'I'd like you three to leave me alone with Andrew for a few minutes. I'll give you a shout when we're finished talking.' The girls and Graham reluctantly left the room. Andrew knelt down on a footstool beside Matty's bedside table. 'Andrew, thank you for agreeing to give me away today. You are such a caring, sharing person. This day is so special to me. I have never been happier in my whole life. Everything is perfect.' She took hold of Andrew's hand. 'I couldn't ask for more – a hearts and flowers wedding day, my life with Cammy, the baby, you walking me down the aisle. The list goes on. Nothing at the moment can stop my pure exhilaration and joy. I want you to know how much of a friend you've been to me over the years and I really do love you so much. If it's the last thing I ever do, I want to walk down the aisle today.' Both Matty and Andrew, tears in their eyes, hugged each other, holding on for a prolonged period of time.

'I am so honoured to be assigning you away today,' proclaimed Andrew through his tears. He rubbed Matty's eyes with a tissue. 'Thank you for asking me to play dad. If I could espouse, I'd be the bride and you'd have to call me Auntie Andrew. Come on, Matty, dry your eyes. I think you'll have to reapply your war paint. Don't fret, you've a profusion of time.'

As Matty's entourage fluttered and flustered like adolescent butterflies on acid, Cammy sat alone in silence. He'd experienced a strange start to the day. Unable to sleep overnight, he jumped out of bed at four in the morning and digested four slices of cheese on toast. While flicking through the Teletext news headlines, two amusing stories caught his eye. Firstly, a man in England was aspiring to beat the world record for being buried alive for six months. Secondly, Edinburgh's fire engines had been called to a city centre cemetery to rescue a married couple absorbed in the passionate act of lovemaking. A gravestone had fallen on top of them! Fascinated by the stories, Cammy fell fast asleep on the settee. During this fleeting snooze, his late grandmother materialised and stood expressionless at the foot of the sofa. A chilly calm descended on him. He was somewhat disturbed because she didn't say anything. This was unusual, as his grandmother had always spoken to him in other dreams. To alleviate his noticeable tension, Cammy decided to have a hot soothing bath. If his first encounter was disturbing, then the second occurrence significantly added to his woes. While soaking in the soapy tub, Cammy experienced a severe bout of *déjà vu*. His feelings of dread were so extreme, he instantly jumped out of the bath, wrapped a large green towel around his body and sat motionless on the wet bathroom floor. Things could only get better.

Cammy collected his confused thoughts in between short bouts of 'ketchup top passing'. He was still staying in Adam's flat, looking after Roger and cats. Mrs Waddel brought Cammy wedding presents – two jars of home-made apple and rhubarb chutney. Even with the aid of an elongated barge pole, he could never in a month of Sundays contemplate eating this condiment, as he'd tasted her cooking before. Cammy and Matty, after the marriage, were planning to stay in Adam's flat for a while until they found a place of their own.

Against all odds, Adam was granted temporary leave to attend his sister's wedding ceremony. He would have to return to prison immediately after the church service. For a short time, Cammy would have a best man.

As the sunny morning advanced in its standard sure-fire manner,

Cammy became happier within himself. A couple of minor mental hiccups would not detract him from the most important day of his life. His kilt, sporran, white socks, bow tie and sgian dhu were neatly placed on top of his camp bed. If you'd merged Matty's mattress with Cammy's camp bed at that exact moment in time, both sets of wedding clothes would have coalesced into a heap of associated fibres.

Cammy took the ornate wedding ring out of a blue box, placed the gold band between his thumb and middle finger and raised the ring to the sun-drenched window as if carrying out a pagan act of worship. The gold ring was taken from the Duncan grave at the Calton cemetery. In fear of major bodily harm, he decided not to tell Matty the muddy origins of her wedding band. 'I am so bloody happy!'

When fate was tempted once too often for a Saturday morning, the telephone rang.

I'm not going to answer the phone decided Cammy. I'll let the answering machine deal with the call. It's always the bloody same, people phone when you don't want them to phone and no one phones when you need someone to phone. The phone rang four times before the answering service switched itself on.

Adam's voice droned out from the machine in a humorous manner. 'No one available to take you're call at the moment. If you are a friend please leave a name and number and if I can be bothered, I'll call you back. If you're someone trying to sell me double-glazing or a kitchen, then fuck off and die yah miserable bastards! Please speak very clearly after the tone.'

There was a short silence followed by the clicking noise of someone placing down the receiver.

'I hate that,' muttered Cammy. 'I wish they'd leave a message. That is so annoying. I suppose I could dial 1471 to see who it was. I won't give the selfish bastard the satisfaction.'

The telephone rang repeatedly for the next five minutes. Cammy had the pleasure of listening to Adam's polite message over and over again followed by the clicking sound of someone hanging up. When the phone rang for a fifth time Andrew left a short message. 'Cameron, please pick up the phone... If you are

there, please pick up the phone... Cameron, are you there? No...
No... Okay, listen carefully, If you get this message please phone
me immediately.....' Cammy picked up the receiver. 'What's
wrong, Andrew? You sound in shock?'

'Cameron, its Matty.'

'What about Matty? What about Matty!'

'Cameron, I'm really sorry I have to tell you this over the
phone, she's dead.'

Cammy surely hadn't heard Andrew properly. 'Andrew, what
do you mean? What did you say?'

'I'm sorry Cammy. Matty is dead. Stay where you are, I'll be
straight over.'

Cammy felt like a lifeless puppet on the end of a string, dangling in sickly dead space. He was dazed on the canvas in suspended shock, a moment of horror never to be erased from his
mind. This brain-numbing bulletin was barely fresh in Cammy's
head when the door opened and Adam, attached by handcuffs to
a prison officer, added his own untimely words of misery.

'Hi, cheery, what's wrong with your face? It's tripping. Has
someone died?'

Chapter Twenty-Four

THE LILY-FILLED CHURCH was laden with startled wedding guests, some sobbing, some sitting hushed staring into space and others praying. The sun was streaming in through the colourful Victorian windows like a set of theatre spotlights. You could see the dust floating through the air. The ushers had the unenviable task of revealing the day's tragic news to the guests as they arrived at the front door of kirk.

The devastated congregation filed slowly into the church and sat on pews situated on both sides of the kirk's main aisle. This was not exactly the wedding day everyone had anticipated. Graham, coaxed into filming the marriage with Adam's video camera decided to pack the Panasonic back in its bag out of harm's way. Filming people crying was not his idea of fun.

Matty had suddenly collapsed in her bedroom and died in Andrew's arms. The post mortem would later reveal the cause of death to be a blood clot to the brain. Cammy and Andrew insisted the day should go ahead as the guests were already on their way. Andrew informed the appropriate authorities including the police before the service and a report was to be sent to the Procurator Fiscal, who in turn would order the post mortem examination. Following the examination, a death certificate would be issued and a bereavement notice placed in the *Gazette*. Andrew hoped to arrange the funeral for a week on Tuesday as he knew the process could take up to seven days.

Cammy, head bowed, walked listlessly into the church and hurried down the centre aisle. The entire congregation held their breath in bewildered silence. At the front of the church, he turned to face the congregation.

'Thank you all for staying.' His voice was faltering. 'Matty always wanted to come down the aisle in a wedding dress. I so wanted to marry her today.' There was a short pause. 'In my eyes, we will always be married. You know I love her hazel eyes. I always wanted to be a dad and a good dad I shall be. He'll grow to know how loving his mother was. My son will carry on her spirit.'

Cameron junior, as he would soon be called, was peacefully sleeping in the minister's arms, oblivious to his sorrowful surrounds. 'Please stay for the whole day because I need you more than I've ever needed anyone before. I know in my heart Matty would have wanted us to have a good time tonight. I don't feel like having a good time. I'm sure you don't either. I don't know what to say.'

Cammy paused to take a sharp intake of breath. He was trying to make sense of the worst day of his life. 'I love Matty so much. I miss her. I don't want to sleep alone tonight.' He broke down into tears. Adam, sitting in the front row of the church, jumped up to help, pulling the prison officer over with him.

'Adam,' uttered Cammy in a soft voice. 'I'm okay. I need to finish what I was saying. Please let me finish. I need to do this for Matty.' The prison officer, now with a sore wrist, sat back down with his mobile convict.

Most people were amazed Cammy was able to speak at all. His human layers were fully peeled, exuding raw emotion. 'Andrew is organising the funeral service at the Calton Cemetery. Please come along if you can. I know a lot of you work during the week, nevertheless, try your best to be there. Everything is out of my control at the moment. Please forgive me if I get a little mixed up today.' He looked up to the roof of the church. 'I normally believe the end of life is part of life. I don't feel like believing that today. I'll miss Matty more than you can possibly imagine. She'll stay in my thoughts and in my heart forever.' Such was his whole-hearted anguish Cammy hesitated and took time to look around the kirk unaware of anyone else in the church. 'Please God, let this be one of my dreams. Maybe I'll wake up in a minute or two?'

Tears were streaming down Cammy's face. He bravely continued. 'Some of you will be aware of Matty's indifferent quest to find her real parents. Andrew found an official envelope beside her bed, which I took the liberty of opening. The correspondence was from the adoption agency giving details of Matty's real parents. Perhaps she didn't want to know what was inside the envelope? Perhaps she hadn't got round to opening the letter? Perhaps she already knew? We'll never know. We now know that her parents are also dead. Perhaps they're all together now? Her real mum and dad were David and Catherine Duncan who are buried in the Calton cemetery. Andrew has gained permission to bury Matty beside her parents.' His grieving voice was barely audible through his tears.

Cammy was horrified to learn that both Matty and he had been present at the funeral of her real parents, Mr and Mrs Duncan, observing the burial from the Calton cemetery watchtower. Furthermore, Cammy would have to live in the solemn knowledge he'd robbed from their grave.

Chapter Twenty-Five

MATTY WAS LYING SERENELY in a fine oak coffin at the front of the funeral parlour. She was wearing her beloved lucky green jacket over the wedding dress. A black silk rose was pinned into her hair and Matty's fluffy yellow microphone was positioned beside the fingers of her right hand. Andrew prepared Matty's body for the funeral as if it was her wedding day. He'd found the next five weeks lottery tickets and some lemon sweets in her jacket pocket. Adam suggested taking the tickets, as they'd be of no use to Matty. Andrew, irked by the very thought, put them back where he found them.

Cammy stepped down to the side of the coffin, took hold of Matty's hand, placed the wedding ring on her finger and kissed her goodbye.

The air was teeming with the trail of freshly trimmed grass.

The ageing stone outlook tower was watching over the city cemetery. It was Tuesday, the day of Matty's funeral, although you could hardly see the Calton burial ground thanks to the dense Firth of Forth fog. This was to be a gloomy day full of tears and remorse. The past continued to cast long shadows over the present.

Three interesting events took place on that melancholy Tuesday morning. A vandalised bench was removed from Princes Street Gardens. Cracked paving stones were replaced in Regent Terrace and scaffolding was erected around the base of the Calton cemetery watchtower.

Cammy agreed to dig Matty's grave by hand, preparing her burial ground on the Monday evening. This was a personal tribute to the love of his life. Andrew's homage to Matty was to make sure her coffin arrived half-an-hour late.

The mourners were gathered in a sombre semicircle around the muddy grave. Standing right at the front of the plot, beside the minister, was Adam, unsuitably attired in white training shoes and attached by handcuffs to a young prison officer called Geoff. The older officer who'd accompanied Adam to Saturday's wedding ceremony requested a transfer due to Adam's regular bowel motions and his irritating repetitive references to *The Great Escape*. Not much fun being attached to a war-crazed, compulsive, fart merchant. Adam was granted permission to attend his sister's funeral. In comparison to the wedding day release, this was an easier request for the prison to authorise.

A large ginger cat was watching the subdued proceedings from the top of the soon-to-be renovated watchtower. An open-top bus stopped on the main road outside the cemetery as a mark of respect.

The service was short and sweet. The heart-warming words had already been uttered on Saturday night.

'Geoff,' remarked Adam, 'would you release me from the cuffs so I can throw earth into the grave?' He paused and looked helplessly at the mourners seeking sympathy for his plight. Andrew caught his eye and smiled.

'Sorry, Adam,' answered Geoff. 'I have clear instructions to keep the handcuffs on for the whole day.'

Adam hadn't been so close to a man since his hot and bothered encounter with homosexuality. After delivering a second-hand loudspeaker system to Andrew at the funeral parlour, they ventured out for a lunchtime drink to celebrate his latest acquisition. One alcoholic beverage led to another and ten hours later as the pub prepared to lock up, Andrew invited Adam back to his cottage where they indulged themselves in a cocaine sniffing competition. After a long speech by Andrew declaring you haven't lived until you've slept with a man, the unlikely duo hopped into bed together. It would be fair to say Adam was somewhat numb in the morning especially when he realised that a pint-sized part of his personality revelled in the adventure. No prizes to learn that Adam had immense trouble accepting this hard-headed fact. Despising gays was the predictable outcome.

'Come on Geoff,' demanded Adam. 'It's my sister's funeral. I'd like to throw earth into her grave.'

'You only need one hand for that.'

'Yeah, and you only need one hand for wanking,' retorted Adam.

'Now, now,' interrupted the minister appalled by the disagreeable diction. 'Please watch your language. Have some respect.
This is a funeral!'

'Sorry, Rev.' Adam apologised. 'Can you have a word with
Geoff?'

'I'm a minister, not the prison governor.' He was plainly
annoyed by the interruption.

'Fair point. Here Geoff,' Adam pointed to his feet, 'these were
my dad's training shoes.'

'What?'

'My dad used to run in these.'

'What do you mean by that?' asked Geoff.

'Come on, Geoff, this is such an important moment in my life,'
pleaded Adam thrusting both hands towards the prison officer.
'Let me out the cuffs. I loved Matty so much. For goodness sake
have some compassion. I'm not going anywhere.'

'No!' Geoff was sticking to his guns. 'It's more than my job's
worth.'

The melancholy gathering weren't happy with the prison officer's
attitude. What harm would it do freeing Adam for a few seconds?
The piercing stares exuding from the many inconsolable eyes were
enough to change the prison officer's mind and release Adam from
the handcuffs. He took a small step forward and picked up a
handful of earth. 'I give thanks to a girl I am proud to call my sister.
My dear Matty if I could swap my body for yours, I would. I'm
the bad apple in the basket...'

'Barrel,' said Cammy.

'Yeah, I'm the bad barrel in the basket. There's no justice in
this world.' Adam threw a handful of earth into the grave; the
mud clattered onto the coffin lid. 'Ashes to ashes.'

'Adam, forgive me for saying,' interrupted Cammy. 'You
should start this sentence with the words earth to earth, not ashes
to ashes.' The poignant moment was lost to a blemished proverb.
Adam looked around at the group of mourners. 'Sorry Cammy,
sorry everyone.' You could sense Adam was up to something, a
man on a mission. He was spouting sentimental twaddle, saying
things about Matty he'd never said before. He was of course sad

to lose his sister although they'd never in any stretch of the imagination been close friends. 'Earth to earth, ashes to ashes, wallet, keys, fags, cock.'

Adam sprinted away from the graveside at full speed, jumped over the cemetery wall and shouted, 'Hold on to yourself, Bartlett, you're twenty feet short.' Before you could say Jack Robinson to a goose he'd disappeared into the misty horizon. The prison officer rushed to follow but tripped over Mrs Waddel's silver-topped walking stick and fell to the ground clutching his ankle. Was Mrs Waddel an accessory to Adam's great escape or was this an unfortunate accident? No one appeared to see what happened through the mist. The impromptu round of applause suggested the assemblage weren't too upset with Adam's swift exit. Although ridden with grief, Cammy thought this was Adam paying his own perfect homage to Matty.

Cammy stepped forward and in tribute to Matty and her parents, produced a four-iron golf club from nowhere, teed up a green Slazenger golf ball and hit it with no accuracy towards the Stevenson family tomb. Fate delivered an amusing blow. The ball bounced off a gravestone and rebounded off the prison officer's head. Geoff was having a bad day. Cammy picked up a handful of earth from the dew soaked grass and took over where Adam had left off.

'Ashes to ashes.' Cammy paused 'I'm getting this wrong myself, thanks to Adam... Earth to earth, ashes to ashes, dust to dust. Getting over someone's death takes time, while the passing of time leads to death. Come the darkness please protect her in the shadows. I love you, Matty.' He threw the earth onto the coffin lid.

'If anyone would like to,' advised Cammy, 'we're all going to visit the pub around the corner; please come if you can. There will be tea, coffee and sandwiches available. Andrew and Graham will lead the way. I would like a few minutes in the graveyard by myself.'

Cammy waited for the cemetery to empty then knelt down beside the grave. 'I am sorry I stole from your parents. I'm sorry I lied to you in Sicily. I'm sorry you didn't know the wedding ring was your mother's. Please forgive me. Whatever I've said and done one fact remains – I love you with all my heart and always will. I'll bring wee Cammy up to see you on a Sunday and I'll make sure your grave is the smartest in the churchyard. I shall always watch the video taken of you in Sicily. I'll miss our long chats. I'll miss our rows. I'll miss everything about you. I'll never forget you as long as I live.'

Cammy spoke to Matty for ages. 'Do you remember the time on the school bus when we passed the cemetery? A large funeral was taking place. The bus stopped to let the coffin bearers cross the road. The mourners followed and we all sat in complete silence for what seemed like an eternity. I burst into tears and you held onto my hand. For the next two weeks, every time we passed that churchyard you grabbed my hand. I'll treasure that memory for ever.'

As the evening sky merged with the onset of night the moon drifted into view from behind the darkening clouds, illuminating the brass nameplate tightly screwed to the coffin lid. ILONA 'MATTY' DUNCAN – RIP

This was no déjà vu.

The following Saturday night, in a grubby two-storey guest-house in Carlisle, Adam sat with his new unemployed friends in front of a broken gas fire, watching the evening's light entertainment on an old black-and-white television. This ragtag bunch of full-time layabouts were poised with cheap plastic pens and lottery tickets in hand, waiting patiently for the National Lottery Live programme to start.

Adam's great escape was originally conceived in Her Majesty's Prison, Edinburgh. From the morning of Matty's fateful wedding to the day of her sombre funeral, Adam's crafty brain was working overtime, spending a week cultivating meticulous arrangements for his breakout. He knew the Calton Cemetery and surrounding neighbourhood like the back of his hand and this proved invaluable to his master plan. When he learnt of his sister's death, he was fairly sure permission would be granted to attend her funeral.

First on the agenda was a focused effort to have the prison officer who'd accompanied him to Matty's wedding replaced. Mr

Stores was a strict authoritarian, following all security regulations without exception and Adam knew this stern individual would never release him from handcuffs. So, he set about making this officer's day a total nightmare by farting and burping as much as he could in the prison van on the way to the church. This fetid offering ushered a day of persistently chattering in the prison officer's ear, quoting long uninterrupted passages from *The Great Escape*. In a definitive attempt to make sure his captor was transferred, Adam, during Cammy's impassioned address in the church, leant over and whispered in the officer's ear, 'I find you very attractive.'

The first stage of his strategy worked; a younger prison officer called Geoff replaced Mr Stores with immediate effect. There was nothing to say that Geoff would show a more lenient streak at the funeral. This was a chance Adam had to take. Thankfully his new bureaucratic attachment demonstrated a smidgen of graveside compassion. The opening section of Adam's fleeing blueprint was aided by firstly, his knowledge of six permanent rubbish bins located on the main street to the east of the cemetery and secondly, his insistence on wearing a black suit and tie to his sister's funeral instead of the normal prison garb. This would aid his breakout.

On the day of Matty's burial, Adam promptly found a wheelie bin on the other side of the crumbling cemetery wall and while Geoff assumed his captive was lost in the foggy distance, Adam was concealed in a stench ridden bucket of rubbish under the prison officer's very nose. Before Geoff could muster any form of official back up, Adam had jumped onto the back of a moving train on the outskirts of Waverley Railway Station.

Smelling like an old kipper and lacking any form of finance, Adam slipped unobserved through a window into the back of the unopened buffet car. He was keen to abandon the train as soon as he could, perhaps at the next station. His departure was provoked earlier than proposed on seeing the ticket collector advancing towards his carriage. With lady luck on his side the train began to slow down and he seized this opportunity for freedom by climbing through one of the carriage doors and leaping down to the grassy embankment below. As the 14.45 Edinburgh to Birmingham – delayed by a technical failure – pulled away, Adam remained hidden behind a small bush until the train was clearly out of sight.

Then, like a peg-legged cross-country runner, Adam stumbled over a newly ploughed field and hid behind a clump of old oak trees. In fear of capture, he decided to wait for darkness before travelling any further. Leaning up against a small grassy mound, tired and hungry, his mind wandered back to earlier in the day, nurturing memories of Matty.

His happiest recollection of her stretched back many years to one of the few days they played together as children. Adam was fifteen, Matty nine, a wealthy schoolmate's house in Portobello the cheerful backdrop. They concocted a game called 'The East of Scotland World Championships' based on the real sport of athletics with one significant difference – they were only allowed to use objects found in the back garden. A short stick was changed into the javelin, a red brick became the shot put, while the rhubarb patch was neatly transformed into the long jump. After pole vaulting with a broom handle, an old discarded mattress was the perfect landing place. A sprint from the main garage to the back gate was the 100 metres and five laps around the sizeable detached house was considered to be a marathon. Hockey consisted of two goal-like tomato boxes, a tennis ball and a couple of rusty golf clubs. Violent blows to the legs were administered at regular intervals. Adam remembered this day for two reasons. He enjoyed Matty's companionship without any mention of their age difference, and for the first time ever he felt at ease in the company of his sister. Basically the day was a one-off. True to form a petty argument followed the next morning.

Fast asleep, curled in a ball at the base of an old oak tree, Adam began to dream. Matty appeared larger than life in her wedding dress carrying a pint of cider in one hand and holding a Cuban cigar in the other. They both hopped on a 750CC Triumph motorbike and drove at high speed through the centre of Edinburgh. She seemed content.

Adam awoke shivering amongst a pile of sodden leaves, having remembered his first dream. His shirt, jacket and trousers were clammy from the moist ground, his mouth full of dirt. He was up and moving within minutes under the shadowy cape of night. After an hour's saunter he stumbled on a desolate farmhouse where fresh clothes were stolen from a washing line and a bicycle from a shed. Not quite Steve McQueen, nevertheless this mode of pedal power would happily assist him for now. His fresh outfit, damper than his old one, consisted of shabby corduroy trousers, a white collarless shirt, a tartan scarf and a well-worn woollen jumper. His new clothes dried out in the morning sun, his old were hidden in a wooden horse trough. By early afternoon, after peddling furiously for hours, he chanced upon the main route heading south. He stopped, dumped the bike in a ditch and clambered up a bank to the side of the road, hoping to stop a passing car. Adam hitched a lift to Carlisle with a Greek sales rep and while the rep went into a motorway service station, Adam stole his car. In the glove compartment Adam found a small leather wallet containing one hundred and twenty-eight pounds cash and four major credit cards. This would help settle a few bills. He ditched the red Ford Fiesta on the outskirts of Carlisle and in the true traditions of an environmentally friendly thief took the local bus into town.

The shabbiest guesthouse in Carlisle, full of dole cheque worshippers and barbiturate addicts, was Adam's chosen place of residence. The whole dwelling house reeked of cat's urine, fried bacon and damp plasterboard. This would be Adam's hostile home for the next couple of weeks.

As Adam sat in Carlisle, Cammy sat at the top of the watchtower steps clutching Cameron junior in his arms, Andrew sat on his treasured toilet seat and Graham sat on a plane heading back to Sicily.

'Would you turn the volume up, Dave,' cried Carl. 'The programme's about to start.' Dave was a tall ex-light middleweight boxer from Bristol. Carl was a squat bearded man from Kent. Neither had worked for four and a half years. The room reverberated to the sounds of the National Lottery Live theme tune. This was nearly the high point of the residents' work-shy week. Collecting unemployment benefit was first past the post followed closely by spending the dole cheque on booze and lottery tickets. Sleeping all day ran in a close third.

'Hey lads,' remarked Adam, 'is the bottle of sauce on the table finished?' To show he was alive and well, Adam planned to send Cammy a bottle top and small plastic turd through the post.

'What was that, Danny?' asked Carl.

Adam was temporarily using his trade name. 'The sauce bottle, can I have the top?'

'You're a weirdo, aren't you,' said Dave.

'I'll take that as a yes, then?'

'Shut it Jock and watch the box,' roared Dave.

'Ladies and gentlemen, welcome to the National Lottery Live,' announced the cheerful female presenter. 'Tonight, live in the studio we have the comeback appearance of Martha and the Muffins. We also have a very special guest to press the lucky lottery button tonight.'

'I'd give her one.' Carl was waggling his tongue like a lunatic.'

'I'd ask her out before you did,' bragged Dave. 'I'd get in there when you weren't looking, give her a quickie at the back of the studio and you'd be standing there like a tit wondering what happened.'

'She'd never shag you two,' protested Tony peacefully. 'Never in a month of Sundays.' Tony was the quiet, unemployable type. Now and again he'd suddenly join in the conversation and invariably leave as quickly as he'd entered, drifting back into his lonely world.

'Bloody right she would,' barked Carl. 'She wouldn't look at you Tony because you're a bowl of rat sick.'

'Yeah, Tony, you're a bowl of r..r..rat's sick. Good one CC...Carl,' added Joan the stammering landlady.

Adam was enjoying the deep intellectual conversation and warm friendly atmosphere. 'What are you eating?' quizzed Adam.

'Chocolate chip ice cream,' spluttered Carl.

'Mmm, nice, very good choice. I know a good supplier of chocolate chip ice cream. I'll get you some before I leave,' replied Adam. 'Any cigs left, Carl?'

'Not a sausage, pal.'

'Danny, who are Martha and the Muffins?' asked Dave.

'Do you not remember 'Echo Beach'?'

'Echo what?'

'Never mind.' Adam didn't wish to show his age. Obviously Carlisle's adopted motley crew were too young to remember Martha and the Muffins. 'Here, Dave, is it easy to train a dog to pick up a ball and place it in a hole?'

'What are you saying now?' snarled Dave. 'Just piss off and watch the programme you piece of Scottish shit.'

Carlisle's unemployed weren't equipped for Adam's intricate scamming brain. The National Lottery Live was on and that was the focus of everyone's booze induced attention. Adam was continuing his quest to find a way of winning a 'hole-in-one' bet at golf. He thought he could train a dog to run on the green, pick up a golf ball and drop it in the hole. Surely there would be no rules against this? Maybe they don't allow dogs on golf courses during main tournaments? I could gain access as a blind man, thought Adam. His animated mind hadn't lost the capacity to rant.

'How do you get three gays on a bar stool?' asked Adam. The room fell silent. Nobody was listening. 'Turn it upside down. Ha...Funny, eh? Do you know there's a place in Ireland called Muff and they've a diving club. Now that's funny.' No one reacted. The Lottery was far too important. Adam was setting low personal standards and failing miserably to achieve them. He decided not to ask any further questions for the time being.

'Our special guest on the programme tonight,' announced the TV presenter. 'Is none other than legendary screen actor and film director, Lord Richard Attenborough.'

Adam jumped out of his seat in delight. 'It's Big X, Big X from *The Great Escape*. That's brilliant. I thought the Germans killed him but he's alive, alive, alive, oh!' Adam danced around the living room. Richard Attenborough's long and distinguished stage, television and film career both as an actor and director were inconsequential to Adam. As far as he was concerned, Richard Attenborough was only one person and that one person was Big 'X' from *The Great Escape*.

The motley crew of brain numbed simpletons turned and stared at Adam. 'Shut it, Jock and listen to the programme,' howled Dave. 'If you don't shut up, I'll put your lights out.'

'Big X, three tunnels and all that,' murmured Adam before returning to his seat. 'Tom, Dick and Harry.'

'Lord Richard Attenborough,' announced the TV presenter. 'Please press the button and roll the balls.'

'Good luck everyone.' The balls whizzed around the plastic machine like mini-planets in a tornado-induced galaxy disaster. The living room fell silent.

Adam, lacking the lottery spirit, paid a prompt visit to the flat's polluted toilet facilities. The guesthouse's lavatory was nothing to scribble home about – most of the writing was already on the wall. Adam added to the lacklustre graffiti by scratching an 'X' onto the back of the hollow toilet door. On returning to the television room, he briefly heard a recap of the winning numbers. 'So tonight's winning numbers in ascending numerical order are one, nine, twelve, fourteen, fifteen, nineteen and the bonus ball is four.' Early indications suggest there is one jackpot winner who will walk away with twelve million pounds.' Cheers echoed from the old television set. 'Next week we have an interview with Larry Foley from Sussex who lost his £1 million winning ticket in his house. Luckily he found it in the dog's basket with two days to spare. Just in time to claim his winnings!'

'I bet he was happy as Larry. Ha, ha, ha, happy as Larry,' blurted Dave. He was about to succeed Adam as the worst joke teller in Britain.

'I always get two numbers,' complained Tony. 'Never three, always two.'

The numbers were very familiar to Adam. Where had he heard these numbers before?

'Dave, what were the numbers again?'

'One, nine, twelve, fourteen, fifteen and nineteen.'

'Four is the bonus ball,' added Carl.

Of course Adam knew the numbers. How could he forget? He'd bought lottery tickets for his sister on countless occasions. A warm sinister feeling swept through his whole body. 'Dave,' quizzed Adam.

'Yeah.'

'If you have a winning ticket, how long can you wait before cashing it in?'

'I think about six months, Adam, yeah about six months.'

Some other books published by **LUATH** PRESS

FICTION

The Bannockburn Years

William Scott

ISBN 0 946487 34 0 PBK £7.95

A present day Edinburgh solicitor stumbles across reference to a document of value to the Nation State of Scotland. He tracks down the document on the Isle of Bute, a document which probes the real 'quaestiones' about nationhood and national identity. The document ends up being published, but is it authentic and does it matter? Almost 700 years on, these 'quaestiones' are still worth asking.

Written with pace and passion, William Scott has devised an intriguing vehicle to open up new ways of looking at the future of Scotland and its people. He presents an alternative interpretation of how the Battle of Bannockburn was fought, and through the Bannatyne manuscript he draws the reader into the minds of those involved.

Winner of the 1997 Constable Trophy, the premier award in Scotland for an unpublished novel, this book offers new insights to both the academic and the general reader which are sure to provoke further discussion and debate.

'*A brilliant storyteller. I shall expect to see your name writ large hereafter.*'
NIGEL TRANTER, October 1997.

'*... a compulsive read.*' PH Scott, THE SCOTSMAN

The Great Melnikov

Hugh MacLachlan

ISBN 0 946487 42 1 PBK £7.95

A well crafted, gripping novel, written in a style reminiscent of John Buchan and set in London and the Scottish Highlands during the First World War, *The Great*

Melnikov is a dark tale of double-cross and deception. We first meet Melnikov, one-time star of the German circus, languishing as a down-and-out in Trafalgar Square. He soon finds himself drawn into a tortuous web of intrigue. He is a complex man whose personal struggle with alcoholism is an inner drama which parallels the tense twists and turns as a spy mystery unfolds. Melnikov's options are narrowing. The circle of threat is closing. Will Melnikov outwit the sinister enemy spy network? Can he summon the will and the wit to survive?

Hugh MacLachlan, in his first full length novel, demonstrates an undoubted ability to tell a good story well. His earlier stories have been broadcast on Radio Scotland, and he has the rare distinction of being shortlisted for the Macallan/ Scotland on Sunday Short Story Competition two years in succession.

FOLKLORE

The Supernatural Highlands

Francis Thompson

ISBN 0 946487 31 6 PBK £8.99

An authoritative exploration of the otherworld of the Highlander, happenings and beings hitherto thought to be outwith the ordinary forces of nature. A simple introduction to the way of life of rural Highland and Island communities, this new edition weaves a path through second sight, the evil eye, witchcraft, ghosts, fairies and other supernatural beings, offering new sight-lines on areas of belief once dismissed as folklore and superstition.

Scotland: Myth, Legend and Folklore

Stuart McHardy

ISBN: 0 946487 69 3 PBK 7.99

Who were the people who built the megaliths? What great warriors sleep beneath the Hollow Hills? Were the early Scottish saints just pagans in disguise?

Was King Arthur really Scottish?

When was Nessie first sighted?

This is a book about Scotland drawn from hundreds, if not thousands of years of story-telling. From the oral traditions of the Scots, Gaelic and Norse speakers of the past, it presents a new picture of who the Scottish are and where they come from. The stories that McHardy recounts may be hilarious, tragic, heroic, frightening or just plain bizzare, but they all provide an insight into a unique tradition of myth, legend and folklore that has marked both the language and landscape of Scotland.

Tall Tales from an Island

Peter Macnab

ISBN 0 946487 07 3 PBK £8.99

Peter Macnab was born and reared on Mull. He heard many of these tales as a lad, and others he has listened to in later years.

There are humorous tales, grim tales, witty tales, tales of witchcraft, tales of love, tales of heroism, tales of treachery, historical tales and tales of yesteryear.

A popular lecturer, broadcaster and writer, Peter Macnab is the author of a number of books and articles about Mull, the island he knows so intimately and loves so much. As he himself puts it in his introduction to this book 'I am of the unswerving opinion that nowhere else in the world will you find a better way of life, nor a finer people with whom to share it.'

'All islands, it seems, have a rich store of characters whose stories represent a kind of sub-culture without which island life would be that much poorer. Macnab has succeeded in giving the retelling of the stories a special Mull flavour, so much so that one can visualise the storytellers sitting on a bench outside the house with a few cronies, puffing on their pipes and listening with nodding approval.' WEST HIGHLAND FREE PRESS

Tales from the North Coast

Alan Temperley

ISBN 0 946487 18 9 PBK £8.99

Seals and shipwrecks, witches and fairies, curses and clearances, fact and fantasy – the authentic tales in this collection come straight from the heart of a small Highland community. Children and adults alike responsd to their timeless appeal. These *Tales of the North Coast* were collected in the early 1970s by Alan Temperley and young people at Farr Secondary School in Sutherland. All the stories were gathered from the area between the Kyle of Tongue and Strath Halladale, in scattered communities wonderfully rich in lore that had been passed on by word of mouth down the generations. This wide-ranging selection provides a satisying balance between intriguing tales of the supernatural and more everyday occurrences. The book also includes chilling eye-witness accounts of the notorious Strathnaver Clearances when tenants were given a few hours to pack up and get out of their homes, which were then burned to the ground.

Underlying the continuity through the generations, this new edition has a foreward by Jim Johnston, the head teacher at

Farr, and includes the vigorous linocut images produced by the young people under the guidance of their art teacher, Elliot Rudie.

Since the original publication of this book, Alan Temperley has gone on to become a highly regarded writer for children.

The general reader will find this book's spontaneity, its pictures by the children and its fun utterly charming. SCOTTISH REVIEW

An admirable book which should serve as an encouragement to other districts to gather what remains of their heritage of folk-tales. SCOTTISH EDUCATION JOURNAL

SPORT

Over the Top with the Tartan Army (Active Service 1992-97)

Andrew McArthur

ISBN 0 946487 45 6 PBK £7.99

 Scotland has witnessed the growth of a new and curious military phenomenon – grown men bedecked in tartan yomping across the globe, hell-bent on benevolence and ritualistic bevvying. What noble cause does this famous army serve? Why, football of course!

Taking us on an erratic world tour, McArthur gives a frighteningly funny insider's eye view of active service with the Tartan Army - the madcap antics of Scotland's travelling support in the '90s, written from the inside, covering campaigns and skirmishes from Euro '92 up to the qualifying drama for France '98 in places as diverse as Russia, the Faroes, Belarus, Sweden, Monte Carlo, Estonia, Latvia, USA and Finland.

This book is a must for any football fan who likes a good laugh.

'I commend this book to all football supporters'. Graham Spiers, SCOTLAND ON SUNDAY

'In wishing Andy McArthur all the best with this publication, I do hope he will be in a position to produce a sequel after our participation in the World Cup in France'. CRAIG BROWN, Scotland Team Coach All royalties on sales of the book are going to Scottish charities.

Ski & Snowboard Scotland

Hilary Parke

ISBN 0 946487 35 9 PBK £6.99

 Snowsports in Scotland are still a secret treasure. There's no need to go abroad when there's such an exciting variety of terrain right here on your doorstep. You just need to know what to look for. *Ski & Snowboard Scotland* is aimed at maximising the time you have available so that the hours you spend on the snow are memorable for all the right reasons.

This fun and informative book guides you over the slopes of Scotland, giving you the inside track on all the major ski centres. There are chapters ranging from how to get there to the impact of snowsports on the environment.

'Reading the book brought back many happy memories of my early training days at the dry slope in Edinburgh and of many brilliant weekends in the Cairngorms.' EMMA CARRICK-ANDERSON, from her foreword, written in the US, during a break in training for her first World Cup as a member of the British Alpine Ski Team.

SOCIAL HISTORY

A Word for Scotland

Jack Campbell

with a foreword by Magnus Magnusson

ISBN 0 946487 48 0 PBK £12.99

'A word for Scotland' was Lord Beaverbrook's hope when he founded the

Scottish Daily Express. That word for Scotland quickly became, and was for many years, the national newspaper of Scotland.

The pages of *A Word For Scotland* exude warmth and a wry sense of humour. Jack Campbell takes us behind the scenes to meet the larger-than-life characters and ordinary people who made and recorded the stories. Here we hear the stories behind the stories that hit the headlines in this great yarn of journalism in action.

It would be true to say 'all life is here'. From the Cheapside Street fire of which cost the lives of 19 Glasgow firemen, to the theft of the Stone of Destiny, to the lurid exploits of serial killer Peter Manuel, to encounters with world boxing champions Benny Lynch and Cassius Clay - this book offers telling glimpses of the characters, events, joy and tragedy which make up Scotland's story in the 20th century.

'As a rookie reporter you were proud to work on it and proud to be part of it - it was fine newspaper right at the heartbeat of Scotland.'
RONALD NEIL, Chief Executive of BBC Production, and a reporter on the *Scottish Daily Express* (1963-68)

'This book is a fascinating reminder of Scottish journalism in its heyday. It will be read avidly by those journalists who take pride in their profession – and should be compulsory reading for those who don't.'
JACK WEBSTER, columnist on *The Herald* and *Scottish Daily Express* journalist (1960-80)

The Crofting Years

Francis Thompson
ISBN 0 946487 06 5 PBK £6.95
Crofting is much more than a way of life. It is a storehouse of cultural, linguistic and moral values which holds together a scattered and struggling rural popula-

tion. This book fills a blank in the written history of crofting over the last two centuries. Bloody conflicts and gunboat diplomacy, treachery, compassion, music and story: all figure in this mine of information on crofting in the Highlands and Islands of Scotland.

'I would recommend this book to all who are interested in the past, but even more so to those who are interested in the future survival of our way of life and culture'
STORNOWAY GAZETTE

'The book is a mine of information on many aspects of the past, among them the homes, the food, the music and the medicine of our crofting forebears.'
John M Macmillan, erstwhile
CROFTERS COMMISSIONER FOR LEWIS AND HARRIS

POETRY

Blind Harry's Wallace

William Hamilton of Gilbertfield

Introduced by Elspeth King
ISBN 0 946487 43 X HBK £15.00
ISBN 0 946487 33 2 PBK £8.99

The original story of the real braveheart, Sir William Wallace. Racy, blood on every page, violently anglophobic, grossly embellished, vulgar and disgus-ting, clumsy and stilted, a literary failure, a great epic.

Whatever the verdict on BLIND HARRY, this is the book which has done more than any other to frame the notion of Scotland's national identity. Despite its numerous 'historical inaccuracies', it remains the principal source for what we now know about the life of Wallace.

The novel and film *Braveheart* were

based on the 1722 Hamilton edition of this epic poem. Burns, Wordsworth, Byron and others were greatly influenced by this version 'wherein the old obsolete words are rendered more intelligible', which is said to be the book, next to the Bible, most commonly found in Scottish households in the eighteenth century. Burns even admits to having 'borrowed... a couplet worthy of Homer' directly from Hamilton's version of BLIND HARRY to include in 'Scots wha hae'.

Elspeth King, in her introduction to this, the first accessible edition of BLIND HARRY in verse form since 1859, draws parallels between the situation in Scotland at the time of Wallace and that in Bosnia and Chechnya in the 1990s. Seven hundred years to the day after the Battle of Stirling Bridge, the 'Settled Will of the Scottish People' was expressed in the devolution referendum of 11 September 1997. She describes this as a landmark opportunity for mature reflection on how the nation has been shaped, and sees BLIND HARRY'S WALLACE as an essential and compelling text for this purpose.

'A true bard of the people'.

TOM SCOTT, THE PENGUIN BOOK OF SCOTTISH VERSE, on Blind Harry.

'A more inventive writer than Shakespeare'.
RANDALL WALLACE

'The story of Wallace poured a Scottish prejudice in my veins which will boil along until the floodgates of life shut in eternal rest'.
ROBERT BURNS

'Hamilton's couplets are not the best poetry you will ever read, but they rattle along at a fair pace. In re-issuing this work, the publishers have re-opened the spring from which most of our conceptions of the Wallace legend come'.
SCOTLAND ON SUNDAY

'The return of Blind Harry's Wallace, a man who makes Mel look like a wimp'.
THE SCOTSMAN

Poems to be read aloud

Collected and with an introduction by Tom Atkinson
ISBN 0 946487 00 6 PBK £5.00

This personal collection of doggerel and verse ranging from the tear-jerking *Green Eye of the Yellow God* to the rarely printed, bawdy *Eskimo Nell* has a lively cult following. Much borrowed and rarely returned, this is a book for reading aloud in very good company, preferably after a dram or twa. You are guaranteed a warm welcome if you arrive at a gathering with this little volume in your pocket.

'This little book is an attempt to stem the great rushing tide of canned entertainment. A hopeless attempt of course. There is poetry of very high order here, but there is also some fearful doggerel. But that is the way of things. No literary axe is being ground.

Of course some of the items in this book are poetic drivel, if read as poems. But that is not the point. They all spring to life when they are read aloud. It is the combination of the poem with your voice, with all the art and craft you can muster, that produces the finished product and effect you seek.

You don't have to learn the poems. Why clutter up your mind with rubbish? Of course, it is a poorly furnished mind that doesn't carry a fair stock of poetry, but surely the poems to be remembered and savoured in secret, when in love, or ill, or sad, are not the ones you want to share with an audience.

So go ahead, clear your throat and transfix all talkers with a stern eye, then let rip!'
TOM ATKINSON

LUATH GUIDES TO SCOTLAND

These guides are not your traditional where-to-stay and what-to-eat books. They are companions in the rucksack or car seat, providing the discerning traveller with a blend of fiery opinion and moving

description. Here you will find 'that curious pastiche of myths and legend and history that the Scots use to describe their heritage... what battle happened in which glen between which clans; where the Picts sacrificed bulls as recently as the 17th century... A lively counterpoint to the more standard, detached guidebook... Intriguing.'
THE WASHINGTON POST

These are perfect guides for the discerning visitor or resident to keep close by for reading again and again, written by authors who invite you to share their intimate knowledge and love of the areas covered.

Mull and Iona: Highways and Byways

Peter Macnab

ISBN 0 946487 58 8 PBK £4.95

'The Isle of Mull is of Isles the fairest, Of ocean's gems 'tis the first and rarest.' So a local poet described it a hundred years ago, and this recently revised guide to Mull and sacred Iona, the most accessible islands of the Inner Hebrides, takes the reader on a delightful tour of these rare ocean gems, travelling with a native whose unparalleled knowledge and deep feeling for the area unlock the byways of the islands in all their natural beauty.

South West Scotland

Tom Atkinson

ISBN 0 946487 04 9 PBK £4.95

This descriptive guide to the magical country of Robert Burns covers Kyle, Carrick, Galloway, Dumfriesshire, Kirkcudbrightshire and Wigtownshire. Hills, unknown moors and unspoiled beaches grace a land steeped in history and legend and portrayed with affection and deep delight.

An essential book for the visitor who yearns to feel at home in this land of peace and grandeur.

The West Highlands: The Lonely Lands

Tom Atkinson

ISBN 0 946487 56 1 PBK £4.95

A guide to Inveraray, Glencoe, Loch Awe, Loch Lomond, Cowal, the Kyles of Bute and all of central Argyll written with insight, sympathy and loving detail. Once Atkinson has taken you there, these lands can never feel lonely. 'I have sought to make the complex simple, the beautiful accessible and the strange familiar,' he writes, and indeed he brings to the land a knowledge and affection only accessible to someone with intimate knowledge of the area.

A must for travellers and natives who want to delve beneath the surface.

'Highly personal and somewhat quirky... steeped in the lore of Scotland.'
THE WASHINGTON POST

The Northern Highlands: The Empty Lands

Tom Atkinson

ISBN 0 946487 55 3 PBK £4.95

The Highlands of Scotland from Ullapool to Bettyhill and Bonar Bridge to John O' Groats are landscapes of myth and legend, 'empty of people, but of nothing else that brings delight to any tired soul,' writes Atkinson. This highly personal guide describes Highland history and landscape with love, compassion and above all sheer magic.

Essential reading for anyone who has dreamed of the Highlands.

The North West Highlands: Roads to the Isles

Tom Atkinson

ISBN 0 946487 54 5 PBK £4.95

Ardnamurchan, Morvern, Morar, Moidart and the west coast to Ullapool are included in this guide to the Far West and Far North of Scotland. An unspoiled land of mountains, lochs and silver sands is brought to the walker's toe-tips (and to the reader's fingertips) in this stark, serene and evocative account of town, country and legend.

For any visitor to this Highland wonderland, Queen Victoria's favourite place on earth.

WALK WITH LUATH

Mountain Days & Bothy Nights

Dave Brown and Ian Mitchell

ISBN 0 946487 15 4 PBK £7.50

Acknowledged as a classic of mountain writing still in demand ten years after its first publication, this book takes you into the bothies, howffs and dosses on the Scottish hills. Fishgut Mac, Desperate Dan and Stumpy the Big Yin stalk hill and public house, evading gamekeepers and Royalty with a camaraderie which was the trademark of Scots hillwalking in the early days.

'The fun element comes through... how innocent the social polemic seems in our nastier world of today... the book for the rucksack this year.'
Hamish Brown, SCOTTISH MOUNTAINEERING CLUB JOURNAL

The Joy of Hillwalking

Ralph Storer

ISBN 0 946487 28 6 PBK £7.50

Apart, perhaps, from the joy of sex, the joy of hillwalking brings more pleasure to more people than any other form of human activity.

'Alps, America, Scandinavia, you name it – Storer's been there, so why the hell shouldn't he bring all these various and varied places into his observations... [He] even admits to losing his virginity after a day on the Aggy Ridge... Well worth its place alongside Storer's earlier works.'
TAC

Scotland's Mountains before the Mountaineers

Ian Mitchell

ISBN 0 946487 39 1 PBK £9.99

In this ground-breaking book, Ian Mitchell tells the story of explorations and ascents in the Scottish Highlands in the days before mountaineering became a popular sport – when bandits, Jacobites, poachers and illicit distillers traditionally used the mountains as sanctuary. The book also gives a detailed account of the map makers, road builders, geologists, astronomers and naturalists, many of whom ascended hitherto untrodden summits while working in the Scottish Highlands.

Scotland's Mountains before the Mountaineers is divided into four Highland regions, with a map of each region showing key summits. While not designed primarily as a guide, it will be a useful handbook for walkers and climbers. Based on a wealth of new research, this book offers a fresh perspective that will fascinate climbers and mountaineers and everyone interested in the history of mountaineering, cartography, the evolution of landscape and the social history of the Scottish Highlands.

LUATH WALKING GUIDES

The highly respected and continually updated guides to the Cairngorms.

'Particularly good on local wildlife and how to see it' THE COUNTRYMAN

Walks in the Cairngorms

Ernest Cross
ISBN 0 946487 09 X PBK £4.95

This selection of walks celebrates the rare birds, animals, plants and geological wonders of a region often believed difficult to penetrate on foot. Nothing is difficult with this guide in your pocket, as Cross gives a choice for every walker, and includes valuable tips on mountain safety and weather advice.
Ideal for walkers of all ages and skiers waiting for snowier skies.

Short Walks in the Cairngorms

Ernest Cross
ISBN 0 946487 23 5 PBK £4.95

Cross wrote this volume after overhearing a walker remark that there were no short walks for lazy ramblers in the Cairngorm region. Here is the answer: rambles through scenic woods with a welcoming pub at the end, bird-watching hints, glacier holes, or for the fit and ambitious, scrambles up hills to

admire vistas of glorious scenery. Wildlife in the Cairngorms is unequalled elsewhere in Britain, and here it is brought to the binoculars of any walker who treads quietly and with respect.

NATURAL SCOTLAND

Wild Scotland: The essential guide to finding the best of natural Scotland

James McCarthy
Photography by Laurie Campbell
ISBN 0 946487 37 5 PBK £7.50

With a foreword by Magnus Magnusson and striking colour photographs by Laurie Campbell, this is the essential up-to-date guide to viewing wildlife in Scotland for the visitor and resident alike. It provides a fascinating overview of the country's plants, animals, bird and marine life against the background of their typical natural settings, as an introduction to the vivid descriptions of the most accessible localities, linked to clear regional maps. A unique feature is the focus on 'green tourism' and sustainable visitor use of the countryside, contributed by Duncan Bryden, manager of the Scottish Tourist Board's Tourism and the Environment Task Force. Important practical information on access and the best times of year for viewing sites makes this an indispensable and user-friendly travelling companion to anyone interested in exploring Scotland's remarkable natural heritage.
James McCarthy is former Deputy Director for Scotland of the Nature Conservancy Council, and now a Board Member of Scottish Natural Heritage and Chairman of the Environmental Youth Work National Development Project Scotland.

'Nothing but Heather!'

Gerry Cambridge

ISBN 0 946487 49 9 PBK £15.00

Enter the world of Scottish nature – bizarre, brutal, often beautiful, always fascinating – as seen through the lens and poems of Gerry Cambridge, one of Scotland's most distinctive contemporary poets.

On film and in words, Cambridge brings unusual focus to bear on lives as diverse as those of dragonflies, hermit crabs, short-eared owls, and wood anemones. The result is both an instructive look by a naturalist at some of the flora and fauna of Scotland and a poet's aesthetic journey.

This exceptional collection comprises 48 poems matched with 48 captioned photographs. In his introduction Cambridge explores the origins of the project and the approaches to nature taken by other poets, and incorporates a wry account of an unwillingly-sectarian, farm-labouring, bird-obsessed adolescence in rural Ayrshire in the 1970s.

Keats felt that the beauty of a rainbow was somehow tarnished by knowledge of its properties. Yet the natural world is surely made more, not less, marvellous by awareness of its workings. In the poems that accompany these pictures, I have tried to give an inkling of that. May the marriage of verse and image enlarge the reader's appreciation and, perhaps, insight into the chomping, scurrying, quivering, procreating and dying kingdom, however many miles it be beyond the door.

GERRY CAMBRIDGE

'a real poet, with a sense of the music of language and the poetry of life...'

KATHLEEN RAINE

'one of the most promising and original of modern Scottish poets... a master of form and subtlety.'

GEORGE MACKAY BROWN

Scotland Land and People
An Inhabited Solitude

James McCarthy

ISBN 0 946487 57 X PBK £7.99

'Scotland is the country above all others that I have seen, in which a man of imagination may carve out his own pleasures; there are so many inhabited solitudes.'

DOROTHY WORDSWORTH, in her journal of August 1803

An informed and thought-provoking profile of Scotland's unique landscapes and the impact of humans on what we see now and in the future. James McCarthy leads us through the many aspects of the land and the people who inhabit it: natural Scotland; the rocks beneath; land ownership; the use of resources; people and place; conserving Scotland's heritage and much more.

Written in a highly readable style, this concise volume offers an under-standing of the land as a whole. Emphasising the uniqueness of the Scottish environment, the author explores the links between this and other aspects of our culture as a key element in rediscovering a modern sense of the Scottish identity and perception of nationhood.

'This book provides an engaging introduction to the mysteries of Scotland's people and landscapes. Difficult concepts are described in simple terms, providing the interested Scot or tourist with an invaluable overview of the country... It fills an important niche which, to my knowledge, is filled by no other publications.'

BETSY KING, Chief Executive, Scottish Environmental Education Council.

The Highland Geology Trail

John L Roberts

ISBN 0946487 36 7 PBK £4.99

Where can you find the oldest rocks in Europe?
Where can you see ancient hills around 800 million years old?
How do you tell whether a valley was carved out by a glacier, not a river?

What are the Fucoid Beds?
Where do you find rocks folded like putty?
How did great masses of rock pile up like snow in front of a snow-plough?
When did volcanoes spew lava and ash to form Skye, Mull and Rum?
Where can you find fossils on Skye?

'...*a lucid introduction to the geological record in general, a jargon-free exposition of the regional background, and a series of descriptions of specific localities of geological interest on a 'trail' around the highlands.*
Having checked out the local references on the ground, I can vouch for their accuracy and look forward to investigating farther afield, informed by this guide.
Great care has been taken to explain specific terms as they occur and, in so doing, John Roberts has created a resource of great value which is eminently usable by anyone with an interest in the outdoors...the best bargain you are likely to get as a geology book in the foreseeable future.'
Jim Johnston, PRESS AND JOURNAL

Rum: Nature's Island

Magnus Magnusson

ISBN 0 946487 32 4 £7.95 PBK

Rum: Nature's Island is the fascinating story of a Hebridean island from the earliest times through to the Clearances and its period as the sporting playground of a Lancashire industrial magnate, and on to

its rebirth as a National Nature Reserve, a model for the active ecological management of Scotland's wild places.

Thoroughly researched and written in a lively accessible style, the book includes comprehensive coverage of the island's geology, animals and plants, and people, with a special chapter on the Edwardian extravaganza of Kinloch Castle. There is practical information for visitors to what was once known as 'the Forbidden Isle'; the book provides details of bothy and other accommodation, walks and nature trails. It closes with a positive vision for the island's future: biologically diverse, economically dynamic and ecologically sustainable.

Rum: Nature's Island is published in co-operation with Scottish Natural Heritage (of which Magnus Magnusson is Chairman) to mark the 40th anniversary of the acquisition of Rum by its predecessor, The Nature Conservancy.

ON THE TRAIL OF

On the Trail of William Wallace

David R. Ross

ISBN 0 946487 47 2 PBK £7.99

How close to reality was *Braveheart*?
Where was Wallace actually born?
What was the relationship between Wallace and Bruce?
Are there any surviving eye-witness accounts of Wallace?
How does Wallace influence the psyche of today's Scots?

On the Trail of William Wallace offers a refreshing insight into the life and heritage of the great Scots hero whose proud story is at the very heart of what it means to be

Scottish. Not concentrating simply on the hard historical facts of Wallace's life, the book also takes into account the real significance of Wallace and his effect on the ordinary Scot through the ages, manifested in the many sites where his memory is marked.

In trying to piece together the jigsaw of the reality of Wallace's life, David Ross weaves a subtle flow of new information with his own observations. His engaging, thoughtful and at times amusing narrative reads with the ease of a historical novel, complete with all the intrigue, treachery and romance required to hold the attention of the casual reader and still entice the more knowledgable historian.

74 places to visit in Scotland and the north of England

One general map and 3 location maps

Stirling and Falkirk battle plans
Wallace's route through London

Chapter on Wallace connections in North America and elsewhere

Reproductions of rarely seen illustrations

On the Trail of William Wallace will be enjoyed by anyone with an interest in Scotland, from the passing tourist to the most fervent nationalist. It is an encyclopaedia-cum-guide book, literally stuffed with fascinating titbits not usually on offer in the conventional history book.

David Ross is organiser of and historical adviser to the Society of William Wallace.

'Historians seem to think all there is to be known about Wallace has already been uncovered. Mr Ross has proved that Wallace studies are in fact in their infancy.' ELSPETH KING, Director the the Stirling Smith Art Museum & Gallery, who annotated and introduced the recent Luath edition of *Blind Harry's Wallace.*

'Better the pen than the sword!' RANDALL

WALLACE, author of *Braveheart,* when asked by David Ross how it felt to be partly responsible for the freedom of a nation following the Devolution Referendum.

On the Trail of Robert the Bruce

David R. Ross

ISBN 0 946487 52 9 PBK £7.99

On the Trail of Robert the Bruce charts the story of Scotland's hero-king from his boyhood, through his days of indecision as Scotland suffered under the English yoke, to his assumption of the crown exactly six months after the death of William Wallace. Here is the astonishing blow by blow account of how, against fearful odds, Bruce led the Scots to win their greatest ever victory Bannockburn was not the end of the story. The war against English oppression lasted another fourteen years. Bruce lived just long enough to see his dreams of an independent Scotland come to fruition in 1328 with the signing of the Treaty of Edinburgh. The trail takes us to Bruce sites in Scotland, many of the little known and forgotten battle sites in northern England, and as far afield as the Bruce monuments in Andalusia and Jerusalem.

67 places to visit in Scotland and elsewhere.

One general map, 3 location maps and a map of Bruce-connected sites in Ireland.

Bannockburn battle plan.

Drawings and reproductions of rarely seen illustrations.

On the Trail of Robert the Bruce is not all blood and gore. It brings out the love and laughter, pain and passion of one of the great eras of Scottish history. Read it and you will understand why David

Ross has never knowingly killed a spider in his life. Once again, he proves himself a master of the popular brand of hands-on history that made *On the Trail of William Wallace* so popular.

'*David R. Ross is a proud patriot and unashamed romantic.*'
SCOTLAND ON SUNDAY

'*Robert the Bruce knew Scotland, knew every class of her people, as no man who ruled her before or since has done. It was he who asked of her a miracle - and she accomplished it.*' AGNES MUIR MACKENZIE

On the Trail of Robert Service

GW Lockhart

ISBN 0 946487 24 3 PBK £7.99

Robert Service is famed world-wide for his eye-witness verse-pictures of the Klondike goldrush. As a war poet, his work outsold Owen and Sassoon, and he went on to become the world's first million selling poet. In search of adventure and new experiences, he emigrated from Scotland to Canada in 1890 where he was caught up in the aftermath of the raging gold fever. His vivid dramatic verse bring to life the wild, larger than life characters of the gold rush Yukon, their bar-room brawls, their lust for gold, their trigger-happy gambles with life and love. 'The Shooting of Dan McGrew' is perhaps his most famous poem:

> *A bunch of the boys were whooping it up in the Malamute saloon;*
> *The kid that handles the music box was hitting a ragtime tune;*
> *Back of the bar in a solo game, sat Dangerous Dan McGrew,*
> *And watching his luck was his light o'love, the lady that's known as Lou.*

His storytelling powers have brought Robert Service enduring fame, particularly in North America and Scotland where he is something of a cult figure. Starting in Scotland, *On the Trail of Robert Service* follows Service as he wanders through British Columbia, Oregon, California, Mexico, Cuba, Tahiti, Russia, Turkey and the Balkans, finally 'settling' in France.

'*A fitting tribute to a remarkable man - a bank clerk who wanted to become a cowboy. It is hard to imagine a bank clerk writing such lines as:*
A bunch of boys were whooping it up...
The income from his writing actually exceeded his bank salary by a factor of five and he resigned to pursue a full time writing career.' Charles Munn, THE SCOTTISH BANKER

'*Robert Service claimed he wrote for those who wouldn't be seen dead reading poetry. His was an almost unbelievably mobile life... Lockhart hangs on breathlessly, enthusiastically unearthing clues to the poet's life.*' Ruth Thomas, SCOTTISH BOOK COLLECTOR

'*This enthralling biography will delight Service lovers in both the Old World and the New.*' Marilyn Wright, SCOTS INDEPENDENT

On the Trail of Mary Queen of Scots

J. Keith Cheetham

ISBN 0 946487 50 2 PBK £7.99

Life dealt Mary Queen of Scots love, intrigue, betrayal and tragedy in generous measure.

On the Trail of Mary Queen of Scots traces the major events in the turbulent life of the beautiful, enigmatic queen whose romantic reign and tragic destiny exerts an undimmed fascination over 400 years after her execution.

Places of interest to visit - 99 in Scotland, 35 in England and 29 in France.

One general map and 6 location maps.

Line drawings and illustrations.

Simplified family tree of the royal houses of Tudor and Stuart.

Key sites include:

Linlithgow Palace – Mary's birthplace, now a magnificent ruin

Stirling Castle – where, only nine months old, Mary was crowned Queen of Scotland

Notre Dame Cathedral – where, aged fifteen, she married the future king of France

The Palace of Holyroodhouse – Rizzio, one of Mary's closest advisers, was murdered here and some say his blood still stains the spot where he was stabbed to death

Sheffield Castle – where for fourteen years she languished as prisoner of her cousin, Queen Elizabeth I

Fotheringhay – here Mary finally met her death on the executioner's block.

On the Trail of Mary Queen of Scots is for everyone interested in the life of perhaps the most romantic figure in Scotland's history; a thorough guide to places connected with Mary, it is also a guide to the complexities of her personal and public life.

'In my end is my beginning'
MARY QUEEN OF SCOTS

'...the woman behaves like the Whore of Babylon' JOHN KNOX

MUSIC AND DANCE

Highland Balls and Village Halls

GW Lockhart

ISBN 0 946487 12 X PBK £6.95

Acknowledged as a classic in Scottish dancing circles throughout the world. Anecdotes, Scottish history, dress and dance steps are all included in this *'delightful little book, full of interest... both a personal account and an understanding look*

at the making of traditions.'
NEW ZEALAND SCOTTISH COUNTRY DANCES MAGAZINE

'A delightful survey of Scottish dancing and custom. Informative, concise and opinionated, it guides the reader across the history and geography of country dance and ends by detailing the 12 dances every Scot should know – the most famous being the Eightsome Reel, "the greatest longest, rowdiest, most diabolically executed of all the Scottish country dances" .'
THE HERALD

'A pot-pourri of every facet of Scottish country dancing. It will bring back memories of petronella turns and poussettes and make you eager to take part in a Broun's reel or a dashing white sergeant!'
DUNDEE COURIER AND ADVERTISER

'An excellent an very readable insight into the traditions and customs of Scottish country dancing. The author takes us on a tour from his own early days jigging in the village hall to the characters and traditions that have made our own brand of dance popular throughout the world.'
SUNDAY POST

Fiddles & Folk: A celebration of the re-emergence of Scotland's musical heritage

GW Lockhart

ISBN 0 946487 38 3 PBK £7.95

In *Fiddles & Folk*, his companion volume to *Highland Balls and Village Halls*, Wallace Lockhart meets up with many of the people who have created the renaissance of Scotland's music at home and overseas. From Dougie MacLean, Hamish

Henderson, the Battlefield Band, the Whistlebinkies, the Scottish Fiddle Orchestra, the McCalmans and many more come the stories that break down the musical barriers between Scotland's past and present, and between the diverse musical forms which have woven together to create the dynamism of the music today.

'I have tried to avoid a formal approach to Scottish music as it affects those of us with our musical heritage coursing through our veins. The picture I have sought is one of many brush strokes, looking at how some individuals have come to the fore, examining their music, lives, thoughts, even philosophies...'
WALLACE LOCKHART

' "I never had a narrow, woolly-jumper, fingers stuck in the ear approach to music. We have a musical heritage here that is the envy of the rest of the world. Most countries just can't compete," he [Ian Green, Greentrax] says. And as young Scots tire of Oasis and Blur, they will realise that there is a wealth of young Scottish music on their doorstep just waiting to be discovered.'
THE SCOTSMAN

For anyone whose heart lifts at the sound of fiddle or pipes, this book takes you on a delightful journey, full of humour and respect, in the company of some of the performers who have taken Scotland's music around the world and come back enriched.

NEW SCOTLAND

Scotland - Land and Power
the agenda for land reform

Andy Wightman
in association with
Democratic Left Scotland

foreword by Lesley Riddoch

ISBN 0 946487 70 7 PBK £5.00

What is land reform?
Why is it needed?

Will the Scottish Parliament really make a difference?

Scotland – Land and Power argues passionately that nothing less than a radical, comprehensive programme of land reform can make the difference that is needed. Now is no time for palliative solutions which treat the symptoms and not the causes.

Scotland – Land and Power is a controversial and provocative book that clarifies the complexities of landownership in Scotland. Andy Wightman explodes the myth that land issues are relevant only to the far flung fringes of rural Scotland, and questions mainstream political commitment to land reform. He presents his own far-reaching programme for change and a pragmatic, inspiring vision of how Scotland can move from outmoded, unjust power structures towards a more equitable landowning democracy.

'Writers like Andy Wightman are determined to make sure that the hurt of the last century is not compounded by a rushed solution in the next. This accessible, comprehensive but passionately argued book is quite simply essential reading and perfectly timed – here's hoping Scotland's legislators agree.' LESLEY RIDDOCH

Old Scotland New Scotland

Jeff Fallow
ISBN 0 946487 40 5 PBK £6.99

'Together we can build a new Scotland based on Labour's values.' DONALD DEWAR, Party Political Broadcast

'Despite the efforts of decent Mr Dewar, the voters may yet conclude they are looking at the same old hacks in brand new suits.' IAN BELL, *The Independent*

'At times like this you suddenly realise how dangerous the neglect of Scottish history in our schools and universities may turn out to be.'
MICHAEL FRY, *The Herald*

'...one of the things I hope will go is our chip on the shoulder about the English... The SNP has a huge responsibility to articulate Scottish independence in a way that is pro-Scottish and not anti-English.'
ALEX SALMOND, *The Scotsman*

Scottish politics have never been more exciting. In *old Scotland new Scotland* Jeff Fallow takes us on a graphic voyage through Scotland's turbulent history, from earliest times through to the present day and beyond. This fast-track guide is the quick way to learn what your history teacher didn't tell you, essential reading for all who seek an understanding of Scotland and its history.

Eschewing the romanticisation of his country's past, Fallow offers a new perspective on an old nation. 'Too many people associate Scottish history with tartan trivia or outworn romantic myth. This book aims to blast that stubborn idea.'
JEFF FALLOW

Notes from the North
incorporating a Brief History of the Scots and the English
Emma Wood
ISBN 0 946487 46 4 PBK £8.99

Notes on being English
Notes on being in Scotland
Learning from a shared past

Sickened by the English jingoism that surfaced in rampant form during the 1982 Falklands War, Emma Wood started to dream of moving from her home in East Anglia to the Highlands of Scotland. She felt increasingly frustrated and marginalised as Thatcherism got a grip on the southern

English psyche. The Scots she met on frequent holidays in the Highlands had no truck with Thatcherism, and she felt at home with grass-roots Scottish anti-authoritarianism. The decision was made. She uprooted and headed for a new life in the north of Scotland.

'An intelligent and perceptive book... calm, reflective, witty and sensitive. It should certainly be read by all English visitors to Scotland, be they tourists or incomers. And it should certainly be read by all Scots concerned about what kind of nation we live in. They might learn something about themselves.'
THE HERALD

'... her enlightenment is evident on every page of this perceptive, provocative book.'
MAIL ON SUNDAY

BIOGRAPHY

Tobermory Teuchter: A first-hand account of life on Mull in the early years of the 20th century
Peter Macnab
ISBN 0 946487 41 3 PBK £7.99

Peter Macnab was reared on Mull, as was his father, and his grandfather before him. In this book he provides a revealing account of life on Mull during the first quarter of the 20th century, focusing especially on the years of World War I. This enthralling social history of the island is set against Peter Macnab's early years as son of the governor of the Mull Poorhouse, one of the last in the Hebrides, and is illustrated throughout by photographs from his exceptional collection. Peter Macnab's 'fisherman's yarns' and other personal reminiscences are told delightfully by a born storyteller.

This latest work from the author of a range of books about the island, including the standard study of Mull and Iona, reveals his unparalleled knowledge of and deep feeling for Mull and its people. After his long career with the Clydesdale Bank, first in Tobermory and later on the mainland, Peter, now 94, remains a teuchter at heart, proud of his island heritage.

'Peter Macnab is a man of words who doesn't mince his words – not where his beloved Mull is concerned. 'I will never forget some of the inmates of the poorhouse,' says Peter. 'Some of them were actually victims of the later Clearances. It was history at first hand, and there was no romance about it'. But Peter Macnab sees little creative point in crying over ancient injustices. For him the task is to help Mull in this century and beyond.'

SCOTS MAGAZINE, May 1998

Bare Feet and Tackety Boots

Archie Cameron

ISBN 0 946487 17 0   PBK   £7.95

The island of Rum before the First World War was the playground of its rich absentee landowner. A survivor of life a century gone tells his story. Factors and schoolmasters, midges and poaching, deer, ducks and MacBrayne's steamers: here social history and personal anecdote create a record of a way of life gone not long ago but already almost forgotten. This is the story the gentry couldn't tell.

'This book is an important piece of social history, for it gives an insight into how the other half lived in an era the likes of which will never be seen again'
FORTHRIGHT MAGAZINE

'The authentic breath of the pawky, country-wise estate employee.'
THE OBSERVER
'Well observed and detailed account of island life in the early years of this century'.
THE SCOTS MAGAZINE
'A very good read with the capacity to make the reader chuckle. A very talented writer.'
STORNOWAY GAZETTE

Come Dungeons Dark

John Taylor Caldwell

ISBN 0 946487 19 7   PBK   £6.95

Glasgow anarchist Guy Aldred died with 10p in his pocket in 1963 claiming there was better company in Barlinnie Prison than in the Corridors of Power. 'The Red Scourge' is remembered here by one who worked with him and spent 27 years as part of his turbulent household, sparring with Lenin, Sylvia Pankhurst and others as he struggled for freedom for his beloved fellow-man.

'The welcome and long-awaited biography of... one of this country's most prolific radical propagandists... Crank or visionary?... whatever the verdict, the Glasgow anarchist has finally been given a fitting memorial.'
THE SCOTSMAN

Luath Press Limited
committed to publishing well written books worth reading

LUATH PRESS takes its name from Robert Burns, whose little collie Luath (*Gael.*, swift or nimble) tripped up Jean Armour at a wedding and gave him the chance to speak to the woman who was to be his wife and the abiding love of his life. Burns called one of *The Twa Dogs* Luath after Cuchullin's hunting dog in *Ossian's Fingal*. Luath Press grew up in the heart of Burns country, and now resides a few steps up the road from Burns' first lodgings in Edinburgh's Royal Mile.

Luath offers you distinctive writing with a hint of unexpected pleasures.

Most UK bookshops either carry our books in stock or can order them for you. To order direct from us, please send a £sterling cheque, postal order, international money order or your credit card details (number, address of cardholder and expiry date) to us at the address below. Please add post and packing as follows: UK – £1.00 per delivery address; overseas surface mail – £2.50 per delivery address; overseas airmail – £3.50 for the first book to each delivery address, plus £1.00 for each additional book by airmail to the same address. If your order is a gift, we will happily enclose your card or message at no extra charge.

Luath Press Limited
543/2 Castlehill
The Royal Mile
Edinburgh EH1 2ND
Telephone: 0131 225 4326 (24 hours)
Fax: 0131 225 4324
email: gavin.macdougall@luath.co.uk
Website: www.luath.co.uk